GRAPHIC

Shane Briant

ISBN: 0-9578826-1-0
ISBN-13: 9780957882614

For Wendy, as ever - my love and personal psychiatrist.

ABOUT THE AUTHOR

Shane Briant has starred in 34 international films all over the world, working for such directors as John Huston, Jack Gold, Roland Joffe, Peter Collinson, Warris Hussein, Glenn Jordan and Ian Barry. He's acted alongside Paul Newman, James Mason, Olivia de Havilland, Jeremy Irons, Geoffrey Rush, Cliff Robertson and Jack Palance. He is the author of seven best selling thrillers, published in America, Australia and Europe.

His autobiography, 'Always the Bad Guy' was published in 2012. The short film he wrote, 'A Message from Fallujah' starring Lance Hendrikson won the Best of the Festival award at the Los Angeles International Film Festival in 1995.

ACKNOWLEDGMENTS

My thanks to the wonderful hotels and restaurants that allowed me to include their names in my novel. They are all out there in real life, to be visited!
The Arlberg Hospiz Hotel in Sank Christoph, Austria.
The Hotel Buci in Paris.
The Hotel Rialto in Venice.
The Blason in Amboise, France.
The Hotel Klosterbrau in Seefeld.
The Tabou restaurant in Sydney.
The Hotel Alter Goldener Berg in Lech, Austria.
The Hernandez Coffee shop in King's Cross, Sydney.

My thanks to Chief Superintendent Deborah Wallace, Barrie Hitchon, Major 'Slip' Mitchell, Michael Commerford, Richard Martin, Denis Saville, Kevin Farasopoulos and Giblet and Freddy.
Nicola O'Dea.

In memory of Denis Liston.

PROLOGUE

My name is Sainte-Claire.

Actually, it's not. It's Robert Howard. Robert Howard is the name written on my birth certificate. I was once loved as Robert Howard. Worked as Robert Howard. But now, at least to the people who live on the darker side of Sydney, I'm known simply as Sainte-Claire.

Sainte-Claire has seen people beaten with iron bars. Picked human body parts from frozen food containers. Watched a human head explode as bullets pierced the skull.

A year ago I'd never have imagined it possible that one day I'd stand toe to toe with violent criminals and be ready to gamble they'd back off first. It's curious to think that this was the result of one crazy mistake: a young girl, a child taking me for someone else. For a tough guy named Sainte-Claire. The creation of my pen.

I'm a crime writer. I write graphic novels. That's crime thrillers with pictures. Not in any way comics. You may have read one of them. A couple have been turned into films.

When it all began, Sainte-Claire was the product of my imagination, only as real as the ink on a page. Now I think he's taken me over.

No, that's not accurate. I know he has.

In my attic office, as I tap away on my iMac, writing my books, glancing at my reflection in the window glass, I'm still mild-mannered Robert Howard. But when I step outside, on to the night streets of Sydney, I'm Sainte-Claire.

I'm drawn to danger now, like a moth to a flame. As mountain climbers are drawn to Everest, skydivers to free falling, and mercenaries to combat zones. I relish being feared. I enjoy the respect I see in the eyes of men harder than me. The prospect of violence brings an incredible rush.

My psychiatrist says I am making progress. But the truth is, I lie — to humour her and cling to my sanity. Maybe I'll understand myself better if I detail the events of the past few months.

1

I was in my attic office, the morning of 11 June, last year. It was past midnight. I always intuitively know when one day ticks over into the next. It's like a stab of fear deep within my psyche telling me I now have one day less to live.

Sainte-Claire had just saved the life of a five-foot-five, green-eyed, leggy prostitute called Sonja Bressel. She would have been the seventh victim of a serial rapist killer. Would have been, but for the fact she'd engaged the services of Robert Sainte-Claire PI, known and feared simply as 'Sainte-Claire'. My Teflon-fisted gumshoe was reholstering his still smoking Glock 17 pistol when the phone rang by my elbow.

"Help me, Mr Sainte-Claire," a tiny voice cried desperately down the phone line. "Please help! Tiggy's not here and I'm frightened."

My first reaction was one of surprise. Who did this small lost voice belong to? She sounded as if her sixth birthday was still a long way off. How did she have my telephone number? And why was she calling me Sainte-Claire?

I tried to clear my head of tawdry images of Kings Cross brothels, where my hero had stalked the night in search of Sonja Bressel's assailants. "What's your name, pumpkin?" I said. But all I could hear were racking sobs.

"They were being horrid to Mummy. Please help, Mr Sainte-Claire. Tiggy's not here. I'm all alone and it's scary."

More sobs.

"Where do you live?" I asked. If she told me I could call the police. The little girl sounded in a terrible state. And let's remember, it was the middle of the night – a time when all little girls should be tucked up in the deepest of slumbers with teddy bears.

"Mummy was crying. And Tiggy's not here!" The small voice was becoming hysterical, punctuated by hiccups.

"Listen to me, sweetheart. Of course Sainte-Claire will help you. But I must know where you are or I can't come and make things right, can I?"

"I'm home, silly! But Mummy's gone. And Tiggs—" More gut-wrenching sobs and hiccups. "I don't know where she *is*!"

"Where's home? What street do you live in? Can you tell me?"

"We live in Roslyn Street. Number 5. Please help us, Sainte-Claire. Tiggs says you're wonderful."

"That's nice," I said in a soothing voice, trying to calm her. "Look, I'll come straight round. You stay where you are — don't go outside. Go up to your bedroom and stay there. Do you understand me?"

There were more sobs, but slightly lower in volume. A couple of seconds later they'd died down to a wet sniffle. "You'll come? You'll really come, Sainte-Claire?" asked the very tiny voice. It was as if she couldn't quite believe it; as if she'd found Santa Claus's telephone number by chance, called him, and he'd told her he'd be round with a bagful of parcels.

"Of course I'll come. But first you must tell me your name. Mine's Robert."

"Don't fib! I know who you are, Sainte-Claire!"

"Okay! Your turn then, smudger — you tell me yours."

"Alice. My name is Alice. Tiggs calls me Ally-Oop."

"All right. Now, you do as I say, Ally-Oop, and wait till I come round. I should be with you in a few minutes. Try not to cry — blubbing's for kids, eh? And don't be afraid."

"I'm not afraid now, Sainte-Claire. You'll help us — I know that. Promise not to blub."

And that was that. Sainte-Claire to the rescue! The question was, what was happening at 5 Roslyn Street? More to the point, what the hell could *I* do about it?

Judging by the tone of the little girl's voice I immediately ruled out a hoax call. She'd seemed genuinely distressed and I doubted very much that I'd been fooled by an adult putting on a kid's-voice. Clearly Ally-Oop needed help.

I dialled triple zero.

"Police, Fire or Ambulance?"

"Police."

"One moment, please."

I knew I'd be answered by one of two designated operators at the Sydney Police Centre. From there I'd be switched on to whichever of the five regions my call applied to. In my case it was Kings Cross. In the old days I'd be asked where I was calling from. But in these days of hi-tech telecommunications, my number would show up somewhere on a computer screen deep within the operations centreWord count and I'd be patched through to the appropriate station.

"Kings Cross Region Centre. May I have your name, please?"

"Look, I hope this isn't serious, but just in case it is, I thought I should call you…" I was strangely tongue-tied when it came to the reality of this crisis. Sainte-Claire would have cut to the chase in a matter of seconds – problem and location, then suggested an answer. Me? I was useless.

"Your name, please, sir," the operator replied flatly.

"Howard. Robert Howard. I just received a call from a little girl. She sounded frightened. She may need help."

"Is this child a relative, Mr Howard?"

Clearly the operator wanted to find out if she was dealing with a domestic.

"No, she's not. I've no idea who she is. It may be a hoax call, but I don't think so."

I was about to continue when the operator cut in. "Do you have an address for this child, sir?"

"I do, yes — 5 Roslyn Street, Kings Cross."

"Can you tell me the nature of the problem, Mr Howard?"

"The girl was crying. She said her mother was crying too a while back, but now she's not at home any more. The kid's alone in the house. I'd say she's about six to eight years old. She's terrified. Hysterical is maybe nearer the mark. She said she has a sister, but she's not there right now — I expect she's out trying to find her mother. Sounds to me as though something bad has happened there."

"How do you know this girl, sir?"

"I don't."

"Then how did she come to call you, Mr Howard?"

It was a good question.

"I've no idea," I replied. Then frustration set in. "Look, it doesn't really matter! I'm telling you that I got a call from a child saying she's scared to death. She told me where she lives. Now I'm telling *you*. Just send someone to check it out!"

The operator was beginning to bug me. What more did she need to know other than what I'd just told her? A little girl was in trouble. I wasn't about to solve the problem with her over the phone.

"Send the police to 5 Roslyn Street. It's an emergency. A child's in danger. That's now a matter of record. I'll meet them there!"

I hung up.

I hurried downstairs and threw open my front door, hotly pursued by Giblet, my marmalade cat, who clearly thought she was participating in some kind of great midnight game. I jumped in my car. Giblet peed on the back wheel, then stalked away as I turned on the ignition.

The streets were reasonably empty. Just a smattering of taxis with party animals making their way from one club to another. Within a few minutes of my call from Ally-Oop, I was turning into Roslyn Street, trying to make out the house numbers in the darkness.

It wasn't difficult to locate where Alice lived – every light in one particular house was blazing, and I could hear the sound of a child sobbing, even though my driver's window was closed.

I double-parked in the middle of Roslyn Street and opened the car door.

A girl of about eleven or twelve was sitting on the steps that led up to the front door of Number 5. She had dark curly hair and big brown eyes that stared down the road like a nervous barn owl.

She'd flung a raincoat over her pyjamas — I could see a patch of teddy bears. As I approached her, she stood and backed away slightly from me. I stopped, making no attempt to open the garden gate. I didn't want to frighten her.

"Excuse me, is your name Tiggs? Or maybe Tiggy?" I asked with a reassuring smile. "You see... I'm a friend of Alice's."

The girl said nothing. She merely stared at me, wide-eyed and confused. I couldn't blame her. Unless Alice had told her of our recent telephone conversation, what on earth would an adult pal of her baby sister be doing asking questions after midnight outside the front gate.

"Perhaps I should explain. Ally-Oop just called me on the phone. She was pretty upset."

That was an understatement – reinforced by the loud sobbing coming from the house. Alice had clearly forgotten her promise not to blub.

"She asked me to come round and help. So..." I paused, not quite knowing what else to say. "Well, here I am. Are you all right?"

The girl studied me from head to toe for a couple of seconds. She was shaking, but trying to act tough.

"I'm waiting for my Aunt Lucy. She said she'd come straight over. Everything's fine, thank you."

She didn't appear frightened of me personally, and I took that as a compliment. I like to think I have a friendly appearance and I've always got on really well with kids. Always wanted some of my own as a matter of fact, but my previous partners never had time for babies, so I've had to make do with the friendship of other people's kids. Jez said she'd change things around one day, but that's another story.

The girl finished her 'up and down' appraisal of me. "Who are you? I don't think we've met, have we? What's your name?" she said with remarkable aplomb.

"My name's Robert, Robert Howard," I replied. "Is everything all right? No one's hurt, are they? Is your mother back? Is Alice okay?"

I watched the girl's face closely. It was possible she was in a state of shock; that inside the front door her mother lay bleeding to death of gunshot wounds. I had to decide whether to walk straight past her into the house and take matters into my own hands, or stay where I was and hope the cops would arrive shortly.

"Sainte-Claire?" she whispered with a look of incredulity. "Robert Howard, you said? My God, that means that you actually *are* Sainte-Claire!"

"How on earth did you find out where I live?"

Her expression of strength crumbled, as if suddenly she'd found a friend who might look after her, make things right.

I was astounded that she'd put me and my graphic hero together so quickly — if at all. My publisher tells me the people who read my graphic novels are aged between fifteen and sixty-five. Looking at this little girl, I would have thought she'd be more familiar with Harry Potter than Sainte-Claire, PI.

"Alice telephoned me just now. I've no idea how she got my number."

Tiggy looked thoughtful.

"She was very upset when she called me. Still is, by the sound of it," I continued, looking over her shoulder through the open front door.

"She'll be fine," Tiggy said, trying to choke back tears that were now welling to fill her eyes. "She cries a lot, you know. Mind you, she had a bit of a fright tonight. Me too. Why don't you come inside, Sainte-Claire, and we'll wait for Aunt Lucy there? She shouldn't be too long — she lives in Edgecliff. She drives quite quickly, you know."

She held out a hand towards me, smiling through her tears. She was a tower of strength again. "It's nice to see you, Sainte-Claire. Makes me feel safe, having you around."

I pushed the gate open, walked towards her and took her hand in mine: then a thought occurred: perhaps it was a better idea to wait outside. After all, I didn't know this girl personally, and the cops would probably be round within minutes. What would Aunt Lucy and Tiggy's mother think when they arrived home and found a total stranger in the house holding hands with a pre-teen child? It'd probably put the fear of God in them. The cops would arrive and cuff me. I could imagine the headline. *Author up on paedophilia charges. "All a huge mistake," claims Robert Howard at committal hearing!*

"I think maybe we should wait out here for Aunt Lucy, don't you?"

Tiggy didn't reply, just smiled up at me. I looked past her again at the half-open front door. The sobbing was relentless.

"Look, on second thoughts, maybe *you* should go inside and see if your little sister is all right – she still seems very distressed."

"Oh, she'll be fine. She's a real crybaby sometimes."

"Are you sure there's no one still in the house? No strangers?" I had to make sure Alice wasn't in any immediate danger from intruders.

"No, they've gone. But it was so scary." She wasn't coping as well now; the tears were now flowing freely down her face.

The headlights of a car turned into Roslyn Street. Tiggy's face crumpled in relief. Quite unexpectedly, she flung her arms around my neck and began to cry hard. This was followed by a torrent of words.

"Oh, please help us, Sainte-Claire! I feel something terrible is happening. Mummy's gone. There was this noise in the night and I woke up and heard people in the house. Mummy was shouting at someone. Sounded like men. Lots of them — two anyway. Then it sounded like they were trying to stop Mummy from shouting — like they were putting something over her mouth — and there was this noise of things being kicked over. I ran to the bedroom door and called to Mummy, but then it went all quiet. Then Ally woke and she… I don't know… Ally's like that, she knows when something bad is happening, and she started to scream. I ran downstairs and all the lights were on. I was so scared, Sainte-Claire."

All of this came out in a cathartic gush, in the space of about three-point-five seconds.

A woman of about thirty-five got out of the car, which she'd double-parked behind mine in the street. She strode towards the gate and pointed a walking cane at my head. "You there!" she shouted loudly. "You let that girl go at once! The police will be here shortly. Leave her alone!"

I tried to let go of Tiggy's hand but she held me fast. I looked lamely at my hand, then at the woman.

Tiggy came to my rescue. "It's all right, Aunt Lucy. He's only here to help. It's Sainte-Claire! He's a friend."

"Well, *I've* never seen him in my life. Would you please let go of the man's hand, Tiger-Lily, and go inside."

Tiggy looked crestfallen and let go of my hand. But she didn't go inside; she stood fast beside me.

"What did Tiggs say your name was? Sainte - something?" Aunt Lucy advanced through the gate towards me.

Almost precisely in unison Tiggy and I said:

"Robert Howard."

"Sainte-Claire!"

Aunt Lucy's lips shrivelled like an oyster doused with lemon juice. "Well, which *is* it?"

"I think we're losing sight of what we should be doing right now, don't you?" I replied. "Little Alice is inside alone, crying her eyes out. I'm here because she called me on the telephone. How she got my number, I have no idea. She asked me to help her because she was afraid and didn't know who to turn to. So here I am, doing my best to help her. My name, for the record, is Robert Howard."

At that moment the police paddy wagon arrived. The doors were thrown open and a sergeant and a young female constable came towards us.

"*Please* go inside and look after Alice," I pleaded with the woman. "It doesn't matter who I am."

The police walked through the gate to join us.

"I'll be right back, officer," Aunt Lucy said to the sergeant, grabbing Tiggy's hand and pulling her up the steps to the front door and into the house.

"Julie. Go inside with the lady," the sergeant said to the constable. She nodded and was off at once taking the steps two at a time.

"Do you live here, sir?" the stout policeman asked me in a brusque but reasonable tone.

"No, I don't," I replied.

"Can you tell me what exactly happened here tonight?"

"Well, actually I have no idea. But I can tell you *why* I'm here, if that's any help." I knew full well that what I was about to tell him wasn't going to sound too credible.

"That would be a start," he replied stonily, reaching for a pad and a ballpoint pen.

"I was at home just a few minutes ago, writing. I'm an author. Graphic novels. I received a call from a little girl who had somehow got my telephone number. She was crying and sounded panicked."

"Do you know this girl?"

"No."

"Then why would she ring you?"

"I've no idea."

He scribbled some notes then looked up at me again. "So, then what?"

"I was concerned for her safety because she sounded hysterical. So I asked her where she lived and immediately called triple zero. Then I came round here myself."

"You're talking about the child that was here just now?"

"No, that's Tiggy. The girl who called me was Alice. I think she's inside crying."

"She told you her name was Alice? On the phone?"

"That's correct."

I looked at the upside-down pad. The names 'Tiggy' and 'Alice' were added under the time and address.

"And your name is?"

"Robert Howard."

He wrote down 'Howard, Robert' in his pocket book.

"And you don't know this girl? Alice?"

"No, I don't. I thought I explained that. She thinks I'm someone else. You see, as I said, I'm a thriller writer—"

He held up a hand. "May I have your address please, sir?"

I gave him the full address, postcode included.

"Just round the corner?"

"Pretty close, yes."

At that moment, the policewoman reappeared at the front door.

"Sarge? Can you come inside?"

"Be right with you," he said, looking up the steps. He turned back to me. "Do you think you could stick around for a moment or two, sir? I'd like to ask you a few more questions."

"Mind if I join you inside?" I replied.

"I'd have to ask the owner of the house first, Mr Howard. How about I do that, while you wait at the door?"

I felt he was treating me like an idiot, but I put my ego on hold for the sake of the children. I felt an instant bond with the two of them, and I hadn't even *met* Alice yet.

So I stood by the gate and waited. I could hear muffled voices inside, but not much more. Alice had stopped crying. Quite a few houses now had their lights on. The commotion, coupled with the arrival of the police truck, had woken the entire street. There were now three cars double-parked outside the house – my 1985 Citroën Goddess, Aunt Lucy's Volvo and the police vehicle. Even though a paddy wagon would be a familiar sight in this district, it still aroused curiosity. It's like helicopters – they've been around for decades yet people still can't resist gawking at them.

Kings Cross is Sydney's red-light area, where drug-related crime and prostitution are the name of the game. Yet, unlike most other red-light areas round the world, the Cross is also home to ex-prime ministers, lawyers, writers, movie stars and every imaginable professional person. You can walk along one street where vagrants lie asleep on the pavement, take a left turn and you're in a street of five-bedroomed, five-marble-bathroomed, two-million-dollar terrace houses. Soho in London was the same in the sixties: the rich and famous living cheek by jowl with the 'crims and prossies'. Greenwich Village and Soho are similar in New York.

Roslyn Street was home to lovely old terrace houses that would average two and a half million dollars at auction, yet fifty feet up the road at the El Alamein Fountain, a cross section of the minority groups of Sydney was singing the night away cross-legged on the pavement, passing booze around. If I'd had children, I'd have chosen to live in a safer area. But then, perhaps sheltering children from the realities of urban life is a problem in itself. It was doubly unfortunate for the parents of these two children that during the past few years

Roslyn Street had become the location of choice for casual drug dealers.

As I waited to be called inside, I noticed someone at a ground floor window two doors down, across the street. I could only see a human torso – the head was hidden behind a lace curtain. The baggy trousers suggested an elderly man. My cat Giblet thinks that if you hide your head behind a curtain and leave your body unobscured, you can't be seen. So did this idiot. I waved at him and smiled. In a flurry of curtain lace, the torso was gone.

"Mr Howard?"

I turned. It was the policewoman.

"Would you like to come inside for a moment or two, sir?"

"Of course," I replied.

She stepped to one side and I walked up the steps and into the house. It was one of those terraces that had had a major designer refit. There didn't appear to be any supporting walls at all; it looked new-age Sydney-minimalist. Polished wood floors, expensive eclectic furniture, cream walls. A Brett Whiteley on the wall opposite. Not an oil or acrylic, it looked more like a colour litho. Nice nonetheless.

Sitting at the far end of the room on one of two three-seater cream-coloured sofas was Aunt Lucy. On her lap was a little girl with almost white blonde curly hair, very reminiscent of Millais' famous painting *Bubbles*. It had to be Alice - the source of the earlier sobbing. She was sucking her thumb and staring at the floor in a daze. Sitting at Lucy's side was Tiggy, hands folded in her lap looking very grown-up. Opposite them, sitting on a small period Chinese chair, was the sergeant.

Tiggy looked up as I entered the house and beamed at me.

There's nothing quite like the ingenuous smile of a child. If a child smiles at you it's because they like you and they simply can't help themselves — like most dogs and some cats. I can recognise a smile on most animals — birds are more difficult. It's the opposite, of course, if children find you annoying. The same goes for the majority of dogs, and all cats. Birds? I'm not sure.

I switched my glance from Tiggs and caught Alice's eye. Her face lit up like a lighthouse.

"Sainte-Claire! Tiggs said you'd gone!" she cried out.

The policewoman gave me a blank look. The sergeant consulted his notes quickly.

"Gone? Me? Nah!" I replied. "Not until I know everything's fine. But how did you know it's me?"

"Just do!" Alice squealed happily. "But you don't look much like Sainte-Claire."

Somehow I felt she didn't mean this as a compliment. Sainte-Claire has sometimes been described as 'way cool' by my younger readers.

"Actually, Tiggs told me you're probably in disguise," Alice went on, and giggled.

All the adults stared at me, uncomprehending.

Alice clapped her hands, then looked at her aunt and hugged her. "He'll find Mummy. He does those sorts of things all the time. Dead bodies too!"

"I'm sure he does, darling," Aunt Lucy replied, as if the words 'dead bodies' had never been uttered. She brushed a loose twist of Alice's bubbly hair to one side. "Do sit down, Mr Sainte-Claire."

"Howard. My name is Howard. Sainte-Claire is my fictional hero. I'm an author, I write crime fiction. Well, graphic novels. That's novels with pictures." Same old spiel.

"You're Sainte-Claire to me and Tiggs! Always will be," Alice shouted loudly. There was evidence of the smallest pout as she spoke.

"Whatever," Aunt Lucy cut in. " It doesn't really matter, does it. I'd just like to thank you so much for coming to the children's rescue as you did. It was very kind."

"Oh, anyone would have done the same. Alice here—"

"Ally-Oop!" Alice interrupted. "You can call me Ally-Oop!" She pointed a finger at the sergeant. "*He* can't!"

The sergeant glanced at me again and I could see the muscles in his jaw working. There was a slight hiatus in the conversation.

"Ally-Oop seemed very upset," I ploughed on, "so I thought I'd call the police, just in case."

Everyone was staring at me, so I felt compelled to continue. "So… what exactly *is* the problem?"

Aunt Lucy turned to Tiggy. "Tiggs, be a darling and take Alice back to bed, would you? I'll just be a few minutes here. Then I'll come and tuck you both in."

"Will Sainte-Claire come and see us tomorrow?" Tiggy asked as she stood. "We could talk about… stuff."

"If Mr Sainte-Claire isn't too busy," Aunt Lucy said, glancing at me. "We'll see if we can arrange something, darling. Now off you trot with Tiggs."

"It's Howard," I said.

"What is?" Lucy asked absentmindedly.

"My name."

"Yes. I know that. You just said so."

"No, you misunderstand me. *You* just called me Sainte-Claire."

"I didn't," she replied crisply.

"Well, it doesn't matter of course. Just thought I'd make sure you knew who I was."

There was a stony silence.

I smiled at Tiggs. "Well, I'd love to see you all again sometime soon and chat about… well…*stuff.*"

Tiggs shot me a look. She obviously didn't appreciate being patronised. That hadn't been my intention.

"Bye, Sainte-Claire. Don't be a stranger now," she said, very grown-up. She'd probably heard the phrase in some American soap opera. She held out a hand to Alice. "Come on, Ally. Bed!"

Alice took hold of Tiggy's hand and they walked past me to the stairs. As they started climbing Tiggs glanced back over her shoulder and winked at me. No smile, just a wink. Very Lauren Bacall.

Now I was alone with the adults. *This* was scary. I'd much rather have been chatting to the kids.

"Thank you again for coming over, and for calling the police, Mr Sainte-Claire."

This Sainte-Claire thing was getting out of hand.

"Look, just so we all know, for the record, my actual name is Robert Howard. The hero of the books I write — they're graphic novels actually — is called Sainte-Claire. I don't know how your nieces came to think of me as Sainte-Claire, but we can probably clear that up some other time. What's more important is this — is their mother all right? Alice told me she woke up and her mother was gone. Then Tiggy told me that she heard her mother shouting and there was some kind of scuffle — as though someone was trying to gag her. And now there's no sign of her. So, what happened?"

The police sergeant gave me 'the look'.

"I was asking that very question when you came into the house, Mr Howard. Perhaps you'd let me continue?"

Aunt Lucy, for the first time, looked worried. I suppose she'd been putting on a brave front for the kids.

"I'm afraid I don't know where Charlotte is — Charlie's the children's mother, my sister. There's no sign of her. It's very worrying."

"Mrs Portman, when did you last see your sister?" the sergeant asked.

"I speak to her every day. Or most days, anyway. The last time we spoke was yesterday morning. She was fine then. She took the children to school, and was working at home when I called."

"What time would that have been?"

"Midday. She was editing a manuscript on Egyptology for Rikards, the publishers."

"Do you think your sister would ever simply leave the house and forget to lock the door behind her?" I asked.

Sergeant Hughes shot me a 'do you mind minding your own business, this is my job' look.

"Of course not," Lucy replied, "Certainly not in the middle of the night. That's what's so worrying."

A thought struck me. "Does Charlotte have a mobile phone?" I asked quickly, before Sergeant Hughes could open his mouth again.

Lucy's eyes lit up. "Yes! Of course. Let's ring it! Good idea."

"It's an idea Sainte-Claire might have come up with," I said. The words were out of my mouth before I realised how asinine they sounded.

Lucy dug into her handbag, snatched up her mobile phone and punched in some numbers.

We all waited expectantly.

Then we heard a mobile phone cheep upstairs and Lucy's shoulders slumped.

"I'll go check it out. Let it ring, please," said the policewoman. She disappeared upstairs.

"Do you mind my asking — is your sister married, Mrs Portman?" I said.

"Of course she is," Lucy shot back. "She has two small children. You've just met them, for heaven's sake."

"I think what Mr Howard means is that she may be divorced," Sergeant Hughes cut in. "Would you be able to tell me where your brother-in-law is tonight?"

"Tiggy said he'd gone to see a friend earlier. Around six. I expect he'll be back shortly."

Then her face went pale. "Of course. We should call Peter at once. Tell him what's happened. Bloody silly of me." She punched some more numbers into her mobile and the ringing stopped upstairs.

We sat in silence for a few seconds. There was clearly no reply to the call. Lucy's expression showed that the message service had kicked in.

"Peter? It's Lucy. Look, there's no need to panic. I'm with the girls right now. Seems that Charlie's gone missing. Not for long or anything, but we can't find her. It's after midnight, or thereabouts. Can you get back ASAP? We don't really know what's going on."

I could tell she was debating whether or not to say something else. Question was, what would it be? She decided to say nothing and hung up.

"Perhaps he left his phone in the car," I said, trying to be positive.

"Perhaps," Lucy replied.

The policewoman came downstairs. "The master bedroom looks undisturbed. Mrs Reid's nightgown is still under the pillow, so it looks as if she was downstairs when she had her argument with...whoever it was. I'll take a look in the kitchen."

"I hope the argument was with someone she knew, rather than an intruder," Aunt Lucy said quietly, more to herself than any of us.

"Tiggy said she heard her mother shouting," I said. "And she could hear furniture being knocked over. Then she said it sounded as though someone was trying to gag her. Sounds more like an intruder to me."

"I wonder if you'd let *me* ask Mrs Portman *my* questions, Mr Sainte-Claire?"

"Howard," I said. "You've got it down on your pad somewhere."

Hughes gave me another of his annoyed looks. I wasn't going to get the full ten out of ten in his 'buddies' poll.

The policewoman returned. "A chair's been knocked over and damaged in the kitchen, Sergeant. And there's some broken crockery — cups and stuff — on the floor."

Lucy put her head in her hands. She was now clearly shaken.

"I don't suppose—" I began, then stopped.

Lucy looked up as if to prompt me to continue.

"Well, it's none of my business, but perhaps your sister and brother-in-law haven't been getting on so well recently?"

"You mean could *they* have had a fight?" Lucy answered.

"I think what Mr..." Sergeant Hughes glanced down at his pad, then up again, hoping no one had seen him, "I think what Mr Howard is suggesting is that it's possible your brother-in-law came home, got into an argument with your sister, they had a fight, and they both left the house in a temper."

"Leaving the children alone? With the door open? No way."

"Well, it has been known to happen. We see these kinds of domestics all the time."

Lucy stared him down. "Not in *my* family. Our family isn't prone to domestics."

"Mrs Portman, this isn't a *class* thing. It's something that happens to us all — kings, queens, grocers, policemen, everyone."

"Well, it doesn't happen to *us*, Sergeant Hughes. Charlie would put her life on the line for those children!"

"But possibly not for her husband?"

"What are you insinuating, Sergeant?" Lucy asked.

"Just that she might love her children more than her husband."

"*All* mothers do," was Lucy's crisp reply. "It's quite natural to prefer one's children and animals to one's husband."

She had a point.

Hughes made some more notes.

"Perhaps," I began, hoping to settle her down a little, "you might have a photograph of Charlotte and Peter handy? One that you could give Sergeant Hughes here. Then he could take it back to the station, make some photocopies and pass them around."

Sainte-Claire would have solved the riddle of the disappearance by breakfast.

Lucy stood and walked right up to me so she stood quite close — almost nose to nose. Deliberately confrontational.

"Look, Mr Howard, Sainte-Claire, or whatever your name is, I'm very tired and overwrought right now. So, while I'm grateful that you should have taken the trouble to come round to make sure the children are all right, I think this has now become a personal family matter — one that is no longer your concern."

She paused, as though daring me to offer any more advice on how to find her missing sister and brother-in-law.

"Mrs Portman," Hughes said, "I take this matter quite seriously. I'd like to hope that the disappearance of your sister will be temporary – perhaps the result of an argument with her husband. However, there remains the very real possibility that there were intruders here tonight. And until we have the opportunity to speak to Mr Reid, we have to consider that your sister may have been taken by force from this house. I'd like to ask your permission for some detectives to come out here and take a thorough look around."

Lucy turned to Hughes, her cross expression reverting to worry. "Oh God," she mumbled, "what on earth happened here tonight?"

I wanted to leave, but I didn't know whether I should interrupt. It seemed a little uncaring to say 'Well, I'll leave you to it' just at that point.

"Will you be staying here until we are able to locate your sister or your brother-in-law, Mrs Portman?" Hughes asked.

"Of course I will," Lucy murmured. "Someone's got to make sure the children are safe."

"If there's any way I can help," I ventured quietly, "do let me know." I reached into my right pocket and pulled out my wallet, drawing out one of my business cards.

She looked at me with a soft half-smile. "I'm sorry I was short-tempered with you just now, Mr Sainte-Claire. It's just so worrying, that's all."

"Howard," I said. "Sainte-Claire is my character's name. But it doesn't matter — I'm Sainte-Claire to Tiggs and Ally-Oop, I may as well be the same to you."

I smiled. After all, it was intended as a joke. However, Lucy stared blankly as though she had no idea what I'd said to her.

"Constable Downe will stay with you for the time being, if that's convenient, Mrs Portman," Hughes said. "I'll go arrange for some detectives to call round as soon as possible. Probably within the hour."

Lucy sat down on the sofa. I felt she was close to tears. Just then Tiggy called from upstairs.

"Auntie? Ally won't go to sleep until you come up."

"I'll be with you right now, darling," she replied. She was on her way up the stairs as I left.

As I walked towards the gate, I saw an elderly man in baggy pants put a scrap of paper under the windscreen wiper of my car. I wouldn't swear to it in a court of law, but he looked very similar to the curtain-peeper I'd noticed a while back. He looked up as I walked towards him, then shuffled off to his house across the way and slammed the front door quickly behind him.

I pulled the paper out from under the wiper. There were just three words scrawled in pencil on the back of a Woolworth's grocery receipt: "Double-parking dickhead!"

2

It was close to two in the morning when I got home. I tried to get back on track with what I'd been doing prior to the telephone call from Alice, but that wasn't possible. I couldn't get those kids out of my mind. I was worried for them — mostly because I felt they had more common sense than the adults who were supposed to be looking after them.

Was I being unfair to Mrs Reid? If she'd been abducted against her will, certainly. But where the hell had *Mr* Reid been when all this was happening? Had he simply gone out to see a friend, as Aunt Lucy maintained, and was having a good time somewhere else? I hoped so. At least the girls would soon have one parent to look after them.

The possibility that Peter Reid had also been abducted was slim. The fact that he wasn't answering his mobile wasn't cause for concern since most people switch off their phones as a matter of courtesy if dining at someone else's home. Peter would know Charlie was looking after the children.

I kept looking at the phone on my desk, without quite knowing why. Maybe I hoped Aunt Lucy would call, tell me that Charlie had returned, and it had all been a big mistake.

But 3 a.m. came and went, and the house remained still.

My mind was full of a jumble of disturbing images: visions of Charlotte Reid struggling in the kitchen, two masked men wrapping a gag round her mouth as she tried vainly to call for help.

As I couldn't sleep, I opened my email to see if Lara, my literary agent in New York, had had any feedback from my New York publishers. The option to film my latest Sainte-Claire thriller, *The Fist Visits the City of Shadows*, had expired and she was now going for a big three-book deal. 'The Fist' was another street nickname for Sainte-Claire — I featured his hands in a lot of my artwork.

I clicked on 'Send & Receive' and the usual flood of trash mixed with treasure flooded in. It normally takes me about twenty minutes to weed out what I need to open and what to delete. Often I get emails from people I've never met who want to ask questions about my graphic novels or are seeking advice about publishing their own material. I answer as many as I can. It's the legacy of the gratitude I feel for all the people all over the world who've helped me with my internet research over the years.

I like genuine feedback from my readers, and so, after my third novel, I put my email address inside my books. After all, if people didn't buy my books I'd have to revert to actually working for a living, and that's a horrifying thought.

As I looked at the subject of the first email in my inbox — 'Is Sainte-Claire a closet queen?' — a thought occurred to me. I clicked open to the sent folder and scrolled down the files. Usually, when I've answered an email I delete it — unless of course it has useful information, in which case I save it to another file.

I looked back one by one at all the emails I had sent recently. I was about a minute into this task when I stopped at one that originated from Reid@aol.com.au. Reid was the kids' name. I clicked it open.

As soon as I saw my reply, I knew it was an email that Tiggy had sent me three days ago. At the time I had known her simply as T-L.

It read:

> *Dear Mr Sainte-Claire,*
>
> *Look, I know you're not really Sainte-Claire, but my younger sister thinks you are real. Anyway, I think your comic books are really wicked! Dad reads them to Alice every night before bed. Sometimes I know there's a bit that he thinks he shouldn't read aloud to Alice – she's my little sister. When that happens he winks at me and I read that bit later.*
>
> *Mummy reads things like Tolkien. She's always preferred fantasy. Maybe she's an escapist. In a way, so am I.*

I just wondered if I might be able to chat with you on the phone sometime. I read your books a second time when I'm alone. And Alice just loves the pictures! I don't really know why Dad edits bits for Ally-Oop, because they're not too violent or anything. That's what's so nice about Sainte-Claire - everyone's so afraid of him he doesn't have to do much to get some answers! Anyway, you probably don't like giving your telephone number to strangers, so maybe if I give you my number at home, you might call me? My Mum's called Charlotte. Everyone calls her Charlie. Am I being too boring? I just love Sainte-Claire. He's so smart. And nothing seems to faze him. My telephone number is **** ****.

Best wishes,

T-L.

I stared at the email. I remembered the day I received it; I'd been very rushed because I'd had to get some proofs off to my publishers. I'd simply replied;

Dear T-L,

Thanks for the email. Glad you like reading my graphic books. They're fun to write. I'd love to have a chat sometime when I finish what I'm doing. All the best,

Robert Howard (Sainte-Claire!)

PS Give my best to your sister for me!

I'd sent it off and had been about to drive round to my publishers when I thought, hell, why not call the girl and give her a big surprise. So I'd picked up the telephone and dialled. After a few moments an automatic message kicked in. The voice must have been Mrs Reid's — Charlie.

I'm afraid neither Peter nor I are able to get to the phone right now, please leave a message, or call me on my mobile… It gave both her and her husband Peter's mobile numbers.

As far as I could remember, I'd said something I thought was amusing — something I hoped would make T-L smile. It was along the lines of: 'This is Sainte-Claire calling T-L. Hope I got the number right. I'll call again sometime soon. See ya around, hey? Bye."

So 'T-L.' was Tiger-Lily. Tiggs. Now I could piece the puzzle together. The telephone at the Reid home probably recorded the telephone number of everyone that called. T-L would have come home that day and either her mother passed on my message, or Tiggs had been the first home and listened to it herself. Either way, she'd probably written my telephone number down on a pad somewhere together with my name – or rather Sainte-Claire's name. Days later when Alice had woken to hear her mummy screaming, she'd run to the telephone to call for help. She'd have seen my name scribbled on the pad and thought all her dreams had come true. Sainte-Claire to the rescue! Whoopee!

It was the only scenario I could make work in my mind.

The telephone woke me the next day. It felt late. I knew immediately that I'd slept in.

It was Jez, the love of my life. Her full name is Jezebel Norman and she was twenty-seven then, I was thirty-six — an age gap I thought just about right. She's a more than reasonably successful Australian painter with a studio just off Crown Street in Surry Hills. A lovely studio, and a still lovelier girl: five ten, skin the colour of a slowly stirred macchiato, Coco Chanel jet-black cropped hair and the longest legs you'll see off a Milanese fashion runway.

Her mother is a Brazilian dancer named Delilah who came to Sydney with a samba troupe in the late sixties. Frank, Jez's father, is a half-blood Aborigine who organised a touring dance troupe of his own around Australia thirty-odd years ago. He took one look at Delilah dancing the salsa on the stage at the Enmore Theatre, asked her out for a drink, got entirely carried away by her crazy personality and asked her to marry him within the month. Delilah didn't think twice. Frank's still a good-looking man; in *those* days he was a knockout.

You may be wondering about the name, Jezebel? Gives you some idea of the mind-set of her mother. When I think of Delilah I always think of that Nina Simone lyric: 'Crazy he calls me, sure I'm crazy, crazy in love with you'. That's Delilah — but crazy in the nicest possible way. Delilah took Frank to Paris a few years back and they formed a dance troupe there. Now she teaches Afro-Cubano dance in the Rue du Faubourg-St-Honoré, and Frank looks after the house and tries to keep up with her.

"So what's up, Pulitzer?" Jez sang down the line.

Pulitzer was the nickname she'd given me. She's a half-hearted Buddhist and believes in a kind of weird karma that if you call people by their deepest desire, their dreams will come true. Occasionally I return the compliment by calling her Sulman, or 'Sulie'. She likes that.

"The usual," I answered, suddenly aware of Giblet stretched across my legs like a long ginger rug. Giblet doesn't take kindly to being disturbed when she's stretched. I christened her Giblet because I found her one Christmas Eve staking out the kitchen door of Buon Ricordo, one of Sydney's most celebrated Italian restaurants. It's just around the corner from where I live. She was looking lost and more than a bit hungry. Well, she was alone and hungry on Christmas Eve. Wouldn't you be glum?

"I have to finish some proofs, then call DHL to collect them. Then I'm free."

"Lunch?"

"Jesus! What time is it?" I asked. My left arm was under the cover and moving it to read my watch risked one of Giblet's swift clawing attacks.

"Take it easy. It's only ten," Jez replied. "Did I wake you, Pulitzer?"

"Nah, I've been up for hours."

"Bullshit, Maestro. I woke you and you can't move because that fat pussy's lying on you. Right?"

"Pretty much."

"Come round to the studio, say, two-ish. I'm hashing out something — I want your opinion. Just charcoal so far, but it could be interesting. Okay?"

"I'll be there. My treat." As if it were ever any other way.

I put down the phone and called out a morning greeting to Giblet. To be fair to her, if you wake her up in a civilised way she usually responds favourably. It's only when you startle her that she inflicts pain. In my book that's fair enough — I don't like being shaken into consciousness either. Jez is the one exception — and only then provided she feels like 'fooling around'.

Giblet raised her head lazily, glanced first at the window, then at me.

"Time for brekkie, kid," I told her. That usually did the trick. The breakfast word was one she understood well.

My normal morning regimen is this. Cut up fresh chicken breast or chuck steak for Giblet. Refill cat milk and biscuit tray. Make coffee. Shower. Then check the email.

Over coffee, as I watched Giblet finish a plate of food that would have defeated a rugby union prop forward, I was again consumed by a mixture of curiosity and concern for the Reid family. Had Peter returned home? Was Mrs Reid okay? Had Aunt Lucy been able to cope? Had the kids been sent to school? Perhaps everything had been a storm in a teacup. Hopefully just some misunderstanding.

My initial thought was to call Lucy. Then I realized calling the Kings Cross police was a more sensitive way to find out what had happened at the Reid home. Who knew what had happened in the interim? Quite possibly someone was lying dead — the victim of a road accident — and the family was grief-stricken.

So I made my first call that morning. A policewoman answered.

"You're not Julie, by any chance?" I asked.

"Julie who?"

I couldn't remember if Sergeant Hughes had mentioned the constable's name. All I could recall was Julie.

"It doesn't matter. Perhaps Sergeant Hughes is available? My name is Robert Howard."

"Can you tell me what this concerns, sir?"

"I was at 5 Roslyn Street last night with Sergeant Hughes and his partner. I made a triple zero call in response to a distress call I received. I just wanted to ask Sergeant Hughes how things turned out."

"Sergeant Hughes is off duty right now. Are you a relative of the people living at 5 Roslyn Street?"

"No, just a concerned friend. Could I speak to someone?"

"I'm afraid it's not police policy to discuss these matters over the phone, Mr Howard. Perhaps you could call in personally?"

"Would anyone be able to help me if I did?"

"That very much depends on the nature of your questions. And the case involved, naturally. My advice is to come in and talk to one of the detectives here."

"Can you give me the name of the detective handling the case?"

"I'm not at liberty to discuss the matter over a phone line, sir. As I said, perhaps you might wish to call in yourself."

It was all so much easier in my books. Sainte-Claire has this pal named Phil Govern, a senior detective sergeant who works at City Central. Sainte-Claire simply phones Phil and calls in a favour.

'Hey, Phil. I need to know what went down last night at 5 Roslyn Street. Can you put in a call and get right back to me?'

'Sure thing, Sainte-Claire. I owe you one. How soon do you need to know?'

'ASAP, Phil. Sorry, but I've got a heap on today.'

'No problems, mate. I'll get on to it right away.'

And that would be that. Phil would call back with all the info within five minutes and Sainte-Claire would know all the 'angles'.

All I knew was that I'd have to schlepp down Bayswater Road to the cop shop and grovel for information, same as the next citizen.

I showered and then checked my emails. I was half-expecting another one from Tiggs telling me that everything was okay and not to worry. But there was nothing from the Reid household and about twenty from my readers. Fifteen were congratulatory; four thought they had found textual flaws of one kind or another. Pain-in-the-arse readers.

The final email I opened was from some woman who wanted me to come round to her place and spray her naked body with low-fat fruit yoghurt. She detailed her choice of flavour and her address. Most of the email was taken up with detailing how exactly to get the yoghurt into the spray gun and avoid 'clogging'.

I was out of the house by 11 a.m. and at the counter of the police station ten minutes later.

All the cops were discussing something in the back room — I could see them through an open door. I was ignored long enough to make me twitchy. This would never happen to Sainte-Claire. People notice him at once — he has that kind of aura. Authoritative.

Eventually, a constable caught my eye and came to the counter. He was about twenty-five and very good-looking; the kind you'd immediately cast in a network TV cop show — blond and in terrific shape.

"Yes? Can I help you, sir?"

"I hope so," I replied with a big smile. It's always a good idea to present one's friendly side initially. Of course, Sainte-Claire is usually pretty brusque, but that's fiction. 'Abrasive' might even be a better word to describe his manner, but it never stops him getting answers. And why? Because people instinctively fear Sainte-Claire. One look from him and they get straight to the point.

The cop looked expectantly at me.

"I telephoned earlier. About the incident last night at 5 Roslyn Street."

"Oh, right." He nodded his head; he had no idea what I was talking about. "Do you have any further information concerning the matter?"

"You are aware of the incident I'm referring to?"

"I'll have to take a look, sir. Could you wait here one minute?"

I could see him chatting with a man in a crumpled suit at the back of the station. The man looked in my direction for a second or two, rubbing his eyes wearily. His suit looked as though he'd run a couple of marathons in it, cooked a banquet for a hundred tourists, then slept in it.

He walked up to the front desk. "I'm Detective Sergeant Chase. Can I help you?"

No 'sir' when it comes to plain clothes. Interesting. I made a mental note to include this 'attitude' in future graphic novels. Maybe it was simply fatigue, I know the hours cops work.

"Yes, I hope so. I was at 5 Roslyn Street last night. A possible abduction case — well, that's what Sergeant Hughes and his partner characterised it as at the time. I was the one that made the triple zero call."

"Characterise? What's that supposed to mean?" He obviously thought I was being a smart-arse.

"Characterise? Means describe. That's what they thought it was, anyway. A possible abduction."

"Mr Sainte-Claire, isn't it?"

"No. Howard. Robert. Look, I'm only here because I was concerned for the family. Is everyone all right?"

"Howard? I seem to recollect the report says a man named Sainte-Claire called it in?"

"Well, the report's got it wrong. My name's Howard and that's the name I gave to the operator. Possibly some mistake crept in at Roslyn Street. You see, the two girls thought I was someone else."

Chase began rubbing his eyes again. Possibly the onset of conjunctivitis. I moved back a tad just in case. It's very infectious.

"Why would they think that? The girls, that is."

I took a breath. It was Groundhog Day — I was doomed to make the same speech forever. "I'm a writer," I began, slowly. "I write graphic novels. My central character is a private investigator named Sainte-Claire. Some of my readers think that I actually *am* the person I write about. They confuse the two. But the majority of my readers realise there's a difference. Last night the girl who called me on the phone was a child, and consequently could be forgiven for thinking I actually *was* Sainte-Claire."

"You're talking of the younger of the two girls?"

"That's right."

"Well, how would she know she needed a private eye? Why not just call the police?"

I tried my best not to sound impatient, but I had better things to do than play these games with Detective Chase.

"She's just a little girl — I'd say she's about six years old. Her father reads the books aloud to both girls. The little sister thinks Sainte-Claire's a guy who helps people. She probably saw my telephone number with a name next to it somewhere, and she dialled the number because she needed help. Her mother was gone and she was afraid. Okay? Make sense?"

I was annoyed. "I think I made the exact same speech last night to Sergeant Hughes – it must be on the record."

Chase looked at me and then began to scrape at something inside his mouth with his left pinkie.

"So, what can I tell you, Mr Howard?"

"Well, I was hoping you could assure me that everything's okay at the house. Has Mrs Reid returned, or is she still missing? Has *Mr* Reid returned? I would like to know, if that's allowed."

I know it sounds as though I was being a bit short, but as I kept the smile on my face, the effect really wasn't so bad.

"Well, Mr Howard. As it happens, it was me who looked into the matter last night. I think I got there just after you left. I'm happy to be able to tell you that Mrs Reid returned home an hour or so later and everything's back to normal."

He looked down at his pinkie – he'd just come across some food particle left over from breakfast.

"So there was no abduction?"

He locked eyes with me. "No abduction, Mr Howard."

"Then what happened?" I asked, curious.

"Let's just say it was the aftermath of a domestic matter, Mr Howard. I'm afraid I'm not at liberty to discuss other people's personal affairs with you. Nor police investigations."

"You're investigating?"

"I don't think I said that."

"You mentioned investigations."

"I said I couldn't *discuss* police investigations — not that there *were* any on-going."

"There are?"

"I didn't say that."

"But *are* there?"

Detective Chase's eyes glazed slightly.

"As far as I'm aware, Mr Howard, everything is just hunky-dory at 5 Roslyn Street. As a private citizen, it is your choice whether or not to visit your friends and check that what I've just told you is the truth, the whole truth and nothing but the truth. But me? I have to go to the men's room – it's been a long night."

He turned his back on me and wandered off.

3

I was in a pretty cranky mood by the time I finished my interview with Detective Sergeant Chase. Curiosity got the better of me as I exited the cop shop, and I turned left and walked down towards Roslyn Street. So much for the sensitive approach. Now I *had* to know if all was well.

The sun was out and the street looked rather picturesque — apart from a small huddle of emaciated addicts at the corner of Roslyn and Bayswater Road looking for a fix. An old man was sitting in an armchair in a front garden while an even older man, who must have been in his eighties, was snipping away at what remained of the seated man's white hair.

There was no doorbell on Number 5, so I knocked.

No reply. So I knocked again — this time more loudly.

Still no response, so I did something I'd not normally do; I looked in the window. The curtains were drawn, but there was an inch or two between them to peek through. The lights were off inside and there was no sign of life. Perhaps everyone was out.

I knocked again, one last time.

To my surprise, this time there *was* a response. But it was behind me, from across the street. The old grouch from the night before — the one who thought he was invisible if his head was behind a lace curtain.

"She's out," he shouted at me through the open window from behind his curtain.

"I can *see* you," I shouted back loudly, as I would to a child playing Hide and Seek. The body disappeared from the window, then reappeared as the front door opened. His expression was angry now.

"I'm just trying to be helpful, you big dickhead! Knock all you like. She's out!" His tone was like something you'd expect from a mutant out of *'The X-Files'*.

31

I smiled hugely. "Well, I'll be damned! That explains why no one's opening the door."

He just stared at me. I was suddenly afraid that some indescribably disgusting life form was about to spring from his stomach.

But — what do you know — at that precise moment I heard a voice behind me. "Yes?"

I turned. A woman had opened the door.

"Can I help you? Are you another detective? I'm afraid I was asleep."

I quickly glanced back and winked at the grouch across the street.

Then I turned back to the woman.

She looked around thirty-six. Conservatively dressed. Harrowed expression that spoke volumes regarding her general state of mind. Logic dictated she was Mrs Reid. Charlie. Despite her rattled expression, I noticed she had nice hair and good teeth.

"No, I'm not a detective. I hope I haven't come at a bad time. My name's Howard. I was here last night. I made the triple Zero call."

The woman said nothing. Just chewed her lip a bit.

"Are you by any chance the mother of Tiggs and Ally-Oop?"

"I'm Mrs Reid. Yes."

The staring continued for a couple of seconds. I don't think she was trying to be rude. Her expression told me she was hundreds of miles away in some nightmare wilderness of storms, windlashed coastline and terror.

"So everything's okay now? That's what they told me at the police station."

I could see the nightmare images slowly fade, the clouds scudded from her mind and she began to register my words — up till then she must have been on autopilot. Immediately a fake smile the width of the Parramatta River transformed her from wraith to quizmaster.

"Oh, yes, everything's *fine*! Just fine. Look, do come in, Mr Howard. I am so grateful for all your kindness last night. My sister

Lucy told me how sweet you'd been, and the girls wouldn't stop talking about you all morning! You're a hero figure to them. They think you're quite wonderful. I had to fight to get them off to school. Come in!"

The house was cold, which made me feel uneasy. Why uneasy? Well, it's the kind of thing Sainte-Claire would notice. A happy house with kids running round is usually kept warm. It was winter, but the heater evidently hadn't been switched on. Even Mrs Reid had her arms wrapped around her for warmth.

"Can I get you a coffee, Mr Howard? Do say yes. It's the very least I can do to thank you for coming out here in the middle of the night."

"That would be great. You're sure I'm not interrupting anything?"

"Absolutely not. I'm working from home today. Doing a little tidying up of a book I'm compiling — a new coffee table number on the Egyptian god Amon. Quite interesting, even to a thriller writer such as yourself. Someone who maybe thinks Egyptology a bit dull? Am I right?"

"Quite the opposite. I love history and all the associated Egyptian fables. Wasn't Amon a fertility god?"

I knew a little about Egyptian gods, though perhaps fertility wasn't the most apposite subject for a first conversation. However, I thought it might forge some literary bond between us as writers, and possibly lighten her up a bit.

She was delighted at my interest. "You're quite right. Amon was one of the eight divine forces of chaos known as the Ogdoad."

"Can chaos *ever* be divine, I wonder?" I said light-heartedly. But she didn't appear to be aware of my presence any more — I could see by her expression that she'd been instantly transported to the banks of the Nile.

"Amon became a national deity in the second millennium. His name was fused with that of the supreme solar deity, Ra, to create Amon-Ra. He was the hidden power who created the gods, you know."

She looked into the half distance as she chatted on. "Would you believe the snake form of Amon-Ra is said to be the earliest being to exist in primeval waters?"

"Wouldn't doubt it for a second," I replied with a warm, reassuring smile. She had a somewhat loopy air about her, even bearing in mind the events of the previous night.

I looked down at an enormous book that lay on the coffee table. It had a picture of the familiar jackal-headed Egyptian god Anubis on the shiny cover. I estimated the cost of the tome at around three hundred dollars and wondered how many had been sold. Even if she achieved half of my sales she'd be ahead of me.

She saw the direction of my glance. "That's mine."

"I can see that," I said, pointing at her name in bold letters. "Very snazzy."

She stared vacantly for a second, then a smile broke through — maybe she thought 'snazzy' was too flip. "What I mean is, I didn't just edit that one. It was the product of my doctorate."

"It looks wonderful. Is it available at Dymocks? Angus and Robertson? My local store is Ariel, on Oxford Street."

This time Mrs Reid giggled, reminding me a little of Alice the night before. Some colour was returning to her drawn features. A good sign.

"Oh, you're pulling my leg, Mr Howard. But, actually, you *can* order it at Dymocks. Of course the sensible thing would be to borrow it from the author, if possible. That would save you two hundred and eighty dollars."

"Sounds great to me. I'd be happy to reciprocate, of course. But that would be a lousy deal — mine sell for around thirty dollars. Pulp fiction, you know."

She clapped her hands together, reminding me again of Alice the night before. "Of course! You're an author too!"

Now I was *really* confused. I thought that had been established a long time ago, and she was way too young for Alzheimer's.

"How absolutely wonderful! My children positively lap up your crime comics. Peter reads them too. I buy them every year as stocking-fillers for Christmas."

Stocking-fillers, eh? Well, I suppose they'd never make the cut as wedding presents.

"They're really a bit adult for children, you know," I said, for want of anything better. "And I like to think of them as graphic novels, rather than comics. Comics are for kids. Graphic novels are for grown-ups."

Actually, I don't consider my books too sexy or too violent for anyone. Simply a bit *sophisticated* for a six-year-old.

"Adult? Oh, come on, Mr Howard!" she replied.

"Let's not be so formal. Why don't you call me Robert?"

"Okay, then. Robert! My opinion — well, Peter's as well as mine – is that we live in the real world. You may as well grow up seeing what's around you and come to terms with it. That's what we teach the children."

"I think you're absolutely right." I held out a hand. "But you haven't told me *your* name. You're Charlotte? Yes?"

"I'm sorry, how rude of me. Yes, I'm Charlie. Well, that's what Peter and Lucy call me. I was christened Charlotte."

She shook my hand warmly.

"Let's go into the kitchen and brew some Hernandez coffee."

Her words were sheer music. Hernandez coffee is, to my mind, the best coffee this side of Madrid. I can drink it any time of the day or night.

"Can I bring the Anubis book through with me?" I asked.

"Of course you may, Richard," she replied, chirpily. She was either very susceptible to sudden mood swings or a great actor. But the name thing was beginning to get out of hand. "Robert," I corrected.

"Oh, I'm such an idiot. Robert! Of course you are!"

"Your husband, Peter. I have this feeling—" I paused, as if trying to recollect having met Peter at some time in the past. Of course I hadn't; I was simply fishing for information.

She didn't bite. She didn't say anything, actually.

"Your husband isn't a lawyer, by any chance? I think we may have met at the Royal Sydney Golf Club?"

"No," she replied without looking up. "Peter's in insurance. A commercial adjuster with the Vandercheltz Group."

I'd never heard of them. I'd hit a dead end, so I dropped the subject.

I couldn't help noticing small fragments of broken crockery lying against the wall under the French windows. Also the back of one of a matched set of three bar chairs that stood against the eating area had been wrenched off. It was propped against the wall opposite.

Charlotte Reid continued to busy herself with the coffee.

"Wasn't Anubis responsible for all those mummys in tombs? And consequently all those English Hammer horror movies?" I said, flipping through the pages of her book.

Charlotte laughed as she filled the kettle.

"Kind of, yes. Some say he was the son of the first Pharaoh. When his brother killed him — the Pharaoh, that is — Anubis embalmed him and wrapped him up in bandages. So I suppose he set a trend. Pity he doesn't get residuals from Hollywood in the afterlife — he'd be worth a fortune!"

The kettle clicked off and she poured boiling water into the glass coffee plunger. The smell would have brought *any* mummified Pharoah back to life.

It was time to broach the subject of the previous night. The question was, how to couch it without appearing too intrusive.

"I found an email that Tiggs sent me a while back when I got home last night. That's how she must have got my telephone number."

Charlie swung her head round, as if someone had discharged a twelve-gauge shotgun behind her back.

"Tiggs? Email? When?"

"Oh, it was no problem. She emailed me a few days ago with your phone number. I telephoned here, but no one was at home so I left a message. I'm just suggesting that's how Alice may have got my telephone number."

Charlie's face was still a mask of apprehension. "What did she say?"

"Tiggs? In her email?"

"Yes."

"Just that she liked my graphic novels. That her father read them to her and Alice. That Ally liked to look at the pictures. You know, cute stuff like that."

I could see she was breathing hard. She looked down at the bench top, her eyes staring wildly. What on earth was worrying the woman? She appeared panicked.

"Are you all right, Mrs Reid?" I asked, moving towards her.

She looked up quickly and put on one of those smiley faces. "Yes, of course. I just was concerned that Tiggy might have been a bother."

"Tiggs could never be that. She's thoroughly charming."

"That's a relief," she said, pouring the coffee.

There was an embarrassed silence as she sipped, occasionally looking up at me from the rim of her cup.

"Must have been a bit of a shock to see the detectives here when you got home," I said after a minute or so.

No reaction. Just more smiley faces. Her grin had become a rictus.

"Did they manage to contact your husband?"

The rictus dissolved and the white mask of apprehension returned.

"Peter? The police contacted Peter?"

I was at a loss how to play this one. Sainte-Claire would have been smooth and reassuring in tone, managing to squeeze every last jot of relevant information out of her within a few minutes. He'd probably have had to fight her off physically into the bargain — Sainte-Claire's very attractive in an irresistibly craggy way. Weather-beaten sexy Jean-Paul Belmondo meets Antonio Banderas. Well, it's fiction, isn't it? People live pretty drab lives, by and large.

"Lucy tried to call him on his mobile phone while she was here last night, but he'd switched it off. I imagine you've seen him yourself since then. He must have been late home."

She put her coffee down and wiped her hands down the sides of her pants. "Of course I've seen him," she said, without looking at me.

"He's all right?"

She drilled me with an almost hostile look. "Naturally he's all right. What on earth do you mean, 'Is he all right.'?"

"I didn't mean to be rude, Charlie. It was a pretty strange evening, that's all. I thought perhaps he'd crashed his car or something, and *that's* why you'd rushed out."

"Who said I rushed out?"

I didn't know how to pursue the matter without being too confronting. "Well, when Alice telephoned me initially she said she thought someone was 'being cruel' to you. Her words. And then later Tiggs told us — the police officers and me — that..." I hesitated as I debated how much to quote. "Let me think. 'There was a big noise in the night,' that's what she said. She woke up and heard you shouting at someone. Sounded like two or more men."

Charlie's face was a picture of frozen horror as she listened.

"She said it sounded as though — I'll try to use her words again, 'as though they'd tried to stop mummy from shouting — like they'd put something over her mouth – and there was this noise of things being kicked over.' That's really why we were all so worried. We thought you'd been abducted, you see."

"Well, of *course* I wasn't abducted." Charlie had recovered some of her composure. "I rushed out because..." She faltered, as though she just couldn't think of anything plausible that would account for her rushing out into the night, leaving the front door open and her two small children alone.

"Gracious, Mr Howard," she said eventually, with a light laugh. "It's really a personal matter I'd rather not go into now. For heaven's sake, we hardly know each other! Yet here I am, being positively *grilled* by you. You'd call it *'the third degree'* in your comics, I expect."

"Graphic novels."

"Whatever. But to get back to what you're asking, it's a personal matter between my husband and myself." The semi-smiley face was back. "Peter's just fine. I am just fine. The *children* are just fine. If you must know, we had a quarrel. A very minor one, I might add. He went to see some friends of his and ended up staying there the night."

"Great," I replied. What more could I say? Sainte-Claire would've squeezed the truth from her. Every last drop of juice. But me? Nah. Mr Nice -Guy.

The initial wraith-like look returned to her face. "Look," she said in a somewhat shaky voice, "it's been a great pleasure to meet you, Mr Howard, but I really have to get moving. So many things to do, you know. So, if you wouldn't mind… "

"Of course. I've got several things to attend to myself. Book stuff. Manuscripts. The usual." I placed my cup on the bench-top and made my way back through the living room to the front door.

"Please give my best to Tiggs and Ally. Tell them to call me any time. Maybe I could take them out on a trip or something. The zoo?"

She didn't reply, simply opened the front door.

"*All* of us, that is, of course," I added quickly. I didn't want her to think I was a 'child enthusiast'.

"That would be very nice. I know they'd love that."

I put on my own smiley face — it seemed like the only suitable response. Then I walked down the steps to the gate.

At the corner of Roslyn it occurred to me that I hadn't had my revenge on the old codger who'd called me a dickhead the night before simply because I'd double-parked in the street.

I pulled out one of my cards. Underneath my name it says simply 'Author', and it gives my email address and lists selected bestsellers. I reached for my silver Tiffany's pen that Jez had given me a couple of years back on my birthday and wrote on the back: *'From a Double-Parker to a Nosey-Parker. One dickhead to another?'*

Then I posted it in his letterbox.

I'd reached the top of Roslyn Street again when I heard a door slam loudly behind me. I glanced round and saw Charlotte Reid run down her front steps, throw open the gate, run to her car and get in.

A couple of moments later she sped off, the tyres squealing as they tried to get a grip.

Stranger and stranger.

Sainte-Claire would have jumped into his customised 1974 Fiat Innocenti and given chase — a few cars back, naturally — but I was on foot. Unprepared. My Citroën Goddess was in the garage, having failed to start yet again the previous morning.

The idiot writer.

4

"I'd drop off if I were you. Hell, you've got enough on your plate right now, Pulitzer, without worrying about crazy people."

Jez was getting stuck into a risotto with seared tuna and porcini mushrooms. Eating and drinking were a serious occupation to her. I'd settled for a simple plate of prosciutto crudo. A bottle of Ciccone Estate Sauvignon Blanc, our favourite, stood between us in a cooler, practically empty already. I was matching her glass for glass, but it was proving hard to keep up.

She looked up from the risotto to judge whether I was considering taking her advice, and poured the last of the white wine into her glass before I could react.

"I'm just worried for the kids," I said. "They're a cute twosome."

"Tiggs and Ally-Oop. Sounds like a music hall team," she replied, laughing. Everything is either a dance or a canvas to Jez.

I couldn't help noticing a young guy around twenty sitting at a far table. Jez and I were eating on the pavement on Bourke Street, under one of those propane heaters. The young buck had been staring at Jez's legs for twenty minutes straight now, possibly hoping she'd cross them, à la Sharon Stone, if he stared long enough. The fact was, he had just the right angle to take advantage of such serendipity.

"I mean, what *really* went on last night?" I said, returning to my former train of thought. "*That's* what I'm wondering."

"Write a book about it."

That's what they all say. Problem was, I didn't have the first idea what I was dealing with.

"Hey, come on, Pulitzer, the cops *are* usually right. It's a domestic, no question. Look, with ninety per cent of murders the killer's usually the victim's husband, or one of the grown-up kids. The motive's usually money. I'd say Petey-boy got himself in a spot of bother last night with a young lady. Charlie got wind of it and it made her see red. So much so, she went out after hubby to beat the living shit out of him. End of story."

She paused to wipe the last of her porcini sauce from the plate with a crust of sourdough bread, then uncrossed and recrossed her legs. The young man opposite swallowed hard.

"Truth and fiction," I murmured to myself. "Which is stranger?"

"Truth's not as entertaining," Jez replied. "Although network execs wouldn't agree with me."

"What would Sainte-Claire do? Come on, what do you reckon?" I asked.

"Hell, I don't know. Probably go see her, wheedle the truth out of her, take care of business — then screw her."

I was disappointed in her for once. "Oh, come on, Jez. Sainte-Claire doesn't simply *screw* women. That's a bit hard-edged, don't you think?"

"I don't know, he always seems to end up in the sack with them."

This was true. But she was putting it in such a tawdry way. In my graphic novels I like some sort of relationship to develop slowly. And I usually made the point that Sainte-Claire ended up in bed with the client — at *her* instigation. She just couldn't help herself.

"Okay, but he doesn't *screw* them," I persisted. "It's better than that."

"Sure is. He bonks them till they can't move. That's my kind of guy."

"We're talking romance here! Women are drawn irresistibly to Sainte-Claire because of his charisma. *That's* the name of the game. *That's* what I write. *That's* my personal fantasy. And that's what my readers like to read, because it's their fantasy too," I protested. "One thing I can assure you, it's got nothing to do with the length and breadth of his dick."

She gave me 'the look', smiling wickedly. Then, to my immense surprise, she stood, walked round the table and kissed me full on the lips. Long and hard. Pressing the top half of her fabulous body into mine. She tasted of cream and porcini mushrooms; she smelled of Gaultier scent and sunshine. It was the sexiest thing.

She returned to her chair and sat as I fought a testosterone rush — could have been embarrassing.

"That's because Sainte-Claire is *you*, Pulitzer. Well, in a way, I suppose. And you screw pretty well too, as a matter of fact."

She smiled and the street lit up. Those teeth. That smile. Those lips. Whoah!

I couldn't help glancing again at the young guy. He was sweating.

So was I.

"Well, thank you, kind lady," I replied.

A woman in a twin set and tweed pants sitting at the next table turned and smiled pure acid at us both. "I'd like to thank you *personally* for sharing that thought with the whole restaurant," she said. "Especially with my husband. He's got this…" She searched for the right word. "This *thing* about coloured people."

Jez turned her head slowly to look at the old bag. "Then maybe he should dip your blue-rinsed head in a strong solution of hot Nescafé and make himself happy."

I walked Jez back to her studio and made all the right noises when she showed me her latest canvas — I'd been too late to look at it before lunch. It was a bunch of charcoal squiggles that looked like some kind of a bird; interesting.

Back home, images of the Reid children still flashed through my thoughts every few minutes. I had to do something to put my mind at rest. I got the number of the Vandercheltz Group from directory assistance and called them.

"The Vandercheltz Group. May I help you?"

"May I speak with Peter Reid, please," I asked the soothing male voice at the other end of the line.

There was the slightest hesitation.

"I'm afraid he's in a meeting at present. Can I take a message, sir?"

I told him I needed some insurance advice and Peter Reid had been recommended by a friend. I gave him my number.

"Have you any idea how long the meeting might last?" I asked.

There was another pause. Too long again. It didn't take a genius to jump to the conclusion that Peter Reid wasn't in a meeting at all.

"I'm sure he'll get back to you this afternoon, sir. Perhaps there's someone else who might be able to help you, Mr…? "

"Sainte-Claire," I replied without thinking, then immediately regretted it.

"Well, Mr. Sainte-Claire, how can I help you?"

"I'll wait to speak to Peter Reid, thanks all the same," I cut in, and hung up.

So, Peter either was in a meeting or he hadn't shown up at work that morning. I hoped it wasn't the latter. Maybe he was in trouble and Charlie had known, but wasn't about to tell me. I tried to think along the lines Saint-Claire would have done, and picked up a pencil to make some scribbled notes. In my graphic novels such scribbling often leads Sainte-Claire to some conclusion — one that's seldom far from the truth.

'Midnight. Mrs Reid missing. Abducted? Perhaps. Mr Reid absent from home. Quarrel? Mrs Reid returns. No sign of Mr Reid. Mr Reid not at work.'

Just then the telephone rang at my elbow.

"Sainte-Claire? Is that you?" a small voice asked.

"Tiggs?"

"Tiger-Lily. Ms, if I'm to be a client."

I couldn't help smiling; she was quite a character. "Oh, so you're thinking of hiring me?" I said, playing along.

"That's exactly right, Sainte-Claire," she replied crisply.

"Well, I don't come cheap, you know."

"Sure, I know that — the best is always expensive."

43

"It is indeed."

"Five hundred dollars a day plus expenses, or a flat fee 'to be negotiated'. No refunds."

She knew her stuff.

"Well, that was *last* year. New rules now. Inflation. I'm charging seven hundred these days. Plus expenses, of course. And there's another new rule."

"What's that? Hit me," she said unfazed, in early Kate Hepburn-speak. She was clearly a *Movie Greats* afficianado.

"It's ten bucks to kids under fifteen. And *no* expenses. The money is negotiable and there are lay-by facilities."

There was a slight pause.

"There's no need to patronise me, Sainte-Claire. I'll pay my way, same as everyone. I just need time."

"You got it. About seventy years, I'd say. Of course, with me being the wrong side of thirty-five already, I'd like to hope you'd be able to settle accounts within ten years. That would help me a lot. Got to think of my retirement."

"You're doing it again," she said.

"Doing what?"

"Patronising me as though I'm a baby. I'm not Rita Rae, you know."

Rita was a character in the graphic novel before last, *Dawn's Early Light*, a beautiful yet tragic airhead who couldn't grasp the simplest logic. Ms Rae made the characters Marilyn Monroe played seem positively intellectual.

"Well, I'm sorry if I appear to patronise. I don't mean to. You're a very bright girl. I saw that last night."

"Which is why I am ringing, Sainte-Claire."

I looked at my watch. It was 2.50 p.m.

"Where are you? School finished early today?"

"I'm not at school. I'm home. I was worried about my mother, so I told the headmistress I felt a bit sick and wanted to go home early."

"They just let you leave if you say you're unwell?" I asked. Not having kids of my own I didn't know the ins and outs of such simple scenarios.

"Well, they ring *home*, of course, to check. What do you think? Really, you ask the silliest questions sometimes."

"Well, if Charlie said you could come home, why are you worried about her? Isn't she there with you now?"

"No, she's not. And *she* didn't say I could come home, because she wasn't *at* home. No one could reach her on the telephone. That's why I'm worried."

"So why did they let you go home?" I asked.

"Because they trust me. Because *they* don't think I'm silly — unlike you. I am actually twelve years old and quite capable of walking half a mile home."

Now I shared Tiggs' concern. The last time I'd seen her mother, she was driving off at speed. Where had she gone? Was she all right?

I tried to gather my thoughts.

"So what is it exactly you'd like me to do for you? You know I offered to help in any way yesterday, so just ask."

"You're sounding like Mr Howard now. I don't want Robert Howard helping me — no offence intended. He's a nice enough person, I suppose, but… " She trailed off.

"Go ahead. Mr Howard won't take offence. Let him have it, straight."

"Okay. I want *you* to help me, Sainte-Claire. You get to the bottom of things fast. That's why you're you."

It sounded to me like dialogue out of a de Niro movie. *The Deer Hunter*. The scene with the gun.

"Shall I come round to your house? Is that what you'd like?"

"You haven't said you'll take on the case yet, Sainte-Claire," she said.

She'd painted me into a corner. I'd been trying to get answers to the puzzle all morning. Now I was doubly intrigued. Plus, I wanted to help the family if they were in trouble. It seemed the only way I was going to get to the bottom of things was to play along with Tiggs. So I played.

"All right. It's a deal. You get the deferred payment option."

"What's that?"

"Last year's prices, deferred till you're twenty-one. And don't get back on your high horse — all my under-age clients get that deal, Ms Tiger-Lily, so it's nothing special. Shall I come straight round?"

"No. We can't meet here, silly. I want to keep our arrangement private. I don't want Mummy to know, just in case things get dangerous."

Dangerous?

"Sure, I understand."

"How about the Hernandez Coffee House at three - thirty, Sainte-Claire? You know the venue?"

"You got it, Tiger-Lily. See you then."

I was about to leave when I caught sight of myself in the hall mirror. I was wearing a pair of Country Road chinos, a taupe Ferragamo knitted jersey, and brown English Lobb brogues. Pretty conservative. But that's me. I left the fashion statements to Jez.

But my new client, Ms Tiger-Lily Reid, would be expecting a meeting with Sainte-Claire, and he certainly did *not* wear beige chinos and knitted jumpers. He was one dangerous looking dude. I had a lot of thinking to do concerning appearances.

I flipped through my wardrobe, searching for the kind of clothes I usually dress my hero in. Lots of black. And edgy. What did I have available?

I found a black suit, single-breasted Italian linen. It had a label, 'Guaranteed to wrinkle', stitched on the inside breast pocket. Apparently a few wrinkles are good. Obviously inferior linen didn't wrinkle so well, hence the label. I matched the suit with a black Diesel T-shirt, nicely faded, and black Dirk Bikkembergs shoes with toecaps you could rest a Henry Moore bronze on. Perfect.

Next, I headed for the bathroom. Saint-Claire has shortish fair hair which has a tendency to stand up in a spiky sort of way that's considered voguish. I'd seen Brad Pitt sporting a similar style at the *Mondrian Hotel* in Los Angeles after some award night or other, possibly the Oscars, and Jez had told me it was the sexiest look around so I changed Sainte-Claire's hairstyle to match in my novel at the time, *New Yesterday*.

I found a jar of some gook that hairdressers affectionately refer to as 'product' — Jez leaves a secondary supply of all her cosmetics at my place. The label said 'Liquid Toffee'. I smeared a palmful into my hair, and smudged it around a bit as though I were replicating twelve hours of fitful sleep in an armchair. Since I'd just had my hair cut — and much too short, despite my protestations — the effect seemed to work for Sainte-Claire.

I stared at myself in the mirror for a second or two, taken by surprise at the difference. I now looked like one of London's sociopath Kray brothers. There was a cold, somewhat brutal, calculating look in the eyes that held my gaze. The spiky, dishevelled hair, together with all that black fabric had generated a very real metamorphosis — as if I'd stepped into the shoes of a complete stranger.

And yet not so, since I had merely stepped into the shoes of someone who had been a close friend for years. My hero, Sainte-Claire.

The more I looked into this man's eyes, the more I enjoyed the feel of the new identity. It was as if Dr Jeckyll was staring at Mr Hyde, but rather than being horrified by the transformation, he was enjoying it. I relished the feeling that now I could face everything that life chose to throw at me. I was unusually empowered. I threw back my head and laughed.

As I stepped into the street I was Saint-Claire.

5

I had twenty minutes to spare, so I thought I'd call in at Solid Fuel Services and see if Nick had finished giving my beloved Citroën Goddess the kiss of life once again.

I got to know Nick Kougios through his dog, Clamp. An aptly named hound: once he fastens on, it's his choice and no one else's whether or not you go free. This dog has to be the toughest-looking in Darlo — half bull terrier, half something much meaner. Mostly white, with bits of brown and black. Stands head high to your hip and is a supermarket trolley in length. He has a look in his eye that tells you he's not going to take shit from any living thing.

My own dog, Coco, died a year ago and loved Clamp with a vengeance. She was a pretty tough hound herself, but in Clamp's company I swear I often saw her bat her eyes. Most days our first port of call was a visit up West Street to pay a courtesy call to 'El Clampo'.

Nick looks as mean as his dog. And in some respects he is — tough as the welds on the inside of a container ship. He stands about six-two, his head is shaved, his body has the consistency of weathered teak, and he looks more Arab than Greek. Clamp is seldom far from his heels.

Apart from owning a garage, Nick is a part-time stuntie, and runs a tae kwon do course for hard men. I only discovered this because our hounds had clearly taken a fancy to each other, and every now and then Nick and I ended up sharing a few coffees at Bar Coluzzi in Victoria Road. He'd read my books, but had his reservations. 'Not nearly enough serious biffo, mate,' he once said without a smile. He liked the pictures.

When I arrived, Nick was leaning an arm inside my Citroën to switch on the ignition. The engine burbled — just.

He looked up at me. "Well, she's turning over, mate. More than that? Dunno. Done my best."

"Can't ask for more, Nick."

"Shit cars. Nice lines but shit cars. *All* Froggy cars."

Nick was a Holden man through and through. I stared at my car. Mechanically, he was correct. It *was* a shit heap.

Nick smiled wickedly. "You wanna take a look at my new beauties, bubba?"

I thought he was talking cars, but instead he pulled open a drawer of a huge red enamelled steel tool chest and beamed. I looked down at the contents, expecting some mechanic's tools, but this was a collection of the most cruel-looking martial arts weapons I'd ever seen — all long-bladed TKD stabbing knives. I was surprised. Martial arts was one thing; this was practically pornographic.

"Wrong friggin' tray," he muttered, pushing it home and pulling out another tray. This contained mostly 'star' throwing knives.

"Mean as all shit, eh? Don't you just love 'em? Personally, I favour the Surgical Star SS4 over the Cyclone Star. Flies truer. Six teeth as opposed to the three curvy blades."

He shoved that tray home and pulled out a third. Axes! He took out a gleaming long-handled chopping tool.

"This one here's a beauty! The Chinese Farsha Star AX. Wide blade. Could slice prosciutto with this bastard. Wafer-fuckin'-thin."

He handed it to me with the same delicacy a young mother would use to pass over a three-week-old baby.

"Feel the weight, bubba. Nick's little helper, eh? Chop-chop!"

I didn't know the martial arts etiquette of how to respond. "Handy at a barbie?"

Nick eyed me curiously. Was I serious?

"Barbie? Nah, mate. Urban warfare!" Then he beamed and punched my shoulder.

"Joke, Joyce!" he said, roaring with laughter.

I smiled for the first time that day. Nick's attack dog farted loudly in his sleep.

Nick looked at me properly for the first time. Up till then he'd been glued to car engines and weapons of mass destruction.

"Hey, bubba. What's with the new look? I'll have to give you some decent wheels. What's up, mate?"

"No time. Gotta go, Nick," I said. "I'll pick up the car later."

Now that I was a heavy-duty P.I, I wasn't about to be late for my first client.

Tiggs had taken off her school hat but was still in uniform. She was seated at a corner table by the window, drumming her fingers. When I entered she stared at me for a couple of seconds, checking me out from head to toe. By her expression I judged I'd passed a test.

"Have you ordered, Ms Reid?"

Her fingers stopped drumming as I stood by the table, towering above her. I noticed that her feet scarcely touched the floor.

"As a matter of fact I have, Sainte-Claire. Double ristretto with a twist of lemon for you, and a macchiato for me. Okay?"

In my day kids drank milkshakes; how times had changed. The double short black was my hero's trademark day-time tipple. Short, and strong as Hercules. Very tasty too.

"I asked the man to bring them over when you showed up."

"Good thinking. Hate cold coffee."

"I know."

I settled down opposite her. The woman at the next table gave us the casual once-over and smiled. Dad and daughter playing charades?

"Well, let's get right to it, Ms Tiger-Lily. What exactly would you like me to do for you?"

"Before I get to that," she replied, rummaging about in her school bag, "I brought a small retainer with me. I'd like you to have it, as a gesture of my good faith."

She pushed her hand across the table, opening it up and offering what was clenched inside. I held out my hand and she deposited two ten-dollar notes and a five into my palm. I glanced at the money for a microsecond, then slipped the notes into my inside pocket with all the finesse of Bogie in *Casablanca*.

"Fine. Now that we've got the formalities over with, shoot."

"This is all in confidence?"

"Most assuredly," I replied. Very formal.

"Well, then. Let's start with my mother. You came round this morning, didn't you?"

"I did, yes."

"Well, the thing is, she wouldn't have told you any important stuff. I mean, *personal* stuff. She's not like that."

"You don't know what we talked about. You were at school."

"Right. But I know Mum — she'd never tell you what's worrying her. Sometimes she shares problems and stuff with me, but seldom with Dad. Theirs is a quite formal relationship."

I couldn't help smiling. What kind of a child would refer to their parents' relationship as 'formal'. How old was she, for Christ's sake? Ten? What did she mean anyway?

"Can you define formal? Just so I know."

"Oh, they love each other and all that. They just don't kid around together a lot. They're not silly, like you and me."

She looked behind me, caught the eye of a waitress and made a drinking gesture with her fingers. Where were the damned coffees she'd ordered?

She returned to her previous train of thought. "Formal? I suppose I mean… not very cuddly. My family has never been very cuddly. As a matter of fact, I don't think I'm particularly 'cuddly'. I mean, I like to cuddle *animals*. And I don't mind if Alice cuddles me — she's very sweet and rather little, you see."

It all sounded a bit upper class English. "Let's get back to Mum and Dad, eh?" I said. "What's worrying you?"

"My father," she continued, deliberately using the more adult word, "is in some kind of trouble, I think. That's what led to the kerfuffle last night."

Kerfuffle. I hadn't heard that word for years. Shows how kids pick up the language of their parents.

"What kind of trouble? Work trouble?" I didn't much want to mention girl trouble – though I was fully expecting Peter to have a major dose of that too.

"Not work, no. At least I don't think so."

"Well, tell me what makes you think he's in trouble at all?"

"My father has recently started betting on horses. About a year ago, my Uncle Sam sold him a racehorse, and ever since then there've been problems. I think that's where the trouble began. You see, Uncle Sam is what my mum has always called a fly in the ointment."

"Really."

"Yes. I think that means he's a bit of a nuisance," she added by way of explanation to the ignoramus sitting opposite her.

"A bad egg?" I said, continuing the old-fashioned dialogue.

Her face clouded with incomprehension. "A what?"

"Bad egg. Means the black sheep of the family. Someone who's prone to getting into trouble. Is that what you mean?"

Her face lit up. "That's it exactly. Uncle Sam's a bad egg!"

"Is he your mother's brother, or your father's?"

"Dad's."

A pretty dark-haired Hispanic girl arrived with a macchiato and a double ristretto. She winked at me without Tiggs seeing, placed the macchiato in front of me and gave the ristretto to Tiggs.

"No, the double short black is for Sainte-Claire. The macchiato is for me, please," Tiggs said. All grown-up.

"My mistake. Any cakes?"

"Not at present, thank you," Tiggs replied. "Though they do look yummy." The childish word was at odds with her haughty expression. Her eyes dwelt for several seconds on the cakes in the glass cabinet opposite, then flicked back to mine. I'd managed not to smile as I saw the adult in her fighting with the child on account of the sticky chocolate mud cake.

"And what exactly makes him a bad egg in your eyes?" I asked, getting back to my case interview.

"Not just *my* eyes, Sainte-Claire. *Everyone* knows Uncle Sam's always in trouble."

"What kind of trouble?"

Tiggs lifted her cup and sipped at the macchiato. When she put it down there was a small blob of frothy milk on the tip of her nose. She was blissfully unaware of it. I managed not to smile.

"He was always very clever. Cleverer than my father, I'm told; though I personally don't believe that. But that's the problem, I think - Uncle Sam always thought he was so clever he could get away with anything."

She took another sip of coffee. The nose smudge got bigger.

"He went to university in Oxford, and then gave it all up to manage a rock and roll band. Not a famous one or anything."

"Who?"

"No, the Grant Hartley Experience," she replied, misinterpreting my question. "Mr Hartley went to Magdalene College with Uncle Sam. Anyway, the band lost all Sam's money making some awful rock albums, so my uncle started selling insurance."

"Nothing wrong with that," I said. "Your father sells insurance too, doesn't he?"

"Quite right. But Uncle Sam was different because there was no insurance company in the first place. He just pretended there was. Then when people wanted to claim, they couldn't, because there was no money. I only know all about this because Uncle Sam was almost sent to prison and it was in the papers. Dad had to bail him out. It was really embarrassing."

"So what's this got to do with last night?" I asked.

"Well, we hadn't heard from Uncle Sam for a long time. Not long enough really, because something horrible always happens when he turns up."

"When did he show up?"

"A few weeks ago. He telephoned and I answered. He said he wanted to speak to my father. But Dad was out, so I put him on to Mum."

She drained the coffee and started spooning out the froth.

"Mum's face fell when I told her who it was. She told me to go upstairs so she could talk in private. I pretended to, but listened instead. All I could hear was Mum saying things like 'we just don't have it', and, 'it may be the chance of a lifetime for all I know, but we're not in a position to risk it. Not now and not ever.' Then she started to cry and said 'please leave us alone, Sam. I can't bear all of this worry.' That was it. Then she put the phone down. I think Uncle Sam was still talking at the time. You know? You can tell."

"You can tell," I nodded in adult agreement.

The waitress walked by. "Can I get you two more coffee?" she asked, then looked Tiggs in the eye and gestured at her nose, girl to girl. Tiggs looked confused for a moment, then wiped the froth away with the back of her hand. Her face coloured.

"Another coffee, Sainte-Claire?" she asked, as if nothing had happened.

"Thank you, no," I replied.

The waitress smiled sexily at me, which made Tiggs smile. Then her face clouded as she remembered the frothy nose.

"Why didn't you tell me?"

"What's a little froth amongst mates?" I replied.

"She fancies you, Saint-Claire. Did you notice?"

I shrugged. Saint-Claire is fancied all the time by beautiful women. No big deal.

"So what do you think it was all about? The telephone conversation, that is?"

"Well, at the time I thought Uncle Sam wanted money. He usually wants money."

I held up a hand. "Hey, wait a second. What's this got to do with the racehorse?"

"Well, Sam sold it to Dad, and that was the start of everything. The horse was called Faithful Hope. Uncle Sam came round one day a long time ago and told us all that he was selling a racehorse for a friend of his, and it was going cheap as chips. He said it had won heaps of races and was set to do really well. Would Dad like to buy a leg, or a fetlock — something like that, anyway. It actually means a quarter share, not — well, you know what I mean."

"I know what you mean."

"I think Dad was pleased that Uncle Sam wasn't just asking him for more money."

"So pleased he bought the horse?" I interrupted.

"Exactly! We all went to the stables and spoke to the trainer. It was a very pretty horse. We had a lovely day out. Dad did all his business with the trainer and was quite excited. Mum wasn't at all pleased, though. She kept telling Dad that Uncle Sam was up to no good again. But Dad said he'd checked all the horse papers and stuff, and the chances were the horse would win a big race at Randwick and we'd all be rich."

"And did the horse win?"

"Well, yes, it did, actually. But not at Randwick. Somewhere called Goulburn. Not the same — that's what they all said. And it *wasn't* a big race and it *didn't* make us rich. But Uncle Sam told Dad to have a big bet on the horse. So even though he didn't make much money from the race, he did win a fair bit on the bet. And so I expect did Sam. And that was the start of the slippery slope."

Slippery slope. Fly in the ointment — she had the eastern suburbs patois down pat. It was in the genes, no doubt.

"Seems to me your Dad did pretty well out of his bet," I suggested.

"He did. At first, anyway. That's what got him going. I remember him telling Mum over breakfast one Sunday that it was all so easy, and why should he bother going to work every day when you could win pots of money betting on what he called 'sure things.'"

"There's no such thing."

"I know!" she exclaimed. "You don't have to tell *me*. But you weren't there to tell Daddy, were you! That's why it all turned out so badly."

I could see that, despite her anxiety, her eyes kept drifting off to the cake stand. I waved at the waitress, beckoning her over.

"Look," I said to Tiggs, "I'm going to have one of those chocolate suckers over there. Want to share? My treat."

She tried to disguise her delight. "Well, if *you're* going to have one, I may have a taste," she murmured obligingly.

"Two more coffees, please. The same as before, and a slice of the mud cake. Two spoons," I told the waitress.

She smiled and gave me a look as she wrote it down on a pad — you know, that extra eye contact that signifies much, *much* more? It must have been the Liquid Toffee in my hair or the black menacing clothes — it certainly wasn't a reaction I was used to. I have to admit I liked it, even though I'd never have done anything about it. Flirting can be fun, I suppose.

Tiggs grinned so widely she brought her hand up to hide her smile.

"She *really* likes you, Sainte-Claire. I can tell."

"Guess she does," I replied with a straight, 'couldn't-care-less' face.

"Anyway, Dad was so excited that Faithful Hope had won, he asked the trainer—"

"What was his name?" I interrupted.

"Can't remember. It'll come to me. It's in the memory bank somewhere. Anyway, Dad rang him up after the weekend and asked him where Faithful Hope would run next. And the trainer told him someone had stolen her the day she came back to the stud!"

"So what did he do?"

"He rang Uncle Sam because Sam had the insurance papers."

"Isn't your dad in the insurance business?"

"Yes, but they insure big buildings and ships. Not small stuff, like horses and cars. "Uncle Sam said he'd insured the horse, but he told Dad later that he'd forgotten to post the cheque and Dad wouldn't get a penny. We never saw Faithful Hope again!"

"Sounds a bit suspicious to me."

"Dead right! Something slimy was going on there, for sure. But by now Dad was hooked on betting on the gee-gees."

There it was again: parent-speak. Very old-fashioned too.

"But tell me this, Ms Tiger-Lily. How does all this tie in with what happened last night?"

"I'm getting to that, Sainte-Claire."

"It's just that time's money, as I'm sure you'll appreciate."

"Certainly do," she replied as the coffee and cake arrived.

The waitress placed the cake between us and gave us each a plate and a fork. Tiggs smiled a thank you at her and the waitress smiled at me, yet again.

"Anyway, the day before yesterday," Tiggs said, sipping her coffee really carefully so as not to dip her nose in the froth, "a man came to the door in the evening. It was between six and seven. I know because Alice and I were watching *The Simpsons*. Mum called down, asking me to see who it was at the door — we have a spyhole, you see. I looked through and there was a huge man standing there."

"Big as in tall, or big as in lots of muscle?"

"Lots of muscle. No hair. And a line down the side of his face that made me think of Captain Hook."

"A scar?"

"Kind of, yes."

"You didn't open the door, did you?"

"No, of course not. I told the man through the letterbox that I'd get my mother. He said to get my father, but Dad wasn't home yet."

"So what happened?"

"Well, Mum came down and she took one look through the peephole and told the man that Dad wasn't home and that he should come back another time. I was listening round the corner in the living room."

"And?"

"The man shouted through the letterbox, 'You tell him he's got till midday tomorrow. Else I'll be back. Tell him he won't want that.'"

During all this she'd managed to spoon exactly half the chocolate cake into her mouth. The spoon was poised over the remaining half.

"Wicked cake, isn't it," she said, smacking her lips.

I ate a fat wedge of my side, made some suitable 'yummy' noises and pushed over the remaining piece. "Here, help me with this bit, will you?"

She popped it in her mouth.

"So your dad owed someone money — that's what you think?"

"Looks like it. And I'd guess the bad guys came back last night to try to get it from Mum."

"You reckon your father borrowed money to buy the horse?"

"Spot on."

"Your dad didn't come home last night, did he?" I guessed.

She shook her head.

"Do you know where he is?"

"Nope," she replied, her face suddenly as long as Faithful Hope's.

"Well, look, I'll put out some feelers. Ask around the traps, as they say. See what I can find out. Then I'll get back to you. I'm sure we can sort this out pretty quickly."

"I'd rather my mother didn't know I'd hired you, Saint-Claire. It might worry her, and she's worried enough at the moment."

My thoughts returned to where Charlie could have been dashing off to in such a hurry that morning.

"So, could you reply though my hotmail address?" she continued. "I can pick up my email at one of the internet cafés in Darlinghurst Road. Gives me a bit of privacy. You know what I mean?"

"Absolutely," I replied. "Can't have everyone knowing what you're up to, can you?"

She gave me a beady look. "You're not patronising me again, are you?" she asked.

"Perish the thought," I replied with a straight face. "What's your hotmail address?"

Her face reddened for no reason I could think of.

"Tiggy-Winkle@hotmail.com," she said. It was the barest croak. "It was Alice's idea - the Mrs Tiggy-Winkle bit. She's a character in the Beatrix Potter series of books, you know. I used to read them to Ally-Oop."

"Know them well," I said with a poker face. "Good writing."

"Ratchett!"

"No, I mean it!" I said, thinking I'd been seriously caught out being patronising.

"Mean what?"

"I mean I've always liked Beatrix Potter."

"Maybe. But Ratchett's the name of the trainer," she shot back and scraped the last of the froth from the inside of her second cup of coffee.

I walked Tiggs round the corner back home. She let herself in. Latch-key kid.

It was four o'clock. I asked after Alice, and she told me that if Charlie didn't show up with Alice by four-thirty she'd go and collect her from pre-school herself. Then she'd call me.

As I turned the corner into Ward Avenue I saw Mrs Reid's blue Saab turn into Roslyn Street and park outside Number 5.

I couldn't read her expression from so far away, but I could see clearly that she had Alice with her, so all seemed well.

I was relieved.

6

I have an old mate called Slip Haverfield. He lives in a ritzy apartment in Darling Point. Rich as Croesus. Family money — most of which he's frittered away on horses and the good life. Owned a lot of bloodstock over the years. Mostly in England, where he was born. For the last twenty-five years he's owned quite a few in Australia as well.

Despite turning eighty-five last February, Slip still commutes between his horses at Lambourne, possibly the finest address for horseflesh in England, and those he keeps in Oz at Flemington and Randwick. If anyone knew whether there was any dirty work afoot regarding Faithful Hope, I fancied it'd be Slip. He earned his nickname at Eton — he was forever 'slipping' down to nearby Slough to place bets for his schoolmates.

Slip's apartment occupies the entire twenty-fifth penthouse floor. Windy on a bad day; breathtaking views *every* day. He's got a butler of the old school called Devers, who lives in, and has travelled the world with Slip. It's rumoured he can pour a martini outdoors at precisely the same ice-cold temperature anywhere in the world, despite the ambient heat, be it in Oslo or Tunis. And malt whisky is invariably served at body temperature.

After a brief chat on the phone, Slip suggested a drink at his apartment — to get stuck into a drop or two of his Avonside ten-year-old malt whisky. I was delighted to accept. I was in his drawing room ten minutes later.

"You've been ignoring me, Robby. Bad thing, that," he said sternly as Devers poured four fingers of Scotch into my glass. "I suppose you're after a bit of my gossip for research on some comic or other."

"Graphic novel, Slip."

"Of *course*, dear boy! Whatever you say."

He screwed up his eyes and took a slug of Avonside.

"Jesus Christ, Robby, what *have* you done to your hair? You look as though you've been caught in the jet stream of a Sabre fighter!" Slip flew Sabres in New Guinea during World War II.

I'd forgotten about the Liquid Toffee. I was still Sainte-Claire on the outside.

"Oh, Jez thought she'd have some fun with some hairdo. It's nothing."

"Lovely girl, that filly. Proper job! Bloody marvellous painter too. Make sure you look after that one. Legs practically as long as *Let's Hurry*," he said, referring to his favourite Group Three filly.

"Ever heard of a trainer called Ratchett, Slip?" I asked as the smooth malt worked its way down to my toes.

He rolled his eyes in thought. It was like typing a name into the 'Finder' function of a database containing horse business only. Three seconds later the rolling stopped and the eyeballs gleamed.

"Shady character. Decidedly shady. Country trainer. Never had dealings with the man, m'self. Wouldn't either. Why do you ask?"

"A friend of mine was wondering if I knew anything about him. Nothing important. He had a horse that won him some money, then the animal was stolen."

"Faithful Lass," he replied, quick as a flash. "That was it, no?"

"Almost," I replied, astounded by his depth of trivial horse knowledge.

"No, wait! *Hope*. Faithful Hope. Ran a few times in the country. Never did any real good. Won a few nothing races. Then it showed up one day at Goulburn and won some quite reasonable handicap at inflated odds. Caused a few bookies some grief."

"How come you're familiar with the horse?"

Slip laughed and drained his Avonside. His glass was empty for all of two seconds, refilled by the ever-diligent Devers. Slip's facility to empty bottles of malt is legendary at Newmarket.

"Bare-faced fraud to my mind. And a damned clever one too! Some very rascally fellows made a bundle of readies out of it all. The poor owner didn't know much about it though. Can't put my finger on the fellow's name right now. It'll come to me."

I had no doubt it would.

I sipped away, trying to keep pace with old Slip.

"Happens all the time at small meets. You hold a horse back a few times at country races till the price goes right out, then you let her rip and make yourself some serious folding money. Problems only arise if the authorities can prove you've been allowing the horse to run below its ability."

He took another slug.

"They had Tim Shehan holding the bugger back for weeks. Then, come Goulburn – the trainer gives her the green light."

"Apparently my friend—" I stopped short, there was no point in holding back. "Well, I'll be frank with you, I don't know the man, merely his daughter. This person bought the horse just before the Goulburn race."

"Yes, well, that's the way it's often played. You need some patsy who doesn't know much about horseflesh." He grinned knowingly. "Am I right there?"

"You are."

"He buys the horse and doesn't know it's all been set up in advance. See, the nag is only going to win that one race. Then it's going to disappear, so that any Jockey Club enquiry won't find out that she was pretty decent and should have won the races she tanked before. They start off by selling the filly to some sucker, make their bets, hide the nag afterwards and the only person who's going to take the fall is the owner. He loses his horse and the money he paid for it. Hopefully he's insured."

"What about the trainer? And the jockey, for heaven's sake? They have to come out of it looking a bit suspect, surely."

Devers topped me up.

"Well, not really. The jockey, Seth Redmond, hadn't ridden Faithful Hope the previous few times, so as far as he knows the horse performed really well. Can't blame him, can you? And the jockeys that rode it before — well, those races weren't videotaped, were they? They don't tape at small potatoes country meets. And as far as Ratchett goes, his manner of training is pretty much in line with his moniker — everyone knows he's a scoundrel. But he's such small fry no one bothers with him.

"Of course, as I recall, there were a few bookies on the day that were seriously annoyed. But apparently Ratchett didn't have a bet himself. Strange, eh?" he said wryly.

"So he couldn't be seen to be making money himself, even though he was part of the conspiracy?"

"Million miles an hour, Robby, my boy," he said, stifling a chortle. "They tore his Aston Martin apart nevertheless. More to let him know they weren't going to wear it again if he tried."

"How do you know all these details, Slip?"

"Oh, I just love all the devilment on the wrong side of the tracks. And believe me there's a lot of it. Ratchett's case was delightful. His car vanished from outside his house one week after the race, and was delivered back, piece by broken piece, over the following three months. Not that his jalopy was worth much. Bad condition, don't you know."

"Who was the bookie who was hit most? Would you have any idea?"

"Neville Lawrence, I seem to remember. And his backer — some shady character up the Cross. We heard on the grapevine that 'Nev' was responsible for the disassembly of Ratchett's Aston, anyway."

"And what do you imagine might have happened to Faithful Hope?"

"Glue factory? Maybe she's running up in Queensland called something else. Hope so. Hate it when the horse wears the blunt end of the stick while the villains get rich."

Slip drained his second helping and looked towards Devers. The man seemed asleep to me; still standing, but his eyes were closed.

Slip snapped his bony fingers lightly. Devers instinctively reached for the bottle and did the honours.

"Who sold him the horse?" Slip asked. "He might be able to sue the bastard."

"His brother, unfortunately. I gather he might be a bit of a conman."

"Well, sadly there are a few about in this business — mostly amongst the cheaper end. We used to call such chaps 'hot'."

The conversation turned from horseflesh to stocks and bonds and the GOD's when he'd owned a house called 'Four Winds' in St James, Barbados. We'd cracked the second bottle by the time I made my excuses.

By the time I got home I was plastered. Slip, by contrast, could probably have chatted away all night. He clearly enjoyed giving his memories a good outing every now and then. I think it keeps him young to remind himself of the days when he was rubbing shoulders with the Queen Mum at Ascot. I believe he once owned the current home of the Prince of Wales.

I checked my email upstairs in the office. The most interesting correspondence was from Tiggy-Winkle@hotmail.com.

> *'Hi Sainte-Claire!*
>
> *All is as well as can be expected with Dad still missing. I keep asking Mum where he is and she keeps avoiding the issue. First she said he was staying with friends in the Blue Mountains. Then later, when I asked her where in the Blue Mountains, she looked completely confused. I expect she forgot what she'd told me earlier. She's very worried about something, but won't tell me a thing. I think Dad's gone missing and she won't admit it to me. But he just wouldn't do that sort of thing — just go off somewhere without telling me. He just wouldn't. That's really why I'm so worried. You've got to find him.*
>
> *Anyway, I found a photo of my Uncle Sam, which I thought you might find useful. When things go wrong Uncle Sam is*

almost always lurking somewhere. Dad's on the left and Uncle Sam's the one who's laughing.
Thanks again for taking on the case.
Hasta la vista
Tiger-Lily
PS Ally-Oop sends her love.

I opened the attached photo. Sam was laughing at the camera. He looked surprisingly normal — but then the best con men always do. Same as the most deadly serial killers; no one ever picks them as cruel monsters. Peter looked as though he had won the lottery. They were standing either side of a nice-looking filly I imagined to be Faithful Hope. With them was a tiny man in racing silks who looked decidedly shady. There are some people whose faces give them away — this middle-aged country jockey was one of those. Crook through and through.

Judging by Peter's jubilant expression, and the sweat on the horse's mouth and neck, I judged the snap to have been taken just after Faithful Hope won her race at Goulburn.

There were a few emails from various people concerning my books. Sol Andrews, the agent who handled my screenplays in Los Angeles, wanted me to seriously consider allowing Miramax to roll over the film option on one of my earlier graphic books *Dead To Rights*. I never knew quite why it had never made it to the screen; I'd always thought it was my best and tightest thriller. It had been optioned by a producer who couldn't make up his mind about any project that didn't involve Julia Roberts and Tom Cruise, and both stars had had better things to do each time the project was mooted, so it had rolled over now for five years. Not bad money, mind you, but I just wanted the film actually produced. I think Sol had given up on the project and was happy to take his commission on the rollover.

My more cerebral literary agent in New York, Lara Sloe — who handled the book publishing deals before they even got to movie deals — wanted the notes I had promised her on my new novel project, a thriller set in St Christoph and Seefeld with the working title, *Snow*. I was quite proud of the artwork.

Then there were emails from various charities, asking if I'd be part of some function or other to raise money for sick kids, sick adults, sick animals, sick geriatrics — dead people, for all I knew. I always try to fit them in if I can. If that's impossible, I usually send a case of signed books to auction off.

I was in the process of making a very hot Bloody Mary — Smirnoff and *Mr & Mrs T's Bloody Mary Mix* poured over crushed ice with plenty of salt pepper, the juice of a whole large lemon, *Lea & Perrins Worcestershire sauce*, *Smack-My-Ass-And-Call-Me-Sally piri-piri sauce*, and a stalk of fresh celery — when my mobile phone cheeped.

It was Jez.

"Hi, Pulitzer. Where are you?"

"Home," I replied.

"Well, you're supposed to be here."

"Where's that?"

"Here is where *I* am."

Good reply.

"Have I forgotten something?"

"Guess you have. I'm here chatting to Michael and I've been drinking for the two of us," she said. Michael doesn't drink. "He's made his speech and we wondered if you were going to show at all." There was a slight pause. "Bearing in mind we discussed the opening quite recently at lunch."

I apologised for my forgetfulness, took a quick shower, washed the gunk from my hair and changed into some comfy clothes.

Back to Robert Howard.

7

The work on show that night at the Commerford Gallery was impressive. Metal sculptures by someone with the androgenous title of AC Hancock. Coincidentally, bearing in mind my afternoon with Slip, the artist's work depicted horses. All were made of polished fragments of motor cars — large and small. I was reminded of Ratchett's Aston — who knew, I might come across his transmission somewhere! One horse's head consisted of a manifold, several bolts and a hubcap. Very clever stuff; it had all the movement and grace of a living animal. The works seemed to have been selling well — there were a lot of red dots next to them.

When I reached the top of the stairs that led to the vast open floor of the gallery, I saw Michael Commerford chatting with a well-known middle-aged Double Bay socialite. There was so much gold around her neck it was dragging her chin down to her pendulous breasts.

Michael glanced over at me as I was served a glass of Semillon — not Ciccone, but passable. I winked at him; he was doing a good job of on-selling Hancock's nuts and bolts and possibly Ratchett's Aston.

I could see Jez on the far side of the room.

The day my blood doesn't race faster each time I catch sight of her they may as well bury me.

She was wearing a chopped singlet that revealed a cocoa washboard tummy, Sass & Bide low-cut jeans and Prada mules with three-inch stiletto heels. She didn't need a follow-spot; the space around her positively shone.

She was talking to a man of about sixty who'd spent all his spare cash on cosmetic surgery, and had nothing left over to pay for a decent wig.

He was virtually drooling.

"Robert, come and meet Todd. My friend here's just bought that big piece over there," Jez said, gesturing to an enormous metal horse rearing up on a plinth to our right. I reckoned it probably consisted of the guts of a couple of Holdens plus a Ford ute or two. The eyeballs were two BMW logos, the nostrils a couple of Mercedes Benz shiny silver emblems. It was one scary nag.

I knew Jez wouldn't be irritated by my forgetfulness; she half-expected my intermittant bouts of amnesia. I'm often so absorbed in my graphic artwork that everything else goes out of my head. Even hunger and sex take a back seat at such times. Well, hunger anyway.

"Robert Howard," I said, shaking the moron's hand.

"Todd Ward."

"It's Todd's horse," Jez added.

"I know, you just told me he bought it."

"No, it's *modelled* on his horse. Cannerby-Lee. She's won races. Lots of them."

I tried to show the right amount of enthusiasm. Frankly, the racing game has never much interested me. "Ever run her at Goulburn?" I asked the old guy, making conversation.

Todd looked as horrified as a rich Englishman might if I'd asked him whether he'd holidayed recently at Bognor Regis rather than Cap Ferrat. Goulburn was evidently not a suitable track for the class acts of the game.

"Goulburn's a bit too 'country' for me. My horses are a cut above that sort of thing."

He sounded English. But you can't always tell. Not all of us Aussies speak with a Crocodile Dundee twang. Maybe it was his school. Maybe he was a South Australian, of good 'bloodstock' himself. Undeniably, he looked as though he was worth a bob or two — his clothes alone must have cost him ten grand. And the metal horse was marked on the list I'd picked up downstairs at fifteen thousand.

"Funnily enough," I continued, "I was chatting to a pal of mine just now about horse flesh. Who's your trainer?"

Todd's smile gave away the fact he simply loved the personal kudos of chatting about the 'Sport of Kings'. New money, I thought in a flash. Probably IT money.

"Neville Cunningham, Francis Gold and Taffy Giffin. Bloody fine trainers, all of them," he replied. "Neville's an Australian, as a matter of fact." His look suggested it was a matter of surprise to him that Aussies could rival the best.

I changed my mind about Todd. He *had* to be English. Too snooty.

"I wonder, have you ever come across a trainer called Ratchett?"

"Certainly not," was the curt reply, the smile evaporating fast.

"I gather from my pal he hasn't got the best of reputations?"

"Nor have most criminals. But you didn't hear that from me."

"But I just did," I replied with a friendly smile, just to annoy him.

Todd looked decidedly uncomfortable. "You're not a friend of his, I trust?"

"My sister's married to him," I replied.

Todd blanched.

"He's joking," Jez intervened.

"I was just curious to know if everyone shared my friend's opinion of him, that's all."

"Who's your friend?"

"Rather not say, Todd. Especially since he just fell short of calling Ratchett a crim himself. You know how these chance remarks can escalate into a libel suit."

"Todd's asked me to ride out at the gallops," Jez interposed, guessing my estimation of Todd wasn't much above a pimp. "Should be great fun."

"Hard work, that's what it is, when you do it every day. But fun for a lovely young thing like yourself on the right kind of morning."

Todd had forgotten his possible libel suit, and was beginning to concentrate once more on Jez. I could see his eyes were focussed on Jez's breasts, and likely to remain locked there.

"Are you here on your own, Todd?" I asked amiably.

His face took a sour turn as he looked up at me. "No, my wife's over there with Michael," he replied, pointing to the fat Double Bay nightmare with the gold chains.

As I glanced across at Mrs Ward, I caught sight of someone who looked vaguely familiar. She was standing with her back to me a good twelve paces away. A second or two later she turned to look at the sculpture to her right and I saw her quite clearly. It was Aunt Lucy. She was clearly having a good time, chatting to a couple of young men half her age.

She caught my eye. I smiled at her, but instead of the returned smile I expected, she turned away from me quite abruptly and pointed out a sculpture on the far side of the room to her two young men.

"I gather from Jez you don't much care for riding?" It was Todd again, at my elbow.

"I like to be in control," I replied. "With horses, most wild animals, some breeds of domestic dogs and swans I've found it's best to be on one's guard. If a horse has it in mind to take off there's not much you can do, is there?"

"Depends on your horsemanship, Robert. Same as everything else in life," Todd replied.

So, it was a contest? Okay.

"I never take anything for granted. Not since a friend of ours was swept off the north face of the Eiger last year. Three times up Everest previously. Then one slip and he was gone. I'd imagine it's the same with racing? Even the best jockey falls from time to time. Piggott took a nasty fall some years back, I seem to remember."

"Correct," Todd admitted.

Jez pinched my arm and smiled at me.

The ensuing lull in the conversation was a good excuse to move on. I thought I'd leave Jez to secure her morning gallop.

"Hope you don't mind — I've just seen someone I know over there. Will you excuse me?"

Jez looked at me curiously after a cursory scan of the room. Who had I seen that she didn't know?

I caught up with Lucy as she was making for the stairs on the far side of the room in an attempt to avoid me.

"Lucy. Nice to see you again. How's everything?" I asked.

The two young men melted away into the crowd.

"Mr Sainte-Claire, isn't it?"

"Almost. That's my character. I'm Robert Howard."

"Of course you are. I'm not normally so stupid. I'm good at names, by and large," she replied, smiling at last. It was as real as Michael Jackson's skin tone. Quite why she should have reacted this way was a mystery. After all, I'd come to help the family when they needed it, and done everything in my power to put them all at ease.

"Wonderful opening," she said. The small talk wasn't coming easily.

"I popped in to see Charlie this morning... " I said and hesitated. Sainte-Claire uses this trick a lot. Usually what happens is that the person he's grilling will give something away. Lucy was an exception to this rule. She was Lot's wife — the pillar of salt.

"She didn't appear too relaxed," I continued. "I hope everything cleared itself up last night?"

"Oh yes, no problems. Peter arrived home only a few minutes after you left. He'd been to see some friends. Bridge. They all switch off their mobiles while they play."

She fixed me with one of the looks she'd given me the night before; the 'you'd better believe what I'm saying or I'll get very angry' type.

"Bridge needs a great deal of concentration," she went on. "Can't have the damned phone beeping while you're counting cards, can you."

"Nothing worse," I concurred with a smile. I'd never played the game, but no recreation is enhanced by the annoying bleat of a mobile.

We stared at each other for a few seconds, during which I suddenly became aware Lucy was a very attractive woman. I hadn't noticed the night before, but tonight she looked gorgeous. She was wearing a knee-length red silk mandarin coat over black coolie pants teamed with black ballet slippers.

"You're staring, Robert," she said. "Do I look peculiar?"

She said it in the nicest possible way. I think she was kind of flattered by my attention.

"No. Not at all. You look great. Last night you looked rather, how shall I say, distracted. As you *would* be, I'd imagine."

No comment.

"Whereas tonight," I lied, "you seem more relaxed."

"Is that your girlfriend over there?" she asked, picking out Jez with her eyes.

"Yes, that's Jez."

Jez was now chatting to someone who resembled an elderly wharfie, except this man's blue denim overalls were perfectly clean and starched. His hair was tied in a snow-white ponytail at the back.

He had to be Hancock. Whoever he was, he was relishing Jez's attention. Quite possibly because he was around five-five tall and his eyeline was presently full of wonderment.

I returned my attention to Lucy. I wasn't about to tell her of my meeting with Tiggy — client confidentiality, you know — so I had to think carefully about the source of my information.

"Charlie's books are very impressive," I said, searching for a way back to the Reid household.

"Yes, my sister's very talented. Are your book covers as nice? I'm afraid I don't read too many comics."

"Graphic novels."

"Well, *thrillers* then." She dwelt on the word a tad overlong, as though it was synonymous with pulp fiction and pornography. "I prefer biographies."

A lot of people say that. By and large, it means they read nothing.

"Yes, fiction is becoming a bit outmoded these days," I said. "You only have to turn on the television to realize that. Real-life dramas — they're the new fad. *Big Brother, World's Funniest Everything, Springer*, dancing contests for soap opera stars, weather girls and ex-pollies, young men left on desert islands with twelve eighteen-year-old near-naked girls for company and expected to make the best of it. Who needs fiction? We can all do without it when we have the real thing."

She didn't seem to get a great kick out of my humour.

"I didn't mean exactly that, Robert," she replied.

Thank God — she'd got my name right. I hoped this was a trend that would continue.

I touched her arm lightly and thought I felt the slightest shiver. "I know you didn't. I was just trying to be amusing," I said.

Right then I could smell Gaultier. Jez. She'd slipped silently to my side. She smiled at Lucy, then looked at me in the expectation of an introduction.

"Jez Norman, Lucy Portman," I said. "Lucy and I met last night."

Jez made that face, coupled with the slightest parting of the lips, the one that signifies suddenly everything is clear.

"Oh, right! Pulitzer told me. It must have been a real worry for you, what with the kids. I hope everything turned out okay?"

"Oh yes. Everything's fine now, thanks," Lucy replied easily.

I was puzzled as to why they were both lying to me — Charlie this morning, Lucy now. I mean, why bother? Why not just tell me to mind my own business? Charlie had said she and Peter had had a 'minor quarrel', and that Peter was still staying with friends. Lucy didn't refer to any quarrel, just that improbable story that Peter had been to a bridge evening. No mention had been made of broken furniture, shouting or a scuffle.

"We quarrel every now and then too. It's no big thing," I said, putting an arm around Jez, who gave me a quizzical look, wondering where the hell I was heading.

"Quarrel? Who's quarrelling?" Lucy did her best to look confused.

"Oh, it's just that Charlie told me this morning she'd had a bit of a tiff with Peter and that it was all a big non-event."

"She said that?"

"Yes."

"I didn't know."

Lucy made a slight movement as if to walk away, so I continued quickly. "How *is* Peter?"

"He's just fine. I think I said that a few seconds ago," was her reply. Then she smiled a goodbye to Jez and wandered off.

"She's a piece of work," Jez said softly at my side.

"What's her game, do you think?"

"You mean, how does she earn a buck, or what makes her tick?"

"The latter."

"I'd say she's anally retentive, wound up like a steel spring and she fancies you."

I was about to interrupt when she added, "And she lies a lot. Predictable clothes, too."

"That's interesting. Why do you say she lies?"

"We're agreed on the other points then?"

I hugged her. She could be irresistible at times. I'm not really one for public demonstrations of affection, but every now and then I can't help myself.

"I don't think she's seen or heard from Peter — whoever he may be — for yonks."

"Glad you picked up on that."

"Why?"

"Because she *was* lying."

"Is Peter part of last night's thing?"

"Yes, he's the girls' father. His wife says he's 'just fine' and staying with friends. His sister-in-law says he's 'just fine' and at home. His office says he's 'just fine' and in a meeting that lasts forever. But I reckon he's anything but 'just fine'. May be dead for all I know. Thing is, everyone's too afraid to tell me."

"Aren't we being a little dramatic?" Jez whispered in my ear.

I was about to answer when I saw Michael approaching, busting to tell us something.

"Just sold a big one! Only got the foal and the emu left. AC is delighted."

I hadn't noticed the emu. "I can imagine. Good for the bank balance. Do I need to ask which one is AC?"

Michael pointed to a woman scribbling on a piece of paper at his desk, at the far side of the room by the French windows. She was about sixty, wearing a sensible skirt, cashmere jersey, a rope of pearls and flatties. An over-sized handbag hung in the crook of her arm, reminding me of the Queen.

"I thought it was—"

"I know. That's her husband. Quite the odd couple, eh? He owns a country garage. The vicious gossip is that when she's short of material, he simply lifts it from whichever car he's working on. Like a surgeon harvesting body parts that might suit a terminally ill patient."

My thoughts drifted back to Ratchett.

"You mean he actually is a fair dinkum mechanic?" I asked.

"Absolutely. She met him when her car broke down in the Western Australian version of Pleasantville, and he happened to own the garage."

I looked at them both, then back at Michael. "Let's take a look at the emu, then get a bite to eat?"

"Sounds good to me, Pulitzer," Jez said. "I'm ravenous."

How this was possible, only a few short hours after that risotto, amazed me.

8

We had dinner at Tabou in Crown Street. It always makes me feel I'm dining in Paris' *Quartier Latin*. The *faison confit* was superb, as was the *raye au beaure noire*. The desserts were miracles.

Jez decided to stay the night. I'd managed to put the Reids out of my mind but during the minutes I waited in bed for Jez to join me, my mind drifted to Tiggy. In order to sort out her problems, I needed to have a word with Uncle Sam and/or her father.

If Tiggs had any ideas how I might track down Uncle Sammy that would be a great help. I presumed his surname would be the same as his brother's. But with con men you never can tell.

Suddenly Jez was beside me and I wasn't thinking detectives.

After Jez had drifted off to sleep, I snuck out of the bedroom and up to the office to send Tiggs an email.

I detailed my questions via her hotmail address, sent it off, then snuggled back in beside Jez. She smelled of Gaultier, love and warm, soft, unblemished coffee skin.

As I began to drift off too, she turned her head towards me, her eyes closed, an arm draped around me. "I love you," she said. The words were the barest whisper.

I kissed her lightly on the cheek.

"Whoever you are," she murmured, then slipped into dreamtime.

Ever the humourist.

Giblet had been in a funk all night. She'd tried to get comfy on Jez's side of the bed, but Jez is a bit of a kicker. Giblet's morning attitude was mollified by diced chicken; Jez's by my eggs Benedict.

Around nine, Jez left for the studio and I checked the emails for a reply from Tiggs.

Dear Sainte-Claire,

Thank you for your email.

Dad drives a boring old Saab. It's pretty old. Red. The plate is ATW 50N.

A Tiggy-Winkle. ATW. That's how I remember it.

Don't know where you'd find Uncle Sam. I found a telephone number in Mum's address book. Don't know how old it is though.

By the way, thanks for the cake.

Regards

T-L.

I didn't bother with the rest of the emails — nothing looked particularly urgent. Instead I picked up the phone and called the number Tiggs had given me. It was a mobile and it had been disconnected. No surprise there.

Next, I called Peter Reid's office.

"The Vandercheltz Group. May I help you?"

"May I speak with Peter Reid, please?" I asked the same soothing male voice I'd spoken to twenty-four hours earlier.

There was slight hesitation, also as before.

"I'm afraid he's in a meeting at present. Can I take a message, sir?"

"He's a busy man," I said, in a tone that clearly suggested I thought he was prevaricating.

"He is indeed," came the crisp, no longer soothing response.

"Have you any idea how long the meeting might last?" I asked.

"I can ask him to call you back when he gets in."

"You must mean when he comes out."

"Out of what?" The voice sounded uncertain.

"The meeting. You said he was in a meeting. You come *out* of a meeting, go *into* a building."

There was a pause.

"We spoke yesterday, didn't we? It's Mr Sainte-Claire, isn't it?"

I wished I had his memory. "That's right," I replied.

"If you give me your number I'll get Mr Reid to call you," he said. "As soon as he is free."

I gave him my mobile number and hung up.

So Peter still hadn't shown up. Not much in itself. It simply added weight to my theory that he hadn't planned to be AWOL.

Next I dialled a mate of mine, Terence, at the *Herald*.

Terry came to my house years ago to do an article on me. We've remained friends ever since. I thought he'd know who was on the crime desk at the *Sydney Morning Herald*, and I might be able to access information I wouldn't otherwise be able to drum up — such as criminal records and license plate numbers. All the stuff that Phil Govern accesses quickly for Sainte-Claire in my books.

As usual Terry was screening his calls — no one answers the phone these days. Except me.

I told the machine who I was, and was halfway through my message when he came on the line.

"Long time, Robert. What's up? New book on the way?"

"Shortly, yes. But this is about something else. I wondered if you could point me in the right direction?"

"Sure, whatever," he replied.

"I need a bit of help with some research and I thought you might know a good contact at Fairfax."

"What kind of research?"

"You don't happen to be pally with anyone who deals day to day with Sydney's crime stories?"

"Sure. James Millar. He handles that kind of material. When the police want a hand publicising a case they usually have a word with Jimmy. He's got his finger on the pulse of the city."

"How well do you know him?" I asked, nervous about my next question.

"Pretty well." Terry was now a trifle wary. "Sounds like you've got a pretty big ask in mind."

"Well, in a way I suppose it is. It's personal, though. I'm trying to find a little girl's father. He's gone missing. The only way I can think of tracking him down is by finding his car. If I asked the cops to keep an eye out for it, they'd tell me to get lost. But if your *pal* asked them as a favour to keep an eye open, that'd help a lot."

"Christ, that's one big ask, Robert," Terry said. "He'd owe them a huge favour."

"That's about it, yes. But I'd owe *him* one of course."

"And me."

"Goes without saying. Tell me, what does he drink?"

"No idea."

"Ask him, can you? Then tell him he'll get a case of it. Anything but Grange, if it's Oz. If it's French, we can negotiate."

"Okay, that's my end of the deal taken care of, what about Jimmy?"

I laughed. "Same for Jimmy," I replied. "The plate number, if he can manage it, is ATW 50N. Red Saab. Belongs to a Peter Reid. Works as an insurance adjuster at the Vandercheltz Group."

"Look, Jimmy's bound to ask. What's he done? Anything illegal?"

"Don't know. Probably nothing."

"Are the police looking for him themselves?"

"Not as far as I know."

"Good."

"But he may be in trouble. Might owe the wrong people money. He had a gambling habit. May have run off with a mistress, for all I know. But I doubt it. I just told the girl I'd try to find her father, so I thought of you."

"I'll do what I can," he said.

Next on my list was a call to Charlotte Reid.

I dialed; the phone rang about six times before it was picked up.

"Hello? Is that you, Charlie?"

There was silence, except for some ambient noise in the background. I could just make out a man saying, 'Put that phone down, Mrs Reid.'

I spoke again. "Hello? Charlie? It's Robert Howard."

Again there was no response. This time I listened harder.

'Don't you mess with us, Mrs Reid, else you'll be very sorry. And put that phone down!'

This time I heard the sentence quite clearly. Then I was disconnected.

I tried to make sense of it. Why would Charlie bother to pick up the phone if she didn't intend to speak? Unless she was desperately hoping someone at the other end of the line would hear the threats and come to help her.

I didn't think twice.

9

Less than ten minutes later I was turning into Roslyn Street again.

Too late. A huge Islander was closing the gate of Number 5 behind him. He headed up the street towards me; I had about ten seconds to assess the guy as the distance between us closed.

His walk was Neanderthal, his arms so muscled they swung at a forty-five-degree angle to the bulk of his body and the veins in his upper arms stood out like cables. He was hunched as he walked, like a pro boxer about to step into the ring. He would have been six three if he'd stood up straight.

I'd been half-expecting to see the bald guy Tiggs had described seeing through the spyhole — the one with the scar. But this monster had hair. Well, about a millimetre.

He looked mean: big forehead, small slits where there should have been eyes. He didn't look happy, and an angry face always makes an adversary look that bit more formidable. He wore a black Hanes Beefy-T and shorts. He should have been thinking of changing up a size to XXXL, as the material over his biceps was digging into the flesh. His thighs were as wide as telegraph poles. A palm tree was tattooed on each forearm.

When he was about five steps away I called out. "Hey, can I speak to you a second?"

He didn't respond. Maybe his twin cauliflowered ears had impaired his hearing, but I doubted it. The slitted eyes had swivelled marginally in my direction as he hunched by.

I called again at his back as he loped away up the hill, this time a lot louder. "Hey, didn't you hear me? I want to talk with you!"

The effect of my shouting at him was remarkable. He didn't slow, he just stopped dead in his tracks — something I'd only seen in *Road Runner* cartoons.

He turned very slowly and the slitty eyes met mine. "You talkin' to me?"

De Niro. He must have seen the movie too.

"Yes, I am."

There was the vaguest semblance of a smile on his face as he moved towards me like one of my comic book anti-heroes. Cruelman maybe.

I was aware of a twitch in my sphincter. Not a good sign. I've never been the violent type. The last time I threw a punch was at school, when I was selected to box in the under fourteen's and got badly beaten. I was a scrawny kid.

He stepped deliberately close — so close that his huge steel-capped work boots scuffed the front of my Lobb brogues. His face was now inches from mine and I could smell his sour beer breath, mingled with his appalling body odour. He'd probably come straight from a training session. His clothes stank of cigarettes, curious considering the probable boxing connection.

"Smoking'll kill you," I said for openers.

He didn't respond to my banter.

"What d'you want with me?" he barked.

"I'm a friend of Mrs Reid."

The man-mountain proceeded to do shoulder rolls, like a slow exercise the Kangaroos do before playing in Rugby League internationals.

"Oh yeah?"

"That's right."

"So?"

"So, I just happened to overhear a little of what you said to her."

He looked confused.

"You wasn't there," he said.

"I heard you threaten Mrs Reid."

"How? You wasn't there."

"You said that."

"So I'm sayin' it twice!"

"It doesn't matter if I was there. Did you threaten her?"

"What if I did? What's it to you, Bum-Fluff?"

"Don't do it again."

"You got to be kiddin' me." He began laughing.

I was trying to disguise my instinct for self-preservation. This man could easily kill me with one hand. I debated whether I should continue. Of course, Sainte-Claire wouldn't have hesitated and it would have been a fun chapter to write. I took the hard option.

"No, I'm not kidding. Just don't do it again. Okay?"

"Or *what*, Bum-Fluff?"

He jabbed me with a finger to the chest. I was taken by surprise, the move was so quick. My body lurched backwards, but I didn't fall. I managed to steady myself by taking one step back. He took a step forward and laughed even more.

"Come on, you big pansy. What yous goin' to do? Clean me up or summin'?"

"You work for someone, big guy? Are you the hired help? Some kind of enforcer?" I kept direct insults to a minimum. I didn't think I was showing a frightened face. At least; I had those few muscles under control.

"You don't want to know, Bum-Fluff," he replied. His nose was touching mine.

"What do you want with Mrs Reid anyway?" I started again, trying to defuse the steadily mounting aggression factor. "Why not just leave her alone?"

I knew I'd painted myself into a corner. It was either a complete ignominious back down or full-on biffo — a fistfight that would probably see me dead or in need of major cosmetic surgery.

What a day.

I suppose all along I had subconsciously hoped a police prowl car would cruise round the corner, or a group of Japanese tourists would walk into the street, and The Blob would think better of creaming me in front of a dozen witnesses. But the street remained empty.

I could hear a vague buzzing in my head. It was probably the blood pounding through my veins at three hundred kilometres an hour.

He jabbed me again in the chest and I felt an unexpected twinge of real anger. It was only the second time in thirty-odd years that someone had jabbed me in the chest with a finger. I hadn't liked it three minutes previously and I liked it even less now. It hit a primal nerve I hadn't known existed.

"Don't you go poking *me* with your stubby little finger, beer breath." The words were the result of instinctive anger — they were out before I realised I'd spoken them. Big mistake.

For someone so bulky, his moves had a surprising turn of speed. I was flying through the air before I was aware he had lifted me clean off the ground.

I landed in the garden of someone's house and rolled a couple of times into a bed of azaleas. By the time I looked up, The Blob was walking up the street without a backward glance. I was lucky that day, really lucky. Just a few scratches. However, as I got to my feet I felt a different man. Something deep inside my psyche was changed.

I'd gone down as Robert Howard. I stood up as Sainte-Claire.

I walked towards the Reid house. A customised Subaru WRX was parked across the road a few houses down, facing the wrong way. Two youths were sitting in the front. They were what newsreaders call 'of Asian appearance'. The car had Simonds mag wheels and a vast Hornet scoupe air intake cut into the pearl red bonnet, under which I knew a turbo blow-off valve rested. A street racer.

The driver looked about fourteen years old, as if he'd never shaved. Both had number one buzz cuts. They were chatting, looking down at something in the driver's lap. Maybe they were divvying up some eckies for a rave party.

I knocked loudly on the Reids' front door.

Charlie took so long to answer that I feared she might be seriously injured. I was debating whether to call the cops, and breaking in prior to their arrival, when the front door opened. She'd been crying hard — I could see that at once, despite the ever-present camouflage smile. I'd been angry when the fat idiot had poked me in the chest a few minutes earlier; angrier still when he'd thrown me over the garden wall. Now I was furious — he'd terrified poor Charlie, she was still shaking.

"Oh, it's you," she said, pretending again that everything was 'just fine'. "Hello. How are things with you, Mr Howard?"

"Robert. I called you a few minutes ago."

"It was you, was it? Yes, I do recollect the phone ringing."

She was in another daze.

"Yes, you picked up, Charlie. I heard what that man said to you."

"What man?"

"The thug who just left your house."

"Oh, him." It was all she could manage.

"I had a brief chat with him down the street. I say brief because his brain functions for a maximum of half a minute at a time, and time ran out. I guess he lost patience with me so he threw me into one of your neighbours' garden."

She looked shocked and her eyes started misting. "Oh dear. I'm so dreadfully sorry—"

I cut her short. "Look, that's no problem, Charlie. I can look after myself. It was concern for *your* safety that made me ring your doorbell. That and the phone call."

"Why don't you come inside? We can't talk like this on the doorstep."

No coffee today. That suited me fine. I wasn't here for coffee and a biscuit this time.

I stepped past her into the hall. She closed the door, then turned to face me.

"What exactly was it you heard that alarmed you?"

"That man was threatening you."

She pretended to laugh. It was pathetically inadequate. "Oh, don't be silly. He wasn't doing anything of the kind."

"Then what was he doing here?"

Her mood changed slightly from embarrassment to annoyance.

"Excuse me, Robert. But what makes you think you can knock on my door and ask me what I've been doing? It's *my* house, not *yours*, and I'll do what I like inside it — and that includes inviting in who I wish."

"'Don't mess with us, Mrs Reid.' That's what I heard that ape say over the phone. *That's* the type of man you choose to invite into your home? Why don't we call a spade a spade, Charlie?"

She stared me out.

"What's got into you, Robert?" she asked eventually.

But I was Sainte-Claire now and showed no mercy. "I came round here today because it sounded on the phone as if you needed help. I came here yesterday because on that particular occasion it was your *children* who needed help. A casual observer might think that in the gratitude stakes you're coming in about fifth."

Her face was no longer fearful, simply surprised.

"What an extraordinary turn of phrase. Are you trying to impress me with glib comic-book rhetoric?"

"Graphic novels." I corrected automatically. "Look, it wouldn't kill you to be frank with me, would it, Charlie? Why not humour me — make me feel a little more assured about the kids' safety. Maybe then they won't need to call me again tonight."

"I've apologised for that already. I've instructed them both never to bother you again."

"That's not my point at all, Charlie."

There was another pause. My change from Howard-sweetness to Sainte-Claire-straight-talker was toughening her up a bit. She knew she couldn't get away with soft-soaping me any more.

"All right. Not that it's any of your business, but I'm having some very personal problems at present that I would rather keep to myself. While I understand you only wish to help me, and I appreciate your kindness, the problems are something Peter and I—"

I cut in hard. "Is Peter all right? Lucy told me he's back." I thought the lie might confuse her.

"I find that hard to believe. She knows Peter's still staying with his friends. I'll say it one last time. Everything's—"

"Just fine, I know. Let's concentrate on the man who was here. What's his name?"

"Why would you want to know?"

"Because he just assaulted me. If the person who owns the garden I was thrown into chooses to sue me for the damage, I'd like to be able to refer them to the ape who tossed me bodily over their fence."

"I don't know his name," she said, looking me defiantly in the eye.

"Who does he work for? Do you know that?"

"If I tell you, will you promise my name won't be mentioned?"

"I can't promise that."

"Then I can't help you. I'm sorry. If anyone sues you, I'll pay for the damage myself. How about that?"

I wasn't going to get any further here. Better to have another chat with Tiggs.

"Well, I'll leave you to it," I said and headed out the front door.

"Thanks for coming. You are a very kind man," she replied, clearly glad I was going.

"One more thing, Charlie. I wouldn't let that man closer than five blocks to your children. He's dangerous."

I walked down the steps and opened the gate.

"I know that. Believe me, I know that," she said, then added, "By the way, you have a flower on your collar. An azalea, I think."

10

Giblet was there to meet me when I got home. Barcom Avenue is definitely her patch. She spends most days strolling up and down the pavement outside a row of eight terrace houses, of which mine is one. She owns them all *and* their owners.

I could hear the phone ringing inside, so I stopped stroking my marmalade monster and made for the door.

"Robert Howard?" the voice asked.

"That's right."

"James Millar. From Fairfax." Terry's friend — the guy on the crime desk.

"Thanks for calling back. Good of you to spare the time."

"No problem. Terry told me what you're after. Matter of fact, I've read a couple of your graphic novels myself."

Hooray — at last someone who knew the genre. My delight was short-lived.

"Well, my wife reads them, then hands them on to me."

That's what my publishers always tell me. Women buy books; men accept them as gifts or take the hand-me-downs.

"They're fun. What I like is that they're well researched, not filled with guff that's a bunch of nonsense."

"I'm glad you like them."

"I passed on your details to my police contact and he said he'd do what he could. I think that means they'll look out for the car. They can't make it a priority, as I'm sure you'll understand, because it's not one. No crime's been committed. Am I right there?"

"Not as far as I know — not yet, anyway."

"Well, the car's on a list now, and unless the vehicle's prestige and criminals are already breaking it down into spare parts in Queensland, it'll probably be spotted quite soon. When it is, my guy will call me and I'll call you."

"That's terrific. Can't thank you enough."

"Yes, you can," he said with a smile in his voice. "Dalwhinnie."

"A case?"

"Sounds good to me. Shiraz. The '95 if possible. I'll be in touch."

I cut in quickly before he could put the phone down. "Before you go, James. A huge Islander guy with two palm trees tattooed on his forearms - mean anything to you?"

"Sure, that's Tug Tutuelo. Well-known Sydney identity. Small potatoes, though. Strictly hired help. Works as a standover man for Tim Brierley. Tutuelo's a handy boxer in his spare time, only three down from the guy who's due to fight Mundine next month. He'll have to lose a bit of weight, mind you. Or go up a division."

"Who's Brierley?" I asked.

"Loan shark," James replied. "Actually, he thinks of himself as a cut above that. Calls himself a capital investment provider — he provides, and you'd better be serious about repayment."

"Or Tutuelo comes a-knocking?"

"That's about the size of it."

"Thanks very much again for putting out the call on the red Saab. I don't know if Terry mentioned it, but I'm doing a favour for a twelve-year-old girl, trying to locate her dad. He's missing and she's worried about him."

"If he's on the wrong side of Brierley, she's got good reason."

"Wouldn't happen to know how I could reach Brierley, would you?" I asked.

He hesitated. I let the silence ride.

"Look, I may be able to point you in the general direction," he said. "His business isn't a million miles from where you live. Terry tells me you're in Barcom Avenue?"

"That's right."

"Well, Brierley's premises are in Challis Avenue. About fifty metres down, past the launderette. Look for Pacific Investment Capital. Then look out for Tutuelo."

"Thanks for the tip. I'll hope to hear from you soon."

"I'll do what I can," he said and hung up.

So Peter Reid had defaulted on a debt. That, or Charlie had ended up owing Brierley money somehow. The latter scenario was more doubtful. Bearing in mind Tiggs' information that Daddy had bought a horse and taken to betting, it looked as though the bets had got out of hand and Peter Reid was now deep in trouble with repayments and had done a runner.

I considered my options. I could go looking for Peter Reid, he could be anywhere in Australia. Or I could go looking for Brierley and try to take the heat out of the repayment situation, give Peter some time to settle his debts. Of course, if I were going to front up on Brierley's doorstep I'd need to dance rather carefully round Tutuelo. Either that or take a crash course in aggressive pre-emptive self-defence.

I found the second option preferable; after all, I was beginning to enjoy Sainte-Claire's more direct approach to life. And I didn't fancy dancing around a nobody like Tutuelo anyway. I'd made a decision as I lay on my back in that garden in Roslyn Street: I was going to toughen up.

And Nick Kougios was going to give me the advice I needed.

It was just after eleven when I found Nick sipping his unlikely morning tipple, a chocolate latte with whipped cream, at the Bar Coluzzi. Clamp was sitting on his haunches at Nick's feet, attending to some annoying itch near his testicles.

We said our hellos and I sat down.

"I need a bit of professional help, Nick," I started.

"What can I do for you, mate?"

"Basically, I need to be able to defend myself."

"Then tae kwon do's just the ticket. How long have we got?"

I hesitated. "How about an hour?"

He put down his latte. I swear Clamp was listening too, because he looked sharply up from his balls and gave me the eye.

"Someone having a go at you, Robby? Just give me a name. You don't need no TKD course."

I ordered a double short black with a twist from the waiter who had arrived at our table.

"It's not like that, Nick."

He raised his thin razored eyebrows and gave me an 'Oh yeah?' look.

"No, really. I just think it's about time I knew a thing or two about taking care of myself."

"Why wait *this* long, mate? You're closing in on forty, ain't you? Thereabouts, anyway. How come no one's killed you before?"

I thought he was joking. I hoped so.

"We move in very different worlds, Nick. I try to keep violence to a minimum."

Nick gave me a look of righteous indignation and threw his arms wide. "Me too, bubba! Me too!"

"Yes, I know," I said.

My coffee arrived and Clamp settled. He usually allowed Nick to handle things until they turned nasty.

"Seriously, though. How long have we got? You want to join the classes?"

"Nick, I *was* serious. I just want a bit of quick advice on what to do if someone has a go at me."

"Think someone might?"

"You never know."

"Come on, you can play straight with me, mate. I've known you for some time now and you've never asked to join the classes before."

"Should have."

"*Course* you should have, ya drongo. Anyway, now all of a sudden you ask me for an instant defence course. Well, I tell you straight, there ain't one. These things take time."

"Pity."

"However, if you give me an idea of what kind of bother you're anticipating, maybe I can give you some useful pointers."

I sipped my coffee, debating how much to share with Nick. I knew that if I mentioned Tutuelo he'd probably go to Brierley's place and see to the guy himself. That was fine, but I wanted to handle things myself rather than have a sidekick do it for me. It was a matter of pride now. I'd written about characters who had minders and I'd never given them much respect in my books. Sainte-Claire had *no* minders. He commanded respect.

"Let's say some evil-looking guy's standing really close—" I began.

"I'll stop you right there. He doesn't," Nick said.

"Doesn't what?"

"Stand real close. No one stands real close to me unless they're friends. *Close* friends."

"So if someone steps in close, I back up?"

"Look, Robby, let's not frig around, eh? What we're talking about here isn't defence. What we're talking here is a pre-emptive strike. If you think someone's going to mess with you, you make sure you give him a hard one before he gets to come in strong."

"Hit him?"

"Shit, yeah! If I even *suspect* some violence — bang, he's history."

"How do you do that?"

"If he's come in close enough for a headbutt, you keep looking him in the eyes, size up the shot you're going to make, look relaxed and easy — not mean at all — then just before your head goes in to spread his face, you glance away as if something's got your attention. He looks off to one side. Blam. End of incident."

Nick sipped at his latte. His foot was tapping now; the mere thought of violence had given him an adrenaline rush. Or maybe it was the chocolate.

"Of course it's best to step back, sharp as you can, else you get sprayed."

"With blood?"

"That's the stuff, bubba." Nick was grinning.

"Suppose he's just trying to scare you? Doesn't intend to fight at all."

Nick just laughed. "Too fuckin' bad. Shouldn't have given me the signals. Tough shit."

"Ever hit a guy by accident? You know, like you *felt* he was going to hit you, but that wasn't on his mind at all?"

"Hundreds of times. But that's war. And I'm often in a war situation, cos I look the way I do. Hell, every hard man in town wants to say he's had a piece of me."

Clamp raised his head and rested it on Nick's knee.

"My advice to you is simple: don't get yourself into any 'situations'. If you get a chance, run. Then, if you feel mad, call *me*."

I wasn't about to do that, so I pressed him for more info.

"What if I don't want to use my head? Or I'm not close enough?"

"Well, personally I like to go for the windpipe. Straight punch to the apple usually does the trick. If they can't breathe, they're putty. If you've got time for a wider arc, give 'em one to the throat with the *side* of your hand. Like a backhand in tennis. Know what I mean? Takes a tad longer to connect, but it's very effective. And if you're up for it, and don't mind takin' a chance that you'll kill the guy — give him an upwards sweep of the side of your hand to the underside of his nose."

"That'll kill him?"

"More often than not, if you connect right. Drives the bone right up into the brain. Mind you, the throat shot might kark him too."

He offered me the side of his hand. "Feel this."

I touched it — it had the consistency of a railway sleeper.

"How do I get mine to feel like that?"

"An hour a day. Hit a brick with the side of your hand. Harder and harder, till it hurts real bad. Then carry on for another ten minutes till you can't stand the pain any more."

"Then do it another ten minutes?" I said.

He smiled broadly. "You catch on fast. Ten years time, you'll have an edge like mine."

He stood and looked down at my Lobb brogues.

"Get yourself some respectable boots. Heavy. Steel caps. Wear 'em tight."

Then he beckoned me to stand up. "Come on. Stand opposite me a second."

I did as I was told. The other coffee drinkers on the pavement watched with interest.

"You see, from here I can pivot on my left leg and stamp right into your knee joint front on with my right heel. It'll snap easier than a chicken wishbone." He laughed. "Down he goes! Snaperoo!"

Just the thought of it made my left knee tingle.

"Mind you, Robby, it takes a bit of training. You don't want to make that move and miss — you'll end up on your backside with someone on top of you, beating your head into guacamole with a tyre lever."

Nick pivotted and lashed out with his leg. His heel stopped about a millimetre short of my knee.

The crowd applauded.

"Thanks for the lesson, Nick. What do I owe you?"

"Tell you what, bubba. You let me fancy-up that crock of Froggy car-shit for cost and we'll call it even."

"Done, mate!"

11

There's no point in asking for advice and then not taking it, so I headed for a shoe shop in Bondi Junction that Nick had mentioned — one that stocked boots fit for a North Sea oil rigger.

The ones I chose didn't look too bad. Since the movie, *Bootmen*, they've become a fashion statement — so Jez tells me, anyway. The Bikkembergs might have been up to busting kneecaps, but I wanted to be sure.

The steel toecaps weren't silvery because they were covered with black leather. However, I was assured they would take the downward force of an RSJ falling from twelve feet, so that was good enough for me. They felt surprisingly comfortable, despite weighing a little less than a Nordica downhill ski boot. Naturally, they looked pretty stupid with my Italian pure wool trousers, so I went home and changed into my Sainte-Claire black linen suit and my black Diesel T — the same outfit I'd worn for tea and cakes with Tiggs.

I was so taken with my new edgy appearance that I spiked up my hair a bit more with Jez's Liquid Toffee. A pair of black Dolce & Gabbana wraparound sunnies completed the outfit.

I didn't see Tim Brierley taking much notice of Robert Howard, Mr 'Nice Guy'. So Sainte-Claire was going to pay the call in his stead.

A few minutes later, I was heading up Liverpool Street. I turned right into Victoria Street and headed up to the Cross and Challis Avenue.

As I passed the Bourbon and Beefsteak I saw an old sailing friend of mine coming towards me. When he was about five feet away I smiled but he walked straight past without a word. I thought for a moment that I'd done something to offend him. Then I realised he simply hadn't recognised me. Why should he? He'd seen Sainte-Claire, not me.

Turning into Challis Avenue, I walked past the launderette. The second house down had a brass plate by the door: 'Pacific Investment Capital'. The door didn't give when I pushed so I rang the bell. A few moments later a French accent purred through the speakerphone.

"PIC. Can I 'elp you?"

I leaned close to the speaker. "My name's Sainte-Claire. Is Mr Brierley available?"

"Do you 'ev an appointment, Mr Sainte-Claire?" Very Froggy accent.

"No, I don't."

"Then I doubt whether a meeting can be arranged today. Mr Brierley 'es a very full agenda."

"He'll want to speak to me. I can guarantee that," I replied. It was the sort of remark I'd put in the mouth of Sainte-Claire.

"One moment please, Mr Sainte-Claire."

I waited. A couple of minutes later, the buzzer sounded by my ear. I pushed the door open and stepped inside.

The walls were blood red, the leather lounges emerald. The carpet was azure. On the walls were several Pro Harts and a big Ken Done. Brierley obviously liked bright colours everywhere, despite the fact that the mix and match was a decorator's nightmare.

Behind a big pale ash desk sat a woman. She had the look of Catherine Deneuve and her clothes were in stark contrast to the interior décor. She wore an exquisitely tailored navy Chanel silk cashmere suit. Her make-up was perfectly understated. She was over fifty and totally gorgeous.

"Mr Brierley will see you in a short while. Perhaps I could get you a coffee, Monsieur Sainte-Claire?"

"Don't worry," I replied with a smile.

"It's no trouble at all," she said. "*I* don't make the coffee. I simply press a button en' someone *else* fetches it." She gave me a look that told me very clearly her job description did *not* include making hot drinks.

"All right, then. Coffee would be great. Thank you."

"Do you have a *préférence*?"

"Very short black?" I asked.

She pressed a button. "A ristretto, please. Right away."

Deneuve returned her attention to a copy of *Vogue* — the Paris edition.

Less than fifteen seconds later a young man came through a door to my left and set my ristretto beside me on an ash coffee table. He had slim hips, black shirt, black pants, gelled hair and a pair of Prada trainers. Looked like a younger gay version of me.

I thanked him.

Deneuve didn't even raise her eyes from the magazine.

I'd been waiting about twenty minutes when I saw her face brighten with a rose luminosity, as though a small light had reflected up at her from the console in front of her.

"Mr Brierley will see you now, Mr Sainte-Claire." She gestured with a lazy arm to the door to her left and behind her.

As I passed her I happened to catch sight of her legs. It was as though a plastic surgeon had succeeded in grafting the legs of a twenty-year-old on to the body of a middle-aged woman. Her ankles were superb. She was wearing a pair of handmade lilac Manolo Blahnik shoes. I only notice such details because I have to dress my characters in my novels, and Jez keeps me up to speed on what women are wearing. The brand names stick.

"Thanks for the coffee."

"*De rien*," she replied huskily, glancing briefly at me. Good teeth, plenty of shine, yet not so over-white you'd question their bona fides.

Brierley's office was the complete opposite of the foyer — white walls and black leather furniture. Big teak Edwardian desk. Several phones and two big silver frames with their backs to me so I couldn't see who were featured — children or celebrities. I mentally conjured up snaps of Chopper Read and Detective Roger Rogerson.

Brierley was sitting behind the desk, fingers interlaced, his expression dark and curious — like a gorilla in a zoo. Behind him was a sixteenth or seventeenth-century portrait of an English gentleman in a wig; maybe he thought some of the class would rub off.

He didn't get up. He merely looked sourly at me.

"Don't believe we've met, Mr…?"

"Sainte-Claire," I replied.

"Well, take a seat, Sainte-Claire. Don't have much time." His accent was fifties' Oz-crim.

He stared at me for a good ten seconds, then tapped his fingers on the arm of his repro Louis XV chair.

"Come on then, Sainte-Claire. Out with it. You told Agnes you could guarantee I'd want to talk to you."

Agnes? Deneuve was called Agnes? 'Good grief', as Charlie Brown would say! Maybe it sounded better pronounced with a French accent.

I held his eyes for a good ten seconds in total silence. I hoped he could make out my eyeballs through the light tint of my D&G's. He was the first to look away; a good sign. Truth of the matter was, I couldn't think of an opener.

"I think you know a friend of mine," I said finally.

"That may well be true."

"His name's Peter Reid."

"Seems to ring a bell. Go on."

"I think he owes you money. Does he?"

"You're asking if his company does business with PIC?"

"In a way, yes."

"What's that supposed to mean?" His tone was becoming tinged with annoyance.

"I'm asking if he owes you money personally. Not whether he's doing business with your front company."

Brierley stopped drumming his fingers and studied me.

"You a plain clothes cop or something?"

"No, I'm an private investigator."

He smiled. "Well then, why don't you just fuck off. I've got no time to spare for private dicks asking me about my private financial business. Fucking cheek!"

"Does Peter Reid owe you money? It's a fair enough question."

"None of your bloody business, mate. Now piss off before I call someone to toss you out."

I saw his hand hover over a button on his desk. "I wouldn't do that," I said.

I was still wearing the sunnies and he probably found it hard to read my expression. He withdrew his hand from the button and his tone relaxed slightly.

"What if he does owe me money? What's it to you?"

"I want you to give him time to pay. Simple."

"He's had plenty of time. There comes a point when you call in the debt collector, repo-man, whatever you like to call him. Happens to the best of us. If it's the bank, you kiss goodbye to house and home."

"Fair enough. But you don't send round an animal like Tutuelo to scare the shit out of his wife and kids. That's out of order." The last phrase was one Sainte-Claire often used.

"Who says I told him to scare anyone?"

"That would be my guess."

"You don't know much for certain, do you, tough guy? *My* guess is you're just here to make trouble."

"I'm asking you to lay off Reid. Let him come home so he can pay off whatever he owes you. Meantime, if you tell me what he's up for, I'll give you something to be going on with. Extra."

Brierley's eyes registered genuine surprise. "What d'ya mean 'let him come home'? Are you suggesting he's pissed off with my cash?"

"He wouldn't do that — he's got kids. He's missing, though. I thought you might know why."

"Well, I don't. And I'm mightily annoyed that he's gone missing. The bastard owes me eighteen grand and his loan is definitely past its 'use-by' date."

"So you have no idea where Reid might be?"

Brierley tilted his chair back and placed his feet on his desk, folding his hands in his lap.

"You know, you're beginning to get up my nose big time. What I know or don't know is beside the point. If I'm still looking at you rather than an empty chair in ten seconds, I'll make sure you leave my office arse first."

"How long would a grand give Reid?"

He looked up at the ceiling. Now that I was talking cold cash, the clock was on hold.

"Okay. Let me see. One grand, you say? One week. Non-refundable."

"You take a cheque?"

He chuckled. "Sure, I take cheques. But get this — no one's bounced one on me in fifteen years. Just remember that. Doesn't make me at all happy."

I wrote out one of my company cheques to Brierley for one thousand dollars. Reid could pay me back as and when he was able to — I could well afford it. My good deed for the day. My signature's an illegible squiggle at the best of times; that day I squiggled more than ever.

I ripped the cheque from the book and laid it on the desk near his foot. He didn't even bother to look at it.

"That's one week from tomorrow morning," I said.

"Not exactly," Brierley replied. "That's one week from... " He looked at his Rolex. "Twenty past twelve this afternoon. Have a nice lunch, Sainte-Claire. Goodbye."

I stood and made for the door.

"You an albino or something?" Brierley said. "World not dark enough for you?"

"I prefer the shadows of the twilight," I replied, suitably darkly. "I don't want to see your hired help scaring the Reid family again."

Brierley held up my cheque and snapped it tight a couple of times.

"No need, mate. No need. Nice doing business with you, Sainte-Claire."

Deneuve, aka Agnes, was still reading fashion magazines as I walked through the reception area. This time her choice was *Vogue Italia*. Her wardrobe suggested she was either very well paid by Brierley, or her services didn't end at five-thirty. She looked up and held my eyes for that microsecond too long, then buzzed the door open for me. I paused at the door.

"*Au revoir*," I said.

She smiled. "*À plus?*" she replied temptingly, in perfect French. See you later?

Hmmm.

12

As I stepped into Challis Avenue I saw Tutuelo turn the corner of Macleay Street and cross the street towards me. He must have come straight from the City Gym; his arms were so pumped they stood out horizontally from his body like wings. If he'd started running, chances were he'd have taken off.

I braced myself for what Sainte-Claire usually refers to as 'a bit of bother'. But as we passed mid-street the goon just glanced at me and walked on. Clearly he hadn't put me and Robert Howard together. Just as well; I wasn't ready for the big lug yet. But I would be, one day soon. I knew that even then. It was a resentment growing deep within my psyche, hour by hour.

On the way home, my mobile vibrated in my suit pocket. I pulled it out.

"Sainte-Claire?"

It was my client.

"Aren't you supposed to be at school, Ms Tiger-Lily?" I asked.

"I *am* at school, Sainte-Claire."

"Where are you calling from - the headmistress's office?"

"Don't be silly. I have my own phone. Can't think why I didn't mention it before. *Much* more convenient than email."

I was astounded. Twelve-year-old kids now had mobiles as a matter of course?

"It's the IT revolution, in case you hadn't noticed, Sainte-Claire. We all have our communicators."

Was that what they called them at school? Maybe Ally-Oop had received her first 'communicator' at kindy. You know — just in case she needed to call her broker.

"Have you turned up anything yet, Sainte-Claire?" Tiggs asked.

I think she was enjoying the game. She liked saying my name — as if Sainte-Claire actually existed. She was a modern day Bacall; I was Bogie. But I could tell by the tone of her voice that she was still worried about her dad. Very worried.

"Dad not home yet?"

"No. And Mum still won't admit that anything's wrong. She just rushes around all the time with a scatty look in her eyes. I wish there was an extension in my bedroom so I could listen in, 'cos she's on the phone all day now. But whispering, so I can't hear properly."

"Have you anything that might be useful?"

"Well, today I heard her say, 'You've *got* to give it to him'. She was pleading. Like when she wants Alice to eat her Brussels sprouts."

"Who was she speaking to? Could you tell?"

"Oh, yes. It was Dad. She said his name a couple of times."

It stood to reason that Peter Reid had gone into hiding because he couldn't pay Brierley. I wondered if Charlie knew where he was. Possibly not. Maybe she was trying to raise the money for him. It was time to tell her that he could come home, that I'd done a deal with Brierley.

"Look, Tiggs, I'm on to a lead here. I think we can work this thing out so your Dad can come home."

"Oh, cool!" she burst out loudly in my ear. "That's really wicked. You're a legend!"

"Hold on," I cautioned. "It's not a done deal yet. But it all seems to be falling into place."

I heard a hand bell ring in the background. "Got to go," she said in a whisper. "Home economics. Yuk! See you soon. Hernandez at four?"

"Done."

The red racer was parked in Roslyn Street, with the same two Asian kids in the front.

I knew Charlie Reid wouldn't be exactly thrilled to see me again, but there was nothing for it. This time I had good news to offer. I took off my wraparounds — I didn't want to scare her.

As I waited for her to answer the door, it occurred to me that the Reids should never have let things get out of hand they way they had. After all, it was only a matter of eighteen thousand dollars all up. Surely a man of Peter's means could come up with that sort of money? After all, he had a decent professional job: and if his cash flow was poor he could surely have borrowed on the equity of the house. And even if the house was double, if not triple mortgaged, why not sell the car, for heaven's sake? Surely anything was better than muscled debt collectors arriving at the door, upsetting the children and forcing you into hiding? The whole affair seemed quite ridiculous.

When the door eventually opened, I was startled by Charlie's appearance. To say she looked agitated was the barest understatement. Her hair was standing up wildly like the Madwoman of Chaillot and she was breathing hard. Her eyes darted left and right, up and down the street, as if she hadn't seen me. Then her eyes came to rest on me and she stepped back suddenly, startled.

"I haven't *got* it yet!" she cried out. "I've told your friends already. I'll have it soon. But you have to leave me alone!"

"Charlie, it's me," I said reassuringly. "Robert Howard."

But she wasn't listening. She was now staring at the red Subaru down the street, panicked. "Make them go away, whoever you are," she begged, tears welling in her eyes. "I just can't bear it any more."

"Charlie. It's me. Robert. Tiggy's friend. Remember?"

Her eyes swivelled to focus on mine. Her mouth gaped. Now she was really confused.

"I think I can help you out of this mess, Charlie. Can I come in for a quick chat?"

Immediately the mask was up again. "What mess? I have no idea what you're talking about, Robert," she replied, attempting to smooth her tangled hair. "Come in, anyway. Can't stand out here all day."

She led the way to the kitchen. On the bench top was a bottle of Scotch and a tumbler. There was still a finger of whisky in the glass. She'd been hitting it pretty hard; I could smell it on her breath.

"Care to join me in a whisky?" she offered.

"Thanks, I'd love one," I replied, to humour her.

She poured two large measures and handed me one, then took a big pull at hers.

"So," she said, "what small jewel of advice have you got for me today? I can't wait."

I was about to answer, when she pointed, first at my hair, then at my clothes.

"Why on earth are you dressed like that? You look like some kind of urban cowboy."

"Felt like a change. I'm having an identity crisis," I said with a smile. That seemed to break the ice a bit. "Look, Charlie. I think I can help you sort things out."

"You can?" she said, with a look that suggested I had no idea what I was talking about.

"I know about Brierley and the money Peter owes him."

Her expression changed from interest to extreme disappointment. "Then you know nothing about anything," she said and took another slug of whisky.

I wasn't about to give up that easily.

"I know that thug who was here earlier today works for Brierley. I went to see Brierley this morning and he told me how much your husband owes him. You can tell Peter he can come home now — I've bought him a week's grace. He can pay me back any time he can. No hurry at all."

"You gave Mr Brierley *money*?" She was horrified.

"Yes. A cheque. I can afford it. Peter, Tiggs and Alice are my readers and I have to look after my support base — they're my potential income."

I was trying to be funny; to relax her a bit. It didn't work.

"Well, much as I appreciate the thought, I'd much rather you hadn't. I have the matter in hand myself. Lucy has just couriered a cheque to Mr Brierley. Payment in full. So that's that."

"Well, it's a pity you didn't feel able to share your problems with me earlier. I might have been able to spare you some grief."

She gave me a pseudo-shocked look. "What on earth makes you think that if I was in financial trouble I'd share that information with you? How dare you! I don't call on the financial assistance of complete strangers."

She had a point.

"I can see where you're coming from, Charlie. I merely offered because your kids asked me to help them, and I felt I could. They're great kids. But you know that."

"I do," she replied flatly, running a hand again and again through her haystack hair.

"So Peter will be coming home then?"

"Peter can come home any time he pleases. It has nothing to do with Mr Brierley." She gave me another withering look. "I tell you what. If I need help, I'll ask for it. All right?"

I nodded.

"Meantime, I'm sure you have other people to advise on how to run their lives, look after their children, etc. Do you get my drift, Mr Howard?"

"I do," I replied. "Just one last thing. Who are those men in the red Subaru down the street — do you know them?"

She looked as though she'd suddenly got a chicken bone stuck in her throat and couldn't breathe.

"Are *they* associates of Mr Brierley too? If so, perhaps I should inform them the cheque's in the post?"

She reached for my hand and clasped it. Tears were flowing freely now.

"I beg you, Mr Howard. Please will you just leave me alone and let me sort out my own problems. Believe me, you can't be of any possible help, and your presence here only compounds my problems. Can you understand what I'm saying? Please go away."

I held her shaking arms and spoke softly.

"Of course I'll go away if that's the way you want it. But let me just say this before I leave you to your own devices." I looked her in the eyes. She was, at least, listening. "I'm always ready to help you. If you or the kids ever need someone, I'm a phone call away. If anyone threatens you, I'm a phone call away. And if anyone actually lays a hand on you, Tiggs or Alice, I'll be around, phone call or not, with a very big stick indeed."

Through the tears I glimpsed the faintest of smiles.

"You're a funny man, Mr Sainte-Claire," she said.

This time I didn't correct her.

13

The goons in the red racer were still parked down the street when I exited Number 5. I wasn't absolutely sure they had anything to do with Charlie's present problems, but I don't believe in coincidences and two young deadbeats looking like the Asian division of Brierley's boys lounging around so close to the Reids' was certainly that. The look of terror on Charlie's face when she'd seen them was imprinted on my mind.

There was only one way to find out what their game was, and that was to ask them.

When I was about twenty feet from them, the car fired up. It had the lumpy sound you'd expect from a rotary engine, on account of its camshafts — they hardly function at idle speed; better at 3000 rpm, best at up to 7000. It sounded more like a drag engine clearing its throat of phlegm. The car began reversing slowly away, keeping a distance of exactly ten feet between us.

I quickened my pace and the Asians quickened the pace of their car to match. I could just make out the passenger grinning at me.

As it reached the bottom of the street, the Subaru made a backward right-hand turn into Roslyn Gardens and stopped. It couldn't go any further because a small grocery truck was parked in the middle of the road.

I stepped up to the passenger side and knocked on the tinted window with the knuckle of my index finger. Neither the driver nor the passenger reacted; they simply looked dead ahead, expressionless.

The driver was a cross between Diana Ross and J-Lo. Perfect skin. A real pretty-boy. The guy in the passenger seat had huge cheekbones, big oval eyes that looked liked pitted Kalamata olives and the barest stubble that passed for a haircut. Two thin razor lines ran from above each eye over his head. He had a small goatee under his lower lip and three silver rings through his upper lip. The ringed effect reminded me of the entries in the Royal Easter Show, cattle division. A pair of cheap green surfie sunnies completed his outfit.

I rapped harder. Nothing. They could have been a pair of tailor's dummies in there. I was beginning to get annoyed. I merely wanted to speak to these guys and they were being deliberately uncooperative.

A few people had wandered out of the launderette to stand on the pavement a few yards ahead of the car. Safely out of harm's way, they were most likely hoping to witness some serious violence. Who knew, it might even be better than reality television.

The other side of the road an elderly couple was looking out a first-floor window, smoking cigarettes and hawking into flower boxes that hung below them.

It was a standoff. The guys in the car weren't about to slide down the windows and chat. And they weren't about to move off either. Meanwhile, I was rapping on the window, looking pretty stupid. This wasn't Sainte-Claire behaviour. He wouldn't have stood for this kind of disrespect.

An idea occurred to me and I looked around the street. Almost immediately I saw a half a house brick. I picked it up and took a position right in front of the car, midway between the chromed headlights. I dangled the brick over the bonnet, which was gleaming like a pearlesque kaleidoscope in the sun.

The effect was startling. The pretty-boy driver immediately sounded the horn. It was one of those road-train air-horns — it scared the hell out of the audience, several of whom jumped. I didn't move. I'd been expecting some stunt or other and was braced to move fast if necessary.

Joe Cool.

A few seconds later, the power windows slid down on both sides and two heads leant out. The invective that issued forth was quite something, the gist being that if the brick were to drop and damage the duco, the two of them would separate my testicles from my torso with bolt-cutters and feed them to reptiles.

"Good. I see I have your attention," I said.

I directed my remark to the driver, but it was the passenger who answered.

"Back off, ass-wipe."

Slowly I bent down, still eyeballing the driver, and placed the brick against the face of the right-hand front wheel. I didn't move from my position midway between the headlights. I was pretty certain they wouldn't dare drive over me with so many witnesses. It was a guess laced with some risk, nevertheless; you try it and see if your heart starts pumping.

"Stand aside, ass-wipe, or I'll tell my man here to drive right through you." His language and accent didn't even hint at his ethnicity — this guy was born in Oz, no question about that.

"Go right ahead," I replied. "You've got quite an audience enjoying the show here today. You'll be looking at ten years in Pentridge. That's a long time bending over, searching for the soap."

Mr Goatee withdrew his head inside the Subaru. Then the door opened and he stepped out.

He couldn't have been over five foot six, even with the Cuban heels. He was wearing a loose floral bowling shirt, faded denim jeans and white snakeskin cowboy boots. Around his neck was a gold chain with a golden skull hanging at the centre. He walked up to me and put his hands on his hips. I had to grin. Who was this guy trying to impress?

"You got some problem with me, pal?"

I looked down on him and remained very still. I remembered what Nick had told me. Don't let them get close. Already, this guy was *seriously* close to me, but I wasn't about to lose the initiative by backing up.

I was fully expecting the head butt. Of course I *shouldn't* have been waiting for it — that was exactly what Nick had told me not to do. But there was no way I could head-butt first — I'd have to drop down around seven inches to connect my forehead with this idiot's nose. Instead I clenched my right fist ready for the throat hit, if it proved necessary.

"You waiting for someone, sonny?" I replied slowly. "Or just reading the funnies with your kid brother?"

"Who the fuck *are* you, pal?"

"My name is Sainte-Claire."

"Well, Mr Sainte-Claire, why don't you get out of my face."

"There's no Mr. Just Sainte-Claire. You'd do well to remember the name."

At the time it never occurred to me I was behaving like some teenage idiot acting out a Clint Eastwood movie. I was the hard man and this guy was about to 'make my day'.

"Fuck off anyway," was the best the small guy could come up with.

"You work for Brierley?" I said.

"Who the fuck's Brierley?"

I studied the guy; the response appeared genuine.

"Forget it. But here's the thing. If I see this shitty little car in this street again, I'm going to take a bat to it."

"That wouldn't be a smart thing to do, arse-wipe."

This guy was the master of the one-liner. Maybe I would have to throat-punch him, just to make him go away. He was that stupid.

I smiled hugely. "Duh."

His eyes were burning with fury, but something was stopping him from mixing it with me. I couldn't pick it. Then it occurred to me that it could be the 'Sainte-Claire Factor' — somehow I was projecting major aggression. I really wasn't afraid of him and he'd picked up on it.

We stood cowboy boot to steel toecap for about another twenty seconds. I could now register fear in Mr Goatee's eyes, and sweat was beginning to roll down the sides of his face. The more he showed fear, the better, and more relaxed I felt.

The driver called out. "Hey, c'mon. Let's get out of here!"

Mr Goatee's eyes flicked from me to something way up the street.

"This ain't over, dickwad," he mumbled.

"You know, shortie," I replied lazily, "I was really hoping you'd come up with something a tad more original."

His lips twitched, then he stepped back and climbed into the car. The windows hummed smoothly upwards.

I moved onto the pavement and looked down at the rego plate. SYCHO1.

Quite the joker. Shame he couldn't spell.

I was expecting the Asian driver to 'lay a little rubber' on the road. Instead, with minimum revs, the red chili car began to move. But Pretty-Boy had forgotten about the house brick leaning against the right front wheel. The WRX lifted slowly over it, tilting to one side, then fell heavily back onto the road. The driver turned to me and pointed a finger that seemed to suggest he would see me again. Perhaps he felt as stupid as he looked and reckoned it was my fault the audience was now laughing at him.

The car glided away up the street.

As it passed Number 5, I saw the reason they'd decided to leave. A white cop car was cruising down towards us.

Back home, there were a few messages on the machine. One from Tiggs — she said she'd try my mobile later. One from my publisher. The last was from Jez. She'd found some superb Parma ham in a new Italian deli that had recently opened down the road from her in Surry Hills. Did I want to join her for lunch at the studio? And could I pick up some sourdough at on the way?

I looked at my watch. I was pushing it, but I could make it.

When I let myself into the studio Jez was standing in front of a big canvas, her head cocked to one side studying it. She must have heard me behind her.

"What do you think, Pulitzer?"

"It's an emu. Definitely an emu."

"Sure, it's an emu, but is it facing you or looking away? Which do you prefer?"

"Looking at me. With crazy eyes like an emu's, why not feature them?"

"Maybe," she mumbled. Turning to me she let out a slow whistle. "Hey, Pulitzer! You look very seriously hot. What's got into you?"

I hadn't changed — I was still Sainte-Claire. And she clearly liked the look.

"Me?" I replied, all innocent. "Same old, same old. You know?"

She stepped up to me and kissed me, then ran her long chocolate fingers through my sticky hair.

"What's with the change of identity? One which, incidentally, I approve of one hundred per cento. I love that hair, Mister P."

Despite her flattery I felt a bit uncomfortable looking the way I did. Maybe if I'd been twenty, I would have felt different. "Couldn't get the plain sourdough, so I settled for the yeasted levain. Okay with you?"

"The bread's fine, sexy."

She kissed me again, then whispered in my ear. "Hey, you got time to fool around?"

"Now?"

"Right now."

I had time.

Thirty minutes later I was lounging on the day bed Jez had set up in the corner of the studio. She'd visited the Brett Whiteley museum in Raper Street eighteen months ago and liked the way he'd set up his workspace. A day bed was a great idea.

I took another look at the canvas. It was beginning to take shape — I could clearly make it out as an emu. The big bird was shaded by a huge gum tree.

Jez set up lunch in the middle of the studio on a folding antique card table and two director's chairs. There was a serving dish in the center of the table on which were arranged about twenty slices of air-cured ham and a pile of green capers. Next to the plate were two smaller dishes. One held cooked asparagus spears — big fat white freshly steamed French suckers that she'd cooked in the microwave. The other held interlaced leaves of whitlof, radicchio and rocket. A pot of white French unsalted butter stood to one side.

"Ready," she called out as she popped the cork on a bottle of Ciccone Gewurztraminer. Then: "You going to tell me why you're dressed like Sainte-Claire, or keep it a secret?"

"It's nothing. It started out as a joke really."

"Ms Tiggy-Winkle?"

"You got it."

"You got all dressed up in fancy dress for a twelve-year-old?"

"It's her fantasy that she's hiring Sainte-Claire, so I thought I'd go see her looking like him." It sounded pretty damned silly, even to me. "Just as a bit of fun, you know."

She gave me a wry look as she poured the wine.

"And today?"

"Today? Well, today, I just felt like it. Call it a whim."

She continued to tease me. "And why did you feel like it today?"

"I don't know. It's nothing to get excited about."

"Sounds like you need a little psychoanalysis, Pulitzer. Maybe I'm witnessing the beginnings of a personality shift."

Jez wasn't serious then, but the thought had actually occurred to me five minutes before and it was beginning to disturb me.

I helped us both to some proscuito, and broke off two pieces of the bread. It smelled wonderful — still deliciously warm.

"You have to admit the way you look influences how people respond to you."

"Ain't that a fact." She was laughing at my ingenuousness.

"What do you mean by that?"

"Oh, come *on*, Pulitzer. If I *dress* sexy, I *feel* sexy and most times people are turned on by me 'cos they think I *am* sexy. If I put on a jogging suit no one pays me any attention at all. I'm just a jogger. We all know that."

"It can't be that simple," I replied.

"Well, think of it another way. Don't you feel better after a nice long bath, when you're wearing a fresh change of clothes?"

"True."

"Well, there you are. It's the same thing with you dressing up as your ace gumshoe. Makes you feel a bit like Sam Spade or Spiderman. What makes street people feel so hopeless is that they're trapped in their despair — they've got no change of anything; no place to shower, not a cent to their name."

Simplistic? Maybe. The Asians I'd had my standoff with in Roslyn Street weren't much different. The image they were trying to project was a violent one, so they'd chosen a violent-looking car and haircuts to match.

"Anyway, I happen to like the new look, Pulitzer. It's cute."

She helped me to some asparagus and poured the melted butter over.

"How's the client, anyway? Are you 'busting the case'? Isn't that the way you put it?"

"Fifty years ago, maybe. But yes, I have another meeting with Ms Tiggy-Winkle this afternoon as a matter of fact."

"Got some good news for her?"

Jez was smiling as she said it. I knew she didn't take the problems of the Reid family as seriously as I did. It wasn't that she didn't care; it was because I hadn't shared sufficient information with her. She thought I was just playing some game, being pally with kids. She knew how much I liked being round kids.

"I think I may have pulled the father out of the frying pan today. That's good news for Tiggs and Alice. At least their dad can come home now."

"How's that?"

"He owed some loan shark a bundle of money and couldn't pay him back. I think that's why he went AWOL."

"So how did you fix it?"

"I paid the guy some money. Peter can pay me back when he's able."

"How much?"

"A thousand dollars."

Jez stopped eating. She looked taken aback.

"You did what?"

"I loaned someone some money. That's all. End of story."

She gave me the incredulous look. "You gave a loan shark a thousand dollars in the hope that he'll ease off some stupid man who's managed to get himself into a situation where he owes a criminal money?"

She was angry. It wasn't the money, I knew that. It was my behaviour. I had to admit I hadn't exactly been acting like an adult since I got out of bed. I should never have continued to probe where I wasn't wanted, and dressing up to look like a hardened professional private dick and fronting up to one of Sydney's most notorious crime figures hadn't been a smart move.

I felt dumb. With some justification.

"I can afford it," I said lamely.

"It's your money, Pulitzer — just don't get yourself into any of Sainte-Claire's 'jams'. Remember, you are you, and fiction is fiction."

"I will."

"And take care of yourself."

"I will."

She reached out a hand to take mine. "I love you, Pulitzer. I don't want to see you in any trouble. You're a kind, sweet man and that's why I love you. I know you want to do what you can for those two kids, but you'll have to learn when to say enough is enough. It's all been a bit of a game up till now. Just keep it that way."

I didn't mention the two lunkheads in the WRX.

14

Jez went back to her painting and I began to wonder what the chances were, realistically, that the idiots in the red car *had* been staking out Charlotte Reid. If so, was it a changing of the guard? Probably not; the Goatee had looked genuinely surprised when I'd mentioned Brierley's name.

But I couldn't forget the terrified look in Charlie's eyes when she'd seen them. These were the guys that were scaring her now, not Brierley. Possibly she'd lied about paying off Brierley, but when I'd told her I'd given Brierley some money so Peter could come out of hiding, she'd said, 'Then you know nothing'. I was beginning to share her opinion.

The more I thought about it, the more I came to the conclusion that I'd actually achieved very little with Brierley — barring handing over a thousand dollars of my own money. So, what was it that Tiggs had overheard her mother tell Peter to 'give up'? Was it money? Or was it something else entirely?

I called James Millar at Fairfax. He thanked me for the wine that had just been delivered to his office, but said he hadn't had any feedback yet from the police regarding Peter's Saab. He assured me the radio cars had the plate number and would keep an eye out.

What was I going to tell Tiggs? I wasn't so certain now that I'd cracked the case at all. Judging by Charlie's general demeanour, things had gone from bad to worse, despite my paying off Brierley for a week.

I was walking down Bayswater Road towards the Café Hernandez just minutes before my four o'clock meeting with Tiggs when I saw a familiar figure cross the road ahead of me. I'd walked on several paces before I realised it was Uncle Sam, the face in the photo Tiggs had emailed me. In the snap he'd been laughing. The man I'd just caught sight of had not been laughing; quite the reverse. His face was as dark as Kostya Tzu's before a world title fight.

I tried to locate him again but there was no sign of him. He'd been walking in the general direction of the Coca-Cola sign, so I jogged back up Bayswater Road.

Finally I saw of him, standing outside the former Millennium Hotel, smoking. Grinding out the butt of one cigarette with his shoe, he immediately lit another.

Should I just walk up to him and introduce myself as a friend of the Reid family? Probably not. It wouldn't be a smart move to show my hand too early.

Uncle Sam glanced at his watch then peered up and down Darlinghurst Road. He looked thoroughly dejected.

It was four o'clock and Ms Tiggy-Winkle would be sitting in Hernandez, her order in place, waiting for me. I had to make a decision. What would Sainte-Claire have done? He would have followed 'the mark'. Tiggs would have to wait.

Uncle Sam stepped off the kerb, and started across the street towards the fire station. I followed. Tailing someone on foot isn't too hard if they don't know who you are. Of course if Sammy decided to jump in a cab or had a car parked nearby I'd be stymied; my car was still in Nick's garage halfway up Palmer Street.

I was hoping he'd stop for a coffee at the Tropicana, so I could somehow engineer a conversation with him, but he kept walking. I maintained a distance of about ten metres between us and had my head down. He looked to be in an agitated state, constantly looking over his shoulder back up Victoria Street to the Coca-Cola sign. Possibly he'd been expecting to be picked up outside the Millennium. Or maybe he was looking for a cab.

At the corner of Liverpool and Victoria, he looked back up the street, his expression changed from darkness to light and he started waving his arms.

It was the red WRX, weaving its way through the traffic with the lack of consideration you'd expect from the punks I'd met earlier. I didn't bother to wait to see if it was going to stop for Uncle Sam; I reckoned it was a lay down misère.

I set off at a run for Nick's garage, hoping that if I headed back down Liverpool and made for Oxford Street via Boundary, Campbell and Glenmore, I'd make contact with them again when they reached the top of Victoria. I knew the WRX would hit the bottleneck at Victoria and Oxford Street. I was very nearly collected by a Telstra van as I ran across the intersection of William and Palmer. The driver leaned on the horn and swore at me.

Thankfully, Nick hadn't started on my Goddess's renos yet — it was still parked in the driveway. I leaped in and threw the car into gear, then headed down the hill. I could faintly hear Nick calling after me — there he was in the rear-view mirror, waving his arms.

My mobile started bleating. At Boundary Street I punched the answer button.

"I'm very disappointed in you, Sainte-Claire."

Tiggs. Very grown-up. Very annoyed.

"Well, you wouldn't be if you knew what was happening. I'm busy earning your money and things are hotting up."

"Which is more than can be said for your double short black," she replied, only slightly mollified.

I turned right into Boundary Street and put my foot down. The Citroën shot forward like toothpaste from a tube. I willed it to go faster. No luck.

"So what's up?" Tiggs asked coolly.

"Look, I can't talk now. I'm tailing someone and I don't want to lose him."

"Who?"

"It doesn't matter."

"If it doesn't matter, then why aren't you here, reporting back to me? Drinking the coffee I've ordered? There's a huge slice of cake. I can't eat it all." There was a two-second hesitation. "Well, maybe I can. Just."

"Okay. It *is* important. I'm following your Uncle Sam and I want to see where he's going to lead me. Call you later."

I heard Tiggs shout, "Hey! Don't hang up!" then I hit the end button and she was gone. I dropped the mobile onto the seat beside me, and made a right into Glenmore.

As I stopped at the lights at the intersection of Oxford and South Dowling Street, I caught sight of the red WRX just beginning to move off with the traffic across my path. I was one car back from the lights and they were third car in their queue. This looked as though it might work out well.

They crossed the intersection ahead of me. I could just make out Uncle Sam sitting in the back seat. He was leaning forward and still looked agitated. The boys in the front seats had that 'I own the world' look. I felt a groundswell of anger but kept it bottled.

I tailed them about four cars behind.

The traffic picked up speed on the freeway to the airport, the WRX continuing to weave between the other vehicles. I managed to keep my distance but it wasn't easy to keep in the same lane — a problem if the WRX suddenly took a left or right exit.

At Daceyville they made a right at the roundabout into Gardeners Road, finally turning right onto the Princes Highway at the end of Canal Street.

My mobile beeped again. Risking a fine, I picked it up. I hoped it was Jez.

"Can you give Uncle Sam a message for me?"

It was Tiggs.

"Look, I don't have a hands-free setup so I can't talk now. Go home."

"That's hardly the way to talk to a client, Sainte-Claire."

I was about to say something stern when she giggled. "Joking!" she said. "Sorry, just curious."

"You don't know where Uncle Sammy's staying right now, do you?"

"No. He's never in the same place for more than a few weeks. Mum says it's because there are always people looking for him to pay back money. So he's always on the move."

We were now passing Arncliffe and approaching Banksia railway station. The red car was driving about twenty ks over the speed limit. Stupid. Especially if you're carrying drugs or weapons. But then, maybe they weren't. My Citroën was practically smoking with the effort.

"Why are you tailing my uncle?" she asked.

"See where he leads me."

"To daddy?"

"Gotta go. I'll call you," I said.

"I had to eat all the cake, you know. I'll get as fat as a pig if you don't show up next time."

"Bye," I said.

Just past Rockdale station the WRX made a right turn into Harrow Road and an immediate right again into a side street called Watkin. I stayed back in Harrow so I could peek round the corner —

I couldn't follow because they'd be suspicious of any car that had made the same last three turns as them.

They halted outside a church and Uncle Sam looked back out of the rear window. He was watching for a tail — just as well I hadn't made the turn. The car moved on and crossed two more intersections, eventually making a slow left turn into another street.

I had a feeling they'd arrived or were close to their destination, so I parked where I was in Harrow and walked down Watkin.

At the corner of Ferrier Street I saw the WRX parked about twenty metres down. It was empty. In front of it was a red Saab, the registration ATW 50N. Peter Reid's car. At that moment I felt a surge of real anger. What the hell was going on? Was I the only person who gave a toss about Tiggs and Ally-Oop? Had Peter Reid actually been abducted, or was he frigging around with his brother and the two goons while his family worried themselves to death?

I walked past the cars on the opposite side of the street, trying to judge which house they'd entered. Unlike my graphic novels, there were no pointers. I saw movement behind the window of the most likely house. Plus the gate was ajar.

Next decision. Wait for someone to come out, or go round the back and see what I could see and hear? I foolishly decided on the latter. There was a boarded-up house next door. I walked down a path to the back, then edged my way towards the fence that separated it from the target house. I could hear male voices. They were pretty indistinct.

I knew that if I tried looking over the fence that divided the properties I risked being seen. But the temptation was too great — especially when, after maybe half a minute of listening, I heard a man say, 'Well, cut a piece off!'

Not a pleasant thing to hear, unless you're a kid waiting for Dad to carve the turkey on Christmas Day.

The voice didn't sound like the guy in the WRX I'd spoken to. It was a mature man's voice, with an Asian accent, so it wouldn't have been Uncle Sam either.

Several males started shouting at each other, then there was an abrupt silence. I could hear a dog barking down the street but nothing else.

I waited for a full minute then reached for a brick lying beside me in a flower bed and stood on it, edging up so I could see over the wooden fence.

I never even felt the blow to the back of my head.

15

It was dark when I regained consciousness. I became aware that my mobile was vibrating in my trouser pocket. I thought I was in a rainforest in Bolivia, being attacked by killer bees. That'll give you some idea of my mental state.

I let the phone ring out.

If you've never been smacked over the head with a blunt instrument you won't appreciate how painful the aftermath can be. Nor will you appreciate that when fiction writers say the victim doesn't know where he is, or what happened, this is a quite normal reaction. All I was aware of was that it was dark and I was in terrible pain.

I rolled onto my back and very carefully touched the back of my head. It felt wet. I tried to focus on my hand but in the darkness I couldn't make out if it was blood or whether I'd been lying in a splash of some diesel oil.

Very slowly things began to come back to me. I checked my watch — it wasn't easy to focus. It had been around 4.20 p.m. when I'd seen the WRX parked in the street – that meant I'd been out for at least an hour.

The mobile rang again. Everything around me — barring the incessant cheeping of the phone in my trouser pocket and the howling dog I remembered having heard before I was hit over the head — was still and very quiet.

The phone ceased ringing for the second time.

As I stood, I stepped on my D&G's and heard that familiar crunching noise that leaves you in no doubt that your sunnies are history. I left them where they lay crushed and walked back round the front of the boarded house. Both cars were gone. The WRX and the Saab.

I walked back to my car in an advanced state of fury. I'd been too hasty, a card-carrying bonehead.

I'd always thought of myself as a pretty calm individual; I imagined I had a higher flash point than most people. But right then I wanted to find any one of those guys and take a shot at him — with a fist or a gun, it didn't matter. If I came out the worse, so be it.

By the time I slid behind the wheel of the slowest 'froggy car' in the world, I'd calmed down slightly and come to the conclusion that perhaps making sure my skull didn't require hospital treatment was my first priority. I was about to call my doctor — an old friend who I knew would fit me in at a moment's notice — when the mobile beeped yet again. This time I answered it.

"Hello?"

All I could hear was crying. I recognised the sobs at once — once you've heard Ally-Oop's 'ooping' you never forget it.

"Ally!" I said happily, pretending I had no idea she was crying at all. "How's things? What a nice surprise!"

"Tiggs is doing her homework."

What could I say? "That's good. You finished yours?" was all I could come up with.

"Guess so," she replied. The sobbing became a snuffle.

"So what's hopping, Ally-Oop?"

I was using the gimmick mothers use on children who've fallen down and are surprised by the pain. The last thing you say is 'Ow! That must have hurt. Are you all right, chicken?' You look in the other direction and say, 'Wow! What was that? Did you see that elephant?' Usually the kid is so surprised they might have missed something as big as an elephant they forget they should by rights be boo-hooing.

She didn't fall for it. "I miss Dad so much," she said after a pause. "I wish he'd come home."

"I know, Ally," I replied. "But he'll be home soon. Sainte-Claire's on the case."

Her tone changed from misery to excitement in a microsecond. I've noticed the very young are prone to fast mood swings.

"I know! Tiggy told me. That's super!"

Then Charlie came on the line. "Who's that?" she asked, warily.

I didn't know exactly how to reply at that precise moment, so I didn't say anything at all.

I could hear Charlie talking to Alice. 'Who are you speaking to, darling? Tell me at once!" Then, a little more crossly, "Do you hear me, Alice?"

Time to intervene. "It's me, Charlie. Robert Howard."

"Oh great! You again — this is barely credible. Why are you calling us? Can't you get through a day minding your own business?"

I was still in severe pain, so it was remarkable that I didn't let fly at her. But I didn't.

"I just called to say hello to the kids," I replied — I didn't want to get Alice into any more trouble. "If you remember, you did say I could keep in touch."

I could almost hear Charlie grind her teeth.

"Well, that's very decent of you," she said.

"How's Peter? Back home?"

"As a matter of fact, he is," she said flatly.

In the background I heard Alice say, 'No he's *not*! He's *not*, Mummy!' Then the phone went dead.

As soon as the line was free it rang again. This time it was Jez.

"Hey, Pulitzer. Where are you? I've been calling for an hour. It's just been ringing out."

"I'm afraid the ambushers got me," I said. It was a continuing joke I had with Jez. Every time I took a different route home, simply for a change of scenery, she'd ask why and I'd say, 'So's the ambushers don't get us!'

I don't think she knew whether I was serious or not this time. Maybe it was the tone of my voice — the pain, you know.

"You okay?" she asked.

"I think so. I'm going to pop in on Julian on the way home. I may have cracked my head open. I fell."

"Jesus!" was the instant reply. Guess I shouldn't have put it so bluntly. "Where are you?"

"Hold on," I replied. "I'm in good shape. Really. May need a stitch or two, that's all. I fell and hit my head. I'll be home in an hour."

"Sure? You don't want me to come and collect you? Can you drive?"

"Sure I can drive. Piece of cake. See you later. Love you."

"Love you too, Pulitzer."

I called Julian and, true to form, he told me to use the back entry to his consulting rooms in Paddington Street. The waiting room was packed with patients who'd been there for the best part of an hour. No one takes kindly to queue-jumpers.

"I'd say this was caused by a metal object," Julian said, as he probed at the hole in the back of my head. "I'm not much used to clubbings, but if it was the million-dollar question, and I couldn't ask the studio audience or phone a friend — a pathologist in this case — I'd say the weapon was a short gun barrel."

I didn't say anything. Sainte-Claire shares his information strictly on a 'need to know' basis.

"Don't you think you should tell the police?" he said.

"Of course," I replied. "I intend to. I wanted to make sure my head was all right first."

"So it was a gun?"

"No comment, Julian."

"Suit yourself," Julian said, adding, "I think we'll need a couple of staples to hold the skin together."

"Fire away," I said.

He did. I felt no pain as the metal rivets went in; my entire body was ablaze with it anyway.

Two Panadeine Forte later I was back in my car, fighting the drowsiness Julian had warned me about. I knew I shouldn't be driving, but I felt I had to keep moving. Dumb. It was close to 7 p.m. and I was thinking about what I should do.

If I contacted the police, what was I going to say? That I was following two young Asian/Australian thugs who had possibly kidnapped a friend of mine? Did I know this for a fact? No. That I then tailed these men across town because the brother of the person I suspected they'd kidnapped had got into their car and driven away with them? That I'd snuck up on them and listened to their private conversation over a garden wall? And had been hit over the head with a blunt object. Who by? I didn't know.

Not too impressive.

I decided it might be better to go home and think things through. After all, tomorrow was another day.

I was just turning into Barcom from Craigend Street when my mobile went yet again. I considered tossing it out the window.

It was my employer. If she'd been an adult, I would have resigned there and then.

"What happened? Tell me everything?" Tiggs sounded excited.

"I tried to speak to Uncle Sam, but I lost him in the traffic. Are you all okay?"

"Sure, I suppose we're okay. Mum's still pretty upset, of course. I think she knows where Dad is, but she won't tell us. Someone just telephoned and Mum answered. Now she's crying again."

"Great." I gave my head about a minute before it fell off my shoulders.

"You said you thought you'd cracked the case?"

I wasn't about to tell her the only thing I'd cracked was my head.

"I thought I had. Maybe I have. We'll see."

"That's not very Sainte-Claire."

"I'm doing the best I can."

I wasn't in the mood to be chastened by a kid, however cute.

"Well, I've got to go and read to Ally. Oh, by the way, please don't call me on my mobile during school hours. Mrs Hampshire doesn't like it. You see, sometimes I forget to turn it off and then I'm in heaps of trouble."

"You'd better tell me the number, you didn't before."

I saved the number.

Less than a couple of minutes later I was stopped by the cops and given a ticket for using a mobile phone while driving. As you can imagine, it made my day.

I dropped off the car outside Nick's garage, put the keys under the mat, where the ambushers would never think of looking, and walked home.

16

Jez stayed the night. I think she was worried about me. She said she thought I might be having a mid-life crisis twenty years earlier than expected.

It took her about half an hour to rinse a pint of dried blood from the back of my T-shirt. Though she liked the new fashionista image, she wasn't so keen on what went with it, which involved getting clubbed over the head by automatic weapons or thrown over walls. What would be in store tomorrow?

On a more serious note, I could see she was as concerned as I was about the kids. No one seemed to be looking after them. Charlie was having a mental meltdown, Lucy was attempting to distance herself from any nastiness, and Peter was still lost in space.

"I hope you won't take offence, Pulitzer," Jez said over toast and Rose's lime marmalade the next morning, "but I think you may have lost the plot a bit."

"You're telling me. And I'm an author, for Christ's sake. Well, there *isn't* one."

"Hey, forget your frigging novels. This is the real thing, Pulitzer! And I'm telling you, you can't solve the Reids' problems all on your own — you don't know a damned thing about them. Go to the police — tell them what's happening. If they don't take you seriously, that's *their* problem. At least you'll have done what you can — and, who knows, they might even think things are serious enough to take the kids into care. That's what the social services are there for, isn't it? To make sure kids like Tiggs and Alice aren't put in harm's way."

She had a point. Though I knew exactly what Ms Tiggy-Winkle would have to say about being taken into care by DOCS. After all, she was twelve years old going on twenty, and she was my client, not a child.

My head felt as though it had been caught in an industrial vice overnight. I hit the codeine again hard, added some Aspirin and washed it down with a Bloody Mary.

Delicious, but it didn't solve a thing.

Despite the explosions in my head and neck, I determined to make three calls. If I didn't get any answers to the questions I was about to ask, I'd head straight for the cop shop and tell them my ridiculous story, at the risk of being taken for a complete fool.

First up was a call to Peter's office.

"The Vandercheltz Group. May I help you?"

It was the same smooth-talker. This time I found his tone smarmy and annoying.

"May I speak with Peter Reid, please?"

"Is that Mr Sainte-Claire?"

"You're good with voices," I replied.

"That's what I do, Mr Sainte-Claire. Listen to voices. I'm afraid Mr. Reid is on holiday."

"Since when?"

"Since you last called."

"When is he expected to return?"

"I'm afraid I don't have that information available. Mr Flanagan is taking over Mr Reid's portfolio in his absence. Perhaps I could put you through to him."

"It's a personal matter. I'm a friend." It wasn't what I'd said before; I hoped he didn't remember.

"Oh, I see," he replied. His tone suggested he *did* remember. "Then perhaps you should call him at home."

I did just that — to make sure Charlie hadn't been assaulted or the house hadn't burnt down since the last time I'd checked. There was no reply. Not even the answering machine.

I called Lucy's number. At least she'd switched her machine on. I left a message asking her to call me on my mobile.

Next was a short walk up to Kings Cross police station. I asked if Detective Chase was available and was told it was his day off. I gave the duty sergeant a brief history about being initially called by Alice at midnight two days ago, plus the details of the first night at 5 Roslyn Street. He disappeared into a back room and I was left alone for at least ten minutes. He returned with a young detective I hadn't met before.

"Good morning, Mr Howard," the detective said. "My name's Dunn. I've had a look at the incident book and I see that the matter of Mrs Reid's disappearance was cleared up two days ago."

"Well, it may *seem* that way, but I wouldn't say *anything's* been cleared up."

I explained that I'd returned to the Reids' house, as suggested by Chase, and that Charlotte Reid had been behaving strangely, that she was in a very disturbed state of mind, that she'd lied to me about Peter Reid's whereabouts, and that I'd not been able to contact Peter Reid since that night. I told him in detail of my several visits to Charlie's house and our conversations on each occasion. I added that Charlotte Reid had at one time told me that her husband had returned, yet seconds later I'd overheard her six-year-old daughter shouting out to her mother in some distress that this wasn't true.

"What exactly are you suggesting, Mr Howard?"

"I think Peter Reid is being held somewhere against his will, and that money is being extorted from Mrs. Reid."

"Initially, you suggested that Mrs Reid was being held against her will. Except on that occasion Mrs Reid returned home a few hours later. Isn't that so?"

I had to agree.

"So now you say that it's *Mr* Reid who's been kidnapped. Do you mind my asking — by *whom* has he been abducted? Do you have anyone in mind? Surely not Mr Brierley? You just told me that Mrs. Reid informed you she has returned the money her husband owed Mr Brierley."

"You're aware of his reputation?"

Dunn smiled imperceptibly. "I know of Mr Brierley, yes."

"When I visited Mrs Reid, I was assaulted by one of Mr Brierley's standover men. He'd been intimidating Mrs Reid."

"You were present, and a witness, when Mrs Reid was intimidated?" Dunn looked genuinely surprised.

"No, I phoned her, and while the phone was off the hook I heard someone threaten her."

"How do you know it was one of Mr Brierley's people?"

"Because I ran round there immediately, afraid that whoever I'd overheard might be about to assault Mrs. Reid."

"But he hadn't?"

"No, he hadn't. I tried talking the matter over with him and then he assaulted me."

"Did you report this at the time?"

"No, I didn't."

"Why not, sir?"

"I thought I'd visit Mr Brierley first, and see what problem he had with the Reids."

"Even though these were problems that were personal to someone else and were possibly none of your business?"

"That's right." What else could I say?

"The man that assaulted you. What was his name?"

"Big Islander guy. Two palm tree tatts on his arms. Name's Tutuelo."

The detective smiled again. "Are you sure he actually assaulted you, Mr Howard? The thing is, when Tutuelo has a mind to lay into someone, we usually take the details of the assault from the victim in St Vinnie's ER. He's a big strong boy."

Dunn was beginning to get on my wrong side. I can usually see the funny side of things, but I wasn't laughing right then.

"How do you know he was acting on Mr Brierley's say-so," he went on, "and not simply off his own bat?"

"I *don't* know that, Detective. I was made aware that this man works for Tim Brierley, so I assumed—"

Dunn cut in. "That's just it. You *are* assuming a great deal, Mr Howard. One way or another."

I was quite steamed up by now. I actually wanted to deck the guy — something that would never have crossed my mind a few days earlier. It wasn't just that he was having a laugh at my expense; it was because he wasn't taking what was clearly a serious matter seriously. I knew I should have trusted my instincts and continued to handle things myself.

"Mr Howard, I appreciate you're concerned for the welfare of Mrs Reid's children. But tell me this. Do you, for instance, know whether the two girls have been attending school the past two days?"

"I believe they have, yes."

"And Mrs Reid, their mother, has been living with them at their home and caring for them?"

"Yes, I believe she has."

"Feeding them?"

"I'd imagine so, yes."

"Well, it doesn't appear to me that this is an occasion to alert social services. I'm not going to go round to Mrs Reid's home and ask her whether her husband has been kidnapped just because you tell me so. Last time Detective Chase went to Mrs. Reid's home she told him it was all a mistake, she was well and had *not* been abducted, that her husband was staying with friends and she knew of his *exact* whereabouts."

What was I going to say? That Mrs Reid's eldest daughter — a twelve-year-old — had engaged my services as a private investigator, without her mother's knowledge? Or that I'd been tailing Mrs Reid's brother-in-law, Uncle Sammy, because Ms Tiggy-Winkle thought he was 'a bad egg' usually involved in some shady business? And then top it all off with the story of my spying on the Oz/Asian drug kids in their red hoonmobile and being hit over the head by person or persons unknown in Rockdale?

I don't *think* so.

"You can handle the information I'm giving you now in any way you like, Detective," I said reasonably. "I'll just say this. It's now a matter of record that I have been in here today. If it turns out that I'm right in my analysis, and the Reid family is in trouble but Mrs Reid is afraid to approach the police for help because her husband is being held captive and she fears for his safety, then the New South Wales Police Department is going to have a lot of egg on its face somewhere down the line. Especially when there are two small children involved, aged six and twelve."

Detective Dunn looked at the ceiling for a couple of seconds.

"Mr Howard, we're here to help the community. We do the best we can, given our resources. I hear what you're saying and I will write up every word you've told me the moment you leave. It'll give me something to do." He raised an eyebrow archly. "Sometime today I will personally visit Mrs Reid and ask her if all's well. I'll classify the visit as a follow-up call. More than that I cannot do. And until I have any evidence at all of child neglect — and let's remember that you have offered me no such evidence — I will not involve the Department of Community Services."

"Look, I'm grateful that you'll go and see Mrs Reid, Detective Dunn." I thought a conciliatory tone would be helpful. "I'm not trying to be a pain in the arse. But when you see her, *you* be the judge of her state of mind. See if *your* instinct tells you everything is 'just fine', as she keeps telling me."

I was turning to leave when Dunn spoke again.

"How long have you known the Reid family, Mr Howard?"

"A few days. That's all."

He wasn't being a clever dick this time; I think he was now genuinely trying to help and wanted some info.

"Just one more thing before you leave, Mr Howard. Next time you are physically assaulted in our area, please keep the police informed. That's what we're here for — to help."

"Thanks, Detective. I will."

"And I wouldn't get into too many arguments with people such as Mr Tutuelo. He's got a long history of violent behaviour."

That was one piece of good advice I chose to toss to the four winds at once. I was going to see Tim Brierley right away, and if that meant getting into arguments with anyone, Tutuelo included, that was the way it was going to be.

17

It was just after ten when I pressed the buzzer at Brierley's office.

"PIC. Can I 'elp you?" That sexy French voice again. Agnes Deneuve.

"I've come to see Mr Brierley."

"You don't ev an appointment, do you, Monsieur Sainte-Claire?"

Maybe the facility to recognise voices is a Sydney quirk.

"No, I don't have an appointment," I replied.

"Then I doubt whether a meeting can be arranged today. Mr Brierley has a very full agenda."

There was a moment's silence. "Unless, of course, you can guarantee Mr Brierley will want to see you again *today*?" There was now a definite teasing sound to her voice.

"I'll take a punt. I like my odds."

"*Eh bien. Entrez, monsieur.*"

The buzzer buzzed and I did as I was told.

This time Agnes was wearing a beautiful Japanese-influenced designer top, a million tiny pleats of aubergine silk. She smiled an inscrutable Da Vinci smile.

"Mr Brierley has asked if you'd wait. He won't be long."

I walked over to her reception desk. "Akira?" I asked.

"Miyaki," she replied.

I could just make out a magnificent multi-layered Alistair Trung skirt. I wondered about the shoes, but it would have been rude to stare.

"A coffee pr'aps?" she asked.

"Why not, the last one was great."

"A ristretto, if I remember correctly?"

"That's the one."

Her slim, beautifully manicured fingers found the call button on her desk.

"Do make yourself comfortable," she said, directing me with a lazy wave to the sofa opposite.

I did as suggested.

Fifteen seconds later a young man came through a service door. It was a different young buck to the one who had brought my coffee the first time, but he was dressed identically to the other boy — black shirt, black pants, identical gelled hair and Prada trainers. Obviously it was the Brierley signature outfit for hired help. I now felt totally uncomfortable in the clothes I had selected as my own signature — like the greeter at some crappy nightclub. So much for tough guys.

He set my short black beside me on the ash coffee table. I thanked him.

This time Deneuve was wearing something in her ear that resembled a hands-free phone attachment, presumably so Brierley could talk directly to her without her having to lift the phone. Interesting.

I sipped my coffee, every now and then looking in her direction. She never once returned my glance. She was engrossed in a copy of *Coté Sud* magazine.

Ten minutes of total silence later she looked up at me. "Mr Brierley will see you now, Monsieur Sainte-Claire."

She hadn't lifted a phone, her lips hadn't moved. Must have been the earpiece.

As I passed her on my way to Brierley's office I smiled down at her and thanked her for the coffee.

"*De rien,*" she replied, without looking up from the magazine. I noticed it was open at the Cap d'Antibes rental section. She had expensive taste in holiday spots, our Agnes.

I closed the door behind me and sat down opposite Brierley. He was writing notes at his desk with a Mont Blanc pen. He looked up at me.

"What can I do for you today, Sainte-Claire? Maybe advance *you* some money this time? Ask away."

"No. I'm here to reclaim *my* advance, actually. Charlotte Reid tells me she's already paid her husband's debt in full."

"Her cheque's not been cleared. So I'll hang on to yours," he replied, concentrating on whatever it was he was writing.

I said nothing. He looked up again.

"Unless you have a problem with that?" It was a leery challenge.

"So you *have* received a cheque from Mrs Reid?"

Brierley gave me the old steely glance. "Seems to me you involve yourself in a lot of other people's goings-on, Mr Sainte-Claire. Any business I have with Peter Reid is private. Whether I have been paid by him, his wife, even his dog for that matter, has nothing whatever to do with you. Am I getting through at all?"

"They don't have a dog."

"Oh, you know *that* much, do you."

"I know that much. And I also know that cheques can be cancelled. I'll be cancelling the one I gave you yesterday."

Brierley stood up and crossed his arms, then walked round the desk and stood very close to me. I hadn't noticed before — he'd always been seated — but standing he was a very big man indeed. Six-four, I'd say. And built like a rower – the one who's usually 'stroke'.

"I'm beginning to find you distinctly annoying, Sainte-Whatsit," he said quietly.

"Oh dear," I replied. "And here's me thinking we were beginning to develop quite a cosy business relationship."

I could see his expression darken. There was a filthy temper lurking beneath the surface. But he was still in control, just.

"I think it's time you were off, don't you, Mr Sainte-Claire? Go do what you usually do round this time of day. Annoy someone else. Take Mrs Reid's doggie walkies."

"She doesn't have a dog, Brierley."

"It's *Mr* Brierley to you."

"Eat me," I said, lightly.

I could see his temper was now closer to snapping point.

"A tiny morsel of advice," he said. "Nobody cancels the cheques they give me. Unless they want to be paid a visit by one of my colleagues, that is."

I stood. I wanted to get right into Brierley's space. See if he could hold back from assaulting me. Being constantly referred to by this piece of horse-shit as *Mr* Sainte-Claire was beginning to get to me. I *was* actually thinking the way Sainte-Claire would have thought. He'd *never* have backed down. He would have had it out with the bastard — and he'd have relished it. And I was just as ready as Sainte-Claire for a bit of 'biffo'. Even if I came off second best I could file a complaint with Detective Dunn just down the road.

We were nose to nose. Brierley had a good three inches on me but I was standing straight and he wasn't. I could feel his breath like an intermittent breeze on my face — we were that close, and he was that angry.

"You mean you'd organise a visit from one of those nice young coffee boys you keep in your kitchen?"

The smile that slowly crept across his face was reminiscent of Ben Kingsley in the movie *Sexy Beast*.

"I employ my 'nice boys' to make dipshits like you coffee while you wait until *I* feel like giving you a few moments of *my* precious time. It's my other staff that look after my more personal requirements — such as debt collection. They are *not* ' boys'. Quite the contrary."

"I know. I've met one."

Brierley looked surprised. "Oh really?"

"Really."

"Did you end up exchanging telephone numbers?"

"Not on that occasion."

"What did he look like?"

"Two palm trees and a bunch of coconuts."

"Mr Tutuelo?"

"The same."

"I'll definitely give him your regards."

"Please do. Nice lad."

Brierley walked to the door and opened it wide.

"Goodbye, Sainte-Claire."

Agnes didn't look up as I entered the reception area. As I reached for the front door, it made a buzzing sound and unlocked automatically. This was clearly the kind of house where you locked your clients in when they were inside and kept them locked out if they were outside. I hadn't noticed this on my previous visit because I'd been concentrating too much on Agnes.

"*À plus?*" I said, as I half turned to her.

"See ya," she replied in broad Strine, still not looking up.

World's chock-full of comedians.

As I walked home, I pondered on whether Brierley would bother to tell Tutuelo to look me up and 'put on the frighteners'. Probably not. Brierley was a pro — he wouldn't ask for a problem unless it made solid business sense. Of course, if I did cancel the thousand dollar cheque he'd probably feel he had to make an example of me. Too bad. I wasn't going to gift a lowlife such as Brierley a thousand bucks of my hard-earned money just because he'd threatened me. I headed for Westpac on Macleay Street and cancelled the cheque.

Back home, ten minutes later, it occurred to me that Brierley knew me as Sainte-Claire, while Tutuelo would only recognize me dressed as Robert Howard. How could Tutelo find me anyway?

Giblet brushed my legs a few times as I walked through into the kitchen. She thinks she may get an extra breakfast if she's super-appealing. She got some smoked salmon off-cuts I found in the fridge. I'm just so easy.

By midday I'd finished my most urgent business tasks. My emails were cleared, and everything replied to.

It was becoming obvious to me that Brierley had nothing to do with the Reids' problems. Much more likely that they lay with the kids in the WRX and their employer. The Asian kids had known where Peter was hiding or being kept prisoner. They'd led me there. Whether or not Uncle Sam had known where his brother was when he hopped a lift with them in Victoria Street was another matter. Sam was obviously up to no good; I was in total agreement with Tiggs there. Based on her testimony, it would be out of character for him to be doing somebody else a favour — even his brother.

Find Peter Reid and I'd find the key to what was going on — that was about the heart of it. Maybe even find Sam, screw the truth out of him and I'd have the answer another way. Of course, if Peter had been in the house at Ferrier Street the day I visited, I'd certainly blown that. I had to recognise the fact that Peter was possibly now dead. Equally possibly, he'd never been in the house at all and someone else had been driving his car that day.

On my way to meet Jez for lunch my mobile cheeped. It was James Millar.

"I've got news. Good and bad."

"The good?"

"We found the Saab."

"Bad?"

"It's been trashed. Burnt out, I gather."

"That's bad."

"No, that's not the bad bit. I'm getting to that."

I had a sinking feeling. "There was someone in the car when they found it?"

Millar laughed. "You've been reading too many of your own books. It's not that bad. But I can tell you there were bloodstains on the back seat. Not a lot, but 'an amount', as they say. The fire brigade put the fire out before it became a shell, so the back-seat material was left intact."

"I was thinking bodies."

"I know."

"Thanks for calling."

"Robert, just one thing. What I've told you is confidential police stuff. Please don't share it with anyone — least of all with the car owner's family. As far as they know — and I'm not sure that they *do* know anything yet — the car was stolen and then found burnt out. And we don't know whom the blood belongs to. Could be animal blood for all we know."

"I won't tell anyone. Where did they find it?"

"Gilmore Street. Early hours of this morning. It had been set alight near Cabravale Park."

"Cabramatta?"

"Close."

They must have driven the car there after they'd put me to sleep.

A chance remark I'd heard that night resurfaced: 'Well, cut a piece off,' someone had said. Cut a piece off Peter? A finger? An ear maybe? Was that why there were traces of blood on the back seat of the Saab? Ears bleed a lot — I knew that from earlier research.

"Robert? You still there?" Millar was still on the line.

"Yes," I answered. "I was just thinking. Sorry."

"That's okay. You appreciate that this is what I do for a living, don't you? That I write crime news?"

"Of course I do, that's what Terry told me."

"Well, if there was something you knew would make a good news story for me, you would tell me, eh?"

"If it wasn't personal stuff — but a good story, sure," I replied.

"We could work together on this, you know. The Saab case."

He had a point.

"Why not? Who knows where this may lead. Tell you what, I'll share anything interesting that comes my way. In return you help me with info every now and then. What do you say?"

"Sounds like you want to know something right now."

"Right. Can you run a number plate, or is that the stuff of fiction only?"

"No, that's easy. Just means I owe a favour. What's the number?"

"SYCHO1."

"That's a car? Jesus, who are you mixing with?"

"It's a Subaru WRX."

"Doesn't sound like a nice person, Robert."

"Asian Australian. By that, I mean they look Asian but speak Oz. Look like ecstasy dealers."

"What's their angle?"

"I think they might have burnt out the car."

"Look, be major careful where you tread here. There are some very dangerous young men around Canly Vale/Cabramatta. Whether or not they're third or fourth-generation Australian, they have a completely different ethos. Get in the way of those criminals? They'll kill you, just for 'face'."

"I may take a drive down there — see if I can spot the Subaru."

"Just because they're Asian doesn't mean they live in Cabramatta, Robert. They could live in Chatswood, Chinatown, Surry Hills — anywhere! We're not talking ethnic ghettos, you know."

"Yeah, I know. But I may as well start with the obvious. Be a help if you could run the plates?"

"I'll call you on the mobile."

I hung up.

18

The burnt-out car and the blood changed everything. And since Charlie had put all logic and good sense out with the recycling a few days ago, I knew I'd have to call Lucy Portman. It was just a shame that Lucy was as eccentric as Charlie was unbalanced.

To my surprise, Lucy picked up at once. Most people don't pick up a phone straightaway, even if they can, simply because they don't want people to think they're waiting for a special call. Generally, people pick up before the second ring only when they're expecting news — good or bad.

"Lucy Portman," she said.

"It's Robert Howard here. Remember? The writer?"

"Of course. We met at the Commerford."

The remark struck me as odd. "Well, strictly speaking, we met before that."

"I'm aware of that," was her cold reply.

"I need to speak to you. Your sister's in trouble. So is Peter. I've offered to help your sister but she won't accept it."

"Maybe not everyone *needs* your help, Robert. Ever thought of that?"

"Look, I'll make this short and to the point. I'm only hanging in here because I think the children are great, and I feel that Charlie can't cope."

"Now you look here, Mr. Howard—"

I cut her short — something I hadn't been in the habit of doing two days ago.

"I know about the debt. I know that Peter's in big trouble. I've tried my best to help and ended up being assaulted twice by people who want me to butt out of Charlie's business. If you don't agree to meet me and discuss the matter, I'll just cash my hand, as they say, and tell the whole story to the police. That means calling in DOCS too. You see, unlike you and Charlie, I feel the kids are being put in a dangerous situation."

Her tone was suddenly very different. "Okay, okay. Calm down. Let's talk." Sainte-Claire-speak certainly got a better reaction than Howard-speak.

"When?"

"How about half an hour?"

"Where?"

"The Lord Dudley."

"See you there," I said and hung up.

On my way to the Dudley I called Jez.

"Hi, Pulitzer. You're going to cancel?"

"That, or be late. Sorry," I replied.

"Be late. I'll paint till I get stomach cramps. Then I'll start without you. Okay?"

She never took offence about the unimportant glitches in life — she was good in that way. The women I'd had relationships with before Jez had always been so particular about punctuality.

In the Dudley I bought a pint of Guinness and sat on one of the comfortable sofas by the open fire situated at the end of the room. I was early by about ten minutes. On the sofa facing me sat a young couple. I guessed they were students. It looked as though she was trying to tell him it was over and he didn't want to come to terms with his loss. She was doing a lot of hand-wringing; he had that 'hurt' face on and was softly touching the side of her cheek every now and then, as though he knew he wouldn't be able to feel her soft skin much longer.

Lucy arrived twenty minutes later. She looked at me as though I'd trodden dogshit across her newly laid Wilton carpet.

"I don't like being threatened, Mr Howard." That was for openers.

"Whatever happened to 'Robert'?" I wasn't about to be cowed.

"I don't take kindly to you intimidating my sister. All this talk about having the children put into care — DOCS and all that. What utter nonsense."

The veins at her temples showed me the blood was pounding round her system. She was seriously angry. Her pupils were dilated, her eyes practically bugging out of her head. The girl across from us was no longer wringing her hands, but looking in our direction. Her partner, by contrast, merely stroked on — her cheek his Holy Grail.

I waited for Lucy to calm down.

"Can I get you a drink?"

"A very large Scotch, please."

'Please'. That was good. No apology for her anger, but some manners remained. A start.

While I waited for a triple Scotch, I could see Lucy reflected in the mirrored beer advertisement above the bar. She was sitting bolt upright on the very edge of the sofa, daring anyone in the room to look in her direction and witness her fury. This was going to be fun. A nice afternoon out.

She lowered the level of her drink by a third in one gulp. I started in slowly.

"Lucy, if only you or Charlie could be civil to me and convince me that the kids are okay, there's nothing would suit me better than to back off. I really do have other things to do, and I only became involved in the first place because Alice called for my help. Help, I should say, that was gladly given."

"Well, everything *is* fine. So why not go away *now*."

"No. Everything is *not* fine. We both know that. You know that Charlie's been lying to me, and you know *you* lied to me when you told me Peter had returned home an hour after I left the house. Now why would you do that?"

I could see her searching for a good reason and coming up empty.

"Possibly I was confused."

"Oh, come on. Let's not dance around each other the way Charlie does with me."

She still wasn't going to volunteer anything.

"Did you know that Peter's car was found burnt out in Cabramatta this morning?"

'Gape' was the only word to describe her reaction. Like a hippo after a long drink at the water hole in the midst of an African drought.

"No, I didn't know that."

"Well, let's start with this. When you told me that Peter returned home from an evening with his friends, that wasn't true. Right?"

"I suppose not," she replied, her eyes downcast.

"Why did you lie to me?"

"It was a personal matter, none of your business. I wanted to get rid of you so I could think what to do."

"Well, that's nice. I come rushing round to help, like Sir Galahad, and all you want to do is get rid of me."

"Is Peter all right?" she asked.

"I don't know. I've been trying to find him." I managed to stop short of adding 'for Tiggs'. "But it would be a help if you'd be frank with me. Who knows, there's always the chance I could help the whole family."

"You want me to be frank?" She drilled me with a steady gaze. "Frank, in what way?"

"How about this? I ask a few simple questions and you answer yes or no."

"Depends on the questions. But basically, okay."

"Good. Is Peter in financial trouble?"

"No more than most people."

"I'll put it more simply. Saves on prevarication time." I knew I was being rude, but that approach worked better than the Robert Howard polite one — it was proving a fast learning curve. "Does Peter still owe Brierley money?"

"So you know about Brierley?"

"I know about Brierley. I met his thugs. You remember? I mentioned being assaulted twice?"

I detected a hint of a smile. Possibly she was relishing the thought that I might have been taught some manners by Brierley's standover men.

"No. That debt has been paid. By me," she said.

"That's nice. Good."

I glanced at her empty glass. "Another?"

"No, thanks. Let's plough on."

"Okay. Is Peter in some other trouble? To your knowledge?"

"What kind of trouble?"

"Is there anyone else who'd wish to harm him?"

"Not that I know of."

"He wouldn't be involved in any way with financing illicit drugs?"

She gave me a look of contempt. "Of course not. Let me tell you this. Peter is a fine man. He loves his wife and adores his children. He has very few failings, and most of those have been brought about by that useless brother of his."

"Which brings us to another question."

"No, it doesn't. You answer one of mine first. You told me that Peter's car had been found in Cabramatta, burnt out. Does Charlie know?"

"Maybe by now, yes. But I haven't told her — she doesn't like it when I call her. I'd say the police would have called her by now."

"How come *you* know about the car, Robert? Do the police confide in writers, choreographers, painters and the like before the next of kin?"

"I have a friend who informed me that the car had been found. That's all."

"That's all? You sure about that? No sign of Peter? No clue?"

She stared at me long and hard. Women can smell a lie at a thousand paces. Jez can smell one across town, on the phone or in an email. I wasn't going to get away with it, but I thought it worth a try.

"Peter's still missing. I thought I'd tracked him down to a house in Rockdale — his car was there."

"Where?"

"Ferrier Street. Ring any bells?"

"No." A pause. "What led you to Rockdale?"

"Sam."

Her shoulders sagged. "Jesus Christ — that bastard."

"Tell me. Is everything all right between Peter and Charlie?"

"Absolutely. I'm not lying, I promise. They live for each other and the kids."

"Then why did she say she'd been arguing with Peter that night?"

"Oh, I don't know. It could have been anything. But it wouldn't have been any *big* thing. They don't fight. In fact, I was round there about a couple of weeks ago — I'd never seen them so 'up'. Peter had opened some lovely champagne and Charlie showed me a wonderful Collette Dinnigan dress she'd bought that must have cost a fortune. Everything was wonderful. Then it was as though they hit the wall."

"They were celebrating?"

"Something like that. Mind you, it wasn't in character for them to be so extravagant — they're usually quite conservative in their spending. Charlie wouldn't go out and buy a designer dress as a matter of course. She looked…" She searched for the exact word. "I don't know. Exuberant! She told me they were thinking of taking the children to Florence for a holiday."

"Perhaps Peter had won on the horses again."

"No. He promised Charlie he'd never do that again. She told me she'd had a serious talk with him. I promised to pay off the debt to Brierley on the condition he wouldn't get into that kind of trouble again."

"Addicts can't help themselves."

"Peter's different from his brother. He knows the meaning of honour. So does Charlie. If Peter says he won't do something again, he won't."

"So why the celebration?"

"Don't know. Maybe they were just happier than usual. Maybe Tiggs won a gold star in class. Who knows?" She sipped at her drink without realising it was empty. "I want to know more about Sammy."

"What's to know?"

"How did he come to lead you to Peter's car?"

"First, *you* tell me about Sammy."

"He's a bastard. If the Cain and Abel analogy holds, Peter's Abel. Sam has always thought the world owes him a living. While Peter has always worked hard, his brother has always thought he can cut corners."

"So where does Sam come into the present equation? Racing? The horse?"

"I wouldn't think so. That's in the past, as far as I know. That time Peter made some money on the bet. But then, so did Sammy. Of course, Peter then lost all his gains when the horse was stolen."

"And no one blamed him — for winning on a shonky bet?"

"You mean the bookies? I don't think so."

"So where does Sammy fit in here?"

"No idea."

We both stared off into space. We were both stumped.

"Sure you won't have another Scotch?"

"You mean another *three* Scotches?" she replied, with a wry grin. "Yes, I think I will. But it's my shout. Another Guinness for you?"

"Why not."

She rose, a trifle unsteadily, and made her way to the bar. She looked as though she'd had a couple at home before coming to see me.

"When did you last see Sammy?" I asked as she settled herself back into the corner of the sofa, this time tucking her legs up underneath her. She hadn't held back — she was clutching another triple.

"We hadn't seen him for some time. Maybe a year or so. Then came the Faithful Hope thing. I knew it would end up badly — so did Charlie — but Peter wanted to give Sammy a chance. He's spent all his life giving Sammy another chance. Being the elder brother, he feels responsible."

"After the horse thing, did he disappear for a while?"

"Yes, he went walkabout. No one knew what'd happened to him. Peter was afraid the bookies had made an example of him. He was worried to death."

She was doing pretty good damage to the second triple.

"Then, out of the blue, he was back."

"Can you remember when exactly?"

"The day after Charlie bought the Dinnigan dress. Made me angry when I heard — they were so happy just then, and he chooses that exact moment to show up on their doorstep."

"What was he after? Money?"

"I don't know. Charlie wasn't even going to tell me he'd showed up. Tiggy told me. Ever since then Charlie's been acting strangely."

"How 'strangely'?"

"Well, to be frank with you, she isn't frank with *me*. She lies to me."

"As if she's hiding something?"

"That's about it. Yes."

"What happened the night I came round? I mean after I left?"

"Well, as you know, Tiggs phoned me and told me Charlie had rushed out. She was a bit confused. I asked her if the people Charlie left with were friends, and she couldn't say. She didn't see them, you see."

"And later?"

"The detectives came and had a good look around. No signs of a break-in — just some broken crockery and furniture. So Charlie must have answered the door, or whoever came in had a key."

"What about the damage to the kitchen?"

"They said it was evidence of a struggle or an argument. They thought it looked like a domestic tiff — no more."

"Then they left you to it?"

"Yes, they left. I put Tiggs and Alice to bed and read to them. Alice went to sleep, but Tiggs couldn't. I sat on her bed for about two hours. Then Charlie came back."

"About three o'clock?"

"Three-ten. I looked at my watch. She was a mess. Shaking."

"What did she say had happened?"

"She didn't want to tell me anything. It was as if she was searching for some fiction to cover what had really happened."

"What did she say?"

"She said that Peter had been out and had returned late with some friends. He'd asked her to join them for a card game at their place. It was late and she'd said no. Then Peter's friend became abusive and broke some plates, and she could see Peter was becoming angry, so she thought she'd better go."

"She left the children alone?"

"I asked her that. It was quite unlike her. She told me she wasn't expecting to be more than half an hour, and the children were asleep."

"You didn't believe her?"

"Of course not. I kept nagging her to tell me the truth, but she kept crying. Eventually I suggested she go to bed. I gave her half a Valium and spent the night on the sofa in case anything happened. It didn't."

"How was she in the morning?"

"Very withdrawn. We took Alice and Tiggs to school. When we came home, she told me everything was okay and she'd spoken to Peter."

"Did you hear the conversation?"

"No."

"Do you think there *was* one?"

"I didn't hear any. I could have missed it, though."

"Did she say where he was?"

"She said he'd spent the night with his ghastly friends. Then went to work."

"He didn't."

There was a sudden flicker of fear in her eyes. "How do you know that?"

"I called Vandercheltz. He hasn't been at work since that night."

"Oh, shit," she said, softly.

The question now was whether to confide fully in Lucy and have her on my side, or whether to keep things close to my chest — like Sainte-Claire.

I chested.

"I think the best idea is for you to keep a close eye on Charlie. Just to check that she and the kids are all right."

"Of *course* I will."

"I'll try to locate Peter, and see if there's any sign of Sammy. I'd say there's a good chance there's a connection."

"How are you going to find Sammy?"

"I think I may be able to track some of his pals."

"And they are?"

"You wouldn't know them."

Sudden attitude. "Oh really, how can you possibly know that?"

"Well, I suppose you might," I said, sarcasm getting the better of me. "Maybe I'm being unfair to categorise you."

She looked pleased to hear my little backdown speech.

"Do you mix a lot with teenage Asian drug criminals? My guess is you don't. But if I'm wrong, I'll run some descriptions past you."

"For one minute I thought you were being pleasant."

"I try to keep that sort of thing to a minimum, Ms Portman," I replied with a grin, then chinked her glass. "*Prost!*"

She smiled. I think she was beginning to warm to me at last.

"*Salut!*" She paused for effect. "Or is it perhaps, *salaud?*" The French for bastard — nice play on words. I was beginning to warm to Aunt Lucy too.

19

The Citroën looked exactly the same — apart from a terrible third-rate matt black paint job. Initially I wondered if he'd had to work on a rush job for someone else. Then Nick appeared from his little office. He looked smug as hell as he pulled up the bonnet. I peered in.

It looked like a rotary engine, though I'd not seen one up close before. And so clean and shiny you could have fried an egg on it and served it at the Ritz.

Nick leaned an arm inside the car and fired up the beast. He then folded his arms and stared proudly down at the guts of the engine. The whole chassis throbbed and pulsed to the low rumble of pure V8 power. I stood beside him, mouth hanging open like an idiot. It was practically alive, if it had been it would've been feral!

"Jesus, Nick," I said. "What have you done to my wheels?"

"It's the best rotary turbo-charged engine available — hundred and seventy kilowatts of raw power," he replied, thrilled. "I've given her a customised five-speed gearbox, front and rear disks. And just so the sound isn't a giveaway, I stuck on an ultra-silent exhaust system."

He ran his hand over the duco.

"But matt black?" I asked. I didn't say anything about the quality of the job.

"That's 'today', mate. Grunge effect took some time. It's like ripped jeans these days — uncool to have anything new. So no shine. Soiled and filthy is the way to go. What can I tell you? Straight-line speed is shit-hot impressive — acceleration's phenomenal. Best brakes and suspension available. All up? Fifteen grand. You pay me eight. But now you got a shit-heap that goes like fuck. Now you got style."

He eyeballed me. "Like it, mate?"

I felt like a big kid again. I liked it.

"Nick, mate... I like it a lot!"

"Get in then. Have a feel of it. Get wet!"

I sat in and looked up at Nick, who was grinning crazily, his expression a tad manic.

"Do you think it's me?" I asked.

"Fuckin' A, bubba!"

It took a while to get used to the feel of the beast. The slightest touch of the accelerator and I felt a kick in the kidneys. But once I got up a head of speed, it was smooth as velvet.

I was about to slip onto the M5 to Cabramatta when my mobile chirped.

"Hi, Robert. Terry."

"Fire away," I replied.

"A friend of mine was in the Cabramatta Force. Name's Ben Morgan. He says he'd be happy to help you with a bit of background if you're unfamiliar with the area."

"I hear the food's great. Never been out there though."

"Thought so. And it is. Ben was plain clothes. Invalided out a couple of years ago. Caught between two cars in a raid. Shame. He works security for Pfizer pharmaceuticals in Ryde somewhere. I called him because I thought you could maybe use some help and he could use some readies. Right?"

"Right."

"What he doesn't know about Cabra isn't worth knowing."

"You got a mobile number for him?"

I punched it into my mobile address book and hoped the cops weren't looking. Then I said my goodbyes to Terry and dialled Ben.

"Ben Morgan? Name's Howard," I said.

"Yeah, Terry called me just now."

"Any chance we can meet today?"

"Sure. Where?"

"I'm on my way to Cabramatta right now. Looking for a WRX. How about we meet for some noodles or something?"

"Why not. I work nights. Now's cool for me. Let's say the Thanh Binh 3 Restaurant. The one on Arthur Street — not John. I'll be there in thirty minutes."

Just then the phone began cutting out — I must have been reaching the edge of a telecommunications signal area. All I could make out was he wanted some kind of Vietnamese soup.

"Sounds interesting. That's Vietnamese for chicken, pork or something?"

"No, it's spelt COP. It's Australian for law enforcement officer. Tell you when I get there."

"How will I know you?"

"It won't be hard," he replied.

It took me another twenty minutes to get there and ten to park. The Thanh Binh 3 was a spacious restaurant packed with over a hundred hungry diners, most hunched over bowls of steaming soup. Everything smelled delicious. The patrons were Asian-looking to a man, woman and child. With one exception.

Sitting by the wall was a weather-beaten forty-year-old Caucasian. His left leg was pushed out straight ahead of him, the right tucked under the wooden chair. Above him a Fox Sports athletics meet was being projected on the blank white restaurant wall. The man smiled at me as I looked around the room for any alternative ex-cop.

"Not too hard to spot, was I? I'm Ben," he said as I approached him.

I shook his hand warmly. "Robert Howard."

"This your first visit to deepest Cabramatta?" he asked.

"As it happens, yes."

"I expect you share the media's view of the village. Drugs, violence and machete-wielding hooligans. Am I right?"

"Not really," I replied, somewhat unconvincingly.

"Yes, *really*. I'll put you straight in a minute. First, let's order. The duck's always great. Lemon chicken's tasty. Me? I always have the same."

"Cop soup?"

"Cop soup. Loverly." The delivery of the last word was pure Eliza Doolittle. "When I was in the job we always came here. Best grub around. Reason for the soup's name is because us cops never know our own minds. So Angie — she runs the joint - invented a soup with everything, just for us. It's literally soup with egg noodles, rice noodles, pork, seafood — fish, prawns, squid — wantons and crispy chicken on the side."

"You cops share things when you eat?" I asked.

"Sure."

"Then I'll have the lemon chicken. With an extra side of fresh chili."

"Won't need to ask. Comes with everything. Chilis hot as a lava flow."

We ordered: lemon chicken, cop soup and two fresh lemon juice drinks that Ben recommended.

The mâitre d', Tiem, shook Ben's hand firmly — they were clearly old mates. Ben even had a few words of Vietnamese; enough to impress me anyway. Above his head, Trulli was leading the rest of the field in some Formula One race somewhere in Europe.

"Cabramatta's changed a hell of a lot since the late eighties. Shit, it was a different place back then. Now it's like a cozy village most of the time. I love the place. Sure, the current affairs shows like to scare all the yuppies in the eastern suburbs by showing ugly footage of a few drug deals every now and then — mostly old stock, I might add. But hell, these things happen everywhere if you look hard enough.

"In the early nineties, Cabra was controlled, more or less, by a couple of very powerful old men. By 'old' I mean guys in their mid *thirties*."

"It's a fucking tragedy that life expectancy amongst Cabramatta Asian street kids in those days was about seventeen."

The lemon drinks came with a tray of differing sauces in small ramekins, together with various bottles of black soy and red chili sambal olek.

"These two old guys controlled the area — half of it 'belonged' to each. All the kids without family worked for them, and there were a lot of these juveniles, straight from the refugee camps overseas into Cabra. Most of the street biz was petty crime then — still is.

"There was normally a pecking order. Four levels. The top man, then about eight lieutenants. They in turn controlled about ten soldiers below them. Beneath them was the rabble."

"When did things change?"

"Turning point was '94. 'Operation Hammer'. The Force went in big time with buy-bust operations. We had to, because suddenly we had a situation where the heroin in the Cross was shit and expensive, and the stuff these guys were peddling was prime grade and cheap as chips. So all the junkies came out west. Well, wouldn't any junkie whose brains hadn't been scrambled already?"

"Did the buy busts work?"

"Sure did. But that wasn't really what changed things. It just kept the lid on."

"What was the real catalyst?"

Just then the food arrived. The cop soup was enough for three big police sergeants. My chicken looked as good as anything I'd eaten in the more expensive chic surroundings of Sydney's Chinatown.

Ben scraped half a dish of tiny fresh red chilis into his soup and started eating — and there was me thinking I was the only non-West Indian in Sydney who could eat Caribbean chilis the same way the Italians eat olives.

"See, the South Vietnamese here are in a different league to those guys in Bankstown. The Beirut Brigade, I call them. Sounds rascist, I know. Maybe it is. But it's been my experience."

"In what way are they different?"

"For starters, the Vietnamese are mostly Buddhists. Second, they have a sense of family and honour. Third, it's all a matter of 'face'. You know what I'm talking about?"

"It's a Chinese thing?"

"Asian, Chinese, Cambodian, Viet — you name it. That's why we seldom arrested and handcuffed anyone in the street. See, we knew all the usual suspects, so, unless we caught them red-handed, dealing hard stuff, or had to step in to stop them carving each other up with choppers, we'd just tell them to present themselves at the station. You know, something civilised like: 'Here! Diem, you come on down to the shop in twenty minutes. Bring Jimmy with you. Okay?' They always did.

In those days I worked with the present boss here, Rachel Willis. She was a sergeant then — Commander now. She was magic on the street. Always a smile for everyone. Always commanded respect. Handled herself better than most men — by that, I mean she was tougher when push came to shove. Dark and kind of sexy when she was working undercover. The local 5T boys always called her 'Madam', even when she had to cuff them."

I'd finished my chicken and was now leaning across and poaching Ben's soup. Poaching as in stealing, not cooking.

"In '94 we had a situation where the South Vietnamese controlled one side of the street and the Cambodians the other. I remember one day I see this wiry Cambodian looking for business on the wrong side of the street. My partner tries to move him on. 'You won't last more than an hour this side, mate', she tells him, 'The 5T boys'll have your guts.' He looks sadly at his shoes. 'This side's where all action is, madam. My side, no business.' An hour later I see him back on 5T territory — that gang ruled Cabramatta in those days — and I worried for the kid. Three hours later we're called to the exact spot we left the Cambodian, and there's the guy with about fifty machete cuts in him. Blood everywhere, and two 5T boys about fifteen years old standing around close by with blood-spattered boots. The Cambodian's throat's hanging off and he looks like he might kark it before we get him to hospital."

"Did he make it?"

"Yeah, matter of fact he did. Had a hundred and seventy staples in his head and fifty-three in his face. Looked like Frankenstein. Never ID'd a soul. 'Face', you know. Knew he'd done the wrong thing. Never worked that side of the street again."

As I snaffled Ben's second to last shrimp I noticed, by sheer chance, a red WRX cruise slowly past the front of the restaurant. I'd never put that sort of thing in one of my graphic novels because I don't believe in coincidences, but here I was searching for the two hoons, and there they were passing by as I pinched my new friend's food!

"Seen something?" Ben asked.

"Yes," I replied. "The car I'm looking for. It just passed by."

Ben shrugged. "Finish your lunch. We'll pick it up this afternoon."

There wasn't much left, so I picked up a few pieces of fresh red chili, dipped them in fish sauce and popped them in my mouth.

Overkill, in retrospect. Definite overkill.

"When did you leave the Force?" I mumbled, waiting for the muscles of my mouth to regain some semblance of function.

"Just after the Olympics. The Force lost a lot of good intelligence during the year either side of the Games. More interested in Olympic security. Took quite a few of our lads off the beat here. Anyway, I left because I was the wrong end of a stolen car one day. Ran me over. Leg's still not right. Pity. I loved the work."

"Are there still gangs? Like the Crips and the Bloods in the States?"

"Nah. That's all history. Just individuals now. No methodology really. We busted the fortified drug houses some time ago — 2001, to be precise. Detective Chief Inspector Willis as she is today, together with Clive Small and some others went to the Premier and told him they needed special powers. The Premier was great — ended up with the Police Powers (Drug Premises) Act 2001. It meant we could put them away if they were in a place that was clearly a fortified drug house, even if they flushed the stuff down the toilet as we came in."

He leaned back in his chair, studying me. "So, enough of my personal history. What's your story here? Why do you want to find these Asian kids? What have they done wrong? Don't *need* to tell me, but I may be able to help."

I didn't know how to cut it all short. I tried anyhow.

"There's this girl I know, aged twelve. Her dad's gone missing. I think his brother — a guy called Sammy — is a bad piece of work. My opinion is that the brother wants something the girl's dad's got. Very badly."

"Any idea what?"

"Must be money, or something that's worth a hell of a lot of money."

"Makes sense."

"Well, I followed Sammy and he hooked up with the two Asian kids I'm looking for. Got into the WRX with them. I'd seen them before, staking out the family home. Had a brief chat with them — not too friendly, those boys."

Ben smiled broadly. "Maybe you didn't show too much respect. It's 'Face' again."

"Yeah, maybe. I didn't feel like showing any respect at the time."

"Sometimes you don't — that's the way it is. Carry on."

"They drove to a house in Rockdale. I tried to check it out. You know, locate the dad and have it out with him and his brother. But someone clubbed me. When I came round everyone and everything's gone away — the father's Saab, the WRX, the Asian kids, Sammy. Then I hear from Terry that the father's car's been found burnt out in Cabravale Park. And the worrying thing is, there were bloodstains in the back seat."

"You think Sammy's up to slicing his own brother?"

"Maybe. I've never met him, but all I hear is bad."

"The boys round here think nothing of a few cuts to get someone's attention. It's part of everyday life. In the bad old days, you got on the wrong side of the 5T, you'd lose a finger, possibly two. Occasionally your dick.

"We used to have what we called the machete run most mornings. In those days we had the old-fashioned rubbish bins all round the city. Great place to stash a machete — down the side of the bin. Meant you didn't have to walk around with one down your pants — it's kind of obvious when you're approached by someone like Rachel or me on the street and you can't show respect by bowing 'cos you'll cut your gonads clean off. So every day, first thing, we used to pick up a dozen or so machetes stashed for later.

"Yes, the 5T were handy with the blade, hopeless with guns. Maybe they're better now, but give them a .22 and the chances were they'd miss you with the first twenty slugs. Might catch you in the butt with the third clip — if you hung around long enough."

Tiem came over, smiling. "Still good soup, hey?"

"Still the best, Tiem."

"Nuff spice, Mr Morgan?"

"Nah, never enough chilis. Kind of bland, really." Ben said it with a straight face.

"We make good fire next time."

Ben smiled. "You do that, Tiem."

My lips felt like wet blubber — not much feeling had returned since the chili hit.

Ben looked down at his bad leg and began rubbing it. "Say, Tiem. You know of a kid round here drives a red Subaru? A street racer?"

In my novels I'd usually say a man's face darkened. Tiem's actually lit up.

"Madonna! Yes. Good boy. Nickname 'cos he's so beautiful and has a mole like famous rock star. The car's beaut too. Why you asking?"

"My friend here would like to meet him, have a chat. No bother, you understand."

"He's Annie Tran's boy. You remember?"

Ben smiled. "She still work the house on Avoca?"

Tiem threw up his hands in mock horror. "No, Mr Morgan. That long ago. No more girls. She's making tourist things now."

"Know where I can reach her?"

"Same house." He laughed. "But different ladies."

I paid the minimal bill. Ben told me not to tip — bad manners, he said — so I didn't. Made me feel unappreciative, but there you are.

"Where's your car?" he asked at the door.

"Not far," I replied. "You willing to come with me to see Annie?"

"That's why I'm here. And the best thing is, I'm not expensive — if you hire me by the day."

"Done deal."

20

When we approached my car a local Vietnamese aged about fifty was appraising my new Sainte-Claire-mobile. He saw me coming and grinned at me, rubbing his hands together.

"Ever thought of an update, mister? New wheels?"

"Think I need a fresh set?" I answered, all matter-of-fact, as though the idea had never occurred to me. By this time I'd slipped on the new sunnies I'd borrowed from Jez — Armani rip-offs she'd picked up in Hong Kong by accident. I was back in Sainte-Claire mode and immediately enjoying the sense of fun, the game. This was going to be great.

The man looked me up and down with a smirk. "Well, I'd say you do need a 'vey-hicle' to match those threads." Now his accent was drifting from Jackie Chan to Shaft.

"Jesus," Ben mumbled at my side. "Threads? Gimme a break."

"You reckon, eh?" I tried to sound interested. "What do you have available? As you can see, I'm not really an 'appearance' guy. I'm a simple 'fast from A to B' man."

He looked at the Citroën. This description of a car that had at least five different chassis colours seemed to confuse him. 'Fast from A to B'? Sure.

"Fast, heh? Yes, I can see that," he replied unconvincingly, presumably to mollify my sensitivities. "What you say about a new Astra? Very sharp. Very clean. One owner. Lady from Double Bay. Nothing to spend. Eight grand all up. No more to pay!"

Ben looked at the ground and mumbled some more profanities to himself.

"Sounds good to me," I replied. "What kind of top speed has it got?"

The Vietnamese looked pleased. This was clearly a selling point — where he thought his used Astra would score. "You like 'speedy'? Well, you got plenty 'speedy'. I driven it myself. Tops one hundred on the motorway. No problemo, mister."

"Mph?" I asked, all innocent.

"He looked at me blankly. "Klicks, mister. Kilometres. We talk Astra here, not Ferrari."

I pretended to reconsider the proposition. With a lot of chin-rubbing, like a third-rate American daytime soap star in a serious close-up. And the joy was, he was actually *buying* the performance.

"How about this? We have a little bet. I drive my heap round the block. When I get back, if you still think your Double Bay shiny Astra can beat it on a straight mile, the eight grand's yours and the Astra's mine."

"Sure thing!" he said, quick as a flash.

"No, hold on," I added, putting a hand on his arm. "I said we make a *bet*."

"Bet?" He looked confused. "Sure. How much?"

"Ten bucks. Just for fun."

He brightened. For a second there he'd thought he was being taken. No way was he falling for any funny stuff.

"Ten bucks? No problem, mister. Then his face clouded slightly. "We'll make the deal when you get back, huh?" He wasn't about to part with as much as a ten spot — as they say in my books — without security.

"Sure thing."

I looked at Ben. "Let's go. It's open."

"Hey. What d'you say you come with us?"

"You bet!" he replied, in a jaunty, jolly fashion.

"Why not give him the front seat, Ben," I said, with a wink only Ben could see.

Ben climbed into the back and put on his seat belt. The dealer got comfy in the front passenger seat but made no move for the belt.

I climbed behind the wheel and turned to the Vietnamese. "Better buckle up, mate. Only thing that saves your life in a high-speed collision is a good seat belt."

The man chuckled gently, but did as he was advised.

I turned on the ignition and looked in my rear-view mirror. Clear street. No cop cars — no cars at all, as a matter of fact. And no pedestrians up front to complicate matters. I stuck her into first, stomped on the accelerator and gunned the rotary turbo engine.

The new tyres left no more than a few inches of black on the road as we shot forward. We made the first left turn doing seventy-five ks in four seconds. Then we speeded up a tad. Ben just gave me a tired shake of the head.

Less than twenty seconds later we'd done the block.

I pulled into the side of the road. The dealer's mouth was sagging open and his pupils were wide as bottle tops. He didn't move for about ten seconds. I touched him gently on the shoulder, which was when he pulled a wad of money from his trousers and, with a shaky hand, peeled off a ten-dollar note. He handed it to me with a deadpan expression.

"Should have seen you coming. The threads, the sunnies, the walk — you know?"

"Threads? Sunnies? Jesus H," I heard Ben mumble to himself.

The Vietnamese stepped out and we pulled back into St Johns Road.

"Feel better now?" Ben queried, as we cruised along.

We turned right into Avoca — a residential street with plenty of houses that had been designed by their owners. Lots of glitz and balustrades.

"That's an old drug house," Ben said, pointing to a smaller red-brick horror surrounded by a heavy-duty chain-link fence. The windows were boarded up and the door looked nailed shut.

"Think they're still dealing inside?" I asked.

"No way. Rachel'd know and they'd be doing time quick as a flash. The point is, no one wants to spend the money tearing it down — it's all reinforced concrete and stuff. Nightmare to demolish."

Ben pointed down McKibbin Street to our right. "That's your car, eh?"

Sure enough, it was the WRX. A kid was leaning against it, chewing gum, flipping a coin. Maybe his grandpa had taken him to a George Raft retrospective recently.

"Where does Annie live?" I asked as we drew up twenty feet behind the WRX.

"The white house opposite the car. Nice, huh? Had twelve bathrooms and twelve bedrooms last time I saw it. Four big spas and plenty of mirror on the ceilings. Not much of a kitchen."

"Not much call for sit-down dinners?"

"Dead right."

George Raft, aged six, was now concentrating his attention on us. He'd picked us for trouble and was wondering when to cut and run to tell the boys. He was fast on his way to a ten-year career on the wrong side of the law. His flipping became a bit more deliberate — flashier.

As we got out of the car I put on my Armani rip-offs and looked directly at him. He swallowed hard and dropped the coin, but was too embarrassed to pick it up again.

"How do you want to handle this, Robert?" Ben said at my shoulder.

I took off my sunnies and turned from eyeballing the kid to Ben.

"Look, this may sound really dumb, but the two WRX kids know me as Sainte-Claire. So, do you mind calling me that — if you call me anything at all."

He gave me the kind of look you might give a teenage girl who thinks she's impressing you by lighting a Marlboro and not inhaling. "Do you have a Christian name? Or is that the 'Sainte' bit?"

"No. Just the surname."

"Like Goldfinger?"

I was beginning to like Ben a lot.

"Similar idea."

As we reached the WRX the kid stood taller.

"Hi there," Ben said in a friendly way. "*Ten toi la* Ben."

The kid screwed up his face as if Ben had spoken in Martian or Venusian rather than Vietnamese.

"You don't speak Vietnamese?"

"Chinese."

Ben gave him the 'are you serious?' look. "What's shaking?"

"Looking after my friend's car," the tiny minder replied. He pulled a rag out of his pocket and showed us. "Keeps the duco shiny."

"Good work, kid. We've come to see Annie. She inside?"

"Sure, she's in."

Ben walked ahead of me, opening the gate that led to the ex-brothel.

"The kid's Chinese? I'd never have picked that," I said as we walked to the double doors.

"A lot of South Vietnamese kids think speaking Chinese is a big step up the social ladder. He's South Vietnamese, and speaks it, I'd say. He's hip — six going on fifteen."

I pressed the bell push. It was pink. Nipple-shaped. Subtle. *Ex-brothel?* I doubted it.

The door opened and a middle-aged Asian woman stood smiling at me.

"Please come in. Thank you," she said. She gestured to a waiting room. "You wait here. I bring."

Ben pre-empted her. "No, we've come to see Annie. I'm an old friend. Tell her Ben's here to talk about old times."

We stood in the hallway for a minute or so. Then the woman returned. "You follow me?" she said.

We followed her up a rear stairway to the private quarters. The house was huge. At the top of the stairs stood a woman who could have doubled for Imelda Marcos. She held out her arms, the fat hanging off them like fresh pork chops.

"Darling! So good to see you, Benny! Come on through to my parlour."

Frankly, I thought we'd just passed through it.

"This is a friend of mine, Annie. Name's Sainte-Claire. He's in the security biz too. Like me."

She studied me in a sort of lip-smackin' way, as though I was a crispy KFC chicken thigh. I should have been flattered, but looking at the porker standing before me, I wasn't.

"Sainte-Claire, eh, honey? You got a *first* name?"

"My mother never gave me one I'm afraid, Annie. It's just Sainte-Claire. Like 'Prince' and 'Sting'."

Writing dialogue again. I smacked myself mentally.

Annie bounced over to a drinks cart with a gold and jade decorated top. Showing guests all the money.

"I know what Benny here likes," she said with a grin, holding up the Baccarat whisky decanter — the inference being that it clearly wasn't a drink. "Thing is, what may I interest *you* in, Sainte-Claire?"

"You have anything soft?" Very deadpan.

"Not much of that round here," she replied with a twinkle in her eye.

"Then I'll join Ben in a whisky."

She glanced at Ben. "Your pal doesn't bat for the other side does he?"

"Nah. He's cool. Likes girls."

"Well, let's warm him up a bit. A Whisky Mac?"

As it happens I like the drink. Whisky and Stone's ginger wine. Good Scottish shooting fare. "A Mac'd be great, Annie," I replied.

Her eyes devoured me.

"That's some fine-looking motor Madonna's got parked outside," Ben said as she handed him his Scotch. "He won Lotto or something?"

"Don't get crazy. That's *my* motor, Benny. I let my baby drive it. Is all."

"Nice rego," I said.

"Frankie's idea of a joke."

"How *is* the kid?" Ben asked.

She handed me my Mac and sat. Then her expression changed and she gave Ben the look. "This why you came to see me? Check out my baby boy?"

"Absolutely not," Ben replied. Boy, was he convincing. Years of experience on the street.

"Well, that's good. Happens Frankie's studying at TAFE now. Computer studies. Doing real well. I'm proud as a stuffed hen of my baby."

At that moment a door at the back of the room opened and the kid I'd eyeballed driving the WRX walked in. He stopped dead in his tracks when he saw me. It wasn't my face — it was the clothes. Instant uniform recognition. Well, as they say, 'clothes maketh the PI'.

"Frankie. You remember Benny, don't you? He's come to see me. Brought a friend with him. Sainte-Claire's the name."

He stood rooted to the spot. Not fearful, just mentally ticking over the possibilities. The angles.

"We met before," he said quietly.

Annie looked at Ben, surprised. "You saw Benny recently?"

"No, Mum. Him. Sainte-Claire. He liked the car. We talked a bit. Nothing much."

"My, what a coincidence," she said. Her face told me she didn't believe in them.

There was a controlled silence. Frankie didn't sit.

"Yes, it's a great car," I said. "We had a chat with a kid outside just a few moments ago — he's giving it a serious polish as we speak."

"Toodles," Madonna murmured, practically inaudible.

"That his name?"

"Nickname, yes."

"Can't recall the name of the guy who was with you the day we met. I think of him as Mr Goatee."

Frankie didn't reply, merely rolled his eyes upwards.

Annie did — angrily. "Frankie! I told you more times than I can think to stay away from that boy. Tri's mean. He's trouble. I don't want him in my car and I don't want you hangin' round him. You understand me!"

I was surprised at her outburst. I could see that Ben was too. This was a serious loss of face for Frankie, aka Madonna.

"I got to go, Mum," he said at last. His whole body was trembling with outrage to be called out like a green kid by his mum. But she *was* his mother and deserved respect.

As Madonna turned to leave, I called out. "Frankie? Mind if I ask you one thing?"

Annie answered: "He doesn't mind."

"You know where Peter Reid is, by any chance? His little girl's looking for him. She's really worried. Thinks he maybe lost his memory or something."

"Never heard of the guy."

He turned to face me. Surprisingly I read confusion on his face.

"Last time he was seen was in Ferrier Street."

Frankie's pupils dilated. "That right?" he said softly. Now he knew what I was on about.

"Yeah, that's right. I was hoping you might ask your friend Tri if he's seen Peter. That'd make me really happy. I hear there's a big reward for info. Make it worth your while."

His wide eyes flicked across to Ben. "The cops involved in all this?"

Ben looked at me.

"Not yet," I said, pointedly. "But I wouldn't want any harm coming to Peter. That'd mean calling in the cops. Major trouble then."

Annie stood abruptly. "Hey, Benny! What's all this shit? This why you came here — to grill my baby boy? Shame on you."

Ben rose and hugged her. "No way, Annie. I came to see you. I'd no idea these guys had met. Okay?"

She wasn't convinced, I could see that. But his words calmed her.

Frankie looked at me. I had his attention at last. "I'll see what I can do," he said.

I handed him my card. "Give me a call if you can help. Strictly confidential. Rewards are worth having. Maybe buy you some wheels of your own."

Frankie didn't reply; he just held up a hand as if to say goodbye and walked out of the room.

There was a pregnant pause. Then Annie spoke.

"So, are you going to fill me in, or am I expected to worry myself to death, Benny?"

"Let *me* explain, Annie," I began. "See, I'm looking after a little girl whose father's gone walkabout. I know the father's brother — the girl's uncle — is an associate of Tri's because I saw him getting in Tri's car. Your car, in fact. So I was hoping Frankie might know her dad's whereabouts. Nothing much to worry about right now."

"*Now?*" she came back at me. "What's *that* supposed to mean?"

"Well, you just told Frankie to steer clear of Tri because he's a mean man. What's he done to make you say that?"

She paused. "This is just between you, Benny and me?"

Ben held up the palm of his hand. "I guarantee that personally." He then looked at me. "That okay with you, Sainte-Claire? This bit's private or she doesn't tell us. Those are the rules."

"That's fine with me," I replied.

I could see the muscles of Annie's jaw working hard — she was debating what and how much to tell.

"Tri's older than you think. He's actually twenty-seven. He looked very different a few years ago. Hung around with the LTH gang. Goatee beard. With three gold rings."

I shot a look at Ben. I could see he was accessing his mental data bank of faces.

"Sure, I know him. Sartor." He shot me a look. "That's Vietnamese for 'killer'. Nickname only. He was a real pussy in those days. Looked mean, but was actually weak as piss. LTH stood for Live To Honour. Not in the same league as the 5T boys. A lot of attitude and not that much muscle. Couldn't cut it eventually. Right, Annie?"

"Right. So maybe a couple of years ago he went independent. Maybe he's watched too many movies — sees himself as a standover man, Viet-style. First up he tried threatening businesses — said he'd wreck their premises unless they paid him money. But several businessmen told Willis. She hauled his arse in and told him to get an education like Frankie. Then let him go."

"So what's the matter with him now?" I asked.

"Word is he does dirty jobs for people outside of our area. Non-Asians. Mostly Lebanese. And those guys can be very mean."

"But Frankie's not involved in that stuff?"

"I hope to Buddha not. I told him I didn't want him mixing with Tri, but now you tell me he's driving the bastard around. That can only mean trouble."

Ben drained his Scotch. "You happen to know who Tri's mixing with right now, Annie?"

"Nah. But I'll ask Frankie later. If I can help find the kid's dad I'll call you. Promise."

"You're a gem, Annie," Ben replied.

"Meantime, if either of you have an hour to kill, feel free to stick around downstairs. My treat."

Jez would have just loved that.

"You can stay up here with me, Sainte-Claire. What you say?"

"If I'd met you three years ago, sure. But I just got myself a new squeeze."

"Sure," she replied, running a hand inside her bra.

21

I drove Ben back to his car.

"Benny, huh?"

He didn't even look at me. "You never heard that. Right?"

"Right."

Rather than him having to talk money, I slipped four hundred bucks into his top pocket while he was looking the other way. His head whipped round.

"Just an advance on security services, Ben. Thanks for everything today."

"No problem, mate." Pause. "I'll have a sniff round, see what I can find out about Tri. I'll also try to find Madonna and have a word in his ear. Surprised he's still knocking around with the likes of Tri. Thing is, I wouldn't want him to think that we're on his case; he's just beginning to come good."

"I know what you mean."

I dropped Ben off beside a blue Nissan Skyline that looked well driven. Poor bugger — maybe the payout for his leg hadn't amounted to much.

"See you, Robert," he said, then held up a hand. "Or should I say, '*Hasta la vista,* Sainte-Claire'?"

"See you, mate."

As I hit the M5 on the return journey it occurred to me I hadn't heard a dicky-bird out of Ms Tiggy-Winkle all day. Nor had I heard from Lucy, but I'd made sure to put the fear of God into her, so she'd ensure the kids were okay.

Just in case I'd screwed up somewhere, I drove by Hernandez — it was just a couple of minutes past four. Who knew, maybe Tiggs was waiting on the off chance I'd come by.

She wasn't. Instead the diminutive figure of Ally-Oop sat at the window table under the fake oil Mona Lisa, her Mary Janes kicking to and fro in space midway between the chair and the floor. Her back was ramrod straight, her 'Bubbles' white-blonde hair everywhere, as if someone had stuck an electric prod into a giant candyfloss on a stick.

The second she caught sight of me through the window she started clapping her hands and grinning.

"Tiggs is on detention," she said, once I was sitting opposite her and she'd calmed down a bit. "Answering back to Mrs. Thompson."

"Oh dear. That's not good."

"Thompie doesn't take doggie-do from anyone."

"I should think not. She's a teacher."

"So I thought I'd come instead. I told Tiggs."

"Tiggs told you we meet here?"

"Tiggs and I are like this," she said, crossing fingers that were no more than an inch and a half long.

"Glad to hear it."

"Shall we have a snackeroo?"

"Why not," I replied. "Hey, that strawberry cake looks great. Fancy a slice?"

Ally-Oop pulled a face. "Tiggs is the sweet tooth. Not me. I like anchovies and olives and all that salty stuff. I usually have an M Pinabo when we come here with Mummy."

"You mean an empanada?"

She thought about the translation for a second or two. "Maybe. Whatever. They're yummy."

"I suppose you'd prefer a lemonade to a coffee?"

"No, thank you. A double latte would be delish."

I signalled a waiter. The sexy girl wasn't on.

"So what's been happening? Any news?"

"About Dad?"

I didn't want to involve her in any of what was happening so I said. "Oh, anything."

"Well, let's see. Aunt Lucy's moved in. She's not as cross as usual. Mum's all right too. Well, she's a bit snappy sometimes. She's worried about Daddy being away so long. He's staying with friends and I think Mum's lonely."

"Well, you'd be lonely too if Tiggs went on holiday without you, wouldn't you?"

"I suppose," she replied.

Fédérico, the owner with the trademark handlebar moustache and Spanish accent that was straight from Seville, came to take our order. I'd known him off and on for five years.

"Mister Howard. How nice to zee you agayn. How sings?"

"His name is Sainte-Claire," Ally corrected. "Everyone knows that."

Fédérico looked temporarily flummoxed. I winked at him so Ally wouldn't notice.

"Oh! Yays! Mister Sainte-Claire! Zat's right!"

Ally gave him a beady look. "What we would like is a double milky latte. A double short something. A slice of strawberry cake for Sainte-Claire, and a M Pinabo for me. Thanks heaps." She beamed at Fédérico and scrunched up her eyes in delight. "Yum-yum!" she added.

"Comeeng right up, missey," Federico replied, and left us to our own devices.

We were sitting inside the coffee shop by the window, overlooking the four tables on the pavement. They're nearly always packed with taxi drivers on a quick break. If you ever want to know where the best coffee's to be had, ask a cabbie. Same as the best short-order food in Europe — ask a long-distance lorry driver. If you've got serious money to spend — consult the *Guide Michelin*.

Just as the coffee, cake and empanada arrived, carried by Fédérico, a shadow fell across the window. For a second or two I thought the sun had gone behind a very black cloud. Unfortunately, I was right.

Tutuelo had claimed a table just the other side of the window. He had his back to us and was looking out at the street. It was simply a question of time before he saw me.

I immediately wondered if Ally-Oop had ever seen the big gorilla when he'd come calling on Brierley's behalf. If she had, and remembered him, she'd be scared stiff.

"It's a bit draughty here by the window, Ally. How about we move to that snug little table at the back by the piano?" I asked.

"I like it here. It's fun to look out and watch all the funny people in the street," she replied. She was now looking directly at Tutuelo's back.

She giggled. "That man's like Stimpy!"

"You watch 'Ren and Stimpy'?" The cartoon just happened to be one of my favourites. Childish, really.

"Stimpy's stinky!" She reached for the salt and shook some on her empanada. "What if Stimpy comes inside? Will he stink us, like Stimpy?"

"He won't come in. Don't be scared."

"I'm not scared!" she replied strongly, with a pout. "Are you? NOT!" She laughed aloud and clapped her hands.

Actually I *was* scared. Scared for her. Though I felt sure Tutuelo wouldn't lay a finger on a child that small, he just might come in and drag me out in front of her. That would scare her all right.

I swivelled my chair so I was half-turned away from him. Ally pulled her empanada into four and began eating. She said something — a word that sounded like 'scrumpty' or 'scrumtilicious' — I couldn't tell exactly because her cheeks were full balloons of pastry. I weighed up what to do in an emergency. I had already eased my mobile out and was selecting the speed dial number of Kings Cross Police. Can't call me unprepared - I'd entered it in that morning.

Ally lifted the glass of latte to her lips with both hands. She then put it down, leaving a big ring of milk round her lips. "Wicked!" she said.

A patrol cop car cruised to a halt opposite. Together with cab drivers, cops make up a big proportion of Fédérico's customers. They need their caffeine hits too.

The two cops sat at the table next to Tutuelo. He appeared unfazed. I supposed that with Brierley as his backup, nothing much fazed a monster like him — unless he was discovered standing over a dead body with blood dripping from his fingers and a human heart in his hand.

Strangely enough, I noticed one of the cops, a young woman, nudge her colleague and nod in *my* direction. Maybe she was worried about a guy dressed in black with gelled hair sitting opposite a six-year-old sweet-faced girl. Paedophilia has a high profile these days.

I caught the cop's eye and smiled my most ingenuous smile. She looked away.

"Tiggs says you followed my Uncle Sammy."

"That's right. I wanted to chat to him about something."

"What?"

"Just some things I wanted his opinion on."

"What things?"

"I'd rather not say. It's secret men's business."

"What's that?"

"It's not important."

"Tis!"

"Isn't."

It was getting to that under-ten's string of endless questions and it was difficult to cope. I was concerned that Tutuelo would turn round at any second and recognise me. Which was exactly what he did at that precise moment. He looked straight at me, through me, round the restaurant and then back down at his coffee.

He hadn't picked me for the man he'd hefted over the Reids' neighbours' fence! I breathed a sigh of relief. Of course, he knew me as Robert Howard — flannel trousers, knitted jersey and brogues. I suddenly felt very smug and grinned. Tutuelo really was a stupid lummox.

"What's funny, Sainte-Claire?"

"Nothing."

"Yes, there is. You're cacking yourself."

"Am not."

"Are so."

"I am not."

"Are so."

When we'd finished this snappy repartee, I became aware that Tutuelo had turned to face me again. There was a vague look of recognition in his eyes. Then he pointed a fat finger at me and mouthed, '*You.*' The smile that accompanied this gesture was probably the vilest thing I'd ever seen. He turned his chair right round so that he now directly faced the window and continued to sip his coffee, his beady eyes locked on mine. He was happy to wait.

I pulled out my phone and selected Lucy's mobile number. Ally-Oop was trying to talk, but her mouth was crammed so full speech was impossible.

"Lucy? It's Robert."

Ally was outraged. I could just make out a muffled, 'Sainte-Claire! Don't tell!'

"I'm treating Alice to afternoon tea just up the road at Hernandez. I have to leave shortly — I'm a bit pushed for time. Do you think you could pick her up? That is, if you're round the corner." For all I knew, she might have been at the Opera House, or Dubbo.

"Of course. But she's quite able to make her own way home," Lucy said. "She's not a baby."

"I know that," I replied. "But today, could you just humour me?"

"Of course. I'll come round. Right now?"

"Soon as is convenient." I lowered my voice so Ally couldn't hear. "By the way, there's a big guy sitting outside. If you recognise him, don't panic."

"Jesus, Robert. What are you saying now?"

"Don't worry. I've got everything in hand. He's just someone who once came asking Charlie for money. He's having a coffee outside. Don't stare at him, that's all."

"As if!" was all she said.

I closed up the mobile and put it away.

"What was all that about? I want to stay longer. And I'm not a baby. I can walk anywhere I like, Sainte-Claire!"

"I know. I'm just being silly."

Ally slurped the last of her latte and wiped her mouth with a paper napkin like a grown-up. Then she burped. "Pardon me!" she said, her face reddening.

It would have made me laugh had Tutuelo not been grinning at me through the glass.

A couple of minutes later Lucy arrived and sat down next to us. "Which one?" she said. "The monster staring at you?"

"You don't miss much," I replied.

She leaned across and kissed Ally on the tip of her nose. "Hi there, Bunny. I've come to take you home. Tiggs is back — you could help her with her homework. What do you say?"

"Me help her? I wish!"

Ally ducked underneath the table and pulled a five-cent piece out of her shoe. She placed it in front of me. "That's my share."

"Very generous, Ally. Much obliged," I replied solemnly. "Times are tough."

"Sure are, Sainte-Claire."

Lucy held out her hand. Ally jumped down from the chair and they walked to the door. Outside, she waved at me then held her nose as she passed behind Tutuelo. Stinky.

Of course, by waving goodbye to Ally and Lucy my eyes again made contact with Tutuelo. I don't think he'd blinked in five minutes. He was like a pointer that had sniffed out a brace of pheasants. He pulled out a mobile and punched in some numbers. Calling Brierley, I guessed.

I left some money on the table and stood.

It occurred to me to call Nick Kougios. It also occurred to me to call the cops. Or Ben. Why did I resist? Call it extreme vanity, coupled with an ego that had so recently become a fixed part of me. I was damned if this man was going to scare me. I wasn't about to call for help and run for cover. After all, I was in a public place with plenty of people around — what was the guy going to do? What *could* he do? We'd just have to see.

As I walked through the door into the street, Tutuelo rose from his seat.

I wasn't about to confront him unless absolutely necessary, so I walked down the road towards the pedestrian overpass.

Tutuelo followed, walking about five paces behind — I could judge the distance because of the click of his shoes. If he came any closer I knew I'd have to turn and face him; after all, he could easily pick up a piece of wood and smash my head in if he was within striking distance.

Five metres short of the overpass logic and self-preservation warned me to walk on by. He could throw me off it, midway across the four-lane highway, and the fall would probably kill me. If it didn't, the traffic would finish the job. So I continued walking down New South Head Road towards Edgecliff.

What was he up to? Was he following me to see where I lived? Perhaps he was waiting for a quieter spot to do me real damage. Possibly others were on their way.

When I reached the other side of New Beach Road I stopped dead in my tracks and turned round. Enough was enough. Time for a manoeuvre.

My move caught him by surprise. He was halfway across the road. He stopped, flexing his muscles and giving his arms a loose shake. His face was one giant grin.

"What's your game, big guy? Something I can do for you?" I asked amiably. Mr Nice Guy. Not looking for any aggro.

"So it *is* you. Bum-Fluff from the Reids' place. Well, blow me down."

I acted cool. "I'll ask you again. What's your beef? Something I can do for you?"

"Put it this way: I have a message from Mr Brierley. He was major disappointed you cancelled payment on a cheque a while back. Asked me to look into it. So I been looking, see? And here you are, Sainte-Claire."

Uh-oh. He'd finally put two and two together.

I couldn't help noticing that he was clenching and unclenching the twin ham hocks that passed for his hands. As if he was exercising them. I began thinking *Nick Kougios Self-Help Manual*.

As I debated how to take things further, an E-type convertible Jag with the top down drove up New Beach Road. The driver clearly wanted to turn into New South Head Road, but was stymied by the bulky Islander standing right in front of him. He tooted the horn twice. First time, short. Second time, insulting.

Tutuelo continued his pre-kill exercises without giving the yuppie a glance.

The driver leaned on the horn again and shouted, "Hey, you! Can't stand in the road all fucking day! Move over, you big boofhead."

This was too much for Tutuelo. His head swivelled very slowly — as if controlled by machinery and then walked towards the passenger door of the Jag.

I knew it was time I made some sort of a move. The moment his back was to me, I crept forward.

The driver looked absolutely terrified as Tutuelo lumbered over. He opened the driver's door and climbed out backwards, initially falling into the road, then scrambling to his feet and staggering away from the car to the gutter opposite.

Tutuelo leaned into the car and wrenched the rear-view mirror off its mounting. He threw it casually across the road into the park, just to the left of the yuppie. The indicator lever was next. Off it came with a snap, and it too flew through the air.

The driver must have been one of those people who live for their car. There was no other logical reason for him risking his life the way he did in the following few seconds. He walked back to the car and grabbed the huge hand that was now clenched around a wing mirror.

"Just you hang on, you dickhead!" he said. "That's my fucking Jag!"

Big mistake.

Tutuelo hit him once across the face with the flat of his hand. Didn't seem like a major blow, but the spray of blood from the young man's nose belied that estimation.

I couldn't just watch the poor sod die, so I straightened my fingers and raised my hand. I guess my luck was definitely in that day because as I swung my hand straight-edged at the back of Tutuelo's head, mirroring the cutting blow Nick had shown me, the big guy swung round to face me. This meant the blow caught him full on the Adam's apple.

Looking back, I was lucky not to have killed him. But it takes a lot to kill monsters like Tutuelo. Either way, he went down like the proverbial sack of spuds. Eyes rolling back into his head, blood seeping from his nose — the whole kit and caboodle. Terrible gargling noise coming from his throat.

The young kid staggered to his feet, holding on to the driver's door. He stared at me — all I could see were two eyeballs in a wash of blood.

"Christ, man. You... just... thaved my thucking....life," he managed.

By now a reasonably big crowd had gathered — standing across the street, in the park, everywhere. Cars were backed up in New Beach Road, about fifteen of them. A few were honking their horns.

Tutuelo lay where he'd fallen. His body was jerking around, fighting for air. Maybe I'd crushed his trachea. I didn't really care. Sounds bad, I know, but I was actually *living* Sainte-Claire now. The bad guy had gone down and Sainte-Claire had triumphed. And *I* was that man! Tutuelo had just monkeyed with the wrong guy.

That's when the cops arrived — the same ones who'd been at Hernandez. The female cop who'd been checking me out in the café, wondering if I was a paedophile, stared down at Tutuelo. She then looked at the E-type, the yuppie — finally at me. There was blood everywhere — except, by some lucky chance, on my suit and shoes.

I was standing spotless in a sea of gore.

22

It took about three minutes for the ambulance to arrive. During that time, one of the cops checked out Tutuelo, attempting to clear an airway, and pumped on his chest.

Another took a statement from the yuppie. The guy kept calling out to me from where they'd sat him down on the kerb. "He saved my thucking *life*! He's a *good* guy!"

Another two cars arrived and the officers directed traffic around us.

"What's your name, sir?" a sergeant asked.

I dearly wanted to answer Sainte-Claire, but thought better of it. "Robert Howard."

"Look, we'll be asking you to come with us to the station," the young sergeant said. "I just want to ask you some quick questions here and now."

"Sure," I replied.

"You know that man?" he asked, pointing to the still unconscious figure of Tutuelo.

"I've met him before. Once only. He assaulted me in Roslyn Street. I reported the matter to Detective Chase at Kings Cross."

"So what happened here, just now?"

"He was following me. I thought he was going to have a go at me when up drives this young guy in the E-type and toots his horn. The big guy was standing in the middle of the road — the Jag couldn't get by."

"And?"

"Well, the Islander guy goes beserk, starts ripping pieces off the car."

"So you struck him?"

"Not straightaway. He assaulted the driver first. I thought he was going to kill him. That's why I stepped in. Had to."

"What did you hit him with?"

"My hand."

The policeman looked down at Tutuelo then back at me.

"Your hand?"

172

"That's right."

"How many times did you hit him?"

"Just once. No need for a second blow." I just couldn't resist. Not often one's in a David and Goliath situation.

"You're martial arts trained? Are you registered?"

"As what?" I was genuinely confused.

"Registered as a martial arts expert. For instance, if you're a black belt, your hands are considered dangerous weapons — you can't go hitting people. You understand that?"

"I see," I answered. "Yes, I have heard that somewhere. But I don't go hitting people as a matter of course. And I've not studied judo or anything like that."

"Lucky shot?"

I pretended to think about it. "Kind of," I replied, with an expression that suggested there was more to me than met the eye. I couldn't help myself.

"You know what this man does for a living?"

"I do. Detective Chase informed me."

"Yet you still fancied your chances with him?"

I shrugged and tried not to smile. Sure, I'd been lucky, I knew that. I didn't much care that Tutuelo was out cold, and I hoped he'd wake up with the mother and father of a headache. But I was enjoying the kudos. These police officers were looking at me with a newfound respect. Perhaps I was talking myself into trouble, but I was enjoying being Sainte-Claire right then.

I spent a good hour with Detective Sergeant Chase. This time he didn't treat me like an idiot. Apparently, getting the better of someone of Tutuelo's calibre earned me a more serious tête-à-tête. On this occasion I shared everything with him – he seemed like a straight-up guy. He listened carefully. When I got to the bit about being hit over the head in Ferrier Street he tut-tutted a bit.

"Stick to writing the comic books, Mr Howard. That way you have control."

"Not so much fun. And they're graphic novels."

He gave me a serious look. "You think this sort of thing is *fun*? Did you see the face of that man in the E-type? He's going to need major corrective surgery. That could have been you."

I gave him a chastened look. He bought it.

"You can see our problem, Mr Howard. Every time we ask Mrs Reid if all's well, she looks me straight in the eye and says everything's fine. We can't keep bothering her when we have no evidence of any wrongdoing."

"Isn't that where private investigators come into their own?" I didn't add that I was working for a twelve-year-old.

"They do, Mr Howard. But you're not a private investigator. You're a writer. And no one has asked you to investigate anyway. By a miracle you escaped a fractured skull in Ferrier Street two days ago. Today you narrowly avoided being beaten to death by the toughest standover man in Sydney, simply because of the chance intervention of an innocent bystander who happened to say the wrong thing at the wrong time. Right time for you, of course."

The phone rang at his elbow. He picked up the receiver. Mostly uh-huhs, okays, and thank yous.

He replaced the handset. "He's going to be fine."

"Mr E-type?"

"No. Tutuelo. They thought they might lose him when he got to the ER His heart arrested."

I was shocked.

"Shit, yeah. You've got a hell of a punch. But now that it's on record, you watch what you do with your hands — that's my advice. Not that I feel any sympathy for that bastard Tutuelo — we reckon he's responsible for four deaths in the past three years. We've never been able to put a decent case together."

"What happens next?"

"Well, as for Tutuelo, he started breathing properly twenty minutes ago, and he asked to discharge himself."

Before I could interrupt he held up a hand. "Hold it! We're charging him with aggravated assault with a deadly weapon. You see, he *is* a martial arts expert. His hands *are* deadly weapons."

"So he's locked up?"

"Not for long. He'll be bailed, I expect. Tomorrow, after a court appearance. Brierley will hire a good bent solicitor — he looks after his own people. Tutuelo'll be back on the streets for a while, then Brierley'll find a good QC and we'll see if we get lucky. I'd say he'll serve time. Road rage and GBH at the very least."

"Any news of the guy in the E-type?"

"Multiple fractures. Nose is pulp. Both cheekbones. Eye socket. Lost the hearing in one ear right now. I'd say that's worth about a year in Pentridge."

A year? Tutuelo had changed someone's life forever, and the price he was going to pay was a year in stir? That was outrageous.

"We're not charging you with anything, Mr Howard, because you merely came to the assistance of a victim of road rage. But we both know it was more than that, don't we?"

I said nothing.

"If the E-type hadn't come round the corner when it did, who knows what might have transpired? 'One punch' may not have been enough."

"I can go?" I asked, after a couple of seconds of dutifully downcast eyes.

"Sure, you can go. But make yourself scarce for a while. There's a mountain of a man going to be looking for revenge very shortly, and it isn't going to be pretty to watch when he catches you."

"Maybe," I replied. I was still in Sainte-Claire mode.

"And leave Tim Brierley alone."

"As you wish."

"I wish."

I put on my sunnies and left.

23

I called Jez on the way home and said I'd play chef if she played around. She liked the idea. She likes my cooking. We settled on her coming over around eight. This gave me time to think about what I was going to tell her of the day's events and what to hold back. More importantly, I could shop for what I was going to cook.

What I find extraordinary now in my saner moments is that I could be thinking of little else but shopping for dinner less than a couple of hours after nearly killing a human being. That wouldn't have been my reaction a week earlier.

Since I didn't have much time, I settled on Tassie salmon on a bed of rocket and whitlof, with a salsa of chili, basil, mint, garlic, soy, lemon grass, kaffir lime leaves, salt, palm sugar, pepper, balsamic and the tiniest dash of fish sauce. Plus ginger-infused rice, garnished with spring onions and toasted pine nuts.

Jez said she'd bring a bottle of something very old and very special. I knew it would be good — she wasn't prone to exaggeration.

Giblet usually hangs around to help me prepare things when I'm handling Tasmanian salmon. It's part of her altruistic nature, I guess. I'd given her shark for dinner, but her nose was pretty good. She knew there was something better going, so she held back a bit when it came to eating, just to keep a place in her tummy free for poached salmon.

I was wrapping the salmon around itself to fit inside the stainless-steel poaching cylinder, when my mobile started beeping. Giblet was watching me from below, rubbing against my leg. I looked at the number display: my employer, Ms Tiggy-Winkle.

"Sorry I couldn't make it today, Sainte-Claire. That's why I sent my deputy."

"Shouldn't upset Mrs Thompson."

"She was being bossy. Wasn't my fault."

I filled a bain-marie with water.

"Ally told me that man was there today."

"What man? Stimpy?"

"You know who I mean. The man who frightened Mum before."

"He had a scar, you said."

"Not him, the other man. Palm trees."

"Ally recognised him?" I was astonished. She'd shown no fear.

"She's tougher than you think, Sainte-Claire. She knew. She thought you *knew* she knew."

"Well, I didn't."

"Oh." She sounded surprised that I could have been so dumb.

"So why are you calling me? I mean, it's always nice to hear from you, but what's up?"

"Not much. Everything's about the same. No Dad. Mum's in a bait. Aunt Lucy's being nice, and that's not like her at all. Ally's fine. Trooper, actually. No boo-hooing."

I held the mobile under my chin and grated some more ginger over the rice, tossed it, then sprinkled the pine nuts and spring onions on top.

"You were supposed to come up with the answers, Sainte-Claire. Excuse my bluntness, but you're proving to be a real slowcoach."

"Well, *ex-cuuuuse* me!" I replied. "I'm dancing as fast as I can."

"Dancing?"

"It's an expression."

"I see."

There was a pause.

"No offence intended, Sainte-Claire."

I calmed my tone. "Well, all right."

"How did things turn out with Mr Stinky?"

What was I going to say? That he'd rearranged the face of some poor bastard in Rushcutters Bay, torn apart his motor car with his bare hands, and that I'd practically killed him with the flat of my hand?

"We had a difference of opinion."

"You showed him what for, I bet."

"I certainly did," I replied as I closed the oven door and set the timer. I could hear the key in the front door. Jez.

It was only then it occurred to me that Tutuelo might be thinking about taking his revenge out on the Reid family, simply because of their association with me.

"Got to go, Ms Winkle. Call you tomorrow."

"Cross your heart and hope to die?"

"Cross my heart — that's all you get."

"See you."

I rang Chase immediately. He explained that Tutuelo wouldn't be on the street for at least twenty-four hours, and that he'd put the word out to keep a close eye on the Reid house.

As I hung up, Jez came up behind me and wrapped her arms around me. She smelled captivating. Green Tea by Bulgari.

She placed a wine bottle on the bench in front of me. "Surprise," she said, holding my face in her hands and kissing me.

It was a bottle of Corton Charlemagne, Domaine Bonneau du Martray, Grand Cru, 1985. Wines don't come much bigger than that.

"You like?" she asked.

"I like a lot. You mortgaged the apartment?"

"No. I bumped into an old pal, Hervé. The family owns the vineyard. Plus the village as it happens. He gave it to me."

"Am I going to meet him?"

"Not this time, Pulitzer. I caught up with him at the airport. I was doing a *Marie Claire* shoot; he was boarding. Shame. He's great."

"He is, eh?" I tried to sound jealous for fun.

"So's his wife. Lizie's crazy — you'd love her."

She took a step back and looked me up and down. "Still Sainte-Claire, huh?"

I'd forgotten to change. It hadn't occurred to me; it felt so natural now. I shrugged and started on the salsa.

"Are we going to be Sainte-Claire forever now?"

"Do you have a problem with that?" I replied, not even bothering to look up. It came out rather snappy. I was immediately sorry.

"No, I don't have a problem," she said without the soft tone she'd presented up till then. She'd taken offence at my edginess.

I stopped chopping garlic. "I'll change if you like."

"It's not the clothes, Pulitzer. It's the attitude."

"Attitude? What attitude?" I shot back. I had no idea what she was talking about and suddenly it annoyed me.

"There you go. Cranky, for no reason. That's not you."

"Oh bullshit," I replied, easing up a bit.

"You can't be someone you're not, Robert, however much fun it might be on 'dress-up' days. I fell in love with Robert Howard, writer, klutz-dresser, sweetheart, do-anything-for-anybody, humourist, sexpot. Sainte-Claire? I don't know the man outside of the pages he fills."

She folded her arms and cocked her head to one side. Cute.

"Am I getting through? Whatever-your-name-is? Or am I going to wake up beside a cockroach tomorrow?"

Very Kafka. I walked over to her and held her. "You're getting through. I am truly sorry."

"Then you're excused changing. Just stay Pulitzer inside the black linen."

I finished putting all the good stuff in the food processor and switched it on. Ten seconds later we had the salsa. I turned off the power and dipped a finger in. I have to admit it was pretty scrumtilicious — to borrow Ally-Oop's lingo.

I then put down a dish of salmon bits for Giblet. If it's possible to hear a cat's lips smack, I heard them that day. The fish was a rhapsody of flavours. I'm good at dips and salsa. Not so good with game and crustaceans.

Now was maybe the time to broach the subject of my head-to-head confrontation with Tutuelo. I took a deep breath. I knew Jez's opinion on violence.

"I had a run-in today with that guy who threw me over a garden fence a few days ago," I said as we ate.

"Run-in? You mean a verbal one or a physical one?"

"The latter."

"Sure you did." She was smiling; she thought I was kidding. I'd described Tutuelo to her before. People didn't survive run-ins with hard men like him.

"Actually, I *did*. He was beating up some poor idiot who'd had the temerity to toot his horn at him, so I had to step in before he killed the guy."

"Hey, wait a minute," Jez said, putting down her wine glass just as she was about to drink — not something she often does when it's so close to her lips. "You're telling me you had a fist fight with that goon, and you escaped without a scratch?"

I couldn't help a tiny grin. "Something like that, yes."

I was enjoying telling the story, lapping up the anticipation of what was to come. Her reaction.

"And how's he feeling right now? A headache, maybe?"

"Oh, he's doing fine. They had to patch him up in the ER, but he'll be fine in the long term."

I couldn't help myself. I started laughing.

"Sure," she said, smiling. Now she *knew* I was kidding.

"No, swear to God it's all true."

Jez's smile faded rapidly. She put down her fork. Her face was white with anger. Well, as white as that coffee skin ever gets.

"You think that's *funny*?" she said, very deliberately.

I should have backed off right then. But I was surprised by her attitude. I actually *did* find it funny that I didn't have a scratch on me and that it was Tutuelo who was recovering in hospital. Served the lowlife right — just for once he was getting his just deserts.

"I suppose I can see the funny side of it, yes," I replied.

"Well, let me tell you *exactly* how I feel about violence, Sainte-Claire. Just so we've got things absolutely clear. In my book you walk *away* from violence of *any* kind."

"I *did* walk away."

"Please don't interrupt, I'm not finished."

"Not fair! You told me you'd have preferred it if I walked away, and I'm telling you I *did* just that. What am I supposed to do — just let you carry on with a speech based on mis-statements?"

"Just let me get to my point, what do you say, huh?" She was getting really worked up. The evidence was plain — she wasn't eating or drinking. Bad signs.

"Okay. Let's start over. You had a fist fight in the street. Is *that* a fact?"

"Kind of."

"And you hit this guy so hard he was taken to hospital?"

"That's about the size of it, yes."

I was trying not to smile again, and not doing a good job of it. This infuriated Jez more.

"I mention hospitals and fist fights and that makes you *smile*? That's *disgusting*, Robert. I think I may have to leave you to it."

She rose to go.

I reached out to her. "Jez. I was put in a situation I couldn't weasel out of."

"Jesus, Robert, we're not talking 'weasel' here. We're talking public punch-ups!"

"The man followed me. I knew he was going to assault me. Question was, how to avoid violence? Then the yuppie shows up and, before I know what's happening, Tutuelo is smashing the guy's face to pulp. I had to do something."

Jez just looked at me. She must have known I had a point, but any kind of violence is a 'no-no' to her.

"What if he'd taken a swing at *you*?" I added, "Wouldn't you want me to protect you?"

"No!" she shouted back at me. "I would have run like hell and hoped you'd be hard on my heels."

"Well, I'm not that kind of person."

"Well, you were *once*! That's my whole fucking point! A soft, sweet man, who would've talked his way *out* of a situation like that, not rolled up his sleeves and got stuck in — then *laughed* about it over dinner."

"I couldn't run, because I was watching a man being beaten to death before my eyes! It's as simple as that. There couldn't *be* any walking away and pretending it didn't matter."

There was a beat. She took a sip of wine. I was encouraged.

"Look, don't think I can't see that side of it. But what's bugging me is that you're sitting there all proud of yourself because *this* time you got lucky. Next time he'll kill you."

"Next time, I'll be ready."

Her eyes danced with fire. "Right! So you *do* see a next time! That's my whole point!"

"Your word — 'next' — not mine. Let's just forget it and finish dinner."

We sat in silence for a few moments. Neither of us knew quite what to say. I could see she was deeply upset, and I was really sorry for having made her feel that way. I knew she was worried for me. She thought I was walking a dangerous line between the fantasy of my books and a very real and violent world. And she was right. What she saw that evening was the beginning of a metamorphosis: I was shedding the skin of Robert Howard right before her eyes, like a brown snake in the bush in spring. And she didn't like the new me.

The thing was, *I did.*

Jez didn't stay long, although I thought I'd played 'the chef' pretty well. She didn't play at all. Because I'd played the fool.

As I lay in bed wishing I could feel the warmth of Jez beside me, I began to wonder what was becoming of me.

I hadn't written a word in all the time since I'd received Ally-Oop's midnight call. I was ignoring all the important people in my life and hurting the one person I truly loved. And for what? Was I really trying to help Tiggs and Ally find their daddy or was I on a weird macho trip?

I drifted in and out of sleep for a good hour. One minute I'd be in dreamworld, busting through the fortified door of a drug house in Cabramatta, State Protection Group cops at my side. Then I'd wake with a start, sweating, and try to go back under. The troubling part of the whole exercise was that I was trying to get back into the dream I should have been relieved to awaken from.

24

Next morning, after cubing Giblet's chicken and making myself coffee, I debated what to do with the next few days of my life. Should I continue trying to help Tiggs, or simply leave Chase to look into things?

The more I thought about it, the more I came to the conclusion Chase would do nothing, because there was nothing in his power he *could* do. He'd been right about one thing: Charlie didn't want his help. And, as far as the police were concerned, no law had been broken.

Maybe the answer was not to be so direct in my approach in future. My visits to Brierley had only resulted in the yuppie kid getting his face rearranged; it would never have happened had I not put Brierley offside enough to persuade him to put Tutuelo 'on my case'. And as far as I could tell, Brierley had nothing to do with Peter Reid's disappearance anyway — so who *was* I helping?

Sammy was the key. He'd been in the WRX that had taken me to Peter's Saab. The only thing I couldn't say one way or the other was whether Peter had been at the house in Ferrier Street that night. Or even if he'd been abducted at all.

What was everyone after? Sammy was sniffing around Peter and Charlie — and he generally did that only when there was something to be had. So, what *was* it that the Reids' possessed?

Then I remembered something Lucy had said. Two weeks ago she'd been with her sister and brother-in-law and they'd 'never been happier'. A few days later it was 'like they hit the wall'. They'd been celebrating: Peter had bought champagne, and Charlie had Lucy upstairs to show her the wonderful Dinnigan dress she'd bought that must have cost a fortune. What exactly was it they were celebrating? They'd certainly been spending big money — big for them anyway. Had Peter received a major salary rise? Had he been promoted to board level? Had he won big bucks on the horses?

Only the last possibility fitted in with the fact that whoever had taken Charlie the other night had been searching for something — and you didn't search for a letter of promotion or one outlining a salary rise. If the win had been at the races, they'd have been searching for a bundle of money, and have found it by now. So why were they still hanging on to Peter? And why were they still staking out the house in Roslyn Street? It was as if they were waiting for Charlie to lead them somewhere. To a pot of gold? What?

I called Lucy on her mobile.

"Hello?" she said. There was that breathy hint of prescience in her voice — like an actor who's waiting for his agent to call him about a movie role.

"It's just me," I said. "Is Charlie with you?"

"She's upstairs. What was all that about yesterday?"

"I'd rather not say."

"Oh really?"

"I'm afraid so, yes. Really. Is everything all right your end?"

"Yes," she answered tiredly. "The kids are at school and Charlie's having a bath. Everything's just hunky-dory. So, end of story. Thanks."

"So Peter's back, is he?"

"No. Why do you say that?"

"Because everything's not hunky-dory then."

She didn't say anything.

"Tell me something. Can you remember exactly when it was that Charlie bought the Collette Dinnigan dress?"

"Well, it was a Wednesday. I know that because I went to the Saville Gallery for an opening. Arthur Boyd retrospective. So…" A pause. "That would mean it was…" Another pause. "two weeks ago today."

"Can you look out the window and tell me if you see a bright red car in the street?"

"Hold on," she answered. A few moments later she continued, "No. No red car. There's someone on an expensive-looking motorbike I've not seen out there before. But no red car."

I thought about this. If someone were still staking out Charlie then they wouldn't be using the same car. A bike would be better. Faster getaway if the cops wanted to question them.

"What's Charlie got on today? Do you know?"

"No idea."

"What car does she drive?"

"A blue Saab."

"The Reids sure love their Swedish vehicles."

"No need to be snooty — they're great cars."

"No question there. I'll speak to you later then," I said and hung up.

It was time for me to stake out Charlie myself.

I parked on Ward Avenue. I could just see a blue Saab parked down Roslyn — I presumed that was Charlie's. If she left on foot, I could follow her and leave my car where it was.

In novels, a two-hour time frame takes me about five seconds to write. It goes like this: 'Sainte-Claire sat in the darkness of the car, sipping from a hip flask of homemade margaritas. It was a warm night, the windows were down, and the night air was heavy with the sweet scent of jasmine." Then you draw the flinty picture.

Pure fiction. Reality's another thing altogether. I found that out quite quickly.

A stakeout in a car is both very boring and very uncomfortable. You can't read because you might miss your target leaving the house. You can't drink margaritas, or any alcohol, because there's a law about booze in cars. And that particular day there was a stiff wind blowing; even with the windows shut I was cold. I could have put on the heater, but you stand out a bit sitting in a car for hours at a time with the engine running and the windows fogging up. And there wasn't any jasmine, just the scent of the street, dog shit, exhaust fumes and garbage.

Down the bottom of Roslyn, I could see a person in leathers on a bike. Looked like a Honda 750. I couldn't tell if the rider was male or female because they were wearing a full helmet with a black visor.

It was ten past midday. I looked up and saw Charlie close the gate of Number 5 and walk to the Saab. As she turned the key in the lock, she looked towards the motorbike.

She drove up the street and the bike started up and followed her. I followed the bike, about fifty metres back.

Sainte-Claire can tail a car round the city three times and no one will ever spot him — same with most fictional PI's. But you try it. Chances are someone will cut in between you, or you'll miss them at the lights. So I got on the mobile and called Ben.

It was only after the sixth ring that I remembered the poor bugger worked nights at Pfizer pharmaceuticals and had probably been asleep for no longer than two hours.

He picked up anyway. "Ben Morgan."

"Hi, Ben. You asleep?"

"No. I'm driving home."

"You work late."

"No. I just went shopping for breakfast."

"Want a day's pay for an hour's work?"

"Sure."

"Where are you?"

"Elizabeth Street," he replied.

"I'm tailing my client's mother. She's got a tail of her own and I don't want them to see me so I need to arrange a changing tail. Can you help?"

"Sure."

I liked his easy answers.

Up ahead, the blue Saab was making a right turn into Craigend Street. It looked as though she was heading down William Street.

"You may be able to pick us up at the end of William Street. She's in a blue Saab, followed by a 750 Honda ridden by someone in black leathers and full face helmet."

"What if she turns off onto the airport access or heads to the tunnel?"

"I'll let you know. Try to hang on to them until you can join up."

"Roger."

I was lucky — the stuff of fiction usually — they kept going down William. It was a great time to have a grungy car because most people don't notice it following.

I was about three cars back. Charlie was in the middle lane, the bike right up her tush. As we approached the CBD and I crossed over Elizabeth Street I saw Ben's blue Skyline pull out from the side of the road and slip into the traffic just behind the Honda.

I'd kept my line to Ben open. "I see you," he said. "I'll pull ahead of the Saab and you can bring up the rear. I'll make the most likely choices. If I'm wrong, you stay with them and I'll join up ASAP."

"Done deal."

Soon we were travelling over the Anzac Bridge towards Balmain. The bike was still right behind her. What kind of an idiot was this guy? I put it to Ben.

"I'd say she's leading him somewhere. Probably arranged."

"If it were the other way round I'd understand — if he was leading her to Peter. But for her to be doing the leading?"

"A safety deposit box. A pile of cash. Buried treasure. Who knows?"

Ben kept going up Victoria Road, across Iron Cove Bridge, through Drummoyne and across the Gladesville Bridge. The Honda had dropped back a car's length but only because a Beemer had snaked in between it and the Saab.

"What do you reckon, Sainte-Claire? Think she's off for a holiday? Could see us in the Alice in a couple of days."

Ben caught me by surprise calling me Sainte-Claire. After all, the Asian kids weren't around. It gave me a definite rush to hear him say Sainte-Claire, which bothered me — just a little. The plain fact was: I was enjoying my new game a lot; one minute standing toe-to toe with standover guys, the next tailing people to mystery rendezvous. Jez was right. A part of me really preferred the charisma that came with Sainte-Claire's persona. I was dressing in black every morning as a matter of course now, and it seemed the most natural thing in the world to smear gel through my hair till it spiked nicely.

And another thing: in the past I hardly ever wore sunglasses, unless I was literally facing the sun on a hot day. Now I was sitting behind the wheel of my custom-built Citroën 'fast car' wearing my Armani wraparound rip-offs. And even though it was a downcast day, black clouds overhead, and I was finding vision a bit of a problem, I hadn't once considered taking the sunnies off.

I heard Ben speaking on my mobile. Since I didn't have a hands-free kit, I had to lift the phone from the passenger seat and ask him to repeat himself.

"I said it could be Parramatta; could be the Blue Mountains."

"Roger," I replied, feeling a bit foolish. Roger, Wilko and all that stuff seemed childish.

"Hold on. She's not there behind me any more. Nor's the bike," he said.

"She's just turned towards Homebush," I told him.

"I'll double back. Hang on to them till I get there."

"Will do." Sounded better than 'roger'.

Charlie, the bike and I crossed over Ryde Bridge. Charlie was a couple of car lengths ahead in the slow lane, followed by the bike. I was in the middle lane behind a two-tonne delivery van. We cruised on a bit.

Less than a minute later I saw the Skyline in my rear-view mirror. Ben must have been driving like Jehu in his biblical winged chariot. He came up fast behind me, then slipped into the left lane, alongside me.

"Nice work," I said into the mobile.

He didn't reply, he just looked deadpan out the driver's window and put out his tongue half an inch.

Five minutes later I heard Ben shout into the mobile, "She's taken the Homebush Bay turn-off."

I was badly placed in the wrong lane for this sudden manoeuvre, so I had to cut right across a Porsche 911 to be able to follow. The Porsche sounded its horn loudly, several times. It wasn't a smart move on my part, bringing myself to the attention of everyone on the road within a fifty metre radius. I swore; Ben would think I was an idiot.

Things got worse at the next intersection. At this time of day, without any sporting event on the calendar, Homebush is a pretty empty place. Not much traffic at all. In our case it consisted of a blue Saab, a Honda 750, a blue Nisson Skyline and a drab-looking Citroën Goddess.

I lifted my mobile, but Ben spoke first. "I'll take whichever turn she doesn't. You follow her. I'll be back on in a couple of minutes."

"Okay."

Charlie turned right on Homebush Bay Drive and made a left on Australia Avenue. The bike followed. There was no way she wouldn't have noticed it by now; she was definitely leading the rider somewhere.

She turned into Figtree Crescent and pulled in to the side of the road. So did the Honda, the other side. So did I — about fifty metres back.

Charlie got out of the car and walked towards a taupe-coloured building. At right angles to the façade of the two-story building was a blue wall. On it was a big sign: 'NSW Lotteries'.

25

I felt really dumb as I pondered whether or not to follow Charlie into the Lotteries office. All the signs had been there for me to follow: as if a whole set of red arrows had been painted in the forest directing me to the road and I'd blundered into the scrub regardless.

Sam had a nose for money, everyone kept telling me that. Charlie and Peter had been celebrating a short while back. She'd bought an expensive dress and they'd been drinking champagne. Ben had even asked Madonna whether the reason he was driving the WRX was because he'd won Lotto. Yet even with the keyword presented to me, did I put two and two together? No way. And why? Because I was still thinking as Robert Howard. Sainte-Claire would have worked it out a long time ago and have staked out the Lotteries office, waiting for Charlie to show, not tailed her blindly from her home, wondering where she'd end up!

I watched the bike rider closely. The visor was still down. Whoever it was was keeping an eye on the Lotteries Office double doors, waiting for Charlie to exit.

Ben drove by and disappeared up the slight incline. The weather had improved and the sun was shining directly into my windscreen. I was glad of the Armanis.

Ten minutes passed. Then another ten. Soon I was wondering what Charlie could possibly be up to. Concerned that I should be doing something, I began to think laterally. I picked up my mobile and called directory assistance, asking for the Lotteries Office of New South Wales. They put me straight through.

"New South Wales Lotteries. May I help you?"

"I'm a writer doing some research on a novel. Can you fill me in on a few things?"

"Such as?"

"If you prefer to remain anonymous after a win, is that possible?"

"Normally, if you're a registered player, you tick the privacy box. That means we don't tell the media that it's you who's won."

"So from then on it would all be private? No one would come knocking on my door with a lot of cameramen and newshounds?"

"I'd better put you through to our media person, Steven Fridley. He can answer the details."

I waited.

"Steve Fridley here. You'll have to be brief, I'm in a meeting."

"Sure. My name's Sainte-Claire. Just a quick question. If I tick the privacy box can I be assured that no one will know I've won the big money?"

"Well, if you're registered we would call you once the draw was over and it was confirmed you'd won a big prize."

"Would you insist you spoke to me personally?"

"Of course," Fridley replied, a trifle annoyed that I might think otherwise.

"But on the phone, how would you know it was me?"

"I'd ask you."

"What?"

"If you were you."

Made sense to him. Not to me. He was missing my point, but I didn't want to get his back up so I back-pedalled.

"Say you'd rung my home number because that was the number on the registration form, and if a man answered, you'd take it for granted it was me? Am I right?"

Fridley sensed a trap; I could hear it in the tone of his voice. "Not necessarily. I'd probably say something like 'Is that Mr. Sainte-

Claire? This is Steve Fridley from the Lotteries Office of New South Wales'."

"Right. But supposing it was someone else who answered and he said 'Yes, Robert Sainte-Claire speaking?' "

"Well…" He hesitated. He had seen what I was getting at. "Well, in actual fact I wouldn't say I was from the Lotteries Office until you told me it was you."

That wasn't much comfort either. Not if I had a brother like Sammy. Ever curious. Ever on the make. If I was Sammy I'd say, 'Sure, that's me. What can I do for you?' Plus I thought it more likely that Fridley would have blurted out who he was up front.

"Then you'd tell me how much I'd won?"

"I'd tell you your registered number had won whatever dividend it was. First, second or otherwise. Then I'd ask if you'd changed your mind about publicity."

"Because publicity is always good for sales of Lotto?"

"Of course. Then we'd arrange a photo shoot sometime soon after the win."

"How long until I can pick up the cash?"

"Cheque. No cash."

"Cheque, then."

"Two weeks after the draw."

"Then what?"

"Then I'd arrange to come by your house with an investment advisor who works for us, deliver the cheque and inform you of all the sensible investment options you have available to you. We do that as a courtesy. One moment, please. " He broke off.

I could hear voices in the background, even though he probably had a hand over the mouthpiece. He was talking to a woman. Then he was back. I heard him sigh.

"Anything wrong?" I asked.

"No, nothing. Can't be helped. Anyway, you now have my full attention. Where were we?"

"Investment options?"

"Right. We have no direct interest in what you do with the money — we just like to look after our less well-educated big winners."

"And if I didn't want you coming round to my house because I didn't want my wife to know I'd won a lot of cash, what would I do?"

There was a brief pause. When Fridley continued, I detected a hint of animosity. Maybe he thought I'd just won a big prize myself and was about to give diddly-squat to my fat old bag of a wife and piss off with my bimbo girlfriend.

"In that case, I would suggest you came to see me here. I'd hand over the cheque. Then I would suggest a short meeting with our advisors."

"How long would that meeting take?"

"Half an hour? Maybe less. No longer than an hour."

As Fridley finished the last sentence, I saw the double front doors open and Charlie emerged.

"Gotta go. Thanks," I said, then dialled Ben.

Almost immediately the bike rider got off the Honda and jogged over to Charlie. I had my hand on my door, ready to jump out if he laid a finger on her. She saw the biker coming, but instead of getting in the car she waited for him.

"Ben, she's back out."

Charlie's expression was grim. I couldn't hear if the biker said anything because he was too far away and he still had the visor down anyway. She shrugged at him and appeared to be telling him something.

"The biker's over with her. They're talking."

"Need help?"

"If I need you I'll call. Let's keep this as low profile as possible right now. I can be with her within seconds if there's any violence."

"Roger."

Whatever she was saying appeared to make the biker angry. He pointed to her handbag with the index finger of a gloved hand. She shrugged again in an exaggerated fashion, as if to say 'Well, what the hell can *I* do?' He kept jabbing his finger at the handbag. She kept shrugging. I was getting angry and wanted to jab whoever it was in the chest, and keep jabbing until he begged me to stop. I was pumped full of adrenaline. But I didn't move an inch — I kept thinking, 'hell, Sainte-Claire, you've intruded enough in this woman's business. Give her a chance to handle matters on her own.'

I immediately experienced a tightening in my stomach muscles — I was now calling *myself* Sainte-Claire. Not good at all. Dr. Jekyll was losing out to Mr Hyde.

Charlie turned her back on the bike rider and leaned down to unlock the Saab door, exasperated. The moment the biker went for her bag I was out the door of my car and running towards them, shouting into my mobile. "Ben, stay with the biker — he's got her handbag!"

By the time I was halfway to Charlie, the guy in leathers was back at his Honda, leg over and starting it up with a roar.

Charlie was lying next to the Saab when I got there. She wasn't hurt as far as I could see; the biker had simply grabbed her bag and pushed her down.

I looked round. Ben's car was coming down the street at a fair pace as the bike raced towards him. As Ben swung the car broadside across the road the biker did a sliding one-eighty and started off in the opposite direction. Then both were gone.

I helped Charlie to her feet. She was crying, her whole body wracked with sobs, reminiscent of Ally-Oop the day I first met her.

Like mother, like child.

Oop. Oop. Oop.

I didn't hear a dicky-bird on the open line to Ben for about thirty seconds. I imagine he had his work cut out following the 750 — a Nissan sedan is no match for a powerful motorbike. I'd placed the mobile on top of the car so I could hear if he got back to me. Meanwhile, several people were looking out of upstairs windows and a security guy had run out of the building to Charlie and me.

"What happened?" he said in a thick Slavic accent.

"Someone on a bike snatched my friend's handbag."

He got on his mobile and made a call — I presumed it was to the police.

Charlie struggled to her feet and pushed towards the security guy. "Please! Don't call the police! Don't! I was promised no publicity. If the police are involved there'll be media everywhere!"

The security guard was just about to say something into the phone. He halted and clicked it off.

A man in a beige suit, lilac shirt and paisley tie walked through the double doors and joined us.

"Mrs Reid. Whatever has happened? Are you all right?"

"Please. I'd much rather no fuss was made of all this. Some young person stole my handbag. It had nothing in it I can't readily replace, so I'd rather leave it at that. If you don't mind."

He made an apologetic face. "I'm afraid I can't just pretend nothing happened, Mrs Reid. I have my superiors to answer to. A mugging outside our premises is something I'm obliged to report to the police. I'm very sorry."

"Was the cheque in the bag?" I asked, quite reasonably I thought.

Charlie looked daggers at me. "What cheque?" She then glared at the man I guessed was Fridley, daring him to dispute what she'd said. He looked down at his brown suede shoes. His aftershave was quite overpowering.

There was a coughing sound on the roof of Charlie's car. It sounded more like a pistol shot than a human voice. I picked up my mobile.

"Ben?"

There was a moment's pause. Then he came on. "The guy's crashed. Went off the road. Doesn't look good. There's people calling the emergency services right now. Better go. I'll call you in a bit."

"What about the handbag?"

"It's on the road some place — as you turn left onto the Western Freeway from Homebush Bay Drive."

"You think he had time to check it out before he dumped it?"

"That's why it's on the road. He was trying to make the turn and look through it at the same time while he outran me. Never made it. Gotta go. The guy needs help. Bad."

Charlie was now in her car and starting the engine — fortunately she had the keys in her hand when the biker went for her bag. Fridley put a hand on her shoulder.

"Why don't you wait until the police arrive? Please, Mrs Reid?"

"I won't be pressing charges. I don't want to talk to anyone."

I stepped back from her car. The last thing she wanted from me was another offer of assistance. She was off down the road before any police arrived.

I walked back to my car and followed her at a discreet distance. I'd done it again: interfered, and disaster had dogged me. It wouldn't have happened to Sainte-Claire. I'd have to sharpen up if I was going to make it in the gumshoe major league.

26

A patrol car was parked across the road next to the Honda. The ambulance hadn't arrived. I stopped behind Ben's car. He was kneeling with a constable next to the fallen biker, cradling his head as the policeman tried to ease off the helmet. He'd been catapulted off his bike as he tried to make a left turn; it looked as though he'd gone headfirst into the freeway stanchion. The helmet had taken the impact but it was badly damaged. There was no sign of any movement from the rider. I tried to get closer but the other policeman held out a hand and told me to keep back.

As the helmet came off very slowly, a cascade of luxuriant jet-black hair fell to the biker's shoulders. A girl, and a lovely one at that.

I won't go into the detail of the events that followed. Briefly, an ambulance came and the girl was loaded into the back. Ben was interviewed and told the patrolman what had transpired — the handbag snatch and everything. A tow truck had arrived well before the ambulance — well, nothing new there.

I found the handbag. It was about fifty metres back down the road. I was mightily challenged not to open it and look through, but somehow resisted the temptation. I handed it to the police.

Half an hour later you'd never have known that an accident had taken place.

"What do you reckon?" I asked Ben as we walked back to our respective cars.

"Bad. Very bad. Maybe we should have waited to take the helmet off. I wanted to wait, but the cop said we had to see if the biker was breathing and the visor was stuck fast. He had a point; she could have been choking to death. I've seen accidents like this before. Broken neck, I'd say. Spinal."

"Was the girl carrying any ID?"

"Yes. Tammi Thurong's her name. The last bit means 'King' in Vietnamese. Mean anything to you?"

I shook my head.

"Think she's a pal of Tri's?" I asked.

"Could be. I'd be guessing though. I might ask Annie. If she's a Cabramatta girl, she'll know Tammi."

He opened the door of his Skyline.

"So Mrs What's-it won the lottery is that about the size of it? And someone wants a piece of the action?"

Or all of it; that was my guess.

"Yes, that's about the size of it," I replied. "Hold on a second — I've got to make a call. Can you wait?" I asked.

"Sure."

I called Lucy. When she answered her mobile I quickly nut-shelled what had happened, and told her to expect Charlie in the next half-hour. I told her she'd be a mess. I added that the police had found her handbag, to tell Charlie that, and that they'd be in touch shortly.

"What was she doing in Homebush?"

"You ask her that yourself. She was at the New South Wales Lotteries building. She told me it had nothing to do with any cheques or jackpot payouts. 'Go figure', as they say in the States."

"I've got to pick up the kids. I said I would."

"Well, if you miss Charlie, that can't be helped. Give me a call later, would you? I want to know she's all right."

"I will. And thanks for looking after little sis. I mean that. You're not such a bad man, Sainte-Claire."

There it was again. I felt another spread of warmth in my chest. Sainte-Claire had done good.

"Take care," I said and hung up.

"Can you use my help a bit longer?" Ben asked as I put my phone away.

"What time do you go back on duty?"

"Not till six. I only need to get my head down for an hour before then. Apart from that, I'm cool."

"You're on," I replied. Having Ben around would be a real plus. He was an ex-cop, he knew his stuff and his local knowledge of Cabramatta was invaluable.

"I'd really like to know who the girl was working for," I said.

"Can I use your mobile?" he asked a bit sheepishly. "My bills are killing me."

I handed it over.

"You free for an hour or so if I arrange a meet?" he asked.

"Of course."

He walked down the road a few metres and I heard him talking into the phone. A couple of minutes later he was back at my side.

"Hope you don't mind my keeping the conversation to myself. You have to respect other people's privacy, and I wasn't sure he'd want to get involved."

"I understand."

"He's a pal. Still works in the job at Cabramatta. Lovely guy called Ercan. Turkish origin — tough as Ataturk himself. I arranged to meet in half an hour in John Street. We can just make it by then. Okay with you?"

"Fine," I replied.

As he handed me back the phone it cheeped.

"James Millar."

"Hi, James."

"The car you asked about. It's registered to a brothel owner called Annie Tran. Avoca Street, Cabramatta."

I thanked him and hung up. No need to tell him Sainte-Claire had got there without his help.

The small coffee shop was about halfway down John Street, situated in a kind of mini square. Ben walked up to a bear of a man who was sitting at a table half his size. The guy's bulk contrasted nicely with the tiny short black he had in front of him. It was a thimble to a sumo wrestler.

Ben introduced us; this time I was Robert Howard. I felt a tinge of disappointment. The waiter took our orders. The giant's name was Turgut Ercan.

Ben explained to Turgut what had just gone down in Homebush, and how we were keen to know if there was any connection between the girl, Tri or Madonna.

"Sure, we know Tammi," Turgut said. "If she weren't halfway to being a terminal junkie she'd be the prettiest little girl in Cabramatta. She's just sixteen, you know. Been a user for only a year or so. Before that she sold caps for various people at the railway station. Record's as long as her black hair."

"So she and Tri know each other?"

"Sure. We busted her only last Friday selling stuff for him."

"How did you know it was Tri's stuff?" I asked.

"We saw him take the money off her after. Pity we didn't see him give the gear to her before. Can't bust the guy for taking her money — that's the shame of it."

The coffee came.

"Does she know Madonna?" Ben asked. I think he was hoping Turgut would say no; he liked the kid.

"Not so that we'd know, no. Frankie's on the way up. He's out of here — we all hope. He wants to make something of himself. And Annie scares the pants off him — he knows she'd rip him open if he got into any serious drug bother."

"Do you know who Tri answers to, by any chance?"

Turgut thought for a while, then shrugged. "The thing is, Robert, there's no real 'Mr. Big' around right now. We've managed to drive them all out of the area. It's just too hard to make a dishonest living here, what with all the public cameras everywhere, and the police profile we have now around the streets. We made it too tough."

"So the bad guys move a few klicks down the road?" I said, somewhat unhelpfully.

"Sure. But what else can we do here than move 'em on? If everyone did the same we'd all be fine. But not everyone's got a great chain of command like we have right now."

So I was still pushing shit uphill. Tammi, the biker, was probably working with Tri. Tri had been staking out Charlie. As soon as I'd busted Tri, he'd got Tammi to take over for him. But Charlie still wasn't thinking about sharing her secret with us.

I looked across the square and saw a newsagency. "Excuse me just a moment," I said, and left Ben and Turgut to their coffee.

A sign on the wall of the shop stated: '$2 lottery now $1,000,000!'

"When did the two-dollar lottery last go off," I asked the bald Asian guy behind the counter.

"Last week. Jackpot."

That was too recent. I wanted two weeks ago.

"Anything happen two weeks ago?"

The guy didn't have to think hard. "No two-dollar win. But Lotto? Yes. Twelve mil. Nice one."

"Local? You sell the ticket?" I said, ribbing him a little.

"Nah. Sydney, though. Makes a change, heh?"

It sure did.

I rejoined Ben and Turgut.

"Turgut says he'll keep an eye out for Tri," Ben told me as I sat down. "Also, he'll ask around for Tri's contacts. Tri'll lead them somewhere pretty soon."

"Tell me something," I said, addressing them both. "What if I'm being threatened, but I choose not to involve the police — what's my legal standing?"

"Depends on whether a crime's been committed," Turgut said. "If it has, then it's not your choice. Not to report the matter is accessorising yourself."

"But would they be charged?" I interrupted. "If it turned out that the person involved was just scared shitless that they or someone they cared for would come to harm if they involved the police?"

"Probably not. Mind you, if I had my way they *would*. Look at it from our perspective here in Cabramatta, or Chinatown for that matter — there's a cone of silence within the Asian community that's really hard to break. The Chinese don't report standover tactics to the police; they think we can't protect them, and to some extent they're right. They report a gang of hooligans to the cops and it's just a matter of time before retribution is handed out. We can keep an eye on the vics for a certain length of time, then they know they're on their own. So I reckon they have to be *made* to tell us what's happening. If the bad guys *know* this, it makes it all so much easier — they know they'll be dobbed in."

I considered this for a moment.

"Are you saying you know of someone who's being threatened, but he's afraid to call us in?" Turgut asked.

I had to tread carefully here. The big Turk seemed like a nice guy, but I knew he had a job to do, and if I shared my knowledge with him he'd feel duty bound to pass it down the line. In many respects, I couldn't think of a good reason not to blow the whole thing wide open to Chase and his people in the Cross. But it always came back to the one problem: proving that a crime of any kind had been committed. Charlie was still clinging to her lie that Peter hadn't been abducted and that all was well. Now she'd be suggesting that she'd driven to the New South Wales Lotteries Office just to have a chat with Mr Fridley — I was sure that would be her story next time I asked her.

So how could I help her, other than finding Peter and setting him free before she felt it necessary to fill a suitcase with money and hand it over to Sammy, Tri and whoever he worked for?

"Nah, just curious," I said in answer to Turgut's question.

27

I drove back to Sydney expecting a stern call from my twelve-year-old client. But she didn't call. Not that we'd arranged to meet — I just expected her to check in with me around 4 p.m. I concluded she was most probably with Lucy and Charlie at home.

I wondered what kind of a brave face Charlie was presenting to her family. It didn't say a lot for the confidence Charlie placed in her sister — she hadn't confided in her yet. Would she do so now?

Ben had said he was going to catch a few z's and then go to work. Turgut had gone back to the cop shop, promising to do a bit of groundwork on Tri and any associates he might have.

I thought I'd stop by Jez's studio and try to make up for my bad behaviour the night before. She'd been quite right — I *had* been acting like a sixteen-year-old who'd just got the better of the school bully. I was ashamed of myself.

I wanted it to be a surprise, so I didn't call to say I was coming; I simply took the M5 back to town and drove directly to her studio in Esther Lane, a tiny street off Crown Street.

I parked with two wheels up on the pavement to allow other cars to get by, and hoped the traffic wardens weren't in the neighbourhood.

The first warning sign was that the two big downstairs doors were wide open. This immediately worried me — Jez would never have left them that way. A quick look at the doors as I passed through showed me they'd been jemmied open. Splinters of wood lay everywhere.

I ran up the stairs to Jez's studio on the first floor, calling her name out loud. There was no reply.

The studio was a shambles. Someone had done a particularly thorough job of vandalising the place. Canvases lay ripped and slashed. Paint had been squirted everywhere. The smell of urine was overpowering.

I pulled out my phone, terrified that Jez might have been in the studio when the place had been turned over.

She picked up after four rings.

"Hi, Pulitzer. What's hopping?" she said casually.

"Jez, there's no need to worry. I'm fine. But I'm afraid to say there's been a break-in at the studio."

A second's pause.

"Shit! I knew I should have taken Kevin's advice and put in the iron bar across the doors. Shit! And more shit!"

"Look, it could have been a lot worse. You might have been here when they chose to break in."

"When did it happen?"

"Don't know. How long have you been out?"

"Since about midday. I've been at the hairdresser's, then at Poppy's — it's her birthday."

"That's nice," I said, my mind a blank. I had a bad feeling this had little to do with petty theft or vandalism; this went deeper.

"Well," she said in a voice that showed passive acceptance of a bit of bad luck. "At least there was nothing to steal but a few canvases, and most of them are too large to carry down the street."

"I'm afraid they trashed the place," I answered. She had to know eventually, and I didn't want her coming round and seeing things the way they were right then — before I'd had a chance to clean up a bit and pay someone to hose out the urine.

"I'll be round in ten minutes," she said.

"Hold on, Jez! I'd like to put the place in a reasonable state for you. I don't want you seeing it the way it is now. It's pretty bad."

"Hell, now you're scaring me to death. I'm coming." She disconnected.

That was that. She was on her way. Couldn't be helped.

I called directory assistance and got the name of a contract cleaner who said they'd send a team within the hour. I told them I'd pay big bucks if they could make it faster. They responded favourably. Half an hour.

Next call was to a locksmith. He said he'd send round a guy called Danny by five.

Then I started stacking the ripped canvases against the wall. It was heartbreaking to see a year of Jez's work shredded and desecrated that way. I couldn't bear the thought of what it would do to her. There was oil paint everywhere: on the walls, the floor, the windowpanes.

I'd stacked about twenty when I heard footsteps on the stairs. In the same moment I saw the words someone had scrawled in oils on the floor by the microwave: *This one's for you, S-C! See yous soon.*

I turned round to see Jez standing at the top of the stairs. Tears were rolling down her otherwise impassive, quite beautiful, face.

I walked over to her, stepping carefully through the detritus, and held her close to me.

We stood like that for about five minutes. I didn't know what to say. Everything can be replaced? It couldn't be. I'd make it all better? I knew I couldn't.

Someone called from downstairs. "Mr. Howard? I'm Danny."

I called to him over Jez's shoulder. "Take a look at the downstairs doors. We want the place secure by tonight. Think about a deadbolt, plus a bar across both doors."

"Will do," came the reply.

"Who would think to do such a thing, Robert?" Jez asked. Well, why would she think it had anything to do with *me*?

I had to come clean. It occurred to me in that instant, with some dread, that it might spell the end of our relationship. But it had to be said — the truth would eventually out.

"I think this has more to do with me than you, Jez. And for that I can't tell you how sorry I am."

She stepped back just enough so she could look me in the eyes. She still held on to me. "What do you mean?"

"Someone is trying to get to me by getting at you."

She looked away. "Christ, this place stinks like a public toilet," she said vaguely, as though in shock.

"I think whoever it was urinated somewhere. I've arranged for some cleaners — they'll be here very soon."

She looked back at me, as if she'd only just processed my previous remark.

"This isn't some kind of Sainte-Claire nonsense, is it? Please tell me it's not. Please tell me that a couple of years of hard, dedicated work hasn't been pissed upon by fuckwits because you preferred to play amateur 'dick' than write 'almost' grown-up books."

I was speechless, waiting for the second shoe to fall. No one who's seen Jez lose her temper will ever forget the experience — or want a repeat performance.

She looked away from me and started picking her way through the broken pieces of frames and crockery, her Jimmy Choos perilously close to the splashes of burnt sienna, ochres and vermilion on the floor.

Then she saw the note. She said the words aloud, one by one, very slowly. She didn't look at me.

A long pause.

Then, "Tell me, Sainte-Claire, what have you been up to today? Anything I ought to know about?"

I was still tongue-tied.

"Rescued any 'dames' recently?"

What was I going to say? Yes, in fact I had rescued one dame, and the second person in two days who'd messed with me was now in the emergency room of a Sydney hospital?

I simply stood there and waited for the cap of the volcano to burst loose.

"Well, let me spell this out to you in very simple language," she said, finally. "I don't like you a whole lot, Sainte-Claire. You may look kind of cute, with your spiked-up hair and snappy clothes, but you are very bad ju ju indeed right now. I'm grateful you called the locksmith and I'm grateful you've called the cleaners. But let me say this just once: you want to be Sainte-Claire and run around getting yourself into a whole heap of trouble, you do it when I'm not around. And I'd be grateful if you could let it be known to the criminal fraternity at large — both in the Cross and Cabramatta — that we are no longer an item. So they can leave me and my paintings alone, and concentrate on beating the shit out of *other* people and their possessions."

"Okay," I said. I knew better than to argue.

"Now go away and let me calm down."

"Can I stay and help clean up?"

"No, you can't."

"Can I see you later?"

"No, you can't do that either."

"Can I see you ever again?"

"We'll have to see. Just go, Sainte-Claire."

I walked to the door, turned and waved a hand. I hoped she'd interpret it as a funny gesture and thaw a bit.

"You can tell Mr Howard he can call me later tonight."

I nodded.

28

My first stop was Surry Hills Police Station. The 'break and enter' had to be reported. The station was in Goulburn Street — I thought of Faithful Hope and the Goulburn races.

The desk constable took the initial details, but when I told him I felt I knew who'd done the damage he asked me to wait while he had a word with the duty detective. Ten minutes later a detective appeared and introduced himself as Popov.

"What makes you think you know who broke into your girlfriend's studio?" he asked.

I explained about the message in oils on the floor and my run-in with Tutuelo, and that everyone at King's Cross station seemed to know he was an enforcer working for Tim Brierley.

"But you just told me that Mr Tutuelo's still on remand."

"I believe so. I don't know for sure. He'll be bailed sometime today I expect. He probably had one of his pals do it for him."

"That's a bit of a quantum leap, isn't it?"

"Not when you consider they referred to me as Sainte-Claire. S-C. My real name's Howard."

"Yes, excuse me, but you're going to have to explain all of the name stuff to me again."

I did so. It took a good ten minutes and it sounded crass.

"You telling me you've been going around telling everyone you're called Sainte-Claire just to please this twelve-year-old girl who thinks she's employing you as her personal private investigator?"

Right on the button. I told you it sounded crass.

"In a way, yes," I replied.

"And Mr Brierley and his mates think you actually *are* Mr Sainte-Claire?"

"Just Sainte-Claire. There's no Mr."

One eyebrow raised slowly. I detected I wasn't his type of person.

"May I suggest you read one of my graphic novels? If you like, I'll drop a few copies in for the staff room."

"I read mostly biographies. Seldom fiction. Never comics. But the boys might like a good read," he said, softening slightly.

That old 'biography' excuse again. I felt sad for a man starved of good page-turning graphic pulp.

"Does anyone else apart from Brierley and Tutuelo know you as Sainte-Claire?" he asked.

He had a point. I didn't know why I'd immediately thought of Tutuelo. Of course, Madonna and Tri also knew me as Sainte-Claire. I had to tell Popov that. And fill him in on the Cabramatta connection. *And* the Ferrier Street story.

When I'd finished, he looked at me as though I was some basket case the beat cops might pull off the street — one who needed to be handed over immediately to DOCS or the Sydney City Mission.

"Are you pulling my leg?"

"Absolutely not, Detective. I swear everything I've told you is true. I just thought it my duty to inform the local police of the break-in — we're not really thinking restitution here. I thought it should be a matter of record, that's all."

"I hope you're not planning to take this further on a personal level, Sainte-Claire. I would advise against that. After all, you aren't sure who did this, are you? You were a few minutes ago — now you're not."

"My name's Robert Howard."

Popov's brow furrowed a second. "Thought you preferred Sainte-Claire?"

"Well…in a way I do, I suppose. Right now, anyway."

"Then you can see why *I'm* confused."

I wasn't so sure who I was myself. I left him to look after his patch and went home.

Giblet was in a foul mood. When I opened the car door, she poked her head inside and practically spat at me — her 'meow' was so loud it was more like a scream. There was also a cannibalistic look in her eyes.

I picked her up and took her inside, wondering what had got into her. After all, she'd had her diced chicken breakfast, same as usual that morning. It was only around six now. Dinner wasn't till at least then most nights.

I opened a tin of tuna and whitefish in a tasty lobster jus. Lobster? Sure. My bet was there were inch-square chunks of the lobster tail mixed in with every fifty-three tonnes of the stuff. Really ace-tastin'. And 'jus'? Gimme a break! Giblet thought the same. She gave me the old 'wall-eye'.

I pulled a box of Cravers from the larder and went to fill her bowl. It was then I realised I hadn't refilled it at breakfast time. No biscuits, no kitty milk. And the tray of water both dishes sat in, so that the ants wouldn't get to the food, smelled stagnant. No wonder she was shitty with me.

I felt super-guilty. I'd just let down my girlfriend in a huge way. I wasn't about to commit the double-whammy and let down the other lady in my life. So I refreshed all the bowls and resolved to go to the supermarket within the hour and get some fresh chicken breast.

In my office later, Giblet looked a bit more relaxed as she sat next to my iMac bathed in the warmth of the desk light that acted as her heater.

I'd showered, changed out of Sainte-Claire stuff, and fixed myself a Bourbon with a twist of fresh lime. During my shower it had occurred to me that I hadn't looked at my emails for two or three days — the fact was, I couldn't remember how many days exactly.

When I clicked on Send & Receive the floodgates opened. It was only then that it became dazzlingly apparent what had been happening to me over the past few days. First, I had forgotten I was a writer. Second, I had put my wonderful girlfriend — the love of my life – at physical risk. Third, I had ignored both my agents — people who had been very good and loyal to me over fifteen years. And fourth, I had forgotten to adequately feed my feline friend. I'd also witnessed one innocent man badly beaten in the street; I'd put another human being in hospital, coming within a whisker of killing the guy; and I'd been the catalyst for an accident that might have killed a young Asian girl. Yet here I was drinking Bourbon and thinking about dinner. What a jerk.

Why had I behaved this way? That was the hard question. Because I wanted to help two little children find their dad? Because I wanted to help Charlie? Not even close.

There were three emails from Lara in New York. The first asked where the notes on the new graphic novel were. In the second she happily informed me that she'd nailed a three-book deal with Random House, including *Things That Go Bump*. The third asked why I wasn't sufficiently excited to respond. She told me she'd telephone if I hadn't got back to her by Friday.

There were five emails from Sol in Los Angeles. He likes writing cut-down messages that sound like headlines in *Variety* – I suppose he's such a part of Tinseltown he actually thinks in those terms.

OZ WHIZ HOWARD'S 'BUMP' HOOKS BIG FISH ROBERTS, REDFORD. That's the headline in today's Variety. *Whadderyathink, buddy?*

That was exactly how he delivered the news of his coup. If you are a normal person who can't decipher Hollywood movie jargon, it meant that he'd done a movie deal for *Things that Go Bump*, and he was major excited.

In the second and third emails his tone became a trifle angry because I hadn't responded. The fourth and fifth were short and to the point: 'Call me,' and 'Will you *fucking* call me' respectively.

I tapped away for about thirty minutes while Giblet watched; she was going to wait me out till I went to buy fresh food. I congratulated Lara and Sol, and told them I'd call them as soon as I'd fed the cat. It must have sounded a lame excuse — not everyone's life revolves around fat, dangerous cats, I suppose.

I was surprised by my lack of enthusiasm. After all, a picture deal with Redford and Roberts involved was the biggest ever to come my way — the stuff of dreams. And a three-book deal with Random House was even more fabulous. Yet my mind was elsewhere; confused, distracted, in need of professional psychiatric help.

I headed off to Coles for the chicken for Giblet and a steak for me. Probably she'd end up having a little of both.

I was on my way back when I bumped into Nick Kougios on the corner of William and Darlinghurst. He grinned at me.

"How's the Sainte-Claire-machine?"

"Great, Nick. Got a lot of guts," I replied.

"Nothing like a wolf in sheep's clothing," he said, chuckling.

I thought for a moment he was talking about me, then I realised he meant the car.

"Heard you got involved in a bit of biffo."

This took me by surprise. "Word gets around," I replied.

"Maaaate! The street's the street. What can I tell you?"

I felt an intense physical buzz, as if someone had congratulated me on winning an Olympic gold medal or something. The 'street' was talking about me? Christ.

"Matter of fact, someone did have a go. I took care of things — like you told me."

"Nearly fucking killed the bastard. That's the word, anyway. Tutuelo to boot. Shit! I'd think twice 'fore I spat in his chops!" He laughed.

"I couldn't stand by and let him kill the kid," I said.

"Course you couldn't, bubba!" Nick said, still chuckling.

"They had to patch him up in the ER. You know that?"

"Sure, I know. I'm proud of you, mate. A short lesson from the maestro and you inspire *fear*! Nice one."

"He'll be fine in the long term," I said.

"Who gives a shit? Thing is, got to see the funny side of things, eh?"

"Well," I began, "it's not really a laughing matter, is it?"

Nick interrupted. "Mate! Let me tell you *exactly* how I feel about violence. In my book, you never walk away from violence of any kind."

"Yeah...well, I suppose I did walk away. Initially."

"Well, that's the whole fuckin' thing! Just don't do it again. This time you threw the dice and won. Lucky. Next time — and there's always a next time — enjoy the moment. You see, once you'd 'ave talked your way out of a situation like that or run away; now you can roll up your sleeves and get stuck in. And now we can 'ave a giggle about it over a schooner or two!"

I was silent, unsure of my emotions. What I should say? I looked at my watch.

"Sorry, mate. I can't stay."

Back home I was about to call Jez and eat humble pie when my phone rang. I picked it up, hoping Jez had had a change of heart and still loved me.

"It's Lucy. Can you come round right away? I'm afraid something terrible's happened."

"What?" I asked, immediately thinking of the kids.

"I've found a human finger in the ice-cream."

Not what I'd expected. Not the kind of line *anyone* would expect.

"Say that again," was all I could manage.

"I think it's Peter's. Looks like a pinkie. Charlie's gone troppo. She won't speak. I have to do something quickly."

I had to *think* quickly. "Put it back in the ice-cream and put the tub in the freezer — keep it frozen for the microsurgeons. You never know. I'll come straight round."

I was out the door and running within a few seconds.

At the corner of Liverpool and Victoria my mobile chirped. I fumbled it out of my pocket as I ran. People were scattering around me — maybe they thought I was a handbag snatcher or simply running from the cops.

My heart sank as I heard Jez say, "Pulitzer? Want to come round and say you're very sorry? We could kiss and make up?"

Good grief…

I was pounding down Roslyn a couple of minutes later. I have to say, Jez wasn't exactly thrilled to hear my news. I'd got as far as 'There's been an accident at the kids' place. I'm on my way right now. I'm running. I'll call you right ba—" when the line went dead. But, hey, what was I going to do — patch up my relationship on the phone and go make love to my girlfriend? Or try to help some poor woman who had just found a severed piece of her sister's husband in the freezer? I knew I was making the right decision.

I was expecting mayhem when I got to Number 5, but the reality was quite the reverse.

Lucy opened the door. Sure, she was looking pale and edgy, but she was calm. Remarkable, really — it's not every day you find a human body part in the freezer.

"I didn't know what to do," she said. "So I called you. I'm beginning to rely on you, I'm afraid."

"Thanks a lot," I mumbled to myself, in the knowledge that my relationship with Jez wasn't just dead but buried — it had a headstone.

As we passed through the living area I saw Charlie in an armchair. Her hands were flat on her knees and she was sitting bolt upright, looking directly ahead of her into Middle Earth. Her mouth was hanging open like a wounded bird's beak. She didn't appear to register my presence.

Tiggs shouted down the stairs. "Who's that, Aunt Lucy?"

"Nobody, darling. Go to bed."

Lucy led me through to the kitchen, then stood beside the fridge with one hand on the door handle. "Do you want to see it now?"

I didn't. Would you? Not really.

"I suppose I'd better," was my grudging response.

She opened the freezer, took out a tub of Cadbury's Luxury Selection Caramello ice-cream and lifted the top. All I could see was ice-cream and toffee goo.

"It's in the middle a couple of centimetres down," she whispered. "I covered it over to keep it frozen."

She dug around a bit with a spoon. A trifle too roughly, I felt, for the good of the finger.

Then I saw it.

It was definitely a human pinkie. Almost white, as though it had been frozen for a while. Quite hairy on either side of the knuckle joints. The cut was clean as a whistle, as though removed with a surgical instrument, or perhaps big bolt-cutters. There was no blood evident at all.

"How did this happen?" I asked Lucy.

"I picked up the kids from school and brought them home. Charlie wasn't here and I was getting a bit worried when she came in."

"Did she tell you what happened at Homebush?"

"No."

"Did she say where she'd been since lunchtime, or why she was late home?"

"No. She was the way she is right now. She simply came in and plonked herself down. Hasn't said a word since then."

Lucy suddenly held up the hand with the spoon, as though she'd forgotten something important. "I tell a lie. I told her I'd fed the kids and that I was going to give them a treat — some ice-cream."

"What did she say?"

"She just screamed out, 'NO!'"

"But you got the ice-cream?"

"Yes. Well, first of all I was really surprised by the volume — it was a big shout. Then I stared at her. She looked crazy at first. Then she gave me a pleading look and said 'no' a bit lower. I heard Tiggs call out from upstairs. I called back that everything was okay, that I'd broken a plate. But I was really shocked by Charlie's outburst. And curious. What was with the ice cream that was so important? So I turned my back on Charlie, walked through to the kitchen and opened the fridge door and took the tub out of the freezer."

She hesitated.

"And?"

"Well, Charlie came rushing at me, clawing at the tub of ice cream. She was acting quite hysterically."

"Did the children hear?"

"Tiggs came running downstairs this time – she was going to see for herself what was going on. Charlie took one look at her shocked little face, held her in her arms and took her upstairs."

"Then?"

"Then Charlie came downstairs and sat in the chair she's sitting in right now. No more tears, not another word. I'm seriously worried about her mental state. Should I call a doctor?"

"Maybe," I said. All kinds of ghastly thoughts were now spinning through my head. The finger had to belong to Peter. The blood residue in the burnt-out Saab was most probably Peter's. It seemed likely that the finger had been sent to Charlie as a wake-up call, so she knew they were serious. How many days had she kept it in the freezer? Presumably she'd put it there so it might be reattached at some later stage. Would brother really cut the finger off brother? It was unthinkable. But at least I now had something to show the police. They'd have to act.

"Look, Lucy, I'm going to walk up to the police station and talk to Detective Chase — he's the one who was here initially, and also the man I spoke to last time. It's better I go to see him than calling the police here — the children, you know?"

She nodded.

"Meantime, do you have a friendly doctor, or is it a more formal relationship?"

"She's very nice. More a friend than a doctor."

"Perfect. Then call her up from somewhere Charlie and the children can't hear the conversation and ask her to come round. Say it's a bit urgent, that something's upset Charlie. Don't tell her about the finger — she doesn't need to know that. Just say Charlie's in a shocked state and may need some sedation."

"Sedation? Looks to me as though she could use a line of speed."

I was surprised. "I wouldn't have taken you for a drug-hound," I said, trying to inject a speck of humour into an ugly situation.

Then a thought occurred to me. "Is Charlie seeing a shrink?"

"Not as far as I know."

"Has she ever?"

"Don't think so. Believe it or not, Charlie's the more down to earth and rational member of our family."

"Well, the times they are a'changin'," I mumbled distractedly

"I missed that," she said.

"Dylan. Doesn't matter."

29

"You wanna bit?" a big girl with pond-green hair in a couple of scrunchies asked me casually as I walked past the Pink Pussycat on my way to the cop station. I smiled back politely.

As luck would have it Chase was on duty. He asked me into an interview room. He'd had his suit cleaned — good thinking. His expression suggested he thought he was in for another waste of time.

I told him exactly what had taken place that day, warts and all. His expression changed as the story progressed, from boredom through interest to disbelief.

"Can you excuse me a moment while I make a call," he said.

Two minutes later he returned.

"There was no cheque in the handbag — nothing that she might have picked up in the Lotteries Office. They checked very thoroughly."

"Maybe the girl picked it out while she was looking through the bag," I countered.

"Did your friend see her do that?"

"I don't think so. He just told me she was trying to open it to take a look when she missed the corner."

He thought about things for a moment.

"So you think the finger belongs to Mrs Reid's husband?"

"Well, that would be my *guess*. It's a male finger. Could belong to a female Russian bodybuilder, but I doubt it."

I know I wasn't helping things along by being flippant, but who the hell else could the finger belong to? Did people usually come across body parts of complete strangers in their freezers? I didn't think so.

"Please don't be smart with me, Mr Howard. If what you're suggesting is true, it's a serious matter — not the time for wisecracks. And while we're talking of serious matters, you might be interested to know the girl your friend was pursuing at speed down the road this afternoon died in hospital an hour ago."

I was angry that his glare seemed to suggest it was my fault or Ben's that the girl had died. I was sorry that she'd died, of course, but we'd never encouraged her to snatch Charlie's bag and do a runner. I told him so.

"Nowadays, we do our best to avoid what's known as hot pursuits, Mr Howard. Too many people are being killed — members of the Force as well as kids who've done little else than hotwire a car or snatch a handbag with a few dollars in it. How fast was your ex-cop pal travelling when the bike hit the concrete pillar?"

"I don't know."

"You didn't ask?"

"There were other things happening at the time."

"Well, it appears to me you make a habit of rushing in all over the place without asking too many questions. And the result? Mayhem."

"I didn't cut off anyone's finger and put it in a tub of Cadbury's Luxury Selection."

He leaned back in his chair. "Gives new meaning to the phrase 'finger food'."

"I was hoping you could resist saying that."

"What does Mrs Reid say about it all? Does she think it's her husband's finger?"

"I haven't asked her yet."

Chase's eyes narrowed noticeably. "You didn't *ask* her?"

"She's in a state of shock. Her sister found it. Right now there's a doctor on the way to their house to care for her."

"Well, let's go see the finger."

"Please, Detective Chase, can you be extra careful around the children? Chances are they'll be in bed, but…well, you know."

"I know very well, Mr Howard. I've been a police officer for twenty-two years. I don't chat about dead bodies with kids present."

"Didn't mean to suggest you'd be insensitive."

"Apology accepted. Let's go see the ice-cream."

I'd only been away for half an hour maximum when we knocked on the door of Number 5. To my immense surprise it was Charlie who opened it. She had on her 'smiley' face.

"Hello, Robert," she said brightly. She then focused on Detective Chase. "It's Mr Chase, isn't it?"

Chase looked confused. He gave me a look, then turned back to Charlie. "Yes. Well, *Detective* Chase. May we come in for a few moments?"

"Please do, Detective."

We walked into the living room. Lucy was sitting in the chair Charlie had been in when I left. They'd swapped positions and mindsets. 'Sheepish' would have been a wild understatement of the look on Lucy's face.

"Can I get either of you a drink? A coffee maybe? I expect you're on duty, Detective," Charlie asked airily.

Chase declined. So did I. I kept trying to make eye contact with Lucy, but she stubbornly refused to glance my way.

"Look, I don't quite know how to say this, Mrs Reid," Chase began in a low tone, so no-one upstairs could hear, "but Mr Howard has just been to see me. He's informed me there's been some trouble here and that maybe we should know about it."

Charlie gave the look of sudden realisation — it's number 132 in the National Institute of Dramatic Arts handbook. "Oh, I *see*! You mean the mugging this afternoon! You have my handbag with you! You're returning it?"

"No, I'm afraid I'm not. I'm sure the police who attended the accident will be returning it to you soon. However, the sad news is that the girl who stole your bag died in hospital from her injuries."

Charlie looked genuinely shaken. "That's terrible."

"Yes, it is. What a waste of a life, eh? To die over a few dollars in a handbag." I sensed that Chase was probing her.

She nodded sadly. "Yes, a tragedy."

"Look, I really hope you won't take offence if I ask you about your husband Peter one last time."

She looked him straight in the eyes. "Peter? Of course. What would you like to know? He's still away on business. I expect him back tomorrow. Would you like him to call in and see you on his return?"

Chase looked taken aback. "Well, yes I would." He shifted from foot to foot. "It's not that I doubt what you're saying, but... " he hesitated. "Well, Mr Howard is still suggesting that your husband is in some kind of trouble."

"Trouble?" she interposed very quickly. "What trouble? I do wish he'd get on with writing his novellas and let us get on with our lives."

Novellas. A deliberate slight.

"He says that... " Chase could hardly bring himself to say the words. "A severed finger he thought could belong to your husband was found in an ice-cream container in your fridge."

Charlie looked blankly at Chase, then at me, then back to Chase.

"Tell me something, Detective Chase. Based on the fact that Mr Howard has been making a complete nuisance of himself for several days, suggesting first of all that I was abducted, then suggesting that it was Peter who had been kidnapped rather than me, why would you give any credence at all to a story such as this? Frankly, I'm staggered you should be asking me this question."

Chase said nothing. What was there to say?

"Did Mr Howard tell you the *flavour* of the ice-cream?"

To give him his due, Chase answered with a straight face. "Just that it was Cadbury's Luxury Selection. Caramel?"

I expected he felt as foolish then as I did.

"Lucy? Do you feel like shedding any light on things?" I called out to the silent figure of Lucy. I wanted very much to ascertain what *her* angle was. At least give her a chance to put things right.

"Not really," she said as she languidly crossed her legs. She didn't look at me.

"Well, I must have just imagined the whole damned thing," I said after a few seconds pause. I must have sounded bad-tempered, to say the least. But I was angry and disappointed with both women. Thanks to them, my life had been turned upside down in the last few days and neither seemed to care a toss one way or another.

"I'll be on my way then, ladies," I said, and turned to leave.

Lucy jumped up. "Please, stay for a drink. Don't go."

I looked at Chase. "Can I have a word outside?"

"Certainly, Mr Howard," he replied. "I must get back to work. I'm just glad that everything's okay here."

"Thank you for worrying about us," Charlie said to Chase, pouring on the charm. What pills was she on? Whatever they were, I wanted a bottle myself — she'd morphed from a certifiable basket-case to a delightfully relaxed and engaging housewife in under twenty minutes.

A miracle.

Outside, I tried to make my peace with Chase.

"You don't buy any of that twaddle, do you?"

He strode on up the rise towards Ward Avenue.

"Because to do so, you'd have to think that I'd made up the whole thing about the finger, and that I need immediate electroshock therapy."

Still no word, just hard, fast walking and hands thrust deep in jacket pockets.

"Call my agent in America! Call my publishers here in Sydney! Ask them if I'm the sort of idiot who would waste your time!"

At Ward Avenue he stopped and turned to me. Surprisingly, he wasn't scowling, but was wearing a thoughtful expression.

"You're not an idiot, Howard. Nor am I. I have no idea what was going through the mind of that woman just now, but I can recognise prevarication when I see it. The thing is, what the hell do you expect me to do? Apply for a search warrant so I can poke through her Cadbury's ice-cream with a wooden paddle for body parts? I'd be the laughing stock not only of my own station but the entire police force. And I doubt very much if I'd be granted such a warrant merely on your hearsay. So… " He held out his arms in a hopeless gesture.

"So the ball's back in my court, eh? Whether or not Peter Reid hangs on to the rest of his fingers and toes — not to mention any softer tissue — is up to Sainte-Claire? Terrific!"

Chase then gave me a strange look and put a hand on my shoulder.

"Hey, listen to me carefully. Your name is Howard. H-O-W-A-R-D. It is *not* Sainte-Claire. You write *comic books*."

"Graphic novels."

"Whatever. Fiction about some kind of a superman or super-sleuth named Sainte-Claire. That man does not actually *exist*. He is not *you*. Am I getting through?"

"Did I call myself Sainte-Claire again?" I said, wearily.

"You did, yes. And if I were you, I'd be worried. I'd actually think very seriously about leaving the Reids to their problems and concentrating on my own, because a shrink might be a real help to you just now."

"You think I'm crazy?" It was a genuine question.

"No, I don't," he replied in the tone a father might adopt when talking to his teenage kid about love problems, "But I think it's time you took a look at yourself and calmed down."

"What about the Reid children?"

"Look, I've taken on board everything you've told me. I believe you when you say you found a finger in the dessert. I think maybe you're right and that Peter Reid's in real trouble. So I'm going to get back to my desk and see what I can come up with to help him.

Meantime, you go home and keep out of trouble. No more fighting. No sidekicks harrying people to death on the roads. Just a stiff drink and bed rest." He paused and grinned. "How does that sound?"

"Not bad."

Chase winked in a friendly manner and walked on, leaving me a solitary figure on a street corner.

30

Normally a stiff drink would have been the right ticket to nirvana, but not that night. The love of my life had left me because of all this nonsense, and that seemed a bit unfair since all I'd been doing was simply trying to help a family in trouble. Whatever sense Chase had talked, it remained a fact that no-one was about to help Ms Tiggy-Winkle and Ms Ally-Oop. Not until something dreadful happened to one or both of their parents and DOCS took them into care. If I got stuck into the bourbon, who was going to make sure the little tykes slept safely?

I was about to walk back home when I felt a hand on my shoulder.

I was so taken by surprise I instantly pivoted on the ball of my right foot, ducked down, swung around and rugby tackled the figure standing behind me. A microsecond later a soft warm body was spreadeagled on the pavement and I was lying on top of it.

It was Lucy.

"Jesus. I... can't... breeeeeathe." Her words came in a series of gasps.

I rolled off her.

Two young female Japanese tourists had appeared out of nowhere and were standing across the street. They held their hands to their mouths and ran up to Bayswater Road. I prayed they wouldn't report the matter to the police.

Lucy stood and brushed herself down — unhurt, merely winded.

"I have to talk to you, Robert, apologise for making you look so silly just now. When you've heard what I have to say, you'll understand. I hope. What do you say we have a bite to eat at the Bayswater Brasserie?"

Personally, I still had visions of severed fingers. With the mention of dinner I saw them in aspic. I wasn't too hungry.

"Please. Don't give up on Tiggs and Alice quite yet."

"That was a low blow and you know it."

She cast her eyes down, then back up. She was pleading.

I debated whether to ring Jez. Then thought better of it. Best to let her cool down overnight.

The restaurant was as full as ever. Like most sensible establishments, they keep a table in case a celebrity such as Keanu Reeves or Elton John walks in with a bunch of people and wants to eat right then and there. It happens all the time now that the American film industry has set up shop in Fox Studios.

Fortunately I eat there a lot and they know me. The maître d' sat us at a quiet table at the back. Just as well — I didn't want anyone to overhear what we were about to discuss.

Lucy picked up the menu and studied it for an inordinately long time. I could only think she was dreading the forthcoming conversation and the grovelling apology she'd have to offer me. Either that or she was capable of dispelling thoughts of iced body parts as soon as a delicious dinner presented itself.

She settled on confit of duck with figs, and I ordered vichyssoise — at least I knew there'd be no human tissue swimming around in it. I also ordered a bottle of Ciccone Scarlato and a big bottle of Perrier.

"Okay. Shoot," I said when the waiter had filled our glasses. "You made me look really dumb just now and I hate that. I'm sure there's a great reason to explain your silence with Chase, so let me in on the big secret. First of all, I trust the finger hasn't been munched down the insinkerator?"

"Absolutely not."

"It is Peter's?"

"Charlie says it's familiar. But when you think about it, would you be able to pick your girlfriend's pinkie?"

"Without a doubt."

A look of annoyance crossed her face. "Shouldn't have used her as an example. Ten centimetre manicured chocolate — you got me there. More to the point though, could she pick yours?"

"My finger? I'd like to hope so." I smiled. She didn't. I felt ashamed.

"Either way, it's back on ice. In a more sensible place, inside a jar marked 'Face Mask'."

"Less likely to be eaten by the children."

She placed a hand on my arm across the table. "Let's get right to the point."

"I wish you would."

"Charlie says they've promised they'll kill Peter if the police are involved. She says that had you not intervened in the first place she could have paid off her brother-in-law and his hired muscle and Peter would most probably still have ten digits."

"There's gratitude for you," I said. I felt extremely hard done by.

"She knows you were only trying to help, but she's so frustrated that you're not getting the message."

"So she knows where Peter is?"

"Not any more. She did early on, but when you came knocking on their door in Ferrier Street they moved him. And chopped off his finger to prove a point."

"Which was?"

"That chopping off body parts comes easily to them. The rest is obvious."

"Is Sammy behind this?"

"Yes."

"Great uncle for the kids. Great brother. Great human being all round."

"He's never gone this far before. This time he's out of control. He can't stop the roadtrain, it's in gear and rolling down an incline."

"Who's at the wheel?"

"A man called Jimmy Chin."

"What do we know about Jimmy Chin? How old is he?"

"Forty-something. Charlie's met him. He sent his right-hand man, a guy called Tri, and a pal of his around the night Tiggs called you. Sammy had told him that he could repay a big debt he owed Chin. Chin asked how he was going to manage that, and he boasted that his brother had come into some money and that he'd have it soon. He didn't mention Lotto at that time."

"How did Chin find out about the Lotto win then?"

"He spiked Sammy's drink with some drug or other the night he mentioned the money. Rohypnol, maybe."

"No, that'd sedate him. Bring on amnesia if anything."

"Well, whatever. Sammy was pissed as usual anyway, and after enough drinks and drugs he started to blab. That's when Tri put a machete to his throat—"

"Hey, how do we know this?" I cut in.

"Sammy told Charlie the night they grabbed her, when Chin was in another room."

"Chin left them alone? No guards?"

"Sammy organised the snatch, so why wouldn't Chin trust him at that stage? Sammy just said he'd get the best results from Charlie if he could persuade her alone."

"Where was Peter?"

"Peter actually *was* at a card game."

"What else did Sammy tell Charlie — in private, that is?"

"That Tri had threatened to cut his throat if he was lying about being able to come up with the money he owed Chin — that's when Sammy had broken down and told him he was talking millions, not just the fifty thousand he owed the Vietnamese. He'd told Chin it was all there for the taking — all they had to do was grab Charlie, call Peter and tell him to cash the Lotto cheque, put half the proceeds into a suitcase and bring it round. Sammy told Charlie he'd only gone along with the idea when they promised not to hurt anyone. So if she played ball all would be well."

"Great guy. Making sure everyone was okay, huh?"

"So they snatched Charlie, and while they were at Roslyn Street they looked around for a ticket, a cheque or whatever."

"Surely they didn't expect her to have cashed the money already?"

"They're stupid. They were checking just in case there *was* a cheque already — one they could get Peter to countersign."

"That would never have worked. Those Lotto people aren't dumb."

"So they made Charlie call Peter on his mobile and Peter rushed round to see her in Ferrier Street. He and Sammy persuaded Chin to let Charlie go. After all, they had Peter instead. There was the question of leaving the children alone — Charlie had heard Tiggs wake and call after her when she left. She was desperately worried for them both."

"So they swapped hostages?"

"That's right. She and Peter agreed that they'd give Chin half the money in cash provided no one was hurt."

"Six million sounds good to me."

"It sounded good to everyone. Plenty to go round."

"So what went wrong?" I had a bad feeling I knew what the answer to that one was.

"You did."

Right.

"You arrived at Ferrier Street, acting all tough, and Chin, Tri and Sammy were worried you'd tell the cops and they'd be arrested for extortion. So they hit you and bolted."

"What about Brierley? Is he involved?"

"He was initially. Sammy owed him money he'd borrowed for bets. Peter owed him money too — he'd borrowed quite a bit to pay for that damned horse. Sammy had suggested PIC for a loan as a favour to Brierley."

She hesitated. "But this is the bad bit."

"You mean the story gets worse?"

"Yes. Chin was so angry at having to find a new place to stash Peter, and angry that you'd been disrespectful of Tri and Madonna outside Roslyn Street."

"Face," I murmured.

"What was that?"

"Nothing. Carry on."

"He was so angry that he thought he'd send a message to Charlie."

"The finger?"

"The finger. Chin was nervous that Charlie would tell you all the details, and that you'd persuade her to call in the police and he'd be busted. So he told Tri to burn the car and chop off one of Peter's pinkies."

It certainly explained why Charlie so adamantly insisted Peter was fine and would be back home soon.

"Who was the girl, Tammi?"

"This is where it gets really bad," she said.

The main courses came at that precise moment. The smell of food right then made me want to heave.

"Who's Tammi?" I repeated.

"Chin's daughter."

"Her name was Thurong."

"So's Jimmy's. Chin's a nickname, because he doesn't have one."

"Shit. That *is* bad. Six million or no six million."

"She was supposed to go with Charlie to pick up the Lotto cheque and bring it back for Peter to countersign. But the Lotto people said they were organising an electronic payment, which would go through exactly two weeks after the date of the win."

"Why did Charlie have to go to Homebush anyway?"

"She had to sign some papers at the Lotteries Office."

"Wait a second — when did she tell you all this? Or have you known all this the whole way through?"

"She only just told me all this stuff."

"Okay. So, there was no cheque for Tammi."

"Right. Tammi was angry because her father had told her not to come back without it, and she thought Charlie was double-crossing her dad."

"So she snatched the handbag."

I was processing all the pieces of the jigsaw as fast as I could.

"So what does Charlie intend to do now?"

"She's terrified that Chin will really hurt Peter, despite the money. She thinks because he's Asian, he'll feel bound to take revenge on Peter because of Tammi's death."

Or maybe he'd think about targeting Peter's children — an eye for an eye. The thought made my spine crawl.

"So she called him on his mobile—"

"Who called who?"

"Charlie called Sammy."

"She has Sammy's *mobile* phone number?" I was incredulous.

"That's right."

"And what did Sammy say?"

"This is the worst bit," she replied, refilling our glasses. I held a hand over mine.

"There's worse? Are you sure we should be sitting here right now doing absolutely nothing while deranged criminals are thinking of chopping more body parts off Tiggs and Alice's father? And possibly sending someone round to hurt Tiggs and Ally themselves, for revenge? What are we? Monsters?"

I was getting pretty deranged myself. Angry that Charlie and Lucy could have let things progress this far.

"Please, Robert. Just listen to me. Another five minutes."

"Ten, tops."

"When Charlie spoke to Sammy, he was in a bad state."

"Drinking?"

"No, he'd been beaten up pretty badly by Tri. Chin told him to work Sammy over, because Sammy had screwed up badly, and now his own daughter was dead. Sammy told him that it wasn't his fault the girl couldn't ride a bike. That was what drove the old guy mad. Lucky to be alive, really."

"So they haven't taken the machete to Peter again?"

"Sammy said no. But he whispered on the phone that he plans to drop Chin 'in the shit', as he put it, by sneaking out during the night and asking Tim Brierley to help him."

My heart sank. Stupid was stupid, but this new thought of Sammy's was bordering on the lunatic.

"He's thinking of telling Tim Brierley that Peter has won twelve mil on Lotto?"

"He thinks he's going to do a deal. First up, he's going to say Peter won four million. Then the agreement will be that if Brierley sends a team round to rescue Peter and fix Chin and Tri, he'll give him half."

"Two million?"

"Right."

"That'll save him four mil. Doesn't matter that the chances are Chin will chop them both up and make them into dumplings — he'll have saved himself four million dollars. Jesus H!"

I pushed my food away from me and considered the options. Not much came to mind. As my eyes flicked randomly from point to point I noticed that the woman at the next table was just getting her food — an Indian curry with okra. Otherwise known as 'Ladies Fingers.'

I excused myself and made for the men's room, where I threw up.

When I returned from the bathroom Lucy was making short work of the duck, removing the last morsels of flesh from the carcass. They breed them tough in Sydney — I was the exception that proved the rule.

As I sat, a waiter passed by. "Anything wrong with the soup, Mr Howard? Too hot?"

Always the joker.

"No, the Vichyssoise is fine. I've just got a lot on my mind and I can't think about food right now."

"Give me a shout if there's anything I can get you."

I said I would.

"So, what does Charlie want us to do?" I asked Lucy. "Sit around and wait for Brierley and Chin to go to war, and hope that Peter makes it out of there with his testicles intact?"

The woman eating the okra gave me a nasty look — maybe I was talking too loudly.

"She thinks that's best for Peter, herself and Sammy."

"Screw Sammy," I said.

The Okra-Lady looked me in the eye. "Can you please watch your language. This is a public place."

Her husband pretended not to be a part of it.

I held up my hands. "I'm truly sorry, madam," I said. "I'm under a lot of pressure."

As she looked away, my mobile rang. This was the last straw. "The man's got absolutely no manners," she said loudly. "Writes well, but a yahoo at heart."

One of my now ex-readers.

The call was from Ben.

"I found out something interesting."

"That Tammi was Jimmy Chin's daughter?"

A pause told me he was impressed — not that I was in the mood right then to try to impress anyone.

"You know who she is, and that she's dead. Right?"

"Yup."

"Jimmy's chin was cut pretty bad in a fight way back in Saigon, before he got here. Hence the nickname. I never knew him as Thurong. Sorry."

"Don't worry. How dangerous is the man?"

"As dangerous as they come. He was one of the Cabramatta originals. Ran the place with one other guy. He only backed off when he realised his own people were becoming junkies and he didn't want his baby Tammi to get the habit. So he went into selling electrical goods. Made just as much. Stores all over Sydney and Newcastle."

"Look, I can't talk right now. Can I call you in fifteen minutes?"

"Sure."

I flipped the handset shut.

"I've got to go," I told Lucy. "Do you have Sammy's mobile number with you?"

I could see her debating whether to be truthful. Then she dipped a hand into her bag and withdrew a scrap of paper. On it was scribbled a number. I took it from her.

Her hand attached itself to my arm. Lucy was stronger than she looked. "Please, *please*, leave it alone now."

My tone was controlled, even though mentally I was screaming. "Lucy," I began, "I *will* think very seriously before I do anything. Believe that. I have Peter's interest at heart. Primarily because I think his daughters are the cutest pair of munchkins I've ever come across. I don't want to see them in a single-parent situation, or orphaned. But whereas *you* may be able to live with the thought that you acted the ostrich when push came to shove, I'm not like that. Thanks to my altruistic involvement with the Reid family, I've probably lost my girlfriend, my mind, my personal identity and at least one solid reader. Plus, I might mention that my career is hanging by a thread and detectives in at least three Sydney police stations think I'm a dangerous nuisance who should be locked up before I kill someone."

Phew! I took a breath.

To give her her due, Lucy had stopped eating for the first time in twenty minutes and was actually listening. Her grasp on my arm was nevertheless vice-tight.

"Don't go after Peter. If Chin or Tri see you, they'll hurt Peter. They may even kill him."

"I'll take that, as I say in my books, under advisement."

I got up to leave. Lucy rose with me.

"No need for you to leave right now," I said. "Finish the wine. Have a pudding. A sticky botrytis, maybe."

Her eyes narrowed. "There's no need to insult me. I'm doing what I can too. Don't think you're the only white knight around here. Who do you think is looking after the children?"

"I'm not trying to insult you — that just came out all wrong. Sorry."

She relaxed a bit. "Okay."

"Just make sure you're around the kids all the time. Don't let them walk home from school alone. Any sign of trouble — people you don't know at the door — call the police. At least we'll know Ally and Tiggs are okay."

"Sure thing, Sainte-Claire," she said with a hint of a grin.

I smiled back. She wasn't so bad.

"Dames," I said, and shrugged.

31

In the street, I called the number Lucy had just given me. I had no idea what I would say, but somehow I had to stop the madness.

I listened to the beginning of the Telstra message: *Your call could not be connected. Please check the number and call—*. I disconnected, then called Ben. He picked up instantly.

"Ben, there's been a development. Turns out Charlie's been in contact with Sammy and the guy's gone totally nuts."

"Why?"

"Longish story. Ends up with Chin telling Tri to teach Sammy a lesson. So guess what Sammy has in mind?"

"Go to the cops?"

"Nah. Ask Brierley in as his protector."

"Christ." Pause. "How much is he offering?"

"Two mil."

I heard Ben exhale. "Peter won quite a bit, eh?"

"He did indeed. But as soon as Brierley knows Chin's involved and where Peter is, he's going to want more moolah. And even if Brierley thinks Sammy's being upfront, he'll want to go get Peter right away."

"And if Chin sees him coming, he'll kill Peter."

"Maybe. But maybe he'll just let him go." I thought out aloud. "Why kill him if there's nothing to be gained? He'd be hunted by the cops for a murder rather than walking away from a kidnapping and extortion."

It was a real point to be considered. If I were Chin, and Sammy was about to change sides, I'd be moving my hostage around so no one could bust him free, not killing him. Unless the loss of my daughter had scrambled my brains.

"Does Chin know Sammy's planning to change sides and cut in Brierley?" Ben asked.

"How would he?"

"Sammy acting strangely. Chin might suspect sabotage."

"That one I'm not sure about. Debatable."

"Has Sammy met up with Brierley yet?"

"Don't know. I'm on my way down Macleay Street right now."

"He won't be there. He'll be at home — unless he's out on the town. But I'd say he'd do business at home if Sammy called him on his mobile. He wouldn't want anyone to see him with a lowlife loser like Sammy."

"Where's his home?"

"No idea. But I can make a call to Kings Cross and ask a mate of mine. He'll know. I'll call you back."

He rang off.

By this time I'd reached Challis Avenue and was looking across at the offices of PIC. The place was in darkness. Not much point in ringing the doorbell.

I'd waited less than a minute when Ben called me back.

"Brierley's got a house on Wentworth Road, Vaucluse. On the right side of the road — money-wise, not geographically. So that's the left side, travelling east. Think major Tuscan. Iron gates with the signature B on both sides."

"Thanks. I may check it out right now. Might get lucky and come across Sammy — if that's where he's gone tonight."

"The security's pretty tight, I believe. Cameras on each corner, so don't think by simply failing to ring a bell he won't know you're out there."

"I'll bear that in mind. Thanks for the help."

"Well, the way I see it, I've got two jobs tonight. Except I have to stick around here. You get my meaning?"

"I'm with you, Ben. You're back on the payroll."

"Nice to be able to help. You get into any serious bother, you call me, mate."

"Will do. Bye."

It took me about four minutes to jog back to the Sainte-Claire-mobile. The bats had crapped all over the bonnet. What can I tell you

— it was bat-crap season and first choice for 'hanging out' if you're a bat was the hackberry tree in my garden.

Giblet came to greet me, looking after her end of the street as usual. She didn't follow me in, so presumably she was still pigged out from when I was home before.

There were no messages on the landline. I hadn't expected any. I knew Jez would call me on my mobile, if she called me at all.

The house was very quiet. Something deep within was telling me I had to do something radical. It was as if a guiding spirit was telling me to follow my instincts and not hold back, that there was something to be done that night and only I could do it. The worrying thing was, the guide was talking to Sainte-Claire, not Robert Howard.

I changed. Black suit, black T, black steel-capped boots.

Then I gelled up.

Five minutes later I was driving through Double Bay on my way to the Brierley manse.

I'd almost forgotten how angry I was with the man — now I was refreshed with new venom. He'd desecrated a year's work that constituted Jez's heart and soul. Brierley was responsible, unless Tutuelo had asked a pal of his to do the job for him, but that kind of phone call from the lock-up would be a problem.

As for endangering Peter, I wasn't doing anything Chin could take exception to, because he wouldn't know I was going to see Brierley. So there was no way Lucy and Charlie could accuse me of upsetting the apple cart.

The lights of the harbour twinkled to my left as I headed up the hill past Kambala School and took a left down Vaucluse Road. The sight of the Bridge and the Opera House at night never fails to warm the heart of a Sydneysider.

There was nothing on the road as my Citroën snaked round to the right by Nielsen Park to Wentworth Street. How many times had I parked down here and gone swimming at Shark Bay? Little had I known then that I'd be here on a very different mission years down the line — one that could cost the life of my new employer's father.

Brierley's house was about six up beyond Coolong Road. The signature 'B' wrought-iron gates were unmistakable. I parked five car lengths up the road, facing the way I'd come, and took a good look at the perimeter walls of the house.

The twin gates of the front were electronic. Opening inwards. Above the gates and at each end of the rendered walls, which stood about three metres tall, were discreet black-box video cameras that would take in anything that moved up to ten metres before it made it onto the frontage. On steel pillars each side of the gates were floodlights, directed downwards so as not to keep everyone in the street awake all night. The only other way into this compound would be via the water at the back of the house, and I was certain the water's edge would be monitored equally well.

Sainte-Claire would have known instinctively how to handle things. He'd probably have found some way to break in and confront Brierley before he had the opportunity to call his bodyguards. He'd have used some state-of-the-art technical equipment.

As a writer, I always spent a lot of time researching what was new on the spy market. A firm in London called *Spy-Catcher* usually kept me abreast of surveillance equipment and phone-tapping hardware. Right then, I wished I could lay my hands on a telephone-tapping device that intercepted calls within a certain radius, so I'd know if Sammy called Brierley from a phone box.

I'd been wondering what to do for about six minutes when a Bentley cruised down the street towards me and the gates purred open in answer to some infrared entry device. There was just one man in the car, the driver.

Brierley was coming home. I hoped it was to meet with Uncle Sammy.

32

It was a long shot to expect Sammy to show up that night, I knew that. Sammy and Brierley could have met already. They could have talked on the phone. But it had been worth a try. I'd had so much bad luck I was due a lucky break. And Sainte-Claire got breaks like that all the time.

Five minutes after the gates had purred shut behind Brierley's Bentley, I saw a dark figure walking furtively down the street towards the house. I couldn't make out the man's face since I was some distance away, but his appearance screamed burglar. Maybe a drunk. Perhaps both.

I tried to conjure up the smiling face Tiggs had emailed me — the photo of Sammy standing next to Faithful Hope. I waited for the figure to stagger into the light at the gates.

As he walked he angled his head deliberately towards the wall. When he reached the entry console he stood with his back to me, glancing every few seconds to his left and right up and down the street. It wasn't enough for me to be able to make out his features clearly. He kept pushing the entry button like an idiot at a pedestrian crossing, thinking the more you pressed it the quicker the lights would change.

Eventually he spoke into the entryphone. I couldn't hear the conversation of course, but I could tell he was talking to someone because he was leaning in closely.

The gates purred open.

Just prior to squeezing through the opening, Sammy took one last furtive look down the street and across the road. This time I saw his face clearly and realised why he'd been staggering. He'd been beaten up badly — one eye was practically closed and his lip was ballooned at one side. He was also holding his side, as though injured there too. Well done, Chin. He'd done himself a big favour smacking Sammy — it had sent him running straight to Brierley to do an alternative deal.

I rang Ben.

"Don't try to bust in," was his immediate advice.

"Wasn't about to," I replied. "I'd say my best bet is to follow Sammy when he comes out. He has to lead me to Peter. I just hope they don't decide to do the biz tonight with some of Brierley's hired muscle."

"These things take time. Welcome to the real world, Sainte-Claire. You can't rustle up a squad of goons in twenty minutes and expect them to go to war. This isn't the fifties, thank God. Or Capone's Chicago. My guess is that he'll listen to what Sammy's got to say, then plan something for tomorrow or even the weekend."

"Let's hope so."

"Where are you parked?"

"Down the street a bit."

"Did Sammy make you on the way in?"

"No, I ducked down."

"How did he get there?"

I hadn't seen. But unless he'd taken a bus, he'd probably parked his car up the road.

"Tailing him isn't going to be easy and I can't help you this time. See if you can spot the car he's using while you're waiting for him to come out. Then find a way to get in front of him till you get to Edgecliff. That way you can keep an eye on him in the mirror and he won't see you following him. He won't turn left or right till at least Edgecliff. Then you can let him pass and follow from behind."

I did as Ben advised. I walked in the direction Sammy had come, but found no warm bonnets or ticking engines. So I backtracked to the car and drove it past Brierley's and reversed into Coolong Road.

It was a quiet night. The air didn't smell of wisteria, nor was there any faint chatter of exotic Aussie night birds. Like the last time, the air was cold, silent and smelled of privileged tomcats.

I looked at my watch. I'd been waiting about fifteen minutes when I saw Sammy exit the house. His gait was a lot steadier this time. Or maybe he'd had a few black coffees. Or a line of cocaine. Maybe just some strong painkillers. He was carrying a black canvas sports bag about thirty centimetres long. What had Brierley given Sammy? An Uzi sub-machine gun to protect himself? That would have fitted snugly in the bag. A down payment of readies? A cut lunch for the following day? A family pack of Nurofen?

He opened the door of a white Astina and got in. I fired up the Sainte-Claire-mobile and waited for him to move off. He was about fifty metres down the road, facing me. As soon as I saw the car move I eased out in front of him.

When I turned into New South Head Road I saw him turn right behind me. I measured his speed and made sure to keep ahead. He didn't seem to be in a rush. I hoped the police wouldn't stop him for DUI — he was driving erratically to say the least.

As I passed the Edgecliff Centre I let a few cars overtake me, including the Astina. I was aching to look across at Sammy and see what expression I could detect — triumph, worry or despair — but I didn't want him to have my face in his memory bank. So all I saw was the back of his head, his body slumped forward over the wheel.

Considering the day I'd had, I didn't feel tired at all. Quite the reverse. I was experiencing the kind of exhilaration I remembered from when I was a child and played cowboys and Indians with the kids next door. Would they find me? Would there be a shoot-out in the OK Corral? It was quite surreal. I *wasn't* a kid; I was an adult. I wasn't playing a game; I was dealing with human lives. There might well be a shoot-out somewhere, but it wasn't going to be with forefingers and thumbs.

Why was I so pumped? Was I completely losing touch with reality? I knew I should be concentrating on Sammy's Astina rather than going through this self-analysis, so I wiped all thoughts of schizophrenia from my mind.

Sure enough, Sammy moved into the turn-right lane at Bourke Street. Looked like he was going to use the Eastern Distributor for a while then cut through Sydenham to Cabramatta. I followed him into the tunnel towards the airport. I was about three cars back, trying to get one space closer. There was a lot of traffic, so I was pretty certain he wouldn't spot me.

I dialled Ben. Something was bugging me. He answered before the second ring.

"Ben, I've picked up Sammy and we're on Southern Cross Drive. The thing is, I was expecting him to head off right towards Cabramatta but he's heading south. Any ideas?"

"The airport?"

That was the most obvious answer.

"Why the airport? He's not going anywhere until he's done the deal with Brierley and the cheque's been cashed."

"Any idea what happened at Brierley's place?"

"No. I stayed outside. But Sammy's now carrying a holdall."

"Maybe Brierley gave him a down payment and he's looking to stash it someplace?"

As the airport turn-off came into sight a black Audi came up fast behind me and then overtook, taking up a position between me and the car immediately behind Sammy's Astina. Even passing at speed, the figure in the passenger seat of the Audi was unmistakable. Tutuelo. He was wearing a neck brace and he looked mean.

Closer to the airport there was a good deal of traffic. It was all bunched up, making it difficult for me to change lanes so I could keep sight of both the Audi and the Astina. I eventually concluded that if I followed the big guy, he'd lead to Sammy.

The Audi went straight ahead when given the option of domestic departures to the left. Curiouser and curiouser. Was Sammy meeting someone off a flight? There weren't many left before the airport night curfew.

The Audi turned into the car park and stopped abruptly. The driver remained in the car; three other men, of whom I recognised only Tutuelo, got out and started running between the parked cars.

I couldn't see the Astina anywhere. Maybe Sammy had seen the Audi in his rear-view mirror and panicked. But why? It didn't make any sense. If he'd just made a deal with Brierley, why would he fear the man's henchmen?

Either way, I wasn't going to get far by staying in my own car and waiting for them to come back to tell me. So I parked a few car lengths back and jogged parallel to the course I judged the goons would be taking. Quite soon I was in one of the more remote areas of the car park where there wasn't so much light. The fact that one of the big overhead fluoros was on the blink only added to the problem.

Two minutes later I didn't know where I was at all in relation to my car nor Tutuelo and his companions. Nor Sammy for that matter.

Last time I'd seen the bad guys they'd been heading back towards the departures building. There was no point in running around like a startled rabbit with no destination in mind — there was every chance I'd run into the guns. So I halted. Should I go directly to departures and see who showed up there? Seemed the best idea. I headed off at a fast jog.

The moment I entered the building I looked up at the board. There were only two flights still scheduled for departure that night. One was an Emirates flight to the Middle East, the other a Thai flight to Singapore.

I approached the first-class check-in desk for the Emirates flight.

"Can I help you, sir?" the girl asked.

"I'm afraid I've just left my briefcase downstairs. I hope it hasn't been lost. The name's Reid. Sam Reid."

I was hoping she'd react automatically and start punching in my name. I was right. She looked up at me. "I'm afraid I don't see a listing under Reid. It is spelled EI?"

"Don't worry, I'll be back in a minute. Thanks," I replied and headed off for the Thai check-in. There, I gave them the same spiel.

"Yes, Mr Reid, but you're really pushing the envelope time-wise. Strictly speaking you should be checking in next door — this is supposed to be purely for first-class passengers. It's past the last call and I shouldn't be checking you in at all really, but since you don't have any luggage—"

"I'll just fetch my briefcase," I said. "Must have left it in the bar. Won't be a minute."

The check-in girl looked at me as though I was a complete imbecile. I walked slowly away.

So Sammy had been thinking about skipping the country. Most likely he was intending to take a fat wad of Brierley's money in his tucker-bag with him. Better a bird in the hand, eh? Typical loser mentality. Of course, he hadn't reckoned on Brierley's lack of faith in him. A man such as Brierley never took it for granted that people were going to do as they said. He wasn't going to bank on it anyway — not if he'd just given that person a whole heap of money on account. So he'd sent Tutuelo and co after Sammy to make sure he went the right way — back to Cabramatta, not the nearest airport.

What a dickhead Sammy was. No lateral thinking whatsoever.

I watched the Thai Airways desk till it closed down and the staff disappeared. Then the flight itself disappeared from the overhead screens. The airport would soon be silent.

I walked back to the car park and took a look around. At first I couldn't see any movement at all. Then I saw a car heading slowly towards the exit. It was black.

I jogged across the car park, cutting the corner to where I knew the black car would eventually emerge after paying the ticket. I didn't make it very far. Halfway across the car park I saw someone lying between two cars in the near darkness twenty metres ahead of me. My heart sank as I got closer.

It was Sammy. His legs were twisted under him and his good eye was staring up at the last flight to Dubai as it screamed overhead. But neither the eye nor Sammy's brain were registering anything. His damaged eye was now completely closed. His head was lying in a pool of blood that was expanding at a rate of approximately a centimetre every two seconds.

Bye-bye Sammy.

33

Half an hour later I was being interviewed at the Mascot Police Station by a detective named Gillian Hannah. She was by far the smartest of the police I'd dealt with so far. Apparently there's a good deal of interchange of information between the various stations, so she'd heard of my run-in with Tutuelo and the break-in at Jez's studio. There was a decent-sized file on me, she informed me with a smile.

"Seems you're getting a bit accident-prone, Mr Howard."

"Looks that way," I replied.

There was simply no way I could now hide anything from the police. Murder was murder, after all. And although I knew Lucy and Charlie were desperate to pay off Chin or Brierley, or both, and be done with it, Sammy was now dead. I couldn't withhold evidence. Even if I did, Brierley had seen fit to tell his muscle to kill Sammy because he'd tried to do a bunk with his money. Why would he care whether or not Peter was killed when they busted into Chin's hideout? I needed police help right then.

"So you last saw Samuel Reid driving his car to the airport? After he'd left Mr. Brierley's residence in Vaucluse?"

"That's right."

"And you saw Tutuelo, together with three other men, as they passed you in the Audi?"

"That's right."

"Did you see Tutuelo in the car park?"

"I saw him get out of the car with his buddies. The driver stayed in the car."

"After that? Did you see Tutuelo again?"

"No, I didn't. I went into the departures building. When the place closed down I came back out to the car park. I could just make out the Audi leaving."

"Then you came across Mr Reid's body?"

"Correct."

"Did you see anyone else in the car park either before or after you went into the departures building?"

"No."

She made some notes.

"It's late, Mr Howard. I'll let you get some sleep. I have your statement, so I doubt we'll need to see you tomorrow. We may call you if there's anything we've forgotten."

I thanked her for her patience. She could easily have had a go at me. After all, I'd been at it again, acting the dumb private dick, staking out the bad guys, tailing people in cars, acting without much responsibility. I'd made all the wrong decisions, all the wrong choices. Yet she hadn't chastened me by suggesting I should have called for police help the moment I'd seen Tutuelo and his pals roar by after Sammy. I should have, and I knew it.

I was once more deeply ashamed.

Rather than wait for the police to telephone Charlie in the middle of the night to inform her of the death of her brother-in-law, I called Lucy's mobile. A very sleepy voice croaked at the other end of the line. It was the wee small hours of the morning.

"Who's this?"

"It's Robert Howard. I'm afraid I have bad news. I thought you ought to know before the police call Charlie."

"Oh, no. What's happened?"

"Sammy has been found dead. Someone struck him on the head." The words sounded softer than 'murder' or 'killed'.

"My God." I could hear her breathing in the hiatus that followed. "No one has called here yet."

"They will, any time. Because as far as the authorities are concerned, Peter hasn't been abducted at all. They'll call as a matter of course to inform the next of kin."

"And ask someone to come and identify the body I expect."

"That's right. Charlie's going to have to know — we can't keep it from her. Of course, the moment she knows Sammy's dead she's going to fall out of her tree entirely. We have to keep her focused on dealing with the problem."

"How do you see us doing that?"

"We pay the ransom and then let the cops catch the criminals."

"Are the police going to stand by and let us?"

"I doubt they're going to stand by, but they might let us. You'd better monitor the phone. If the police ring, take the call yourself, then tell Charlie in your own words. Tell them she's under sedation."

"Thanks, Robert. We can't thank you enough. I mean that."

"I couldn't have done otherwise. Take care."

Next was a quick call to Ben. I told him what had happened. He said he'd been afraid to call in case I'd forgotten to turn off my mobile and it caused a problem. He was shocked to hear about Sammy's murder.

"Is there any way you can access Turgut; see if they're keeping a watch out for Chin and Tri? We can't afford to miss them if they decide to move Peter."

"I'll call him right now. They're a very cooperative bunch down there. They'll do all they can. By the way, maybe it's not the time for levity, but when I was a cop we always tried to take the piss a bit when the going got tough — it was the only way we could cope emotionally, I suppose."

"You about to take the piss out of me?"

"Sure. You know what the detectives call you at Kings Cross?"

I waited.

"Sainte-Klutz."

I had to admit, the nickname had merit.

"And at Surry Hills?"

"Surprise me."

"Devil-May-Claire."

I chuckled dutifully, didn't want to be a spoilsport.

"Call me if you hear anything, okay?"

"Sure."

I couldn't stop thinking of Jez. I had no idea whether she'd ever speak to me again. After all, she'd phoned me as I was rushing round to the Reids' place, trying to bring us back together, to call me back to sanity. Yet I'd turned her away because I was still obsessed with my alter ego. I could fool myself into believing that I'd done it all for the kids — and of course, it was true to a certain extent — but basically I'd been drawn once again to the drama of my graphic novels.

I lay on my bed in the darkness wanting desperately to call her but dreading another rejection.

An hour later I couldn't stand the loneliness any longer. I rang her landline. There's a switch on her phone that allows her to turn off the ringer, yet the machine is still able to take messages. I left one.

"I'm so very sorry for last night. I just *had* to help Lucy — she was desperate. The kids needed my help. You'd have done the same — I know it." I couldn't think of anything else to say — I was hardly going to mention that Sammy was dead. "I love you more than I can say."

A minute later my home phone rang. I picked up.

"It's me," Jez said.

"Hello." I was pretty much tongue-tied.

"Question is, who are *you*?" she asked.

It was a test.

"Robert?" she prompted.

"Yes. Robert Howard."

"Good. I'll talk to him."

"Jez, I think I need help."

"My help?"

"Yours — and a psychiatrist's."

"Don't be so dramatic," she replied. There was softness and sweetness in her voice. The warmth and caring I loved this woman for. She'd never walk away from me; in the darkest corners of my mind I felt sure of that then. But for one fleeting moment I'd been so very scared that she might.

"Would you like me to come round, Pulitzer?"

"I'd like that more than I can tell you," I replied.

Cats have an instinct, as do most animals, about human sensibilities. Giblet sensed my emotional confusion and panic. She'd been snuggled into the back of my legs as I lay on the bed.

When I put down the phone and felt that surge of relief that I was not alone, and the tears flowed, Giblet looked at me and knew she had to do something to show her love and understanding. She stood and padded up to my face and sat on my chest.

And purred.

34

"You don't even know the difference," Jez said as she held me in her arms in bed some short time later.

"Sure I do," I replied. "Neurosis is a personality illness, when you're aware that a problem is present. Psychosis is when you're *unaware*."

"And you *are* aware, Pulitzer?"

"Sure I am."

"Okay, tell me. What's the problem?"

"Well, it's a problem that really isn't one, in that I'm in control of it."

She made a face at me, then kissed me on the nose. We were entwined, face to face. "Then it's psychosis, sweet thing. Not neurosis. Fact is, you don't really think you *have* a problem."

"Oh, come on, Jez. I started dressing up as Sainte-Claire for a joke. For fun. To humour the kids. There was nothing more to it than that."

"But you got a buzz out of it, isn't that right?"

"It was fun, yes. I don't know about a buzz," I lied. I knew I'd got a buzz — but that had come later. With the violence. That was the fact that disturbed me most of all.

"Do you think women prefer Sainte-Claire to Robert Howard?" she asked me quietly after a few moments. "Tell the truth."

The remark was couched as a teasing question, but I knew she was serious. I tried my best to be frank.

"I guess I do, yes. I'd say that most women would find Sainte-Claire more attractive than me. He's more, how shall I say... dangerous?"

"You think women find dangerous men sexy?"

"I know at university most undergraduates preferred the wolves to the lambs."

"And you think of yourself as a lamb?"

"I'm a pacifist at heart, yes. You know me, I abhor violence."

"But Sainte-Claire's a very different type."

"Sure, he is."

It was true; I'd made him so. Deliberately.

"Has it ever occurred to you that you may be living out your fantasies — a wish fulfilment through your writing?"

"Oh, Jez." Her naïvety was almost childish. "All writers do. It's a *sine qua non* of being a creative animal. It's the same in every branch of the arts. Look at Arthur Boyd, Bosch, Dali, Greene, Kafka, Borges. But delving into the mind of a serial killer doesn't make me worry that there's a part of me that would harm anyone."

"How did you feel when you could hear the Islander's footsteps behind you and you expected at any moment that he might smash your head in?"

I thought about it. Adrenaline suddenly flooded through me, exactly as it had on the day. Just the memory was enough.

"I was apprehensive."

"Frightened?"

"Frightened? Strangely enough, no."

"Why was that, do you imagine?"

A good half-minute passed. Her searching questions required a great deal of thought. I didn't know the answers straightaway. And when they began to present themselves, I became unsettled.

"Because you were not, at that moment, yourself," she continued. "You were Sainte-Claire, and you felt secure in that personality. Secure enough to know that Tutuelo couldn't hurt you because you were invincible. Right?"

"It's possible," I conceded, but here I wasn't sure she *was* right. At the time I thought he might kill me with a single blow.

"And how did you feel when Tutuelo struck that young man?"

"Angry." I said the word without a second thought. There was no doubt there.

"Not revolted and sickened by the violence and the blood?"

"Yes," I protested. "Of *course* I was sickened by it."

"No, you just said your emotion was anger."

"I simply knew I had to save the young man from being killed."

"You felt that was likely?"

"Yes, I did."

"Or were you just angry that the big bully was taking it out on someone else?"

"No."

She was talking to me in very soothing tones, stroking my face with her lovely fingers. I was practically in a trance. The whole effect was like taking a polygraph — I had no option but to tell the truth, I felt so secure.

"When you hit Tutuelo and saw him fall, how did you feel looking down at him? Can you recall?"

"I felt... exhilarated. I felt... a sense of fulfilment." I searched for the words. "It was... a *wonderful* feeling."

I felt a clutch of despair in my chest. How was it possible that I could have felt wonderful at the exact moment I might have ended someone's life?

"I felt redeemed," I continued as I reflected deeply, almost to myself. "Worthy, warranted. Justice and good had triumphed. Against all the odds. I'd taken a risk and been rewarded."

"By whom?"

I didn't know. Certainly God didn't reward one side in a test of war, no matter how many armies over the millennia had prayed.

"Is the buzz you get out of the violence at all Freudian, do you think?"

"Sexual, you mean?"

"Possibly, yes."

"No. That I *can* tell you."

"Are we through being Sainte-Claire?"

"I think so," I replied.

"Is that affirmative?"

"Yes," I lied.

I couldn't sleep. If you'd watched hot blood pool around your feet you wouldn't be able to sleep either — the vision would haunt you.

I watched Jez drift off in my arms, then waited for her to find a sleeping position that wasn't using my torso as a bindweed would a honeysuckle. This took thirty minutes.

I walked to the French windows and stood looking out at the night. Barcom Avenue was quiet as the crypt of St Mary's Cathedral. I knew Giblet would be somewhere down the street, acting out her security detail — she'd left the bedroom to give Jez and me some 'quality time' alone.

Around the city, people would be calling each other dirty names, fighting, arguing; young kids were overdosing; women were being encouraged to sell their bodies for money; children were being neglected; the streets were littered with homeless people with little hope. By contrast I was in my quiet nest, with plenty of money in the bank, a beautiful woman asleep in my bed, and a film starring screen idols would soon be made of my fantasies. Sammy was lying in a morgue, a victim of his own greed. How much money had he wanted? Wasn't Peter going to give him a huge wad of money anyway? Wasn't that enough?

The truth was, things had moved very fast in a week. Events had reached a crisis point. Chin had raised the stakes by beating up Sammy, and Brierley had raised them still further by killing him. Now there were two separate criminal camps after the prize and neither would rest until they had Peter's money. All of it. And sandwiched between them were Peter, Charlie and those little girls.

What would be the next move? Now the police had picked Sammy off the airport car park concrete, they too were sitting at the poker table with Chin, Brierley and me. They were players. I wouldn't have said there was any question of the cops continuing to humour Charlie and her silly stories of everything being 'fine' and Peter being 'on holiday'. She had a rude shock coming to her.

I caught sight of Giblet snaking down the road between the cars. She was on a mission. She'd most likely spotted another street-moggie hangin' out on her turf and she had murder in her heart.

So did Brierley, most probably.

There were still so many unanswered questions. How much had Sammy confided in Brierley before he'd left with the bag of cash? Had there actually *been* any money in the bag? The latter was pretty certain — otherwise why would Sammy cut and run? The bag had never been found, which added to the certainty that Tutuelo had been told to pick up the money if Sammy looked as though he was thinking of legging it out of the country. Of course, the biggest question was whether Sammy had told Brierley where Peter was being held. If so, we were in trouble, because I didn't know where he was, and I didn't think Charlie did either. Chin had moved him from Ferrier Street, and I didn't think Sammy had told her where her husband was now.

I put myself in Chin's place. Sammy had pissed off in a huff after he'd been worked over. What might I expect? A double-cross? If so, I'd move Peter Reid pretty damned quick and start talking direct with Charlie, cutting Sammy out of the picture entirely. And as soon as word reached me that Sammy was dead, I'd move Peter double-quick.

So we were back to square one. Where was Peter Reid?

35

Saturday, 7.30 a.m. I was asleep. Jez was asleep. Giblet was asleep. Our bed was cosy and warm.

The phone rang on my side of the bed and I picked up.

"Robert? It's Lucy."

"Who else?"

Silence. I immediately felt guilty.

"I don't know who else to call. I'm sorry." I heard her speaking to someone her end, but couldn't make out the exact words. I could, however, make out the gist of it — she was telling the kids to go outside while she had a private conversation with me.

"That's better," she continued after a few seconds.

"What happened last night," I asked.

"The police called at six this morning. I sat by the phone in the living room with a blanket around me all night. I told them Charlie was on Valium and couldn't be wakened. They insisted she come to the phone; said they'd have to come round if she didn't answer personally. So I put her on."

"How did she take it?"

"She went bananas. She's a mess, I'm afraid. Did a good job on the phone at the time, though. She could never stand Sammy, but she thought he was the only thing keeping a lid on Chin. They told her they'd come round at nine. Can you possibly look after the kids? Take them out for McDonald's or something while the police interview Charlie?"

McDonald's? How little did she know Tiggs and Ally.

I told her to hold, then turned to Jez, who by this time was awake and listening, her ear glued to the back of the handset.

"How about brekkie with the kids?" I asked her. "The cops are —"

"I heard. The woman's audible across the room," she replied in a whisper.

"Want to come with me?"

"Sure, let's play mummies and daddies."

I gave the kids the McDonald's option, but Alice had informed Lucy and Charlie that there were no M Pinabos available there. Besides, the coffee was as 'weak as dogpee' — to quote Ally. Just for a change, Jez suggested the Tropicana. As Tiggs observed, a change was as good as a holiday. She loved her grown-up aphorisms.

We found a table almost next to the fire station. Ally was delighted when the siren went off within seconds of our arrival and the street was alive with action. When it had returned to normality she turned her attention to Jez.

"And where is your *real* home — Africa?" she asked.

Tiggs nudged her with her elbow. "Don't be rude, Ally. She's Australian, same as you and me."

Ally gave Jez the sweetest smile of embarrassment. "Oh, phoo. Didn't mean it like that. That came out *all* wrong."

Jez smiled at her. "Don't worry. I know *exactly* what you mean, Alice, and no offence taken. You want to know where my mother was born. That's a country called Brazil, in South America. My dad's an Aborigine."

Ally clapped her hands. "How exciting! I'd *love* to be an Aborigine!"

"Yes, it's fun," Jez replied.

Then Ally focused on me and screwed up her eyes. "You look funny."

"Really? How?" I asked.

"Not like Sainte-Claire at all. Nerdy. Uncool."

I looked at Jez and smiled. No hair gook. No black threads. No reinforced boots. No sunnies. I was nerdy. "I rest my case," I said.

"I expect you can sit in the sun for as long as you like?" Alice asked Jez, as she tucked into her French toast. "Mummy makes me keep a hat on all the time."

"No, I have to wear a hat too."

"You have such long fingers. Look!" Alice held out her small hand and Jez placed hers against it, finger to finger. The overlap was about three inches.

"Wow, that's really *chewy*!" Ally exclaimed.

Tiggs was very subdued. She had been ever since we'd arrived at the front door of Number 5.

"I'm sorry I don't look like Sainte-Claire today, Tiggs. I'm undercover, you see."

"That's quite all right. And there's no need to treat me like a child. I know who you really are."

She glanced at Jez, then looked deep into her cappuccino and was silent again. Was she jealous of Jez? A girl thing?

"Can you walk with me to buy a paper, please?" Tiggs asked after a few moments. "Mum asked me to get one."

"Of course," I replied, putting down my coffee. "Will you two ladies excuse Tiggs and me for five minutes?"

We walked round the corner into Darlinghurst Road to the newsagent.

"I know about Uncle Sammy," she said as we marched up the hill.

I wasn't going to continue treating her as a child — it made no sense.

"How do you know?"

"I heard Mummy and Aunt Lucy whispering. It's all right, Ally doesn't know."

"You're going to have to be very strong, you know; look after Mum and Alice."

"I know," she replied. No trembling lip, no teary eyes, just the brute strength of a gutsy twelve-year-old.

"So you caught up with Uncle Sammy at last?"

"I guess I did."

"But you haven't found my father?"

"Not yet. I'm trying really hard."

"I know, don't worry," she said, taking hold of my hand. The odd thing was, I felt at that moment she was looking after *me*, rather than the other way round.

"Is Daddy in danger?"

"I think maybe he is, yes. But there are a lot of us making sure that he won't come to any harm."

"What can I do, Sainte-Claire? I feel so useless."

"You're being the best use possible — looking after your mum and Ally-Oop. Right now I'm not sure your mother can cope as well as you can, and it's vital she doesn't fall apart. You know what I mean?"

"I know what you mean," she replied.

We reached the newsagent and she picked up a *Sydney Morning Herald*. "Is all the weekend stuff inside?" she asked.

"Yes, it's all there," the young girl behind the counter replied.

On the way back she was silent for a while. I held out my hand to her this time and she clutched it tightly.

"I like you a lot, Sainte-Claire. I think you're my new best friend."

"I think you're mine too."

"No, Jez is yours," she replied. "But I understand that."

We walked back across the street.

"Do you have children, Sainte-Claire?"

"No. Not yet," I replied.

"Can *we* be your children?"

"Of course. It would be my honour." I was deeply touched.

"I mean Ally-Oop, really. She's still a child. I can be your *second*-best friend."

"Either way. Or both. Whichever."

She stopped abruptly and tightened her grip on my hand.

"Will you always look after Ally, Sainte-Claire? I mean, if anything happens to Daddy. Will you make sure she's all right?"

"Every breath she takes," I replied. "I'll be watching."

Her smile was a mile wide. "That's a song, isn't it?"

"Guess so," I replied. "I'll be watching *you* too – every move you make."

Then she did the cutest thing. She put her other hand on mine, raised it to her lips and kissed the back of my hand. "We'd better get back. Coffee'll be cold."

Her face had gone all red.

We took the kids back to Charlie and Lucy at around ten-thirty. The hour and a half had included breakfast at the Trop, and a trip down to Harry's Café de Wheels in Woolloomooloo. Ally'd been told they stacked the mushy peas on top of the mash and pies, and she didn't think 'all that stuff' would stay on top and not fall down her front. I told her it did stay on top — most of the time, anyway — but she wouldn't believe me. So we walked along Victoria Street and down the steps to the harbour foreshore so she could see for herself. I had a child on the end of each arm, tugging at me and it felt great. I had kids at last.

Charlie looked drained and Lucy had a befuddled expression as they opened the door together.

"I'm pogged!" Ally exclaimed as she hugged Charlie. She meant she'd eaten too much.

"Can we have a quick chat outside?" Lucy whispered to Jez and me as Charlie took the children inside. She closed the door behind her.

"I don't believe Charlie knows where Peter is. Really. And that's what she's told the police. I asked her when they'd gone whether she was going to cooperate and she said she *had* to now. Whether or not *that's* the real truth is another matter. Now that Sammy's dead she's got no way of negotiating — that's her big worry at present."

"It's a pity she didn't cooperate before," Jez said.

"As I explained to Robert, Charlie thought *that* would endanger Peter. She believed that once they had the money they'd let him go. And she didn't care about the money anyway."

"So what did the cops say they'd do?" I asked.

"Oh, you know the police; they're not going to tell us everything. All they've said is that they'll interview Tim Brierley and ask him if he knows the whereabouts of Mr. Tutuelo. Meantime they have a warrant out for the Islander's arrest, based on the evidence in your statement."

"What about Chin?"

"They're liaising with the Cabramatta police, so they said. They assured Charlie they're looking everywhere for Peter. They're convinced he's still somewhere in Cabramatta."

Over Lucy's shoulder I saw the front door open. "Where's Cabramatta?" Ally asked with a puzzled six-year-old face. "What's happening there?"

"Nothing, darling," Lucy said, "It's a suburb of Sydney miles away where a friend of Jez's lives, that's all."

She turned back to Jez and me. "I'd better take Ally inside. Keep in touch, won't you? I mean, if you hear anything."

I told her I would.

Lucy and Ally waved goodbye and we left.

"They *are* mighty cute," Jez conceded as we walked home. "I can see why you're torn."

"What do you have in mind for today?" I asked.

"I may paint a bit. What about you?"

"Stick around home. Look after my emails. Wait and see if anything develops regarding Peter."

"And if it does?" She was now giving me the eye.

"I'll do whatever I can to help the police."

"No more playing Sainte-Claire?"

"No," I replied.

Lying was becoming a habit.

36

I knew I was on probation as far as Jez was concerned. I had to plan my day carefully.

First of all, dress code. What could I wear that Jez couldn't construe as Sainte-Claire, but achieved the same purpose? I settled on black denim jeans with a plain black T-shirt. Black shoes? Well, I could hardly wear white sneakers — I'd look like Seinfeld. So I settled for black trainers. And since the sun was shining, the Armani rip-offs were a must.

The hair was the major problem. If I gelled and spiked it at all, *any* jury would convict me of dressing up as Sainte-Claire. So I came up with the idea of washing my hair and leaving it wet. Every now and then I could duck into a men's room and wet it down, giving the gelled effect. And if Jez chanced by, I'd simply tell her it was wet. Liquid toffee gel? Nah! Water.

I had two choices. I could hang about in Cabramatta on the off chance that either Tri or Chin or both might show themselves — which had to be a very long shot — or stake out Brierley's house and see what was hopping in that quarter. I didn't call Ben because I thought the poor guy was probably catching up on some sleep. If he had any new information to share with me, I was sure he'd ring.

So I drove on down to Vaucluse. I did one drive-by to scout the area, with the Armanis off — no need to stand out as a thug. On Wentworth Road I spotted what I thought was an unmarked police car about seven houses down from Brierley's place.

I turned round when I reached Parsley Bay reserve, parked, and debated how best to keep an eye on Brierley's gates. I could hardly hang out any closer than the cops, and if I parked behind them and sat in the car they'd wonder if I was as stupid as they were — two men in suits sitting in the front of a stationary car? Good grief.

I was about to get out and stretch my legs when someone tapped on the driver's window. It took me completely by surprise. I jumped, both mentally and physically.

A man of about sixty-five was standing by the car; a man I'd never seen before. He had a friendly face and a bushy moustache. In his right hand was a sturdy walking stick. Standing beside him was a bulldog. It was panting.

I wound down the window. "Can I help you?"

"Matter of fact, you can."

He smiled at me amiably and said no more. I thought for a moment he was mentally disadvantaged, so I smiled back at him.

"It's a great day, eh?" It was — the sun was shining.

"I wonder if you could spare a few minutes of your time?" the old guy asked very politely.

"Well… sure," I replied, not knowing what he was going to suggest. Now I was thinking an elderly gay guy on the prowl.

"My employer would like to have a word with you, Sainte-Claire."

Uh-oh.

"And who might that be? Brierley?"

"Mr Brierley, yes."

I looked a little deeper into the old fellow's eyes. There was indeed a twinkle there.

I opened the door and got out.

"You'll come, then?" he asked.

"I don't see why not. One question though."

"Be my guest."

"My information is that the police have an arrest warrant out for an employee of Mr Brierley. I wouldn't want to come across him today — it could be very embarrassing all round. I'd have to turn him in, you see."

"My employer has already informed the authorities he has no idea of Mr Tutuelo's whereabouts. Nor is he Mr. Tutuelo's employer." The tone was very pukka.

"In that case, I'll have a chat with him," I replied.

I started off towards Brierley's house, but immediately felt a hand on my arm.

"My employer is presently lunching at the Nielsen Park kiosk. He wondered if you'd join him and his wife."

"Bit early for lunch, isn't it?"

"They do a very good brunch, I believe. Perhaps we could travel in your car, for convenience? It's just down the road, as I'm sure you know."

I *did* know. What I *didn't* know was how the old retainer had spotted me so quickly and where he'd sprung from. And how the hell did he know what I looked like?

We parked at the bottom of Greycliffe Avenue, walked through the park and along the beachfront to the restaurant. I put on my Armanis.

I spotted Brierley sitting inside by the window as I walked up the steps to the restaurant. He smiled at me and held up a glass of rosé, as though toasting me. Sitting with him was Agnes, the woman I'd thought was his receptionist.

As I approached the table, the old guy hung back. Brierley nodded in his direction. "Thanks, Patrick, I'll take over from here," he said.

Patrick and his dog left us.

"You've met my wife, Agnès, Sainte-Claire," he said, accenting her name as one would in France. She wore a classically simple black dress and a pair of black Audrey Hepburn Chanel sunglasses to match — I couldn't see the shoes. Even through the dark glass I detected a very searching look, the kind you'd present to someone you didn't quite trust.

"Yes, we've met," I said. "Of course, at that time I didn't know you were Mr Brierley's wife."

"Please, won't you seet?" she said.

There it was again, the cod-French — the accent was even more third-rate daytime soap than before.

I sat and was immediately offered a menu. I didn't look down, instead keeping eye contact with Brierley.

"Seems like you're more dangerous than I initially thought, Sainte-Claire," he said. "Do you always wear sunglasses indoors or is it all part of the hard man image?" He said it in a teasing, rather than offensive way.

I flicked my eyes to Agnès and smiled politely. "It's a bright day. However, nowadays I believe they're a fashion accessory. Your wife, for instance, looks fabulous in her Chanel classics. Très soignée."

"Touché," Agnès said quietly, enjoying Brierley's discomfiture.

Fifteen — love.

Brierley hadn't blinked since I arrived. I was determined he would be first. Childish, really. Especially considering my eyes were beginning to water while his were dry as liquid nitrogen.

"Definitely a man to be reckoned with," he added.

Obviously, my condition was psychosis rather than neurosis, because at that moment it seemed perfectly natural to feel proud at being flattered by Sydney's leading criminal identity.

"Is that *your* judgement?" I asked.

"As a matter of fact, it's a friend of mine's. Man by the name of Tutuelo. An acquaintance only, naturally. I'm told you finally had it out with him?"

"In a manner of speaking," I replied. I was enjoying this strange 'Phillip Marlowe' repartee. It was straight out of my graphic novels, but now it was *for real*.

"Seems you got the better of him," he said, sipping his rosé. "Well, there's a first time for everything."

The waiter hovered.

"What can I get you, sir? May I suggest the fresh fruit, followed by the eggs Benedict?"

"I won't be brunching," I replied.

"Pour my friend Sainte-Claire a glass of rosé. It's from Anjou. My wife's neck of the woods."

I blinked.

Damn. Fifteen all.

"Where exactly?" I asked, flicking my eyes to her. "I know France quite well." I was determined to catch out our ham actress.

"Angers," she replied casually. "My family comes from Montreuil-Juigné. It's eight kilometres from Anjou. You 'ave been there, pr'aps?"

Interestingly, I had. And she was correct, to the kilometre.

"It's a very pretty village. I stayed in Avrillé, just down the road," I replied, already feeling foolish.

"*Eh bien. Vous connaissez l'Auberge d'Evenard, peut-être?*"

I had to think. But yes, she was right on the button again. I'd been there with Jez a year before — the food had been great. "Certainly. I believe he was awarded the Lauriers du Terroir recently?" These laurels are awarded to chefs serving traditional local dishes.

Agnès looked genuinely delighted. "*Absolument*! I must email Jean-Pierre tonight!" She held up her glass in a toast. "Just fancy, you 'aving dined at the resturant of my friend! *Salut*, Monsieur Sainte-Claire!"

I took a long pull of my rosé and felt an ass. Fat lot *I* knew about accents.

"Much as I love to listen to your French cuisine banter," Brierley said, a trifle sourly I thought, "perhaps we could get back to *this* neck of the woods for a moment."

"Why not," I replied. "Perhaps you'd tell me why you've asked me here?"

"Because I have a proposition."

"Which is?"

"I'd like to reunite Mrs Reid with her husband. Simple as that."

"Where do I come into the equation?"

"You were helping her — now you help me."

He was no longer staring at me, he was getting stuck into his swordfish. Despite the breakfast at the Tropicana, watching him eat was making me hungry. But I was damned if I was going to break bread with a murderer. I had to admit, though, it did look good. So did Agnès's steak tartare. Presumably if you pay enough extra, you can have whatever you like for brunch — raw steak included for the delectation of the committed carnivores.

"How can I do that? Help you, that is."

"You liaise with Mrs Reid and help me find where Mr Chin is hiding Mr Reid. Not so hard to grasp, surely."

His language was a far cry from the last time we'd met. Not so much of the threats to see me chucked out 'arse first'. Very hoity-toity for a Sydney crim.

"Didn't Sammy share the location with you, Brierley?"

"Tim, please. We're having a pleasant lunch. Let's not be rude to each other."

"He didn't, did he?" I persisted, ignoring his invitation to get more chummy.

"As a matter of fact, he didn't."

"But he nicked off with a bagfull of your money. Right?" I kept my voice down low.

As far as Brierley was concerned, I was just like him — a man of shadows, a criminal, a muscle guy sent by Peter's wife to get the heat taken off her husband's debt. No more, no less. If he'd thought for a second I was a writer masquerading as a tough guy, he wouldn't have been chatting to me the way he was. Right then he thought he could buy me. I played along.

"What's in it for me?"

"A percentage of what I'm getting."

"Which is?"

"One million dollars. You get twenty per cent."

What had I expected? The truth?

"My, that's pretty generous. Tell me, who negotiated the price?"

"Sammy. His brother's agreed to the sum involved."

"How do you know he'll pay you when this is all over?"

Brierley just chuckled and sipped his rosé. "He'll pay. He wants to live, doesn't he?"

Fifteen, thirty.

"So did Sammy," I replied.

Thirty all.

Agnès pretended not to be listening, looked out the window at a lorikeet that had just landed in the tree outside.

Brierley cocked his head towards me. "Sammy was greedy. Sammy tried to steal from me." He leaned back in his chair and snapped his fingers at the waiter. "Hey! More hollandaise over here!" he shouted, suddenly angry — the thought of anyone stealing from him had stirred his juices. Then his mood softened — he'd thought of something funny.

"My friend wants to kill you. Did you know that? It's right at the top of his 'things to do' list." He chuckled again.

Agnès nudged him in the ribs. "Tim. People are leestening."

"Tutuelo doesn't scare me," I said. Easy to say when he wasn't in the room.

"So I believe. Well, why should he? One blow from you and he's history — well, that's the story going around town. And that's the story my friend is trying to…" He searched for the word.

"Expunge?" I offered.

"The very word."

He ate in silence, waiting for a reaction from me.

"I wouldn't even consider working alongside your Islander friend."

"I can understand that. Fact is, my Islander acquaintance will be leaving these shores for a well-deserved break shortly. I'd like you to step into his shoes."

"Where's he off to? Somewhere hot? Hell, maybe?" I quipped.

"Very droll. Vanuatu, I believe."

I stored it in the memory bank — the police would relish that bit of information.

"I think we could work together on this one project, Tim."

"I'm delighted to hear that, Sainte-Claire. Let's drink to it."

The three of us clinked our glasses.

"To good fortune!" he said.

"To *a* fortune," I added. "My cut is two hundred thousand."

"Nice play on words. You drive a hard bargain," Brierley conceded.

I hadn't expected it, but he'd taken the bait.

"You find him, I'll do the rest. No need to get your hands dirty — I have people who don't mind the odd bit of 'hand-to-hand'. Incidentally, you don't already know where Peter Reid is, by any chance?"

"I believe he's been moved. That's my information at present. But Mrs Reid trusts me — she'll tell me when she knows."

"When will that be, I wonder?"

"She's been asked to put together a bag of money — similar to the one Sammy Reid was carrying last night when I saw him at the airport."

"Really? You saw Sammy?"

"Yes, both before and after, as a matter of fact."

"Before and after what?"

"His death."

Forty, thirty.

Brierley's expression was one of genuine surprise; evidently he had no idea that it was me who had found the body. It left him in doubt as to whether I'd actually witnessed the killing itself.

"So, Charlie's waiting to be told where to drop off the cash?"

"Correct. However, I would emphasise that my client doesn't have the money at her home at present. And I might add that she's quite happy to up the ante if Peter's released unharmed. So it wouldn't be a smart move to think of changing plans once we've agreed on our terms — where and when to collect etc."

"Wouldn't dream of it. Why complicate matters? Easy money is just that — easy."

"Good," I said as I got up. "I'll leave you to your dessert."

"How can I reach you, Sainte-Claire?"

"I'll call you. You have a mobile?"

Brierley pulled out a card, wrote another number on the back and handed it to me. "That's my private line. Very private."

I put it in my wallet.

"Don't even think of cutting me out now that we've agreed terms," he added. "My reach is very long. I have friends on every continent."

I didn't bother to look at him; the man was quite foul in every sense.

I nodded to Agnès. "*Au revoir*," I said politely.

"Oo-roo," she replied.

Deuce.

37

I was exhilarated as I walked back along the promenade. Quite a few people were sunbathing on the sand, even though temperature was only about nineteen degrees. There was no wind and the sky was clear. The water was as blue as Giblet's wide moonlit eyes at midnight, and quite pristine. I felt like ripping all my clothes off and swimming to Manly with no stops. Thoughts were racing through my brain so fast I couldn't access them individually as they passed through the viewing area.

As I strode past the stone steps that led to the beach, a classic teenage beach babe passed me going in the opposite direction. My eyes met hers by chance and she smiled coquettishly at me. I was sure it was the incredible energy coursing through me that subconsciously compelled her to look at me. Perhaps she'd seen my aura — shining, visible, despite the strong sun. Either way, I felt at that moment that nothing was outside my capabilities. I was on a mental power trip and it didn't scare me at all.

It should have.

I knew that if I played the cards I'd suddenly been dealt, I could somehow find a way of working things out to everyone's advantage — everyone's but Brierley's and Chin's. The Sainte-Claire in me thought I could handle everything single-handed — but you have to bear in mind my mental imbalance at the time.

I could now call the shots. Brierley wasn't going to move until I told him to, till I gave him a location. Unless Chin had acted irrationally, prompted by the death of Tammi, Peter was still alive, still a hostage somewhere in Cabramatta. My guess was that he wouldn't allow a personal matter to get between him and six million dollars. The stakes were too high.

By now Chin would know of Sammy's murder – it had been on all the television and radio news program. Up to now, Sammy had been his link to Charlie. Would Chin contact her himself now that Sammy was dead? He'd have to communicate somehow. And soon.

It was time to have a serious chat with Charlie, before she got any ideas to go off on her own.

I bought a hands-free kit for my mobile phone in Double Bay and immediately called Ben. You know how sometimes you're busting to share good news with a friend? Well, that's what I felt like that day. Who could I tell, though? Jez? No way.

"He actually thinks you're a 'fellow traveller'?" Ben asked. He was incredulous. "You must have put on quite an act."

"Look, I took out his right-hand man the other day, as if it were so easy. He doesn't know it was a lucky punch — he thinks I'm some kind of an enforcer, hired by Charlie to protect her and the children. So he tried it on – persuading me to change sides and take a slice of the action from him rather than a fee from her. I agreed. "Look at it from his perspective — it makes sense."

"So all you have to do now is find where Chin's stashed Peter Reid."

That burst my bubble a bit. It was as if I'd filled in my own particular Lotto form and ticked Random Pick — all I had to do now was win first prize. Ben was right to bring me back to reality.

"Anyone surfaced in Cabramatta?" I asked.

"No one's called me. Mind you, if something big spiked, the Force might cut me out of the information food chain. I mean, Turgut's a good mate but the job comes first. Should, anyway."

"So we're by no means certain to hear about it if they spot Chin or Tri?"

"Maybe not. I've put out feelers everywhere. Annie's got her ear to the ground too. She's got Madonna out looking for Tri. But, as yet, Tri hasn't made contact."

"Get some rest. If I need you, can I call you?"

"Sure, Sainte-Claire. Any time. The tab's rising though."

"Understood."

Then I remembered the snippet I'd picked up from Brierley. "One more thing, Ben. "Pass on to your sources that Tutuelo has it in mind to leave the country. Vanuatu. They can pick him up at some airport or other — probably Brisbane. Less security."

I hung up and put the hands-free kit in my pocket. I'd reached Roslyn Street, and I needed to have my serious conversation with Charlie and Lucy, together.

We had to have a very clear plan of action. Charlie needed to know exactly what to say if and when Chin or an associate of his called her. And we had to decide whether we were going to call in the police when it came to the exchange.

Either way we had to decide what story we were going to offer the police.

Charlie opened the door to me. She seemed much more controlled, putting a finger on her lips and nodding towards the stairs as I stepped through the door. I knew she meant 'don't let the kids know you're here'. I could hear television noises from upstairs. I nodded a response.

We walked through into the kitchen where Lucy was making cheese and pickle sandwiches.

During the drive from Nielsen Park I'd been debating which cards to chest when it came to sharing my information with the police and which to chest when it came to Charlie and Lucy's 'need to know'. I didn't want anything to get out of hand, and if only *I* knew where every piece of the jigsaw fitted, then I'd feel happier.

But fitting the jigsaw wasn't going to be a cakewalk. I wanted to make damned sure that Peter was unharmed when the exchange took place. That was pre-eminent. I also wanted to make certain that Brierley, Chin and Tri were caught red-handed extorting money from Charlie. To achieve my second aim, the police would have to be somewhere very close when the exchange took place. I planned to set things in motion and inform the cops only at the last moment. That way, they couldn't screw things up by going in heavy with an armed SPG unit that might scare Tri into opening up with an Uzi and killing everyone. It wasn't that I thought the Cabramatta cops weren't up to it; I was simply worried that some higher-ranked officer from Central might take over. And who knew what dickhead would put himself in charge — quite possibly someone without any day-to-day experience of the subtle way things were done in Cabramatta.

"Want a toastie?" Lucy asked.

"Sounds scrumptilicious. Isn't that what Ally would say?"

They both smiled.

"Has there been any contact?" I asked Charlie as she made me coffee.

They both answered in quiet unison. "No."

"What exactly did Sammy outline to you would happen?"

Charlie handed me a coffee and leaned against the Welsh dresser.

"At first it was very simple. I was to go to the Lotteries Office and organise an electronic transfer of the money to my bank. Then I'd go to my branch and arrange for a big withdrawal. Sammy knew that would take time. I have no idea why the girl snatched the bag. I was told she'd escort me to Homebush. Even that seemed pointless, but I suppose they wanted to keep an eye on everything and know what stage things were at. When she asked me to hand over the cheque I was surprised. That was never part of the plan."

"Must have been a breakdown in communications between Sammy and Chin."

"I suppose."

"So you told her you didn't have it?"

"Well, I didn't, did I? I told her I'd just arranged an electronic transfer. But she wouldn't believe me. So she snatched the handbag to see for herself. She wanted to take a cheque back to get Peter to countersign it. But it would have been made out in my name anyway, not Peter's. Sammy knew that — maybe Tri didn't. You see, it was I who won, not Peter. I tried to tell the girl but she wouldn't listen."

"If things had worked out the way Sammy had suggested, what would have happened next?" I asked.

"Well, next I would have withdrawn some of the money on Monday and waited for Sammy to tell me where to go with it."

"He must have realised you couldn't withdraw six million in cash."

"Of course. But Sammy knew that if I gave him my word, it would be honoured. He'd get it all in instalments. Half for them, half for us. There was plenty for everyone."

"You'd have given him more, even after Peter was released?" I was staggered.

"I'd never renege on a promise. Never. Sammy knew that."

"Chin may not be so certain of that, but let's not be negative. You never knew where Peter was?"

"I did initially. Ferrier Street. That's where they took *me*. But after your intervention, they moved him."

That was right — Lucy had told me. I suddenly wished I hadn't asked that question.

"So now we have to wait for Chin to call me?" Charlie asked.

"Unless the police spot him or his associates before then," I replied.

I could hear the unmistakable voices of Ren and Stimpy floating through the house. Ren was calling Stimpy 'Stinky' and Ally was hooting with laughter.

"Have you made enquiries about getting the money together?"

"Yes, I have. And that wasn't easy, I can tell you — you have to look pretty composed when you go into the bank and ask them to arrange to withdraw a million dollars in cash."

"*One* million?" I asked. "When did you initially ask for withdrawal arrangements?"

"Last Wednesday. I told the manager the prize money would be electronically transferred from the State Lotteries account to my personal account, and that he could check with them if he wished. He then asked me if I'd considered other means of transferring the million — anything over ten thousand is a large sum in that branch. It was his way of asking why I wanted so much cash."

"What did you say?"

"I told him I was happy with the arrangements I had in mind and that I'd arranged adequate personal security. I added that if there was any problem withdrawing a small percentage of the money, maybe I would consider depositing the lot elsewhere. That shut him up."

"But the security arrangements seemed to satisfy him?"

"Not too much, judging by his expression. This is the Cross, after all. He told me he'd have to fill out an FTR — that's a Financial Transaction Report. Any sum over ten thousand dollars has to be registered with Austrac – some governmental regulatory authority."

"When will the money be available for collection?"

"Monday," she replied. Then a thought occurred to her. "Do you think the bank will inform the police that I've asked to carry out a million dollars?"

"In Europe, once you've made arrangements, and signed for the cash, you can carry out the notes in a wheelbarrow as far as the bank's concerned. I'll have to find out about Australian banking etiquette. My guess is they'd only inform the authorities if they felt a criminal act was involved. Perhaps if the police asked the bank to keep them appraised of any large withdrawals by you, they'd be in danger of obstructing justice if they didn't cooperate. Otherwise I'd imagine client confidentiality would rule. Banks are pretty close with their information generally — I don't think they like the police twisting their arm to share it."

"So, what do we do now, Sainte-Claire?" Lucy said. She handed me a toastie.

"It's not going to be easy, but we have to wait till Chin contacts you, Charlie. The police have all possible manpower looking for Peter, Chin and Tri. My source at Cabramatta's told me that."

"You don't think Chin might—" Charlie began.

"No, I don't think so," I cut in quickly, I wanted no thoughts of butchery right then. "Why should he? He's got two options. Let Peter go, or continue to hold him and ask you for the money. He'd have nothing to gain by harming Peter. But nothing's going to happen over the weekend."

"How are you so sure?" Charlie asked.

"Because of the money. He knows you haven't had time to collect it. No point in starting the ball rolling until he knows you have the cash and can deliver. Meanwhile, he can make secure arrangements for the exchange and organise a fall-back situation, such as a getaway, in case anything goes wrong."

"Goes wrong?" This time it was Lucy asking.

"A double-cross or a police trap," I answered.

"But we're not going to do that, are we?" There was desperation in Charlie's voice. "Please, Sainte-Claire, allow me to spend my money getting the father of my children home."

"I'll do everything I can to help you, you know that."

"Including keeping the police out of it?"

"You've done a pretty good job convincing them you're now cooperating. I can do the same."

She relaxed her shoulders. "Have you decided what you're going to do? What *we*'re going to do, I should say."

"I'll give you the bare bones and you can tell me what you think. Bear in mind, things have a way of not panning out *exactly* as they should."

Lucy began eating her toasted sandwich. Charlie looked too worried to eat.

"Monday morning we go to your bank. Just the two of us. We'll be watched, I'd say. I can almost guarantee Chin will have someone out there somewhere keeping an eye on you. But this time Chin will be smarter than before. He'll most likely use a Caucasian, and he or she won't be sitting in a car down the road. And I'd wager my house that Tim Brierley will be keeping tabs on you too."

Charlie's shoulders sagged. "Jesus Christ," she murmured.

"It's actually not so bad, Charlie. I had a meeting with Brierley today. He thinks I'm a gun for hire, so to speak," and that you've paid me to protect you and the kids. He asked me to change sides and work with him — without your knowledge, naturally."

"Why did you go see him?"

"Because it's good to know what your enemies have in mind," I replied. I didn't need to tell her that in fact he'd found me.

"We may now be in a position to control the course of events," I went on. "Brierley thinks he's bought me, so he won't do anything until I tell him where the exchange is going to take place. That takes a lot of pressure off us."

"You're going to play Brierley off against Chin," Lucy said flatly. She was way ahead of Charlie.

"Yes, I am. And I want them both to go down. Peter will be safest if we're completely hands-on at the time of exchange. When we collect the money from the bank, Chin's people will see you do it. When Chin calls you, you can tell him you have the money, and it'll be confirmed by the watchers.

"Chin will come up with his exchange plan. Then we'll come up with what suits us. We'll insist we do it our way."

"Easy to say," Lucy interrupted. "What if he insists we do it his way?"

"We have the money. He wants it. He has Peter, nothing more. We walk away, he's got nothing. He can bluff all he likes, but killing Peter will gain him nothing but a manhunt."

"So, what's 'our way'?"

I gave them a rough rundown of my plan. I wanted to put Chin and Brierley together in a confrontational situation at one location. I'd meet Chin with the money, while Charlie and Ben freed Peter at another location. I was hoping Chin and Brierley would shoot each other up a bit — maybe a few swipes of the old machete would be involved too — then the cops would arrive to arrest those left standing.

"I'll have an associate of mine drive you near to where Peter's being held."

"How will you know where that is?" Lucy asked.

"I'll ask Chin. Not where he's being held *exactly*, but roughly, so you can be in the area and ready to pick him up as soon as he's freed."

"So I won't be handing over the money at all, personally," Charlie said.

"No. *I'll* be doing that. You'll be looking for Peter with my friend Ben."

She liked that bit.

"When Chin's checked out the money, he'll call his associates and tell them to free Peter — and I'll call you to tell you where to go. I'll tell Brierley to hold back till I give him the signal to move in, which is after I call you and you go to Peter."

I didn't add that I'd leave it to Ben's judgement whether or not to call in the State Protection Group to flood the area where Peter was being held — that would depend on how things panned out that end. But in any case, he'd call the cops in on Chin and Brierley my end when I asked him to. By the time they arrived, chances were the two hard men would be well stuck into each other.

It was a nice idea. Plans like that worked in my books all the time. Problem was, in real life something always went wrong.

"Now we just have to wait," I concluded.

"I've been waiting so long already," Charlie said in a tone of utter hopelessness. "I don't know *what* to tell the children any more. Tiggs is no fool, she knows her father's in trouble."

She sure did. That's why she'd hired me several days ago. If Charlie had the common sense of her twelve-year-old daughter, she might not be in this pickle herself.

Incidentally the toastie was delicious.

38

On the way home I rang my bank manager in Paddington and asked him whether he'd inform the police if someone asked to withdraw over half a million dollars from his branch. He was circumspect in his reply, said it would depend on the client. If Murdoch or Packer asked for a million, he'd oblige no problem. Someone dubious, he'd think about it. Basically, if the money were sitting in the account, he'd make arrangements to call in the cash after he'd suggested suitable security arrangements for his client.

I asked him what his attitude would be if the police had asked to be kept abreast of any big withdrawals, and he replied he'd cooperate. Since the police would have been keeping close tabs on Charlie since Sammy's murder — probably ever since an abduction was indicated — they'd know of the withdrawal arrangements. This complicated matters: they'd be watching her, every move she made.

Finally, I called Ben and gave him the precise details of my plan. I fully expected him to tell me to get nicked, that there was no way he'd cut out the Force at this stage. But he surprised me by agreeing to help, without reservation. I'd left him a big say in when exactly to call in the police reinforcements in Cabramatta, and that seemed to satisfy him. I wanted the final say on when to call in the cavalry at the cash exchange — I wanted to give Chin and Brierley and their people enough time to kill each other. They deserved it.

Ben said he'd be driving around the Kings Cross area from 9 a.m. on Monday and would be ready to pick up Charlie at a few minutes' notice.

I took some smoked salmon and a Semillon round to Jez's studio. Somehow she'd transformed the place. The ripped canvases had been rolled and stacked. The broken frames had been thrown out, and the floorboards had been steam cleaned and sanded back. The walls had been painted dead white.

Jez was working on a massive canvas that must have been stretched inside the studio. Three metres square, at least. The work was in its very early stages: a stark white and taupe background with a figure outlined in charcoal. Her arms — she was clearly a female — were stretched outwards and upwards in despair. I'd never seen Jez paint anything that was negative, so I was surprised. I thought better than to comment on the subject matter; it probably mirrored her reaction to Sainte-Claire.

My hair had dried, so it didn't look at all like her *bête noir*.

Jez opened the huge floor-to-ceiling double doors to let in the sun and we ate our lunch at a small table she set up by the opening.

Conversation didn't come easily. There was a distance between us that I'd never felt before, and it saddened me. I didn't want to even *think* about the Reids or their problems, but Peter's situation was a constant — I couldn't shake it.

We talked about Bush, Iraq, the G8, footy, world hunger, terrorism, Tim McGuire's art, Nigella Lawson's 'comfort food', what Jez was going to buy Giblet for her fifth birthday, our friends in New York and Paris, her father — a million things. But I couldn't concentrate on anything but a vision of Peter Reid, locked up in some basement, terrified, waiting for someone to help him.

I'd told Charlie to call me in the unlikely event she heard from Chin. Also, if Brierley contacted her or the police wanted to interview her. Meantime, I'd suggested they have the quietest of weekends possible. They were to keep all the doors and windows locked and stay indoors. The children wouldn't like it, but it had to be that way to guarantee their safety.

After lunch I cleared the plates away and Jez got back to her canvas. I drew up an armchair and sat in the sun by the window, gazing out over the Surry Hills rooftops. I could hear children playing somewhere close by; their clamour reminded me of Ally and Tiggs.

At four o'clock I went for a walk. Even though I didn't expect any calls from Chin or Brierley, I was as tense as Nigel Kennedy's E-string. But I didn't want it to show in front of Jez.

I walked up to Crown Street and mooched around. I saw several copies of my novels in a secondhand bookstall. One was inscribed, *'To Scooter. As good a friend as one could hope to meet. Best wishes, Robert Howard.'* Unless Scooter Solomon had been burgled recently, the presence of the book here didn't say much about his present opinion of *me* as a buddy.

I nipped into the Clock Hotel for a beer.

At five I went back to the studio. Jez was fleshing out the figure now with some broad strokes of oil paint. Even at this early stage it was a scary picture. Reminded me of a photo I'd seen of a New Yorker running from the World Trade Center on September 11. I didn't comment — I simply looked at it thoughtfully.

"What's up, Pulitzer?" she said after a few minutes of my silent staring. "What you got planned?"

"You mean for us? This evening?"

"Sure. What else?"

"I thought you were referring to the Reids' problems."

"Well, now I am. What's up with them?"

"Charlie's going to pay the ransom. Monday, probably. Depends on when the bad guys tell her they're ready. I'd say it'd be Monday."

"The police are going to be setting some kind of a trap?"

"I'd say so. They don't always. Sometimes they let the money be exchanged to see if the kidnappers release the hostage safely — after all, that's their first priority."

"Sure. But what I mean is, are the police setting up all of this, or do you have it in mind to act like Dirty Harry and do it all yourself? You know — zip into wherever it is he's been tied up, pull out a Magnum .45, blast away, kill everyone, and set the good guy free?"

I was relieved to see from her expression that she was joking. The shame of it was that what she'd outlined was pretty close to the truth. All barring the Magnum bit — this was Australia, after all, and PI's don't carry firearms. The bad guys, sure. The good guys? Nah!

"That's up to the police. It's all up to them now," I lied.

Then, a few moments later. "How about we see a movie?"

"The Truffaut retrospective's on tonight — *Les Quatre Cents Coups*. How about we stay home?"

"Done. How about I order take-out from Fat Duck?" Their crispy whole Peking duck was magic.

So Saturday night passed uneventfully. *Four Hundred Blows* ended as sadly as ever on that French beach. I wondered if Brierley's childhood had been similar to that of the child in the film — it might account for his choice of career. Jez was, as ever, moved to tears. The duck was great.

Sunday morning came and went. I had my mobile in my pocket but it didn't ring, so I hoped and prayed that all was ticking over uneventfully in the Reid household.

Jez and I walked in Centennial Park in the afternoon, and had a drink at the Woollahra Hotel at around six and listened to the jazz. While Jez was taking in the second set, I walked outside and called Charlie.

"It's me," I said at once. "I'll call over at 8.30 a.m tomorrow. Is that okay with you?"

"That's fine. Lucy's staying here, so between us we can get the children to school and do whatever needs doing."

"I'd like to be at the bank with you the moment it opens. Then we'll go back to your house and wait by the phone. Wear flat-soled shoes or sneakers. Whatever's comfortable."

"In case I have to run?"

"You got it."

39

I lay in bed that night, Jez asleep beside me, trying to think of every conceivable combination of future crises. What if Chin didn't call at all? What if he refused to accept just the one million? What if Brierley pulled some unexpected stunt?

273

Of course, my greatest concern was that I knew I should be calling in the police right now.

The way I saw it, Chin would telephone in the morning sometime. I'd tell him we only had a portion of the money — one million dollars in cash. I'd explain again — in case Sammy hadn't been clear about the amount – that Charlie couldn't give it *all* to him right away without alerting the police to the fact she was about to pay the ransom. There was no reason to point out that the police probably already knew of the proposed withdrawal. I'd tell him the cops had been keeping an eye on Charlie ever since Sammy was found dead, and that was why she couldn't withdraw more. I'd also tell him he'd get the rest in installments — it was now a 'take it or leave it' situation. Then I'd add the part which might make him go for the plan — that I'd personally guarantee he'd get the other five if he cut me in for half a mil.

Quite possibly I wouldn't have to tell him half of this stuff, but I needed to have an answer for everything.

I couldn't be sure that Chin would have an associate watching Charlie and me at the bank. It would be nice, but not vital; it just might make him a little more assured that we really *did* have the money to give him.

That's when things might become difficult. I knew Chin would want to choose the rendezvous where the money was to be delivered. But I needed this to be somewhere other than where Peter was to be released.

In a normal thriller, the changeover would take place simultaneously. I didn't want this because it would put Charlie and Peter in the middle of a firefight. So I planned to suggest meeting Chin myself with the money, and as soon as he'd assured himself that the cash was all there, he'd call Tri and tell him to release Peter somewhere else. He'd then tell me Peter's location and I'd telephone this through to Ben, who'd be looking after Charlie.

This separated the two major Asian players, Tri and Chin. Of course, as soon as Chin had told me where the exchange was going to take place, I'd call Brierley and fill him in, telling him to hold back until Chin had told me where Peter Reid was being held. I'd make sure that Brierley was close enough to show up almost immediately with his heavies, and hopefully all hell would break loose. I'd just have to look after myself when the bullets started flying.

The joy of this scenario would be that I could also safely tell the Kings Cross police of the exact location where all this was going to happen — but at the time of *my* choosing. When the shit hit the fan, they'd be there to clear up and arrest both Chin and Brierley. Even if Brierley didn't show himself, he'd be sure to be charged with being an accessory or conspiracy. Certainly as far as my testimony was concerned.

And the money? Well, it was never the most important part of the plan. The chances were odds-on that it wouldn't get lost. Even if it blew away, providing it blew across the dead bodies of the bad guys, who cared?

As far as Peter and Charlie were concerned, as soon as Chin told me where Peter was being held, Ben would call the Cabramatta police and they'd flood the immediate area with SPG units. Even Tri would see there'd be no point in harming Peter — his best bet would be to clear out damned fast.

That was the plan. That was why I fell asleep at six and woke at seven.

Jez, Giblet and I had an early breakfast. All night long I'd debated whether to tell Jez the details of what was about to happen. She had a right to know, I was aware of that. My life, as well as Peter's, might be at risk, and that definitely impacted on her.

At midnight I'd decided to tell her everything. At 2 a.m. I'd decided it was better she *didn't* know. At four I again decided to tell her *everything*. At six, I changed my mind, afraid I might lose her. At seven I knew she should know regardless of the consequences.

Over breakfast I couldn't make up my mind. Howard wanted to tell her everything. Sainte-Claire wanted to keep my lip buttoned.

As I put the dishes in the machine, she kissed me on the cheek.

"Lunch?" she asked.

I opened my mouth — I knew I had to tell her.

"Same time, same place?" she cut in before I could speak.

"Sure. I'll call you," I replied, as my brain buzzed with conflict.

She kissed me again and the door closed behind her. I wondered if I'd ever see her again.

I went upstairs again and changed clothes.

It was Sainte-Claire who left the house to see Charlie.

40

Lucy was on the way to school with the kids when I arrived. Charlie was dressed in Levi's, sneakers and a red jumper. She made us some coffee in the kitchen.

"When you're in the bank try to appear as relaxed as possible," I said. "Be chatty."

"Then we come back here and wait?"

"That's right."

I walked beside her to the bank in Darlinghurst Road. We were there five minutes after it opened for business. I waited outside like a security detail while Charlie entered. She was only inside about ten minutes. During that time I glanced up and down the street to see if I could spot anyone watching. I couldn't pick any likely suspects.

I rang Brierley on his 'very personal' mobile.

"Yes?"

"It's Sainte-Claire. She's inside the bank right now, withdrawing the money."

"When was that arranged?" he asked.

"Last Wednesday."

"Okay. Now, the payoff. Where and when?"

"I don't know. He hasn't called. I'll be in touch."

"I'll be waiting."

As I disconnected, Charlie walked out of the bank and I escorted her back to Roslyn Street. She was doing a terrific job. She looked relaxed and happy, though I knew she'd be boiling inside.

Back in the house, Charlie sat on the sofa, closed her eyes and began meditating. I leafed through one of her Egyptian art books.

After twenty minutes she brought out the vacuum cleaner and started in on the housework. The happy carefree face she'd presented to the world a few minutes ago was gone, in its place the drawn expression of a wife afraid her husband might die that day. I wished I could give her some comfort, but it was out of stock.

Between ten-thirty and eleven there were five telephone calls. Each time it was as if someone had touched Charlie with cardiac electric paddles. But each time it was some friend or other.

At eleven thirty-five the phone rang for the sixth time. Charlie picked up. I knew immediately by her expression that it was Chin. She listened, at the same time waving a hand at me and making signs. I picked up the phone in the hall.

"Who's that?" It was a distinctly Asian voice, aware a second line had been picked up.

"My name is Sainte-Claire. Don't ring off. I'm handling the financial arrangements for Mrs Reid."

"I deal only with Mrs Reid."

"Then you've got no deal. You have two choices. One is that we agree on arrangements and you receive the money. The other is that we do not agree, in which case we'll be forced to call on the help of the police. We prefer the former. You get the money; Mrs Reid gets her husband back."

Silence.

"You do not tell me how things shall be," the Asian voice said finally.

"We have a bagfull of money, Mr Chin. Mrs Reid has a say."

More silence.

"I tell you where to bring the money. When I have money, Mr Reid is released."

"No. I *show* you the money. Then you tell your associates to free Mr. Reid. I tell Mrs Reid where he is and she goes to her husband."

"Where we meet, Mr Reid will not be there."

"That's absolutely fine with me. You must safeguard your position." I was sucking up, hoping he'd like it.

"You don't show me one million dollars, I tell you nothing. If I don't call my associates, Mr Reid's in bad trouble. Another few fingers. Maybe more."

"That's fine too."

"Mrs Reid has agreed to give the rest of the money when her husband is freed. This is correct?"

"It is. You have her word of honour."

There was a brief moment of silence. Maybe he believed her, maybe not. Maybe at this stage one million dollars in unmarked bills looked pretty good anyway.

Charlie spoke up. "Please keep Peter safe. The money is not important to me. You have my word," she pleaded.

If I'd been Chin, I'd be happy she'd play along. All she had to lose was her husband. Quite what she proposed doing when Peter was released, I didn't know. All this talk of word of honour suggested that she fully intended to write Chin a cheque for the other five million dollars if he wasn't arrested in the meantime. I knew I might have to change her mind on that one at some later date.

"Where do we meet, Mr Chin?" I asked.

"There's a parking area on the ground floor of Officeworks in Ebley Street, Bondi Junction. We will meet there at midday. I will be in a silver BMW. You will park away from me and approach the right side of the car. You will bring money to the car. I will see if all is in order."

"One thing," I interrupted. "I'll have the money bag chained to my wrist. When you have made your calls and Mrs Reid has been reunited with her husband, I will unlock the money."

"Should you not, we will drag you and the money to Bondi Beach, Mr Sainte-Claire."

"We are agreed then?"

"We are in agreement. No police involvement?"

"None. One last thing, though. I will deliver the money alone. Mrs Reid will be at the location of Mr Reid's release. Give us the general area now, so Mrs Reid can be there quickly.

"Canley Vale."

"I will see you shortly then."

"You will see me in twenty-two minutes precisely." He hung up.

It was entirely possible that the police had applied for a court order allowing them to tap Charlie's phone. I hoped this was not the case. It was just another imponderable.

I called Ben on his mobile.

"It's arranged. Can you be here in five?"

"Sure. Where are we going?"

"You're going to Canley Vale somewhere. I'm meeting the main man at Bondi Junction. Officeworks at midday."

Canley Vale was just a few kilometres east of Cabramatta.

"I'm on my way," Ben replied.

I picked up the leather moneybag, attached a slim chain round its handle and snapped the lock round the steel bracelet of my Rolex.

I was the bagman now.

41

Ben's Skyline pulled up outside two minutes later. Just as it did, my mobile went off.

It was Lucy.

"Ally's missing," she said.

I thought my heart had actually stopped beating for a moment; perhaps it had. A whole variety of terrible possibilities rushed through my mind: Brierley had snatched her to guarantee Charlie's and my compliance; Chin had done the same.

"How long has she been gone?"

"Half an hour, maybe slightly longer. The school just called me. They thought she was in the playground."

"So they've no idea if she was snatched?"

"No."

I could see Ben outside, gesturing at his watch — Bondi Junction was a good deal closer than Canley Vale. I looked at my own watch: I had twenty minutes exactly before I was to meet Chin. This wasn't the time to tell Charlie.

"Who's that?" she asked, turning towards me.

"Nothing to do with this."

I motioned her forward to Ben's car and saw her get inside. A few seconds later the car was gone.

"Stay on the line," I told Lucy, as I slammed the front door behind me and strode out to my car.

"It may not be as bad as you're thinking," Lucy said as I reached the Goddess and climbed in.

"What do you mean?" I asked, as the car shot up the street.

"I have Tiggs with me. I just collected her from school. I'll put her on."

"Tell her to make it very quick."

"She's gone to find Dad, Sainte-Claire," Tiggs said. "We have to go get her."

"How do you know where she's gone? Did she tell you?"

"No, but I just *know* that's what she's done. You see, we've been talking the problem over for days and—"

I stopped her short. "What does she think is happening?"

I was heading up New South Head Road. I now had nineteen minutes.

"We've known for ages that Daddy's being held hostage. We see things like that on television all the time. Ally knows you're on my payroll, but she thinks you're being a bit of a slowcoach. She heard you talking to Lucy on Saturday morning, and she asked me where Cabramatta was. I told her I didn't know exactly but that it was somewhere you took a train to. She *must* have gone to find Dad. I just know it."

"Put Aunt Lucy back on, will you, Tiggs?"

"It's me again," Lucy said almost immediately.

"Call the police. Tell them that Alice is missing from school and that you think she may be alone on the rail network somewhere between Kings Cross and Cabramatta. Explain she's only six years old. Where are you now?"

"On the M5, heading to Cabramatta. I guessed your mindset. Should be there in fifteen, twenty minutes."

"See if you and Tiggs can spot her exiting the railway station or on the street somewhere. I'd better go. Don't worry too much about

Ally — she hasn't been snatched. Just try to find her and keep her out of trouble."

"I'll do my best," Lucy replied.

I was about to end the call when Tiggs came back on the line. "Can't you come and help us?" she pleaded. "You work for me, Sainte-Claire."

Insistent.

"Sorry. Can't right now."

"That's an order!" she said. She was quite a character.

Seventeen minutes left.

"I quit," I replied.

"You can't quit."

"Can."

"Can't."

"Can and no returns."

I clicked the end button, made a right into Ocean Street at Edgecliff, and called Ben.

"First glitch. Little Alice has decided to go find Daddy. She's on her way to Cabramatta by train; may already be there. Lucy's driving over there now. Don't tell Charlie. Stick to our plan and don't go looking for her. Hopefully the cops will pick her up — they've been told."

"Roger," Ben replied. That was all. I kept the line open.

I reached the top of Ocean and Oxford with fifteen minutes to go. Now I was early. I pulled over.

"How far are you from Canley Vale, Ben," I asked.

"Had a dream run. I'd say fifteen minutes."

"When I call you with Peter's location, you call Brierley's number." I gave it to him. "I'm going to jump Chin, or whoever's got the phone, so they can't stop the release order. When you've let Brierley's dogs of war loose, call the cops in double-quick — I don't want to be the meat in the sandwich."

"Roger," Ben replied.

I checked the time. Twelve minutes to go. Time to give Brierley the general location.

He picked up almost at once. "Yeah?"

"Sainte-Claire. The meet is in Ebley Street. You'll get a call very soon with the exact location from an associate of mine. Chin'll be in Ebley Street somewhere at midday."

"Jesus H, that doesn't give us much time."

"You can make it. Wait for the call, then jump him. Come in heavy."

I disconnected. There was just enough time to get in a very quick call to Lucy.

Tiggs answered. "Tiger-Lily Reid. Who's that?"

"It's me. You almost there?"

"I don't know." I could hear her talking to Lucy. "Yes. Very close. Aunt Lucy can't talk 'cos she's driving. It's against the law, you know."

"Tell her to start at the railway station then move outwards. I'll get back to you in fifteen minutes or so. Bye."

I dialed again, this time Ben.

"Sainte-Claire. I'll keep the line open from now."

"Roger," came the familiar reply. "We're under ten minutes away."

I looked at my watch. Eight minutes. Time to judge the traffic lights ahead and get moving. I took a deep breath. Surprisingly, I wasn't afraid; rather, energised. Maybe that was how soldiers felt just before action — there was simply no space for fear.

I pulled out into the traffic and was soon halted by the lights at the top of Oxford Street.

Five minutes to go.

The lights seemed to take an age to change. By the time they did there were just over three minutes left. I could feel my heart racing. The adrenaline rush was quite something — I'd never felt anything as strong as this before and it was fucking incredible.

I turned into Ebley Street with under a minute to go. Perfect timing. I could see the Officeworks sign up ahead.

The entire ground floor of the building was designated for parking. Stairs and an elevator took the shoppers up to where all the goods were. There were still plenty of spaces as I nosed into the undercover parking entry lane. I'd been to this place before, so I had an idea where Chin would be waiting. I flashed my headlights and immediately the headlights of a silver Beemer flashed back at me.

It was parked, engine running, just to the left of the exit. The driver had a quick escape from where he was positioned, and there were no boom gates. It was exactly on midday.

I parked on the opposite side to the Beemer and reached for the leather moneybag, which was chained to my wrist. Then I put on my Armani glasses — not to be cute, but so Chin couldn't read what I was thinking when I got close.

I slipped my mobile phone into my inside jacket pocket and ran the hands-free cord up behind my neck and into my left ear. I did a quick sound check.

"Ben?"

"Here."

"I'm in position. I see the car."

"Roger. I'm waiting for you now. Over."

It really was the best game in town!

I walked slowly over to the Beemer, approaching it from the right-hand side. Because of the tinted windows I couldn't see who was sitting where.

When I was ten feet away, both front windows slid down. The man in the passenger seat was a middle-aged Asian. A much younger man was at the wheel. The driver wasn't looking at me, but was staring steadfastly at the exit.

"Jimmy Chin?" I asked. It was remarkable: the man had practically no chin at all.

"Sainte-Claire?" he replied. "You show me money now!"

I placed the bag on the cement floor and unzipped the top. Then I unclipped the chain and let it fall free. I stepped back a pace. All that money must have looked *very* tempting.

"No!" Chin said. "You bring to me!"

"Nah. Come and see yourself," I replied with a smile and stepped back another pace.

He stared at me for a few moments. But the lure of all that cash was just too much. The Beemer door opened and he stepped out.

His eyes stayed locked on mine as he walked slowly forward, also as he picked up the bag. His hand dipped inside and he rummaged, presumably to pick a bundle at random. Lifting it to his nose, he sniffed it, eyes still locked on mine. Then he smiled. He could tell the real thing with just one sniff — quite the currency sommelier.

He picked out three more bundles at random, sniffed them, then zipped the bag shut and shook the smallest mobile phone I'd ever seen out from his sleeve.

"I am man of my word. I trust you to be the same," he said, staring at me.

Sadly for him, I wasn't. Not when I dealt with criminals. I was a dirty double-crosser.

He spoke into the handset. It was in some language I didn't understand, which put me at a disadvantage. In my novels, Sainte-Claire speaks Mandarin, Japanese, Javanese and five European languages including Estonian. I speak French, German and a smattering of Mongolian. That's life in the real world, I guess.

"I have told my associate to free Mr Reid," he said.

"Where shall I tell Mrs Reid to go?" I asked.

"Vale Street. Facing Bareena Park."

"Vale Street. Facing Bareena Park?" I repeated it for Ben's ears — he was still connected. It was unlikely Chin had seen the hands-free — he wouldn't know I'd already passed on the information.

"I will expect the rest of the money soon," he said, "Or I come again for Mr Reid. You tell Mrs Reid."

Chin turned back to the car with the money. I leaped at him and immediately all hell broke loose.

42

Chin fought to break free like a man possessed — and he was stronger than I'd thought. I was trying to pin him face down while reaching into his pocket for the mobile, but he was wriggling his body around like a Sumo wrestler, trying to free one hand to chop at me karate style. I smashed his forehead into the cement and a little of the fight went out of him — not much, but enough to give me the upper hand.

The driver of the Beemer started screaming at Chin, and an Asian I hadn't seen before, because of the tinted glass, leaped from the back seat and ran towards us yelling like a banshee. I noticed the he was carrying a short-handled machete. I butted Chin's forehead down hard for the second time into the cement.

At the exact same moment I managed to close my hand over Chin's mobile, two Merc E-class four doors swung into the car park, one sliding across the exit, the other skidding to a halt just behind it.

Several Caucasian men ran towards Chin and me. One took a shot at the machete-wielding Asian and the bullet crunched into him between the shoulder blades. He fell a couple of inches from us, face down, his forehead splitting open on the cement in a flower of red blood.

Brierley's boys took positions behind their cars and the car park pillars and pumped a stream of bullets into the Beemer. A second Asian leaped out — this guy was carrying an Uzi. He began spraying a mag at Brierley's men. As he tried to jump back into the Beemer for another mag, he took a shotgun blast to the head. It simply exploded.

The Beemer driver clearly thought the time had come to get out fast. He gunned the engine, directing the car away from Brierley's men, who were blocking his exit, with a view to driving out through the entrance. He missed me by a few inches but caught Chin's legs, crushing them. It sounded ugly.

Chin screamed in my ear. I guarantee it was louder than the combined roar of the Olympic crowd when Cathy Freeman won her four hundred metres gold medal. Tinnitus was a gimme. Chin let go of the moneybag. Obviously it took a whole lot to separate a dedicated crim from his cash.

I heard another four shots ring out as the Beemer roared past. Glass exploded over us both as the slugs took out the rear and driver's windows, then the car slewed sharply left and hit a concrete stanchion hard.

There were two seconds of eerie silence. Then the place erupted.

State Protection Group police had appeared out of nowhere and were screaming from both the entrance and exit. "POLICE! GET DOWN! EVERYONE GET DOWN! NOW!"

There must have been eight to ten of them, maybe more, and they were all over the place, dressed in black battle fatigues with black full-face helmets.

I got down fast.

Three of the SPG guys ran to the side of the lead Mercedes. All were yelling like SAS troops in a Fallujah firefight. Three more leaped round the second car, ready to fire, but holding back till they could see what the reaction was going to be. Two more SPG with small fully automatic weapons had taken up positions behind concrete pillars.

One cop was aiming his weapon at the wrecked Beemer.

"OUT OF THE CAR! NOW!"

The driver's door opened and Chin's wheelman fell out, blood pouring from his back.

The other cop was aiming at Brierley's two goons, left stranded in the open, telling them to hit the ground. Since they now had no cover, they dropped their guns and spreadeagled themselves.

As I smashed Chin's mobile on the concrete, another two cops pulled Chin and me apart and held guns to the back of our heads, screaming at us to lie face down.

The whole thing had taken under thirty seconds from start to finish: the area had been secured and the cops were pulling down the flaps over their Kevlar vests that covered the fluoro 'Police' markings. I tell you, those SPG guys know their game.

Chin was rudely dragged away, still screaming. I guessed his crushed legs were causing him some discomfort. That pleased me a lot. I felt a hand on my shoulder.

"You okay, Sainte-Claire?" Chase said, as he helped me up. "Or is it Howard?"

"Where's Brierley?"

"He sent his boys. Wouldn't expect him to get his own hands dirty."

"Shit," I muttered under my breath.

"Yes, I'd say he's deep in it. Don't care how he gets lawyered up, he won't beat this one."

He smiled at me. I was too shaken even to register an expression. I'd never been in a war zone and seen people killed left, right and centre, right before my eyes. Maybe it was just another day at the office to Chase and the team.

"Thanks for keeping us in the game, second by second."

I didn't know what to say — he sounded so genuine.

"Good idea to relay everything through Ben. He's a good man. Meant we could stake the place out well before you even got here. Nice move. Good timing."

So Ben had been playing his own game. Just as well it all worked out for the best, otherwise I'd have had to kill him. That was the way it worked in my graphic novels.

"Any word on Peter?" I asked.

"We picked him up. Walking across Bareena Park — just like the man said.

I heard a couple of ambulances arrive. The medics raced inside, one pair to Chin, one pair to the Beemer driver. Brierley's people were being led away.

"What about Tri?"

"Not yet. They'll find him. They've got a square mile flooded with people — there's no way out."

"And Alice?"

"Reid's youngest?"

"Yes."

Chase's expression changed just enough for me to know something was up. I felt a tsunami of dread course through me.

"Come on. Tell me. Now. We're in this together. Spit it out, for Christ's sake — you owe me that much."

He looked at me for a few seconds.

"Okay. There's ... well ... a situation."

"Tell me," I said again.

"They're holding the little girl hostage. Seems they stumbled on her as they were trying to escape."

"Who exactly? Tri?"

"And Frankie." He paused. "We have things in hand down there, don't worry."

I turned immediately and ran for the Goddess. As I slammed my driver's door shut and gunned the engine I heard Chase shout out.

"Hey, Sainte-Claire! Remember — you can't do it all alone! Teamwork's the thing, mate!"

I felt like Ali before the Rumble in the Jungle. My entire body seemed to fibrillate in waves.

As I drove I made some calls. Somehow I'd got disconnected from Ben's open line. Ben was first on my list.

"Ben? What's going down?"

"Tri's got Alice, he's using her as a shield. He's got a bowie knife to her throat, so no one's going in. They've got a big SPG team ready. There's no way out for Tri."

"How's Alice holding up?" I asked.

"You gotta love her, mate. No sign of fear whatsoever. Gutsy kid. She keeps shouting out to the cops that they should wait for you, then go in hot and heavy. Her words. She's something else. Been reading too many Sainte-Claire comics."

"Frankie?"

"He's right by them. They've got a Kawasaki fired up and ready to go, but I reckon Tri's afraid to leave without his shield. Even *with* her – where the hell does he think he can go?"

"I'll be there in minutes. Use whatever influence you have with the incident commander there — keep them back."

"Sure thing," Ben replied.

43

It took me under fourteen minutes to get to Bareena Park. I picked up a patrol car on the M5, but I pressed the pedal full down and it dropped back and was soon gone. That's my rotary engine. That, and maybe I had a death wish that day.

I saw a cordon of cops and tape as I approached the park, but reckoned I could drive straight through without injuring anyone. Besides, I wasn't about to be told what to do by the cops on the scene. I was all Sainte-Claire now. Full on. Every fibre of my body was tingling with anticipation. If someone wanted to shoot me, they were welcome to. I could take a bullet or two and still function!

I drove straight onto the grass, breaking through the tape. The SPG guys pointed their weapons at me but didn't shoot. I'd figured they wouldn't — by the time I was past them I was no longer presenting any danger, and if they were to discharge their weapons the bullets would fly in the direction of Alice.

I fishtailed to a halt, gouging up a ridge, and jumped out. I was now midway between the cops and the bad guys. I stood on the grass, legs wide apart, my black jacket flapping open in the breeze, my hands clenching into fists. My eyes were pure steel.

There was a curious silence as everyone focused on me: Sainte-Claire.

That's when Ally-Oop spotted me. "The cavalry's here! Sainte-Claire! The Fist!" Another of Sainte-Claire's nicknames.

A small crease of a smile spread across my face. She was quite a kid.

Alice turned her head to Tri. "Now you got no chance!"

Tri had a knife at Ally's throat. It was a classic standoff. In my peripheral vision I could see Charlie and a man I presumed to be Peter Reid desperately hugging each other, terrified. There were cop cars and SPG personnel everywhere — keeping their distance about twenty yards behind me. The negotiator was on a megaphone.

"Let the girl go, Tri! There's no way out!"

But Tri had one arm around Alice and the other holding the knife to her little neck. The gutsy little tyke looked unafraid, struggling like fury. Frankie was standing beside a Kawasaki 500 nearby. The engine was running. He was staring angrily at Tri. I could just make out what he was saying — the cops were too far away.

"Fan-fuckin-tastic idea that was!" he said.

"Shut the fuck up!" Tri shouted back at him, then turned to look at me. "And who the fuck are *you*?"

"You know me, Tri. Put down the girl before I get real mad and make you."

He screwed up his eyes, then I saw a gleam of recognition.

"You the guy that was thinking of dropping a brick on Annie's car? You got to be kiddin'. That you?"

"That's me."

"Sainte-Claire?"

"The one and only."

Yes, I actually said the words. Today I cringe. But on that day, I was a dangerous peacock and I knew I could handle anything.

"I'm not afraid of you, dickhead," Tri spat out at me. But his expression told me otherwise.

He turned his attention to the cops and screamed orders at them. "You let us through! Okay? Or it's bad for the kid. You understan'!"

That's when Charlie broke free from Peter and started to run forward. My head whipped round.

"Grab her!" I barked at the cops. An SPG guy raced forward, tackled her to the ground and walked her back behind the police line.

Tri looked again at me. "Hey, man. You *own* the cops round here?"

"I reckon," I replied.

A few seconds passed. Then I heard the megaphone behind me.

"Sainte-Claire! Please step back."

I paid no attention, rather focusing on Tri.

"Chin's in custody, Tri. There's nowhere to run. Let the little girl go! Do it before I come and take the knife off you. You use it on the girl and I'll take it off you and cut you into a thousand pieces. You feel lucky today? You want to try me?"

Again, seconds passed. The police were standing their ground, waiting for someone to make a decision that could result in the death of a six-year-old. Tri was debating his next move."

"We're driving outta here on the bike, Sainte-Claire. All three of us! You or anyone come close – I stick the kid. Understan'?"

Frankie's head whipped round. "No fuckin' way, Tri!"

I knew I could use Frankie. I started to walk forward, very slowly, step-by-step.

As Ally saw me move closer she shouted out. "Take the shot, Sainte-Claire! Take 'em out! These punks don't scare me!"

It was classic fearless Sainte-Claire tough-talk. Except I didn't have a gun.

I saw a look of astonishment register on Tri's face.

I kept walking.

"We're gettin' out, Frankie. NOW!" Tri screamed. "You drive. We're all outta here!

I could see Frankie wasn't buying it.

"No way, Tri. We leave the kid."

"Way to go, Frankie," I said smoothly and calmly as I closed on them. "Think of Annie. It'd kill her. Do the right thing, Frankie."

The kid looked at me, then back at Tri. "She *stays*. *We* go, Tri," he said.

"You crazy, Frankie? Without the kid, we're both dead!"

"No!"

"Nice thinking, kid," I heard Alice say. Then she actually winked at Frankie.

I knew Frankie was the key — the weak link, the one with any sense of morality.

"Hey, Frankie," I said as I walked ever closer. "Do the right thing. Think of Annie!"

I was a few metres from them when Frankie made a grab for the knife. I dived forward and threw Alice to one side. As I did so, Frankie lunged at Tri with his own short knife. Tri stuck Frankie in the chest and suddenly they were speared together, impaled by their two knives. I stood over them as the blood poured from their chests. Then the SPG guys were all over the place.

I picked up Alice and held her tightly to my chest, walking away from the bloodbath. The cops didn't try to separate us — they concentrated on the two bad guys. A couple of medics raced past me. Charlie and Peter broke free of surrounding cops and ran towards us.

I put Alice down and directed her to her parents. The three embraced like desperate refugees at a border crossing. I stepped back, allowing them a private moment. There was a tap at my elbow. Tiggs was standing there with Lucy.

"Excuse me, Luce," she said. "Okay if I have a private word with you, Sainte-Claire?"

Lucy backed off to give us some space.

"Jesus, " I began. "How did you find us here?"

"Your pal Ben. Couldn't keep up with him. Driving too fast. But he called Luce."

I locked eyes with Tiggs. Then I had the weirdest sensation — kind of like an out-of-body experience. I was there with Tiggs one second, then I was somewhere else. Reality and fantasy were fused. My mind was fogged — I had no sense of the present at all. I was outside the departures building on the tarmac at Casablanca airport, a plane's propellers turning over in the distance, ready to taxi. I was Rick Blaine — Tiggs was Ilsa Laszlo. We stood facing each other in the darkness. The wind that gusted through Bareena Park that day was the propeller wash of Ilsa's waiting plane. Ben stood in the shadows — Captain Louis Renault. As ever the facilitator.

"Been a pleasure doing business with you, Sainte-Claire," I heard a small voice say.

"The pleasure's been all mine, Ms Tiggy-Winkle," I replied dreamily.

There was a beat.

"You know, this could be the beginning of a beautiful friendship," I said, still in some misty dreamworld.

Then reality swept back into my consciousness and I knew where I was. It felt quite extraordinary.

Tiggs looked at me. "Are you okay, Robert?"

I stared back at her. I hadn't been called by my real name in what seemed like a century. She was so damned smart, she probably had a better idea of my mental state than anyone — including me.

"Sure, Tiggs, I'm cool."

She smiled. "Glad to hear it, Sainte-Claire."

Then she pulled out a ten-dollar note and offered it to me. "Its all Dad had in his pockets, I'm afraid. Sorry. That's on account, anyway. Isn't that how it's done?"

"Sure is, kid."

Suddenly Alice was at my side. She took hold of her sister's hand, her candy-floss hair whipped up crazily in wind. I felt strangely sad. It was the end of the road as far as this case went. Maybe there'd be others. But not with my two most precious clients.

"You two make a cool team," I said, keeping up the tough face.

"Yeah. S'pose. Oops and me — we *are* a team. Always have been, always will be."

"Can I come and see you two sometime — take you for coffee every now and then? Maybe an M Pinabo?"

"Mad if you don't, Sainte-Claire," Tiggs replied.

"Here's lookin' at you ... *kids*," I said finally, with a small smile.

We stared at each other, grinning like idiots. I could see Tiggs' eyes beginning to mist, while Oops was hanging tough. Then they both hugged me and I whirled them both around like on a Ferris wheel.

I put them down gently. There was a second's pause.

"Give hugs to Jez for us," Tiggs said.

"She's really chewy!" Alice added.

That word again. New kid-speak?

Then Charlie and Peter joined us. It was like a halftime footie huddle.

As the Reid family walked away I caught sight of Ben's car. It was parked near the police incident truck. Ben was behind the wheel, asleep from exhaustion.

I rapped on the window. He awoke with a start and rolled it down.

"Hi! I hear you excelled yourself. Real hero stuff."

I didn't mention what Chase had told me about his having leaked everything to the cops. I'd keep a few chosen words up my sleeve for later.

"Thanks, Ben. For everything."

"Nah, mate. *You* did the job, I had the easy bit."

"No, for keeping tabs on my craziness."

"How do you mean?" he replied.

"Sometimes, Sainte-Claire, you have to separate fact from fiction. We couldn't have done it all on your timings without the boys in blue behind us all the way. They had to know up front."

"I understand that now."

"You did good. Don't believe otherwise."

"Think they'll nail Brierley?"

He grinned. "They'd better, or he'll have your guts."

"That's what I was thinking."

44

So, that was that: Sainte-Claire came to the rescue. Two of the bad guys died from gunshot wounds at Ebley Street; the others there were arrested. Tri died of his stomach wound. Frankie was lucky, but is looking at a long jail term.

'End of song, end of story', as Louis Armstrong says at the end of *High Society*.

Peter was freed, but his finger wasn't reattached. They dug it out of the Clinique Face Mask. The pinkie was fine; it was the stub that wasn't so crash hot.

Brierley was arrested later at his office at PIC. He denied any knowledge of the incident at Ebley Street, and none of his muscle-boys disputed a word he said. I knew it was going to be hard pinning anything on him, but word on the street a few weeks later was that his wife had met and fallen for an obscenely rich Argentinean polo player and was considering turning Queen's evidence.

Tutuelo was picked up trying to charter a private plane to Vanuatu from Darwin. He was charged with Sammy's murder. Sometime in the future I'll be looking across a courtroom at those beady little eyes and seeing murder reflected there. I look forward to it.

I know I'm a marked man from now on. I've done all that myself and I'm going to have to wear it. I've managed to give myself a huge reputation among both the police and the criminal community of Sydney — one I'll have to live up to. No more 'Sainte-Klutz'. Sure, I have to watch my back now. But that's not the problem. It's Jez.

The day I reunited the children with Peter and Charlie, I drove straight round to Jez's studio. She's the sort of person you can only talk straight with. There's no beating about the bush with her.

Once she knew something big had happened, and that I'd been personally involved, she asked me to tell her everything.

I did.

Of course, it came out that I'd lied to her, kept facts from her and gone off yet again and put myself at risk. And, in the washup, I'd put *her* at risk again because everyone was sure Brierley would exact revenge — be it from inside or outside prison walls.

She didn't shout at me, or call me names. She was simply silent for a while.

"I can't live like this, Pulitzer," she said eventually.

"I can change," I replied.

"I'm not sure you can any more. You love the life too much. Sainte-Claire's too deeply embedded in your psyche now. I loved Robert Howard and he's gone some place."

"I was just trying to do what I could for those children. You know that. I couldn't let them down. They were helpless."

"I know that. But the thing is, you enjoyed it all so much. And that's what saddens me. You're such a big kid, and this isn't a playground — it's the real world, where people die doing things the way you do them. And so do those around you — the people you're supposed to love and care for. You took care of the kids. But you never thought to take care of me."

She turned and looked out the open window.

"Tell you what," I said, "I'll go home and change. You ever see me with gunk in my hair or wearing black clothes, I'm out. What do you say?"

"I say I need time."

"You can *have* time," I replied.

"A *lot* of time, Pulitzer."

Epilogue

It's October now, and I haven't seen Jez for several months. Word is she's happy and painting full on.

Tutuelo's trial is set for next January. It doesn't look as though Brierley will 'beat the rap' as they say. Agnès has been granted immunity, and has promised to return from Buenos Aires for a big 'Sydney-Crim' trial. She's going to dob in Brierley big-time.

Chin didn't make bail. He's still in prison hospital with metal pins and clamps holding his crushed legs together. Frankie promised his mother he'd finish his TAFE course in prison — so Ben said anyway.

Redford and Roberts withdrew from *Things that Go Bump*. It was re-titled *The Signal*, and starred two virtual unknowns — supposed to be a nice cool meld of animation and reality. But somewhere way down the line, a twenty-two-year-old wunderkind comic book cum commercials writer was called in by the producer to 'clean up' my screenplay, and I ended up taking my name off the project. I made a heap of money though, and Sol was one happy camper. The movie was a big box-office winner, but it simply wasn't my work.

Good ol' Hollywood.

I've been seeing a shrink now for two months. She thinks she's making progress with me. Thing is, I lie to her and I know that's not healthy.

I say I'd never do it again. I tell her quietly that I no longer feel the urge to get myself in dangerous situations and feel that incredible A-rush. But I do. I want it like a junkie needs a hit.

How come it's labelled psychotic to want to shoot it out with bad guys, yet heroic to risk your life climbing Everest without oxygen?

I rest my case.

OTHER BOOKS BY SHANE BRIANT.

The Webber Agenda
The Chasen Catalyst
Hitkids
Bite of the Lotus
Worst Nightmares
The Dreamhealer
Always the Bad Guy